Outstanding praise for the urban fantasy novels of Richelle Mead!

SUCCUBUS ON TOP

"Like all great heroines, Georgina Kincaid is an intriguing blend of contradictions; sexy but sweet, an immortal who remembers her humanity, and a girl who knows exactly what she wants in a man and a drink, but who can still lose herself to both. (More than once I found myself thinking, 'I'll have what she's having'. . . and I wasn't talking about the gimlet!) With sharp prose and a powerhouse voice, Richelle Mead took a death grip on my imagination and refused to let go. I, too, fell prey to the enchantments of her succubus, and couldn't stop thinking, wondering, and caring about her until I turned the final page. In short, Georgina Kincaid has been my ruin . . . now no other succubus will do!"
—Vicki Pettersson, author of *The Scent of Shadows*

"This urban sextacular is a hoot."
—*Publishers Weekly*

"Mead has a real gift for character-driven storytelling, for subtle shading and for creating a uniquely believable story world. Georgina Kincaid is a creature of Hell and a genuinely likeable protagonist. This is one of those series that I'm going to keep following."
—Jim Butcher, *New York Times* bestselling author of *Small Favor*

"Richelle Mead's writing is just as dangerously seductive as her characters—*Succubus on Top* is a hell (literally) of a book, compulsively readable and packed with style, humor, suspense and grace."
—Rachel Caine, author of *Gale Force*

"Entertaining . . . imaginative and entertaining to read."
—*Romantic Times*

"Mead and Georgina just keep getting better! *Succubus on Top* delivers a smart observation of relationships and human folly under a deceptively light style with a scorcher of an ending. Georgina Kincaid is a smart, gutsy heroine you can't help but root for, even if she does work on the wrong side of the Good/Evil tracks. A surefire hit for Mead and a delicious read for Georgina fans—I couldn't put it down."
—Kat Richardson, author of *Poltergeist*

"Don't take this book to bed—you'll be up all night. Richelle Mead delivers sexy action and tongue-in-cheek hellish humor—if damnation is this fun, sign me up!"
—Lilith Saintcrow, author of *The Devil's Right Hand*

Please turn the page for more oustanding praise for Richelle Mead!

"Mead cooks up an appetizing debut that blends romantic suspense with a fresh twist on the paranormal, accented with eroticism."
—*Booklist*

"An excellent paranormal."
—*Romantic Times*

"One of those books that had me engrossed from the very first page."
—*RomanceJunkies.com*

"*Succubus Blues* is great fun."
—*The Romance Reader's Connection*

"An engaging read."
—Jim Butcher, *New York Times* bestselling author

"Deliciously wicked! Dysfunctional, funny, and sexy. I look forward to reading more tempting morsels about this succubus with a heart of gold."
—Lilith Saintcrow, author of *Dead Man Rising*

"What an incredible debut novel! *Succubus Blues* is exciting, witty, sexy, intriguing and had me captivated from the first page."
—Cheyenne McCray, author of *Seduced by Magic*

"*Buffy* meets *Sex and the City*. Guilty pleasures don't get much better."
—David Sosnowski, author of *Rapture* and *Vamped*

"Sexy, scintillating and sassy! Richelle Mead is now on my must-buy list."
—Michelle Rowen, author of *Bitten and Smitten*

"Take a beautiful, sassy immortal. Mix in suspense, murder and plenty of hot sex. Pour yourself a great read and enjoy the hell out of this story."
—Mario Acevedo, author of *The Nymphos of Rocky Flats* and *X-Rated Bloodsuckers*

"Writing this good tempts me to believe in angels . . . or deals with the devil. *Succubus Blues* is original, exciting, seductive stuff, filled with characters I'd sell my soul to meet."
—Rachel Caine, author of *Firestorm* and *Glass Houses*

SUCCUBUS DREAMS

RICHELLE MEAD

KENSINGTON BOOKS
http://www.kensingtonbooks.com

KENSINGTON BOOKS are published by

Kensington Publishing Corp.
850 Third Avenue
New York, NY 10022

ISBN-13: 978-0-7582-1643-4
ISBN-10: 0-7582-1643-2

First Kensington Trade Paperback Printing: October 2008
10   9   8   7   6   5

Printed in the United States of America

For Christina, whom I suspect owns more copies of my books than I do. Your friendship and support mean so much to me.

Acknowledgments

It takes a village to write a book, sometimes even a whole suburb. I'm grateful for all of the friends and family who have helped me along the way. Mega-thanks go to my speed-reading feedback team: David, Jay, and Marcee. I appreciate you guys being there to do quick reads for me and reassure me that it's all still doing what it's supposed to. I also appreciate you letting me know when it isn't doing what it's supposed to, whether it's a bad word choice or Georgina being "all emotional and stuff."

Many thanks are due my agent Jim McCarthy, who is always there with fast email responses, solid advice, and reassurance that I really am good enough and smart enough. Thank you as well to my editor John Scognamiglio, who is also quick with email and very, very generous with deadlines.

Lastly, I owe a big shout-out to the readers who encouraged me on a daily basis via email and my blog. Getting all those messages about how you were excited to read the book made me excited to write it.

SUCCUBUS
DREAMS

Chapter 1

I wished the guy on top of me would hurry up because I was getting bored.

Unfortunately, it didn't seem like he was going to finish anytime soon. Brad or Brian or whatever his name was thrust away, eyes squeezed shut with such concentration that you would have thought having sex was on par with brain surgery or lifting steel beams.

"Brett," I panted. It was time to pull out the big guns.

He opened one eye. "Bryce."

"Bryce." I put on my most passionate, orgasmic face. "Please . . . please . . . don't stop."

His other eye opened. Both went wide.

A minute later, it was all over.

"Sorry," he gasped, rolling off me. He looked mortified. "I don't know . . . didn't mean . . ."

"It's okay, baby." I felt only a little bad about using the *don't stop* trick on him. It didn't always work, but for some guys, planting that seed completely undid them. "It was amazing."

And really, that wasn't entirely a lie. The sex itself had been mediocre, but the rush afterward . . . the feel of his life and his soul pouring into me . . . yeah. That was pretty amazing. It was what a succubus like me literally lived for.

He gave me a weary smile. The energy he'd had now

flowed in my body. Its loss had exhausted him, burned him out. He'd sleep soon and would probably continue sleeping a great deal over the next few days. His soul had been a good one, and I'd taken a lot of it—as well as his life itself. He'd now live a few years less, thanks to me.

I tried not to think about that as I hurriedly put on my clothes. Instead, I focused on how I'd done what I had to do for my own survival. Plus, my infernal masters required me to seduce and corrupt good souls on a regular basis. Bad men might make me feel less guilty, but they didn't fulfill Hell's quota.

Bryce seemed surprised at my abrupt departure but was too worn out to fight it. I promised to call him—having no intention of doing so—and slipped out of the room as he lapsed into unconsciousness.

I'd barely cleared his front door before shape-shifting. I'd come to him as a tall, sable-haired woman but now once again wore my preferred shape, petite with hazel-green eyes and light brown hair that flirted with gold. Like most of my life, my features danced between states, never entirely settling on one.

I put Bryce out of my mind, just like I did with most men I slept with, and drove across town to what was rapidly becoming my second home. It was a tan, stucco condo, set into a community of other condos that tried desperately to be as hip as new construction in Seattle could manage. I parked my Passat out front, fished my key out of my purse, and let myself inside.

The condo was still and quiet, wrapped in darkness. A nearby clock informed me it was three in the morning. Walking toward the bedroom, I shape-shifted again, swapping my clothes for a red nightgown.

I froze in the bedroom's doorway, surprised to feel my breath catch in my throat. You'd think after all this time, I would have gotten used to him, that he wouldn't affect me like this. But he did. Every time.

Seth lay sprawled on the bed, one arm tossed over his head. His breathing came deep and fitful, and the sheets lay in a tangle around his long, lean body. Moonlight muted out the color of his hair, but in the sun, its light brown would pick up a russet glow. Seeing him, studying him, I felt my heart swell in my chest. I'd never expected to feel this way about anyone again, not after centuries of feeling so . . . empty. Bryce had meant nothing to me, but this man before me meant everything.

I slid into bed beside him, and his arms instantly went around me. I think it was instinctual. The connection between us was so deep that even while unconscious, we couldn't stay away from each other.

I pressed my cheek to Seth's chest, and his skin warmed mine as I fell asleep. The guilt from Bryce faded, and soon, there was only Seth and my love for him.

I slipped almost immediately into a dream. Except, well, I wasn't actually *in* it, at least not in the active sense. I was watching myself, seeing the events unfold as though at a movie. Only, unlike a movie, I could *feel* every detail. The sights, the sounds . . . it was almost more vivid than real life.

The other Georgina was in a kitchen, one I didn't recognize. It was bright and modern, far larger than anything I could imagine a non-cook like me needing. My dream-self stood at the sink, arms elbow-deep in sudsy water that smelled like oranges. She was hand-washing dishes, which surprised my real-self—but was doing a shoddy job, which did not surprise me. On the floor, an actual dishwasher lay in pieces, thus explaining the need for manual labor.

From another room, the sounds of "Sweet Home Alabama" carried to my ears. My dream-self hummed along as she washed, and in that surreal, dream sort of way, I could feel her happiness. She was content, filled with a joy so utterly perfect, I could barely comprehend it. Even with Seth, I'd rarely ever felt so happy—and I was pretty damned happy with him. I couldn't imagine what could make my dream-self feel this way, particularly while doing something as mundane as washing dishes.

I woke up.

To my surprise, it was full morning, bright and sunny. I'd had no sense of time passing. The dream had seemed to last only a minute, yet the nearby alarm clock claimed six hours had passed. The loss of the happiness my dream-self had experienced made me ache.

Weirder than that, I felt . . . not right. It took me a moment to peg the problem: I was drained. The life energy I needed to survive, the energy I'd stolen from Bryce, was almost gone. In fact, I had less now than I'd had before going to bed with him. It made no sense. A burst of life like that should have lasted a couple weeks at least, yet I was nearly as wiped out as he'd been. I wasn't low enough to start losing my shape-shifting ability, but I'd need a new fix within a couple of days.

"What's wrong?"

Seth's sleepy voice came from beside me. I rolled over and found him propped on one elbow, watching me with a small, sweet smile.

I didn't want to explain what had happened. Doing so would mean elaborating on what I'd done with Bryce, and while Seth theoretically knew what I did to survive, ignorance really was bliss.

"Nothing," I lied. I was a good liar.

He touched my cheek. "I missed you last night."

"No, you didn't. You were busy with Cady and O'Neill."

His smile turned wry, but even as it did, I could see his eyes start to take on the dreamy, inward look he got when he thought about the characters in his novels. I'd made kings and generals beg for my love in my long life, yet some days, even my charms couldn't compete with the people who lived in Seth's head.

Fortunately, today wasn't one of those days, and his attention focused back on me.

"Nah. They don't look as good in a nightgown. That's very Anne Sexton, by the way. Like 'candy store cinnamon hearts.'"

Only Seth would use a bipolar poet as a compliment. I glanced down and ran an absentminded hand over the red silk. "This does look pretty good," I admitted. "I might look better in this than I do naked."

He scoffed. "No, Thetis. You do not."

I smiled, as I always did, when he used the pet name he coined for me. In Greek mythology, Thetis had been Achilles' mother, a shape-shifting goddess won by a determined mortal. And then, in what was an astonishingly aggressive move for him, Seth flipped me onto my back and began kissing my neck.

"Hey," I said, putting up a half-hearted struggle. "We don't have time for this. I have stuff to do. And I want breakfast."

"Noted," he mumbled, moving on to my mouth. I stopped my complaining. Seth was a wonderful kisser. He gave the kind of kisses that melted into your mouth and filled you with sweetness. They were like cotton candy.

But there was no real melting to be had, not for us. With a well-practiced sense of timing that you could probably set a watch to, he pulled away from the kiss and sat up, removing his hands as well. Still smiling, he looked down at me and my undignified sprawl.

I smiled back, squelching the small pang of regret that always came at these moments of retreat.

But that was the way it was with us, and honestly, we had a pretty good system going when one considered all the complications in our relationship. My friend Hugh once had joked that all women steal men's souls if they're together long enough. In my case, it didn't taken years of bickering. A too-long kiss would suffice. Such was the life of a succubus. I didn't make the rules, and I had no way to stop the involuntary energy theft that came from intimate physical contact. I could, however, control whether that physical contact happened in the first place, and I made sure it didn't. I ached for Seth, but I wouldn't steal his life as I had Bryce's.

I sat as well, ready to get up, but Seth must have been feeling bold this morning. He wrapped his arms around my waist and shifted me onto his lap, pressing himself against my back so that his lightly stubbled face buried itself in my neck and hair. I felt his body tremble with the intake of a heavy, deep breath. He exhaled it just as slowly, like he sought control of himself, and then strengthened his grip on me.

"Georgina," he breathed against my skin.

I closed my eyes, and the playfulness was gone. A dark intensity wrapped around us, one that burned with both desire and a fear of what might come.

"Georgina," he repeated. His voice was low, husky. I felt like melting again. "Do you know why they say succubi visit men in their sleep?"

"Why?" My own voice was small.

"Because I dream about you every night." In most circumstances, that would have sounded trite, but from him, it was powerful and hungry.

I squeezed my eyes tighter as a swirl of emotions danced within me. I wanted to cry. I wanted to make love to him. I wanted to scream. It was all too much sometimes. Too much emotion. Too much danger. Too much, too much.

Opening my eyes, I shifted so that I could see his face. We held each other's gazes, both of us wanting more and unable to give or take it. Breaking the look first, I slipped regretfully from his embrace. "Come on. Let's go eat."

Seth lived in Seattle's university district—the U-district to locals—and was within easy walking distance to assorted shops and restaurants that lay adjacent to the University of Washington's campus. We found breakfast at a small café, and omelets and conversation soon banished the earlier awkwardness. Afterward, we wandered idly up University Way, holding hands. I had errands to run, and he had writing to do, yet we were reluctant to part.

Seth suddenly stopped walking. "Georgina."

"Hmm?"

His eyebrows rose as he stared off at something across the street. "John Cusack is standing over there."

I followed his incredulous gaze to where a man very like Mr. Cusack did indeed stand, smoking a cigarette as he leaned against a building. I sighed.

"That's not John Cusack. That's Jerome."

"Seriously?"

"Yup. I told you he looked like John Cusack."

"Keyword: *looked*. That guy doesn't look like him. That guy is him."

"Believe me, he's not." Seeing Jerome's impatient expression, I let go of Seth's hand. "Be right back."

I crossed the street, and as the distance closed between my boss and me, Jerome's aura washed over my body. All immortals have a unique signature, and a demon like Jerome had an especially strong one. He felt like waves and waves of roiling heat—like when you open an oven and don't stand far enough back.

"Make it fast," I told him. "You're ruining my romantic interlude. Like usual."

Jerome dropped the cigarette and put it out with his black Kenneth Cole oxford. He glanced disdainfully around. "What, here? Come on, Georgie. This isn't romantic. This place isn't even a pit stop on the road to romance."

I put an angry hand on one hip. Whenever Jerome interrupted my personal life, it usually heralded a series of mishaps I'd never wanted to be involved in. Something told me this was no exception. "What do you want?"

"You."

I blinked. "What?"

"We've got a meeting tonight. An all staff meeting."

"When you say 'all staff', do you mean like *all* staff?"

The last time Seattle's supervising archdemon had gathered everyone in the area together, it had been to inform us that our local imp wasn't "meeting expectations." Jerome had let us all tell the imp good-bye and then banished the poor guy off to the fiery depths of Hell. It was kind of sad, but then my friend Hugh had replaced him, so I'd gotten over it. I hoped this meeting wouldn't have a similar purpose.

He gave me an annoyed look, one that said I was clearly wasting his time. "That's the definition of all staff, isn't it?"

"When is it?"

"Seven. At Peter and Cody's. Don't be late. Your presence is essential."

Shit. I hoped this wasn't actually *my* going away party. I'd been on pretty good behavior lately. "What's this about?"

"Find out when you get there. Don't be late," he repeated.

Stepping off the main thoroughfare and into the shadow of a building, the demon vanished.

A feeling of dread spread through me. Demons were never to be trusted, particularly when they looked like quirky movie stars and issued enigmatic invitations.

"Everything okay?" Seth asked me when I rejoined him.

I considered. "In as much as it ever is."

He wisely chose not to pursue the subject, and he and I eventually separated to take care of our respective tasks. I was dying to know what this meeting could be about but not nearly as much as I wanted to know what had made me lose my energy overnight. And as I ran my errands—groceries, oil change, Macy's—I also found the strange, brief dream replaying in my head. How could such a short dream have been so vivid? And why couldn't I stop thinking about it?

The puzzle distracted me so much that seven rolled around without me knowing it. Groaning, I headed off for my friend Peter's place, speeding the whole way. Great. I was going to be late. Even if this meeting didn't concern me and my impending unemployment, I might end up getting a taste of Jerome's wrath after all.

About six feet from the apartment door, I felt the hum of immortal signatures. A lot of them. My friends' auras, familiar and beloved, sang to me instantly. A few others gave me pause as I tried to remember who they belonged to; the greater Puget Sound area had a host of hellish employees that I almost never interacted with. One signature I didn't recognize at all. And one . . . one seemed almost familiar. I couldn't quite put my finger on who it belonged to, though.

I started to knock, decided an all staff meeting deserved more than jeans and a T-shirt, and shape-shifted my outfit into a brown dress with a low-cut, surplice top. My hair settled into a neat bun. I raised my hand to the door.

An annoyed vampire I barely remembered let me in. She inclined her chin to me by way of greeting and then continued her conversation with another vampire I'd only met once. I think they worked out of Tacoma, which as I far as I was concerned might as well be annexed to Hell itself.

My friend Hugh, dark-haired with a large frame, paced around while chatting animatedly on his cell phone. Jerome lounged in an armchair with a martini. His little-seen lieutenant demonesses stood in a corner, keeping to themselves as always. Peter and Cody—my good friends and the vampires who lived here—laughed about something in the kitchen with a few other hellish employees I only distantly knew.

It could have been an ordinary cocktail party, almost a celebration. I hoped that meant no smiting tonight since that would have really put a damper on the atmosphere. No one had noticed my arrival except for Jerome.

"Ten minutes late," he growled.

"Hey, it's a fashionable—"

My words were cut off as a tall, Amazonian blonde nearly barreled into me.

"Oh! You must be Georgina! I've been dying to meet you."

I raised my eyes past spandex-clad double-D breasts and up into big blue eyes with impossibly long lashes. A huge set of beauty pageant teeth smiled down at me.

My moments of speechlessness were few, but they did happen. This walking Barbie doll was a succubus. A really new one. So shiny and new, in fact, it was a wonder she didn't squeak. I recognized her age both from her signature and her appearance. No succubus with any sense would have shapeshifted into that. She was trying too hard, haphazardly piling together an assortment of pseudo male-fantasy body parts. It left her with a Frankensteinian creation that was both jaw-dropping and probably anatomically impossible.

Unaware of my astonishment and disdain, she took my hand and nearly broke it in a mammoth handshake.

"I can't wait to work with you," she continued. "I am *so* ready to make men everywhere suffer."

I finally found my voice. "Who . . . who are you?"

"She's your new best friend," a voice nearby said. "My, my look at you. Tawny's going to have a tough standard to keep up with."

A man elbowed his way toward us, and whatever curiosity I'd felt in the other succubus' presence disappeared like ashes in the wind. I forgot she was even there. My stomach twisted into knots as I ID'd the mystery signature. Cold sweat broke out along the back of my neck and seeped into the delicate fabric of the dress.

The guy approaching was about as tall as me—which wasn't tall—and had a dark, olive-toned complexion. There was more pomade on his head than black hair. His suit was nice—definitely not off the rack. A thin-lipped smile spread over his face at my dumbstruck discomfiture.

"Little Letha, all grown up and out to play with the adults, eh?" He spoke low, voice pitched for my ears alone.

Now, in the grand scheme of things, immortals like me had little to fear in this world. There were, however, three people I feared immensely. One of them was Lilith the Suc-

cubus Queen, a being of such formidable power and beauty
that I would have sold my soul—again—for one kiss. Someone else who scared me was a nephilim named Roman. He
was Jerome's half-human son and had good reason to want
to hunt me down and destroy me some day. The third person
who filled me with fear was this man standing before me.

His name was Niphon, and he was an imp, just like my
friend Hugh. And, like all imps, Niphon really only had two
jobs. One was to run administrative errands for demons. The
other, his primary one, was to make contracts with mortals,
brokering and buying souls for Hell.

And he was the imp who had bought mine.

Chapter 2

For a few seconds, I was no longer at the party. My mind's eye flashed back to where I stood on a cliff outside the town I'd grown up in, barely old enough to be called an adult by today's standards. And Niphon was there, smiling at me, promising me he had all the answers and could make my problems disappear. . . .

I shook my head, driving off the memories and returning to the party at hand.

His smile grew, an evil smile that promised even more evil things. I could have been facing Eden's serpent himself.

"I knew you had it in you," he continued, stepping toward me. His voice stayed soft. "I knew it the minute I saw you. I can't wait to find out firsthand just how . . . experienced you've become."

My defenses snapped into place, and I stepped back. "Touch me, and I'll break your fucking neck."

"Such ingratitude, considering I made you what you are."

"Stay away from me."

He started to move forward again, and my heart leapt to a pace that would have killed most humans. Suddenly, Jerome's voice fell over us, and I realized the room had become silent. "Leave her alone, Niphon. She said no."

The imp paused and made a pleading face. "Aw, come on, Jerome. What kind of demon doesn't share his goods?"

"You aren't here to fuck my succubus. If you can't do your job, I can replace you."

Jerome's voice held a warning note that even an asshole like Niphon couldn't ignore. Maybe someone would be consigned to Hell tonight after all. Disappointingly, the imp inclined his head in obeisance and backed off. The look he gave me warned we would have a later conversation.

I walked over to Jerome. "Maybe you should have given me a heads up earlier."

"And ruin things for you lovebirds? Hardly something a die-hard romantic like me could do. Besides, I *told* you to come early."

Hugh snapped his cell phone shut and wandered over to join us. He kissed my cheek. "Hey, sweetie. Big things going on here."

My already enormous sense of dread grew by leaps and bounds. "Such as?"

"Re-org. Seattle's lines have been redrawn. We're getting another succubus. Or, well, we've got one."

My jaw dropped, and I replayed Niphon's earlier words. "You are so joking."

"Afraid not. This is Tawny."

Robo-Blonde pranced over on her stiletto heels and tried to shake my hand again. I kept it out of reach, fearing for my bones. I forced a smile. "Hi, Tawny." I turned back to Jerome and jerked my head at Niphon. "Why is *he* here then?"

"I acquired her," the imp explained. "Acquired" was a nice way of saying he'd bought her soul for Hell, just as he'd purchased mine. "It's my job to stay and watch her until she's settled in and taken her first victim."

"No one ever did that for me," I recalled. "You sort of threw me to the wolves." I'd had to be some innkeeper's sex toy in Constantinople for a few years until I'd learned the succubus ropes.

Niphon shrugged. "HR's new policy. Just think of all the time it'll give us to catch up."

Giving Tawny a sidelong glance, I hoped her adamant desire to destroy men everywhere meant she'd be a quick study. Eyeing her leopard-skin skirt, I had my doubts.

"Well. Fantastic. Now that I'm up to speed, I guess there's no need to stay—"

Hugh shook his head, suddenly becoming my-friend-the-imp as opposed to the all-business imp. I could tell from his expression that I wouldn't like what he had to say next. "There's something else you need to know. For the next year or so, you have to be her . . . uh, mentor."

"Mentor," I repeated flatly.

He nodded, looking sympathetic. Jerome watched our exchange with amusement.

"What, um, does that mean for me exactly?"

Hugh set his briefcase on a coffee table and pulled out what looked like the kind of copied-and-bound manual Kinko's would run off. He tossed it to me. I caught it and nearly keeled over. The thing had about eight-hundred pages.

Mentor's Official and Complete Procedural Handbook on Initial Succubus Intake and Probationary Period (Abridged).

"Abridged?" I spun toward Jerome. "Tell me you're getting back at me for the time I accused you of wearing Old Spice."

"That one's still coming," said the demon. "This one's for real."

"I can't do this, Jerome. I don't have the time! Do you know how much stuff I've got going on? I'm still training the new assistant manager at work—"

He stood up with speed a vampire might have admired. He leaned toward me, the amusement gone from his face.

"Oh gee, Georgie. How inconsiderate of me to take you away from your human boyfriend and your crucial-to-the-world bookstore job and all the other fucking absurdity in your life! Let me just go ahead and tell my superiors that you've got more important things to do than answer to the powers *who control your immortal soul* and could wipe out your existence in the blink of an eye."

Heat flooded my cheeks. I didn't really appreciate being verbally bitch-slapped in front of Niphon and Seattle's entire dream team of evil. "I didn't mean it like that. I just—"

"It's not up for debate any longer." His words crawled over my skin.

I swallowed. "Yes, Jerome." Even I knew when to back down.

Silence fell. A smirk played over Niphon's face. "A human boyfriend. How terribly quaint. I can't wait to hear all about it."

"I think it's cute," said Tawny. "I hope you're making him suffer."

"Their romance is a great tale of *self-exploration*," remarked Hugh, straight-faced.

I shot him a glare. As a sexual workaround, Seth and I found we could do unto ourselves what we couldn't do to each other. I'd never actually told my friends about this solution, but they'd kind of figured it out.

With the drama complete, the rest of the room lost interest in me. Tawny did not, however, and immediately began talking to me about the joys of ripping out men's hearts and watching them cry. I left her as quickly as I could, working the room and talking to those I hadn't seen in a while. I was good at smiling and making people laugh while all the while, my mind spun and processed this new complication. When I finally found Cody, Peter, and Hugh huddled in a corner, I breathed a sigh of relief. I could tell from the looks on their faces that this was the most hilarious thing they'd seen in a while.

Cody, young for a vampire but ancient compared to Tawny, threw an arm around me. His shaggy blond hair was tamed into a short stub of a ponytail. He was perpetually laidback and upbeat, and his "youth" always made the rest of us want to baby him. "Oh, man. This is going to be great. You are so screwed."

"As if," I said, squirming away. "You think I'm afraid of her?"

"I am," said Peter with a shiver. He had thinning brown hair and wore casual yet exquisitely coordinated clothes, all the way down to his argyle socks. He was an old vampire, close to my age, and was Cody's mentor. I'd never thought much about their mentor-apprentice relationship before. It always seemed pretty effortless, but then, Cody was no Tawny.

I followed Peter's gaze to where the new succubus animatedly told a story to a stone-faced demoness named Grace. From the dangerous jiggling of Tawny's breasts, it looked as though the structural integrity of her shirt could only last so long.

"I don't think you're afraid," said Hugh slyly. "I think you're jealous."

"Of what exactly? Bad fashion sense? An ergonomically unsound bustline? I have nothing to be jealous of."

"Whatever. I saw your face when you heard we were getting a new succubus. Looks like someone isn't going to be the only girl in our little clique anymore."

"So?"

"So, we'll have a new little sister to fawn and fret over. You'll have to share the spotlight."

"I'm not sharing anything," I said huffily.

Peter laughed. "So it *does* bother you. Can't wait until the fur starts flying."

"Her fate is in your hands," said Cody.

"You should make her call you 'Miss Georgina,' " added Hugh with a mocking southern drawl. "Or at least 'ma'am.' "

Niphon's presence and Jerome's lecture had put me in a grouchy mood. "I'm not doing any mentoring. She's so gung-ho to take on the world's male population, she doesn't even need me."

The three men exchanged more smirks. Cody made some hissing and meowing sounds, scratching at the air.

"This isn't funny," I said.

"Sure it is," said Cody. "Besides, don't you want to help others? Where's your sense of goodness and charity?"

"I think I cashed that in when I, you know, *sold my soul to Hell.*"

Peter waved his hand. "Details, details. 'Tis the season to put aside petty rivalries and animosity. You've got to get into the holiday spirit. You probably haven't even put up your Christmas tree yet."

"I'm not getting a tree this year."

The smile slipped from Peter's face. "What?"

"Oh, shit. You've done it now," said Hugh. "I already got lectured earlier for not having one."

"You're a Scrooge," Peter told him while still looking at me. "No one expects that kind of festive cheer from you. But Georgina . . . didn't you have a Christmas tree last year?"

"Yeah. Somebody burned it down. At my Christmas Eve Martini Party."

"I was there," said Peter. "I don't remember that."

"You were drunk. You'd already passed out."

"What kind of sick bastard burns down a Christmas tree?"

Hugh and I exchanged glances. "That's an excellent question," I said dryly.

Peter looked startled. "Was it you?" he asked Hugh.

"No," said the imp. "It was Carter."

"Your Christmas tree was burned down by an angel?" asked Cody. He hadn't been with our group last December, so this was all new to him. And Peter too, apparently.

"Yup. The irony isn't lost on me," I said. "He had his ashtray too close to where a branch was hanging down."

"Well, I think he did you a favor," said Hugh. "You can get a fake one now. They're easier. No watering. No woodland animals. Besides, you can get them to match your décor. Did you notice Peter's is 'pissed-off ocean green'?"

Peter sighed. "It's 'jaded sea green.'"

I followed their gazes to Peter's monstrosity of a Christmas tree. Nine feet of perfectly shaped needles draped in gold tinsel and red glass ornaments. Everything on it coordinated. In fact, I suddenly realized, it matched Peter's outfit. The tree looked like a display model from a department store. The green in the multicolored bejeweled star on top even seemed to bring out the blue in the 'jaded sea green.'

"At least you don't have an angel on top," I said. "Because that would have been kind of wrong. And possibly a fire hazard."

"Joke all you want," the vampire said, "but you *have* to have a Christmas tree. Oh, yeah—you also have to draw a name for Secret Santas."

I groaned. "Are we doing that again?"

"Let me go get the cup," he said, trotting to the other side of the kitchen.

I looked at the other two. "A vampire obsessed with Christmas. That has to be the weirdest thing I've ever heard."

"No weirder than an angel burning down a Christmas tree," pointed out Cody.

Peter returned with a reindeer mug that held a few folded pieces of paper. He held it out to me. "Not many left. Pick."

I pulled out a slip and opened it. *Carter.*

"Son of a bitch," I swore. "I hate Christmas."

"You do not," said Peter. "You just have to get a tree. Then you'll feel better."

My eyes drifted from the star, down to Tawny and Niphon. "What I have to do is get out of here," I told them, setting my glass on the counter.

I made my good-byes to them and endured a bit more teasing about my new mentoring job. As I walked to the door, I overheard Jerome saying to Grace, ". . . but I'll be out of town for a few days."

I suddenly realized I needed to ask him something. "Hey, Jerome."

He turned from the demoness, shooting me an impatient look. In as few words as possible, I recapped how I'd woken up without the energy I'd stolen the previous night. Jerome listened, looking bored.

"What'd you do last night? Bursts of shape-shifting? Rocket science? Heavy lifting?"

I didn't need him to tell me what sorts of things would burn through my energy. "I didn't do any of those things. I just slept. I did dream, though."

"Dreams only suck the life out of humans, not us," he remarked dryly. "It's what keeps Hell in business." Seeing my expression, he sighed. "It's probably nothing, Georgie. Mental exhaustion'll do it. You probably spent the whole night unconsciously wrestling with sexual temptation."

I didn't appreciate his flippant answer, but there was nothing I could do about it. I left the party, driving home at a reasonable speed limit this time. As soon as I cleared the door, I tossed that ridiculous manual to the floor. It landed with a ground-shaking thump that made my cat Aubrey puff up her tail.

"Sorry," I mumbled, scratching her black-speckled head in consolation.

Traipsing to the bedroom, I promptly dialed Seth on my cell phone.

"Hey," he said.

"Hey. You have to come over here tonight."

A pause. "Well, I could, but . . ."

"Oh, come on! You won't believe what I just went through. We're getting another succubus."

He paused again. "I'm not really sure how to respond to that."

"Respond by getting your ass over here. I need you."

"Thetis . . . I'm so close to the end here. Four chapters away. And I got this idea while we were having breakfast . . ."

I groaned. Cady and O'Neill had defeated me again. Before actually meeting Seth, I'd worshipped him from afar as a literary genius, reading his novels over and over. Now I knew the dark truth about being a bestselling author's girlfriend.

Hearing my silence, he reluctantly added: "But, I mean, if you really need me . . ."

"No, no. Don't worry about it. It's okay."

"You don't sound like it's okay. I know how women work. You say that, then you'll hold a grudge against me forever. Literally."

"No, really. It's fine. I'll be seeing you tomorrow anyway. Besides, as soon as I get out of this dress, I'm just going to pass out anyway." No way was I starting that procedural tome.

"You're wearing a dress?"

"Yup."

"You weren't wearing one earlier. What's it look like?"

I started laughing. "Ooh . . . are you trying to have phone sex with me?"

"Phone sex? Hardly. We haven't even had a phone first date."

"It's not that hard. You see, I tell you how the dress has a really low neckline with nothing underneath. Then, you tell me how you'll reach out and peel it off and stroke my—"

"Oh my God. No. We are not doing this."

Typical Seth. He could write sex scenes that set the page on fire or dialogue clever enough to impress even me. Make him vocalize any of it, and he choked up. He was shy around others, fearful in large groups, and much happier staying an unnoticed listener. I sympathized but sometimes had trouble really comprehending it, considering how often I became the center of attention. I liked to think he'd improved a bit since we got together, but he had a long way to go.

"It just takes practice. Here, I'll help you. Picture it. I'm getting on my knees and slowly unfastening your pants—"

"Okay, look. If you really want to go through with this, I'd be happy to, you know, go get on my computer and IM it . . ."

"Oh good grief. Go work on your book."

I hung up the phone and sat down on my bed. Good Lord. My weekend had taken an abrupt U-turn. Like it or not, I supposed it had been only a matter of time before a new succubus joined the ranks here. Seattle had grown significantly over the years, and I could only do so much. But a green succubus? One I had to train up? If I hadn't known such administrative decisions were out of the demon's hands, I would have accused Jerome of doing it on purpose. It was on par with his sense of humor. Why couldn't we have just gotten some antisocial pro who did her job without ever interacting with me?

And Niphon . . . well, that was the *coup de gras*. I didn't like being reminded of my past, and I didn't like him. Something told me he had it in for me, though I couldn't entirely fathom why. He'd bought my soul and recruited my eternal services. What more was there? *Wait and see*, a warning voice whispered in my head. I shivered. Tawny couldn't make her first score a moment too soon.

Suddenly, I didn't feel like passing out after all. I wanted to *go* out. Not for a victim or anything . . . just to, well, be out. Grab a drink. Do a little flirting. It might salvage the train wreck I'd just endured.

I headed downtown to the Cellar, a favorite watering hole for local immortals. After Tawny's coming-out party tonight, I doubted anyone I knew would be there. A little alone time suited me just fine. Yet, as I entered the crowded bar and slipped through the drinking, laughing patrons, I felt a cool sensation tickle my immortal senses. It made me think of crystal and ozone.

Scanning around, I finally found Carter sitting across the room at a round table. Seattle's most powerful angel—and the one who had burned down my Christmas tree—had sensed me too, and a slight smile curled his lips in greeting. Although he naturally hadn't been at Hell's all staff meeting, he did have a tendency to hang out with my little clique. It had weirded me out at first, but I'd since come to view him as a normal fixture in my life, albeit a strange and badly dressed one.

More startling than seeing him out tonight, however, was his assortment of companions. Three angels and a human—none of whom I'd ever met before. All of them watched me, displaying curiosity and—for one of them—scorn at my presence. Whatever. He could scorn all he wanted. It would take more than an angel posse to get to me after everything I'd experienced today. Carter's company did strike me as odd; I'd never known him to work with others. A grudging curiosity rose up within me, wondering what could have brought them all together—with a human, no less.

Noting my scrutiny, Carter winked and made a small gesture of invitation, much to the astonishment of two of the angels. I nodded back in acknowledgement, first stopping by the bar to get a vodka gimlet.

When I walked over a minute later, I put on my best saucy succubus attitude and pulled up a chair beside Carter.

"Well, well," I said. "I feel like it's Rush weekend or something. We're all entertaining guests, huh?"

"So I hear," he said. He absentmindedly ran a hand through his chin-length blond hair. Unless I was mistaken, it had been washed for the first time in six months. These guests must be serious. "I also hear one of yours is of a more permanent nature."

I pulled a face. "I don't really want to talk about that, if it's all the same to you."

"Can we expect a cat fight soon?"

"That joke is so one hour ago. You want to introduce me to the rest of the class?"

This made one of the angels laugh. She had deeply tanned skin and black hair that shone like silk. A merry glitter danced in her eyes as she extended a hand to me.

"Yasmine. And you're Georgina."

I nodded back, unable to help a smile. The one she gave me in return filled me with warmth and joy. Maybe some angels weren't so bad after all. It was a good thing, too, because her companions seemed less thrilled to make my acquaintance.

"I'm Whitney," said another slowly, a pretty black woman whose hair consisted of myriad tiny braids. She dressed with a fashion sense that met my standards and wore cat-eye glasses that made her look both cute and wise. Her handshake took a moment in coming, but it did come.

I glanced at the last angel expectantly. He had dark brown hair and blue eyes, paired with a long and narrow face. His expression conveyed clear disapproval and a haughty coldness. Now *that* was behavior I associated with angels. For a moment, I didn't think he'd speak at all. Then, with great stiffness, he said, "I'm Joel." No handshake followed.

I turned to the human. He grinned back with as much enthusiasm as Yasmine and flipped his longish dark hair out of his eyes. "Vincent Damiani. Nice to meet you."

"You too." I cut Carter a sly look. "And all this time, I didn't think you had any friends."

"You're jumping to conclusions, Daughter of Lilith." He sipped from what looked like whiskey straight up. "They're here on business."

"Ooh. Top secret angel business, huh? What're you going to do? Dance on a pinhead? Lobby for National Cute Puppy Day?"

Joel's cold look dropped another ten degrees. "As if we would discuss our affairs with a dark seductress of evil."

Yasmine elbowed him with an eye roll. "She's joking."

"That's what she wants you to think," he warned ominously. "I for one am not going to let my guard down while she attempts to use her wily and sinister powers of seduction on us."

Fixing him with a slow, languid smile, I leaned back in the

chair, crossing my legs so the skirt rode up my thighs. "Baby, if I were using my wily and sinister powers of seduction, you'd be the first to know."

A dark flush stained his cheeks. He fixed his gaze on Carter. "I don't know what game you think you're playing, but you need to get rid of her."

Carter stayed unfazed. "She's harmless—unless you're a drug-pushing god or a nephilim. Or an introverted writer."

Yasmine flinched, her cheerful countenance becoming sober. "Don't joke about nephilim."

"In fact," Carter obliviously continued, "she might fix that little logistical problem. Georgina, I don't suppose you'd mind playing hostess, would you? Vincent needs a place to stay while he's in town."

I arched an eyebrow in surprise. Misinterpreting my silence, Vincent hastily added, "It's okay if you don't want to. I mean, you don't even know me. I can see how that'd be weird."

"I don't know," I told him, even more curious as to what was transpiring with this odd group. "If angels vouch for you . . . well, you can't really get a better recommendation than that. If you don't mind sleeping on the couch, it's fine by me."

"You're a pearl among succubi," Carter declared.

Joel nearly choked on his drink. Considering his stick-up-the-ass attitude, I doubted he had anything alcoholic. Probably Kool-Aid or Pepsi. Diet Pepsi, at that.

"Are you out of your mind?" he exclaimed. "She's a succubus. You can't subject him to that. Think about his soul."

"She's not really into nice guys," Carter said. "Usually. You won't have a problem."

Yasmine offered Vincent a playful look. "He's not that nice anyway."

"Carter—" began Joel.

"I told you, she's fine. Let it go. You have my word. Besides, she won't ask any questions, and it'll give him an accessible place to stay while you guys search."

I jumped on the word "search." Now we were getting somewhere. "What are you guys looking for?"

Dead silence met me. Whitney crossed her arms. Vincent sipped his drink.

"Okay, I get it." I finished the gimlet with a gulp. "Need to know basis. Mum's the word. Hush-hush and all that."

Yasmine's easy grin returned. "I love her, Carter. No wonder you keep her around."

She then started talking about another succubus she'd met in Boston, smoothly changing subjects as deftly as Carter could. Guessing what I was thinking, Carter caught my eye and grinned. I rolled my own eyes in exasperation.

Nonetheless, as the evening progressed, I found myself liking Yasmine immensely. She, Vincent, and Carter carried most of the conversation, and while angels weren't nearly as fun as the rest of my friends, I found this group entertaining in their own way. They also swore and drank a lot less, but well, nobody's perfect.

When the bar closed, I took Vincent with me, but not before Joel issued warnings about the sanctity of the human soul. Vincent listened to it with a patient face, nodding along at the key parts.

"Is he always like that?" I asked on the drive home.

Vincent laughed. "He can't help it. He means well. He's just worried about me."

"Are you worried?"

"Nah. You're pretty cute, but no, I'm not worried. I'm already in love with someone."

I started to joke that that was no protection against anything, that I'd seduced plenty of guys who thought they were in love. Something in his voice stopped my quip. The way he spoke implied that being in love was indeed protection from me and all the other evils of the world. He spoke like one who was invincible. I suddenly felt sad.

"Good for you," I said softly.

He cut me a sidelong look. "You're okay for a succubus."

"Okay enough to tell me what you and the Super Friends are doing in town?"

A smile flashed back over his face. "No."

At home, I set him up on the couch, producing piles of blankets to keep him warm. I kept my apartment at a steamy temperature most of the time, but it was December, and the part of me that still remembered huddling around meager fires in days gone by felt one could never have enough blankets.

I soon went to bed, buried under my own stash of covers. This time, I didn't dream.

Chapter 3

After a good night's sleep, I went to work the next morning, feeling a bit more optimistic about life. I decided Tawny had probably already scored last night, and Niphon was on his way to the airport. Plus, I'd get to see Seth soon since he had made my place of employment, Emerald City Books & Café, his writing headquarters. Yes, it wouldn't be such a bad day.

Due to my ex-manager's complicated pregnancy, I'd recently inherited her position. This had left my old assistant-manager position vacant, and we'd ended up hiring Maddie Sato who just happened to be the sister of Doug Sato—the *other* assistant manager. It had been a stunning display of favoritism, and Doug had thrown a fit, complaining how we'd just lowered his coolness rating by ten points. As it was, Maddie already lived with him. She'd come to visit after his recent hospitalization and never really left. She had a second job as a freelance writer at a feminist magazine, and working at Emerald City gave her a more stable source of income.

I liked Maddie. She was smart and capable and had a twisted sense of humor that spoke to mine. She worked well with customers and was always very polite in a professional capacity. For example, she could get caught up talking with Seth about 'writerly' topics and function beautifully. But, when it came to friendlier and more interpersonal stuff, her social skills were a bit lacking. After a particularly analytical writing discussion, Seth had once made an off-hand comment about her childhood, and she'd frozen up. Seeing him with someone even more socially awkward than he was had been amusing, but mostly I'd felt disappointed at her relapse. I'd made good progress in getting her to come out of her shell and knew how fun she could be. I wanted everyone else to see it too.

Today I found her upstairs in the café, sitting at the table Seth had staked out with his laptop. It apparently wasn't a writerly day because Doug sat with them. He and Maddie appeared to be in some sort of heated argument. Seth sat between them, looking like he desperately wanted to be somewhere else. Catching my eye, he gave me a pleading look. I purposely slid a chair up beside him, forcing Doug to scoot his own chair over. No one knew Seth and I were dating, and the Sato siblings were so caught up in the discussion they didn't think anything of the chair placement.

"What's going on?" I asked. "It had better involve the fate of the store to be detaining the entire management team." The holidays were nearly upon us, and business was insane lately.

Maddie had the grace to look embarrassed, suddenly remembering her duties. She opened her mouth to speak, but Doug interrupted her.

"My illustrious sister's an insensitive bitch."

Maddie rolled her eyes. "He has some crazy ideas about Beth."

I sighed. "Look, if this is about the time Beth wore leg warmers here—"

"Don't remind me of that," grumbled Doug.

"My illustrious brother has this crazy idea that Beth just broke up with someone," explained Maddie.

Both looked at me as though they expected me to set this matter straight. Puzzled, I glanced back and forth between them.

"Why's that crazy?"

"Because she has a cold," said Maddie. "She said she has a cold. That's why she's sniffling."

"She's *pretending* to have a cold," cried Doug. "What kind of sick and twisted world is this when an asshole like me is the one to notice heartache in the masses? For God's sake, her eyes are all red."

"Cold," Maddie repeated firmly. She considered. "Or maybe allergies."

"In December?"

The two of them bickered on. Beside me, Seth fought—and failed—to keep a straight face. I studied the way his lips curved into a smile, liking their shape and recalling how they felt. I turned my attention back to the siblings, enjoying the show. Finally, after about five more minutes, I remembered I was an authority figure and not a slacker employee.

"Why is this a big deal?" I asked.

"Because she's wrong," Doug said. "I'm just trying to prove that."

Maddie sighed. "You're like a twelve-year-old."

"Am not." He jabbed her in the arm.

"Okay, enough." I pointed to Doug. "You, register." I pointed to Maddie. "You, my office."

"Ooh . . . you're in trouble," Doug told her.

"I'm going to show her how to process orders," I growled.

Maddie's eyes gleamed with anticipation, dimples appearing in her round cheeks. She ate up new tasks.

"Female favoritism," said Doug. "You like her better than me, don't you? It's okay. You can tell me. I can take it."

"Go. Both of you. I'll be down in a sec."

I looked at Seth when they were gone. "This is why I don't have children," I told him. That wasn't true, of course. Not true at all. Children simply weren't in the cards for succubi.

"Although . . . I think Doug's actually right," I mused. "As crazy as that is. I saw Beth on my way in."

Seth smiled. "Maddie's a good writer and super smart, but she's kind of oblivious to other people."

I gave him a wry look. "I thought that was true about all writers."

"Some are worse than others."

"Shocking. You rode in a car with her for, what, four hours? What'd you guys talk about?"

"Writing."

I sighed. "I wish she'd relax around people other than Doug and me. She's hilarious. She came up with the idea to Silly String Doug's car after he said Betty Friedan was PMSing when she wrote *The Feminine Mystique*."

"I'm not sure I'd describe that as 'hilarious' so much as 'scary.' Besides, that was your idea," he reminded me. "You two are dangerous. Your whole soul-stealing act seems kind of softcore compared to the stuff you and Maddie concoct."

I grinned. It was true. I hadn't really hung out with a lot of women in the last century or so and was discovering I'd been missing out. "You have no idea. Social awkwardness or not, she's the best thing that's happened to me in a while."

"Oh?"

"Well, present company excluded of course."

"Sure. Whatever you say."

"Hey." I almost grabbed his hand, then remembered we were in public. "There's no competition. You're a better cook. And a better kisser."

"I didn't realize you'd tried her out."

"Well, you know how much I like writers."

My smile slipped a little as my mind switched subjects. I'd been thinking about my energy loss all morning, particularly since I'd probably be seeking my hit tonight or tomorrow. Jerome had blown the matter off, but like usual, I couldn't let it go. I decided then that I'd go visit my friend Erik Lancaster, Seattle's local mortal source of occult knowledge. He seemed to know more than my cronies half the time.

I extended the invitation to Seth, and he agreed to come with me. I was glad. I had often thought it might do him some good to talk to another human who regularly dealt with the supernatural. This was as good of a time as any.

Seth met me at my place after work, and we microwaved a quick dinner before heading out. As we walked down the stairs of my building, he teased me about Maddie again.

"You guys were working in the office a while. Sure you weren't making out?"

"Not too much," I assured him.

He laughed and caught hold of my hand. I jerked him toward me. Our lips met in a kiss, and as the warmth of his body stirred mine, I had no doubts about what the best thing in my life was. After a few sweet moments, we followed the drill and separated, our reluctance making the disentanglement a bit awkward in execution.

"Yeah," I told him. "She's definitely not as good a kisser as—"

I cut myself off, grimacing as I felt Niphon coming toward us. His immortal aura felt slimy and musky. I stepped farther away from Seth and glared down the sidewalk at the approaching imp. Seeing me, he waved a hand in greeting.

"Excuse me a moment," I muttered. I skipped down the steps and blocked Niphon from getting within earshot of Seth. "What do you want?"

"Attitude, attitude, Letha," he tsked. "Succubi should be charming and cordial at all times." He peered beyond me. "Is that the human boyfriend? Can I meet him?"

"You can go the fuck away. You're supposed to be keeping an eye on Tawny."

"I have been," he said cheerfully. "That's why I came to see you. I followed her last night. She was quite confident in her abilities but had some difficulty arranging an assignation in the end. Poor thing. It seems she may take longer than suspected in getting established. Fortunately, I'll stay with her until the end."

His mocking concern dug into me, just as he'd intended. "Is that all you came to tell me? Because I'm leaving now. I've got to be somewhere."

"Of course, of course," he simpered. He gestured vaguely in Seth's direction. "I didn't mean to interrupt your heated moment, even if it looked like it was about to cool down." A sudden look of realization crossed his face. "You don't sleep with him, do you? You've got some sort of noble sense of duty about absorbing his life. That poor, poor man." Niphon laughed. "Oh, Letha. You are one of the most fascinating creatures I've ever come across."

I turned my back on him and stormed up to Seth. "Come on, we're leaving."

"Who was that?" he asked as we walked away.

"He's an imp. And an asshole."

Even almost a block away, I could still just barely catch Niphon's taunting laughter. I tried to ignore it as Seth and I walked to his car. Listening to my friends tease me about Seth was annoying enough. From Niphon, it was unbearable. Fortunately, I calmed down by the time Seth and I got on the road. I instead focused on seeing Erik and hopefully getting my mystery solved.

Erik ran a store up in Lake City called Arcana, Ltd. Unfortunately placed in a strip mall, it nonetheless possessed a warm, cozy feel. Dim lighting shed a tranquil air, and the bubbling of small fountains mingled with the soft sounds of a CD player emitting harp music. Books, jewelry, candles, and statuary cluttered up every inch of free space. The sweet scent of nag champa hung in the air.

"Neat," said Seth, peering around as we entered.

Erik glanced up from where he was kneeling behind a stack of books. He'd grown a mustache since last I saw him, and I liked the way the gray hair stood out against his dark brown skin. A gentle smile bloomed on his face.

"Miss Kincaid, what an unexpected pleasure. And you

have a friend." He rose and walked to us, extending his hand toward Seth.

"Erik, this is Seth Mortensen. Seth, Erik."

They shook. "A pleasure, Mr. Mortensen. You keep good company."

"Yes," said Seth, smiling in return. "I do."

"If we're lucky," I said silkily, "Erik will have time for tea. He only serves decaf, so that should make you happy."

"Of course I have time," said Erik. "I doubt there's any man who doesn't have time for you, Miss Kincaid."

I shot Seth a teasing look when Erik left to put the tea on. "Ah, now there's someone who appreciates me. You wouldn't see him shirking me for a book."

"If memory serves, you worship those books. Besides, how else am I supposed to keep you in the lifestyle you're accustomed to?"

"If memory serves, *I* paid the last time we went out."

"Well, yeah. I was just letting you play liberated so that you and Maddie wouldn't go vandalize my car."

When our tea party commenced around Erik's small corner table, I was surprised to hear Seth engage Erik in conversation on what it meant to be a mortal among immortals. Seth wasn't usually so forthcoming, and I wondered just how much immortal weirdness troubled him.

"It puts my sense of time awry," remarked Erik. "I see people like Miss Kincaid who stay young and beautiful forever. It makes me feel as though no time has passed. Then I look at myself and see the new wrinkles. I feel the aches in my bones. I realize I will be left behind . . . they will go on and continue to shape the world without me." He sighed, more with bemusement than sadness. "I wish I could see what will happen next."

"Yes," Seth said, surprising me. His eyes looked dark and solemn. "I know what you mean."

I glanced over at him, seeing something I'd never noticed

before. I knew he must think about the future and his own death—all mortals did—but only now did I realize how much he *really* thought about those things. Looking at both men, I remembered they would eventually die, and it made something in my chest grow cold. For the space of a heartbeat, I could almost see Seth as wrinkled and gray-haired as Erik.

"Morbid much, you guys?" I asked, trying to affect a blasé air. "I didn't come here to bring everyone down. I've got to pick Erik's brain."

"Pick away," he said.

"Well . . . you know how I need, uh, life and energy to survive, right?" An idiotic statement. Of course he knew. "Yesterday morning, I woke up, and my entire stash was gone."

Erik considered. "That's normal, isn't it? It fades over time."

"Not this quickly. Especially since . . ." I stopped, suddenly realizing having Seth here might not have been so wise after all. "I, um, had just gotten a refill the night before."

Both men kept neutral expressions. "And you did nothing out of the ordinary?"

"No, Jerome thinks it was mental stress." I shrugged. "I don't think I was that stressed. I dreamed . . . a weird dream . . . but nothing stressful."

"Dreams are powerful," Erik said. "And sometimes stress can take more out of us than we realize. Unfortunately, I know little about dreams, but . . ." He frowned, and his gaze suddenly turned inward.

"But what?"

"I know someone who might be able to help. Someone who specializes in dreams."

"Who?" This sounded promising.

Erik took a long time in answering. When he spoke, he seemed unhappy to give up the words. "Someone who might as well be signed and sealed to your side. His name's Dante Moriarty."

I snickered. "That can't be his real name."

"It's not, though I'm sure some of your imp and demon friends would know him by any name. He's a con artist . . . among other things. Considers himself a magician too."

"I deal with corrupt people all the time," I pointed out. "Doesn't bother me much."

"True," agreed Erik. He still looked troubled, which I found puzzling. Although not evil himself, he interacted with me and others of my ilk on a regular basis without blinking. I wondered what it was about one human that would bother him so much. "I'll get you his contact information."

He sought out Dante's card, and I browsed around the store while Seth used the bathroom in the back. The old storekeeper handed me the card when he found it.

"I like Mr. Mortensen a great deal."

"Yeah. So do I."

"I know. I can tell."

I looked up from a display of bracelets, waiting for more.

"You talk and move around each other in a way you're probably not even aware of. It's like how lovers usually inter-act . . . but it's something more too. You have a continual sense of each other, I think, even when not together. There's a burning in the air between you."

I didn't know what to say to that. It sounded nice—but a little intimidating too.

"I've never met another of your kind who's exactly like you, Miss Kincaid." He hesitated, his normally wise-and-competent expression flickering into uncertainty. It was a rare look for him. "I don't know how this will turn out."

Seth emerged then, picking up that he'd interrupted something. He glanced between the two of us, and I rested a reassuring hand on his arm. "You about ready to go?"

"Sure."

I scanned the rest of the jewelry counter, only half-noticing the contents. Suddenly, I did a double-take and leaned over one of the cases. "Erik, where do you find this stuff?"

He and Seth looked over my shoulder.

"Ah, yes," said Erik. "The Byzantine rings. By the same artist who made your ankh necklace."

"Your artist has a real knack for historical detail. They look just like the originals."

He walked around the counter and lifted out the tray with the rings. I picked one up. It was an ordinary gold band. Rather than any sort of mounted gem on top, it bore a smooth and flat disc, almost the size of a dime. Greek letters were engraved into the metal.

"What do they mean?" asked Seth.

I tried to explain the long-lost custom. "It's a benediction. Like a prayer for the couple. This would have been a wedding ring."

I examined another depicting Christ and the Virgin; still another showed a tiny man and woman facing each other.

"I used to have a ring almost like this," I said softly, turning it over in my hands. Neither man said anything, and I finally returned it to its tray.

On the way home, Seth gently asked, "What happened to your ring?"

I stared out the window. "It's not important."

"Tell me."

I didn't respond, and he didn't ask me again. When we got back to my place, I saw no sign of Vincent and figured he was out investigating with Charlie's Angels. Newspapers were scattered across my kitchen table; he apparently liked to keep up on current events. Morbid events, at that. One of the headlines was a story I'd heard the other day about a crazy man who'd killed his wife after having a vision of seeing her with another man. Mortals did creepy things sometimes. Okay, a lot of the time.

Seth sat on my couch and leaned forward, hands clasped together. I'd sensed his mood shift when I wouldn't answer in the car.

"Thetis . . ."

"You want to know about the ring."

"The ring doesn't matter so much. It's just . . . well, I've seen you get like this. Something bugs you, something you re- member. But you won't talk to me about it. There are days I feel like you don't tell me anything."

I sat down next to him, avoiding eye contact in a way he often did. "I tell you plenty."

"Not about your past."

"I have a lot of past, and I talk about it all the time."

"Yeah . . . I guess." He absentmindedly stroked my arm. "But you don't talk about your mortal past. Before you were a succubus."

"So? Does it make a difference? You're with me *now*. You know the kind of person I am now."

"I do. And I love that person. And I want to know what's important to you. What made you who you are. I want to know what hurts you so that I can help."

"You don't need to know that to know who I am. My human past doesn't enter in to anything," I said stiffly.

"I can't believe that."

Again, I didn't answer.

"I don't know anything about that part of your life," he continued. "I don't know your real name. What you really look like. Where you grew up. I don't even know how old you are."

"Hey, it's not just me. You have plenty of things you don't talk about," I pointed out, trying to deflect the attention.

"What do you want to know?"

"Well . . ." I groped for something I didn't know much about. "You never talk about your dad. How he died."

Seth answered immediately, without hesitation. "Not much to tell. Cancer. I was thirteen. According to a therapist Mom made us see, I withdrew into a world of fantasy to cope."

I leaned my head against his shoulder, knowing he'd ex- pound on anything I wanted to know—in a subdued, Seth sort of way. It was ironic considering his normal conversational reticence, but that was how he operated. He believed relationships had to have an open exchange of honesty and baring of souls. I supposed he was right, but there were too many dark parts of my soul I didn't want to share. Parts I was afraid would scare him off.

I knew Seth well enough to realize he wouldn't push this issue anymore tonight, but I could also sense his hurt and disappointment. He didn't ask me these questions to upset me; he did it out of sincere affection. That didn't make it easier, unfortunately, and I fought my anxiety and long-buried pain to try to offer him something. Anything. Anything to show I was making an effort in this relationship. My original face and name were dead to me, obsolete reminders of the woman I'd left behind, never mind Niphon's insistence on calling me Letha. Seth would never know those things.

We sat together for a long time while I decided what I could give up. Finally, with the words sticking in my mouth, I said, "I grew up in Cyprus." The air grew tense as we both waited for more. "In the early fifth century. I don't know exactly what year I was born. We didn't really keep track of those things."

He exhaled. I hadn't realized he'd been holding his breath. Slowly, carefully, he put an arm around me and pressed his lips against my hair. "Thank you."

I buried my face against his shoulder, not knowing what I hid from. I'd barely given him anything—just a couple of pieces of trivia. Nonetheless, yielding that tiny bit from a place in me I wanted to hide from was powerful. I felt exposed and vulnerable without fully understanding why. Seth gently stroked my hair.

"Is the ring from around that time?" he asked.

I nodded against him.

"It'd be worth a lot then, I suppose."

"I lost it," I whispered.

He must have picked up on the anguish in my voice. He held me tighter. "I'm sorry."

We stayed together a while longer that night, but I knew he wanted to go home and work at his own place. Unable to deny him, I shooed him away, though I had a feeling that he would have stayed if I'd asked it.

Once he was gone, I went into my bedroom and closed the door. Kneeling in front of my open closet, I pulled out box after box, setting them haphazardly around the room. My organization lacked something—like, say, organization—and it took me a while to sift through the clutter of junk. Finally, I produced a shoebox covered in dust.

Lifting the lid, I felt my breath catch. Old, brown letters lay stacked with a few photographs. A heavy gold cross on a fraying string lay among the papers, along with other small treasures. I carefully hunted around until I found what I wanted: a bronze ring, green with age.

I held it in my hands, still able to discern the engraved couple atop the mounted disc. It was a cruder job but still very similar to Erik's modern renditions. I ran my fingertips along the ring's edges without knowing what I did. I even tried it on, but it didn't fit. It had been made for larger fingers than I had now. I refused to shape-shift to the right size.

I kept the ring out for a few more minutes, thinking of Seth and Cyprus and all sorts of things. Finally, unable to stand the ache within me, I put the ring back into its box and buried it once more in the closet.

Chapter 4

The next day, I went to the address on Dante's business card. It was in Rainier Valley, which wasn't exactly run-down but wasn't upwardly mobile either. The directions led to a narrow shop jammed in between a barber and a shady-looking convenience store. PSYCHIC hung in red neon letters in the window. The "I" had burned out. Underneath it, a handwritten sign read: PALM READING & TAROT CARDS.

I stepped through the door, making bells ring. The interior proved to be as barren as the exterior. A narrow counter flanked one wall. The rest of the small, stark space was empty, save for a round table covered in red velvet that had cigarette burns on it. A tacky crystal ball sat on top. This place was a wasteland compared to Erik's warm, inviting shop.

"Just a minute," a voice called from an open doorway in the back. "I've just got to—"

A man entered the room and stopped when he saw me. He was about six-foot, with black hair pulled back in a ponytail. Two days worth of facial hair covered his face, and he wore jeans and a plain black T-shirt. Early forties, maybe, and pretty cute. He looked me over from head to toe and gave me a sly, knowing smile.

"Well, hello. What do we have here?" He tilted his head,

still studying me. "Not human, that's for sure. Demon? No, not strong enough. Vampire? No . . . not this time of day."

"I . . ." I stopped, surprised that he'd sensed something in me. He had no immortal signature; he was definitely human. He must be like Erik, I realized. A mortal who could sense the immortal world, though he didn't have enough skill to pinpoint what I was exactly. Deciding there was no point in subterfuge, I said, "I'm a succubus."

He shook his head. "No, you aren't."

"Yes, I am."

"You aren't."

I was a bit surprised to be having this conversation. "I am too."

"No. Succubi are flame-eyed and bat-winged. Everyone knows that. They don't wear jeans and sweaters. At the very least, you should have a bigger chest. What are you, 34B or something?"

"C," I said indignantly.

"If you say so."

"Look, I *am* a succubus. I can prove it." I let my form change, shifting through several different female variations before returning to my usual one. "See?"

"Well, I'll be damned."

I had a feeling he was playing with me. "Are you Dante?"

"For now." He approached and shook my hand, holding on to it. He flipped it over. "You here for a palm reading? I'll show you how to shape-shift your hand to get a good future."

I took my hand back. "No, thanks. I'm here because I have some questions . . . questions that Erik Lancaster thought you might be able to answer."

Dante's smile dropped. He rolled his eyes and walked over to the counter. "Oh. *Him.*"

"What's that supposed to mean? Erik's my friend."

Dante leaned his back against the counter and crossed his

arms over his chest. "Of course he's your friend. He's every-one's friend. Fucking boy scout. If he could have shaken his holier-than-thou attitude and worked with me, we could have made a fortune by now."

I remembered what Erik had said about Dante being a con artist and a Hell-bound person. I didn't pick up any evil vibes off him, but there was a definite abrasiveness to his attitude that made Erik's assessment more plausible.

"Erik has standards," I declared.

Dante laughed. "Oh, great. A holier-than-thou succubus. This is going to be fun."

"Look, can you just answer my questions? It won't take long."

"Sure," he said. "I've got time—at least until the next rush of customers." The bitter tone in his voice as he gestured to the empty room indicated that there hadn't been a rush in a very long time.

"I had a dream the other night," I explained. "And when I woke up, all my energy was gone."

"You're a succubus. Supposedly. That kind of thing hap-pens."

"I wish everyone would stop saying that! This wasn't nor-mal. And I'd been with a man the night before. I was charged up, so to speak."

"You do anything afterward that would have depleted the energy?"

Everyone kept asking that too. "No. I just went to bed. But the dream . . . it was really strange. I don't know how to explain it. Really, really vivid. I've never felt anything like it."

"What was it about?"

"A, um, dishwasher."

Dante sighed. "Did someone pay you to come here and mess with me?"

Through gritted teeth, I related the dream.

"That's it?" he asked when I finished.

"Yup."

"Lame dream."

"Do you know what it means?"

"Probably that you need to fix your dishwasher."

"It isn't broken!"

He straightened up. "Sorry. Can't help you then."

"Erik said this was your specialty."

"It is, I suppose. But, sometimes a dream is just a dream. You sure you don't want me to read your palm? It's all bullshit, but I can at least make something up so you feel like the trip wasn't wasted."

"*No*, I want to know about my fucking dream. How can it be just a dream if I woke up with no energy?"

Dante walked back over to me and flicked a piece of escaped hair out of his face. "I don't know. You aren't giving me enough to go on. How many times has it happened?"

"Just the one time."

"Then it may be just a fluke, kiddo."

I turned toward the door. "Well, thanks for the 'help.' "

Hurrying over to my side, Dante caught my arm. "Hey, wait. You want to go get a drink now?"

"I—what?"

"I'll risk upsetting the masses and close up shop for the day. There's a great bar around the corner. Draft Budweiser—only a dollar a glass during happy hour. My treat."

I scoffed. I didn't know what was more absurd. That Dante thought I'd go out with him or that he thought I'd drink Budweiser. His attractiveness wasn't enough to make up for his weird personality.

"Sorry. I have a boyfriend."

"I'm not looking to be your boyfriend. Cheap sex is fine with me."

I met his eyes. They were gray, similar to Carter's but without the silvery hue. I expected a joke here, but despite the perpetual smirk, Dante appeared to be perfectly serious.

"Why on earth do you think I'd have cheap sex with you? Do I look that easy?"

"You say you're a succubus. You're easy by definition. And even without the bat-wings and flame-eyes, you're pretty cute."

"Aren't you worried about your soul?" Even if he was as corrupt as Erik had insinuated—and I still wasn't really seeing that—Dante would take some kind of hit from sleeping with me. All mortals did. Of course, I'd met plenty of men—good and evil alike—who'd been willing to risk their souls for sex.

"Nope. My soul's pretty far gone. This would just be for fun. Look, if you want to skip the beer, we can just get right to it. I've always wanted to do it on the table over there."

"Un-fucking-believable." I pushed open the door.

"Oh, come on," he pleaded. "I'm pretty good. And hey, maybe your boyfriend's poor sexual performance is what's stressing you out and taking away your energy."

"Not likely," I told him. "We don't have sex."

There was a moment's silence, then Dante threw back his head and laughed. "Did it occur to you that maybe *that's* stressing you out? Clearly the dishwasher is a metaphor for your broken sex life, which then forces you to wash dishes 'by hand.'"

I left, heading back to the bookstore where I could get a little respect. Some dream expert Dante had turned out to be. I could see now why Erik didn't really like him. I was also starting to wonder if maybe everyone was right. Maybe I had mentally burned myself out. Maybe the dream was really just a dream.

I was almost at the bookstore when I got a phone call.

"Miss Kincaid?" asked a pleasant female voice. "This is Karen from the Seattle Children's Alliance, calling to confirm your participation in our auction this week."

"Your what?"

There was a pause. "Our charity date auction, to raise money for the Alliance."

I was still baffled. "Um, sounds like a great cause, but I have no idea what you're talking about."

I heard papers being ruffled. "We have you listed as a volunteer."

"For what, to be auctioned off for a date?"

"Yes. It looks like . . . here we are. Your name was submitted by Dr. Mitchell."

I sighed. "Let me call you back." I hung up and dialed Hugh. "Hey, Dr. Mitchell. You volunteered me to be auctioned off?"

"It's not that different from what you usually do," he argued. "And it's for charity."

"I buy the peace-on-Earth-and-good-will-toward-men thing from Peter and Cody—but not from you. You don't care about those kids."

"I care about the group's director," Hugh said. "She's a fucking fox. I get some high quality candidates to raise money, and I can probably get her in bed."

"You're using a children's charity to further your sex life. That's horrible. And why didn't you ask Tawny? If anyone needs a date, she does."

"Her? Jesus Christ. It'd be a disaster. We're trying to make money here. Do you hate kids or something?"

"No, but I don't have time to do it. I'll write them a check."

I hung up on his protests, just as I turned onto Queen Anne Avenue. I was a little early for my shift and decided to stop home and grab an apple and a granola bar. Last time I'd worked, we'd been so busy that I'd skipped my lunch break. I figured that this time, I should come prepared. My immortality wouldn't let me starve to death, but I could still get lightheaded and weak.

Halfway down the hall to my apartment, I felt a shock wave of crystalline goodness. Angelic auras. I opened my door and found the whole gang: Carter, Yasmine, Whitney,

Joel, and Vincent. None of them spoke; they were all just watching me expectantly. The angels would have sensed me long before I sensed them. They all sat in my living room, casually occupying my sofa and chairs as though they weren't a host of heavenly warriors. Well, not all of them were casual. Joel sat as stiff and formal as he had the first time I met him.

"Oh, man," I said, shutting the door behind me. "It's just like that They Might Be Giants song."

Vincent grinned. " 'She's an Angel'?"

I nodded. "Somewhere they're meeting on a pinhead—"

"—calling you an angel, calling you the nicest things," he finished.

"What are you doing here?" demanded Joel, interrupting our jam session.

"Or not so nice," I muttered. I turned from Vincent and glared at Joel. "I live here, remember?"

"We're having a meeting," he said.

"Hey, when you asked if Vince could stay here, you never said anything about making this your top secret tree house headquarters. I don't care if you guys hold your choir practice here or whatever, but don't try to throw me out while you do."

"Sorry," said Yasmine. I did a double-take. Apologies from angels were about as rare as from demons. From the look on his face, Joel was about as surprised as me. "We probably should have asked first. We can go somewhere else." She leaned over my coffee table and started gathering up newspapers. Interesting. Apparently Vincent's fixation with the news was more than just a personal hobby. I glanced back up at Yasmine and tried to act like I hadn't noticed anything.

"No, it's fine. I'm actually heading right back out. I just came by for some food."

She pushed strands of long, black hair out of her face. They'd slipped out of her ponytail. "You want Vince to make you something?"

He turned to her, startled, wearing an astonished, yet still-amused look. "What am I, your personal assistant?"

"Not with the kind of respect you show us," she grumbled.

I hid a smile. "Thanks, but I'm fine. I don't have the time."

"Good," said Joel. "Then hurry up."

Whitney sighed and looked a little embarrassed—but not enough to contradict him. Yasmine had no such qualms and elbowed him in the ribs. "What was that for?" he exclaimed.

"You have no manners," she scolded.

Grinning broadly, I went to the kitchen and found an apple. When I opened the cupboard to look for my granola bars, I found the box empty. "Hey," I said, carrying it out to the living room. "Did somebody eat these? I had two left this morning."

Carter spoke up for the first time. "I was hungry."

I stared at him, incredulous. "You ate *both* of them?"

"I was hungry," he repeated, not looking contrite in the least.

"Does it ever stop with you?" I exclaimed. "First the Christmas tree, now this? You didn't even throw the box away!"

"I was hoping you'd forgotten about the Christmas tree. That was an accident, and you know it."

I sighed loudly and put the apple in my purse.

"I'm going to the grocery store later," said Vincent helpfully. Aubrey jumped up and settled herself between him and Yasmine. Both their hands instantly moved to pet her. Aubrey gave me a smug cat look at the attention. "I'll pick you up some more if you want."

"Pick *him* up some more so that he doesn't go rob the food bank next. See you guys later. No wild parties while I'm gone." Carter, Yasmine, and Vincent laughed; Whitney and Joel didn't.

When I'd shut the door behind me, I paused in the hall,

wishing there was some way to spy on angels. There wasn't, unfortunately. I couldn't even hide from them. They could mask their signatures from me, but not vice versa. In fact, they all knew I hadn't left yet. Annoyed, I headed downstairs, curiosity burning in me. Why were they all here? Why did they need a human? And what role did the newspapers play?

Figuring out what angels did with their time was always difficult. With my side, it was pretty straightforward. We were always looking to commit souls to Hell and did so in a well-monitored, micro-managed manner. Heaven's forces moved in mysterious ways, though. Carter's purpose in Seattle was a continual puzzle for my friends and me since none of us ever saw any evidence of him doing anything particularly noble, aside from sharing his cigarettes. He did always show a lot of interest in my love life and was quick to dispense cryptic pieces of advice, but I suspected that was more curiosity than altruism.

Work was only a few blocks away. Since it wasn't raining, I simply walked down there. As soon as I entered Emerald City, Maddie approached me, an uncomfortable expression on her face.

"Hey," she said uneasily. "I, um, need your advice. I'm going to a wedding tomorrow and don't know what to wear. This is so stupid . . . but could you take a look at my options?"

Peering around, I decided the store could function without us for ten minutes, particularly since it had taken Maddie a fair amount of courage to broach this subject. I'd never actually seen her dress up before. "Okay. Let's see what you've got."

We went back to my office, and she tried on three different dresses. No doubt Seth would have been amused to know she was changing clothes while I was in there.

When she'd finished, I gave my honest opinion. "They don't do you justice."

"Which is a nice way of saying they look awful on me."

Maddie balled one of the dresses up and tossed it to the floor. "I hate this sort of thing. How can I write about women's issues and not be any good at them?"

"Well . . . you write about different kinds of issues. The problem here is that you're wearing clothes that are too big for you."

Her dark eyes widened in surprise. "*I'm* big. They're loose. They hide it."

Maddie wasn't big, not really. She was a size ten or twelve, if I had to guess, and her short height emphasized that a little. But her curves were all proportioned correctly, and she had a very pretty face. Of course, compared to the anorexic models so popular among humans today, I could understand her attitude.

"You are not big. But those dresses make you look it. Something smaller's going to make you look better."

"I can't wear tight clothes."

"They don't have to be tight. They just have to fit."

Maddie sighed and ran her hands down the sides of her thighs. "You don't know what it's like," she said, the slightest accusatory note in her voice. "You're beautiful and tiny. Not all of us have the luxury of looking perfect all the time."

"No one looks perfect all the time," I argued. "I certainly don't." Okay, I kind of did. "You've just got to find the right things. And really, half of beauty is attitude. You feel sexy, then you *are* sexy."

Maddie looked dubious. "I don't think it's that easy. Guys aren't exactly chomping at the bit to ask me out. You know how long it's been since I was on a date?"

"That goes back to attitude," I said. "Look, I don't mean to sound harsh, but you don't always give off friendly vibes. I mean, you do to me. And to Doug. Sort of. But really, that's it."

"I know I'm not the best with people," she admitted, crossing her arms over her chest. "But I just can't do meaningless small talk."

"Yeah, but you still have to do *some* talking. It's a fact of life."

"Well, if guys came and actually talked to me, maybe I could try. But they aren't really lining up." She gestured at her body. "Because of this. And now we've come full circle."

"What if I could guarantee you a date?" I asked, suddenly inspired.

Her lips quirked into a smile. It instantly transformed her face. "Are you asking me out?"

"No, but someone else will, I'm certain of it. You just have to let me pick out your outfit."

"I'm not wearing anything slutty."

"It won't be," I promised. I stood up from my chair. "Look, I've gotta run. Wear the yellow dress to the wedding. With a belt. I'll give you details later about the date plan." She left, looking skeptical, and I threw myself into work.

The rest of the day flew by. I never saw Seth in the café and presumed he was working at home today. We had a date later on, so I knew I'd see him then. Since becoming manager, I spent a lot of time holed up in my office, which was hard on the social part of me. But, every once in a while, I got to escape to cover someone's break or arrange a display.

While near the self-help section, a guy carrying some books stumbled near me and dropped the stack. Hoping he hadn't tripped on a bump in the carpet and was planning a lawsuit, I hastily knelt down to help him.

"No, no," he said, cheeks burning. He was the age I looked, late twenties. Early thirties at most. "You don't have to . . ."

I was already stacking them, though, and quickly understood his discomfort. They were books on all sorts of fetishes—in particular, exhibitionism and voyeurism.

"Oh God," he said, as I handed him the books. "I'm so embarrassed. I feel like such a pervert."

"It's okay," I told him. "It's your business, and we've all got our . . . ah, preferences."

He looked mildly reassured but still clearly wanted to bolt. There was a wedding ring on his hand, and I expected I was dealing with a fetish he probably didn't share with his wife. Honestly, I was surprised he'd resorted to actual books when he could find a hundred times more sources on the Internet. Most likely he and his wife shared a home computer, and he feared discovery.

It was Georgina the succubus, not Georgina the bookstore manager, who asked the next question. Georgina the bookstore manager would have gotten fired for it if caught.

"You like the watching or the doing?" I kept my voice low.

He swallowed, studied me for mockery, and must have decided I was serious. "The, um, doing."

For half a breath, I considered going for it with him. I needed the energy, badly. He'd be an easy mark, consumed with a secret obsession he couldn't fulfill anywhere else. But, it'd mean doing it in *this* body, and I didn't like that. This was my preferred, everyday shape. I didn't want to sully it with business.

So, I smiled and sent him on his way, silently wishing him well in fulfilling his sexual desires.

I called Seth later while I was walking home from work to confirm our date. We were going to meet over at the Pacific Northwest Ballet to see *The Nutcracker*. While he appreciated the performing arts, getting him to go out while his book's ending loomed had been a Herculean task, and I still couldn't believe he'd agreed. He'd only conceded after I'd promised he could show up at the last possible minute.

Only, we apparently had different definitions of "last possible minute" because when the lights went down, he still hadn't surfaced. The ballet started, and I craned my neck each time I heard one of the doors open. The chair beside me stayed empty, unfortunately. It was a sign of my agitation that I missed a lot of the performance and couldn't appreciate Clara's dream—a dream as vivid for her as mine had been for me. I loved the ballet. I'd danced in a few shows over my lifetime and never got tired of watching graceful muscles and elaborate costumes.

At intermission, I turned on my cell phone and saw that Seth had tried to call. I dialed him back without even listening to the voice message. When he answered, I said, "Please tell me a crazy fan kidnapped you and broke your legs with a sledgehammer."

"Um, no. Didn't you get my message?"

"Well, no, seeing as my phone said it came in a half-hour ago. I didn't have it on because I was busy watching this thing. You know, *The Nutcracker*?"

He sighed. "I'm sorry. I couldn't leave. I was too wrapped up. I thought if I, uh, gave you enough notice . . ."

"Notice? This was more like a belated birthday card. Six months after the fact."

Silence fell, and I felt some satisfaction in knowing he was quietly acknowledging his wrongdoing.

"I'm sorry, Thetis. It was . . . I shouldn't have done it, busy or not. I'm really sorry. You know how I get."

Now I sighed. He was so damned sincere and adorable that I had a hard time holding a grudge. This wasn't, however, the first time he'd stood me up or otherwise neglected our social life. Sometimes I wondered if I allowed him too much indulgence. I spent so much time worrying about my transgressions taking advantage of him; maybe I was the one being walked over without even realizing it.

"You want to meet up after the show?" I asked, trying not to sound mad. "Cody invited me out to the bar with them. We could hang out there for a while."

"Um . . . well, no."

"No?" The annoyance I'd tried to quell shot its head back up again. "I just forgave you for standing me up and wasting the money I paid on your ticket, and now you're turning down my conciliatory offer?"

"Look . . . I really am sorry, but watching you and your friends get drunk isn't exactly appealing."

I sat for a moment, too stunned to respond. He'd spoken in his typically mild way, but I'd heard the slightest bit of derision underscoring his words. Seth didn't drink. He always tolerated my excesses good-naturedly, but I suddenly wondered if they irritated him after all. His meaning came through as haughtiness to me.

"Sorry we're not up to your standards. God knows we can't expect you to do anything outside of your comfort zone."

"Please, stop. I don't want to fight with you," he said with exasperation. "I'm really, really, *really* sorry about all this. I didn't mean to stand you up. You know that."

The lights flashed, signaling the end of intermission. "I've got to go."

"Will you . . . will you please come over tonight? Go out with your friends, let me finish, and then I'll make things up to you. I promise. I . . . I have an early Christmas present for you."

The hesitancy in his voice softened my heart. A little. "Yeah. Okay. It might be really late when I get there."

"I'll wait up."

We said our good-byes and disconnected. I watched the rest of the show in a grumpy mood and decided drinking and bitching with the gang couldn't come a moment too soon.

Chapter 5

Peter, Cody, and Hugh already had a table when I arrived at the Cellar. Tawny sat with them, much to my dismay. I'd completely forgotten about my apprentice. At least she didn't have Niphon in tow. I hoped that meant she'd finally bagged a guy, though her lack of a post-sex succubus glow suggested otherwise. Neither Carter nor Jerome had deigned to show. I recalled that Jerome was out of town and figured the angel was out with his colleagues. They could all still be at my apartment for all I knew.

"Hey," Cody called in greeting, making room for me beside him. "I thought you said you were busy."

"Yeah, well, plans change," I grumbled. I gestured to Hugh. "Got a cigarette?"

He tsked me. "No smoking in public places anymore, sweetie."

Groaning, I flagged down a waitress. Smoking was an ugly habit I'd given up for the sake of the mortals around me. Still, after smoking for over a century, I found I craved the occasional hit during stressful times. The city smoking ban was good for Seattle but damned inconvenient for me and my bad mood.

Cody couldn't let my vague answer go. "How'd your plans change? Weren't you and Seth going out?"

Hugh laughed when I didn't answer. "Uh-oh, trouble in paradise."

"He had things to do," I replied stiffly.

"Things or people?" asked Peter. "Didn't you give him the go-ahead to sleep around if he wanted?"

"He's not doing that."

"Tell yourself that if it makes you feel better," teased Hugh. "No one can write as much as he claims to."

Since my friends apparently had no lives of their own, I had to endure a number of other pokes and jibes. They probably didn't mean to do any real damage, but their words hurt anyway. Seth had already upset me enough without their help. Anger simmered within me, and I tried to channel it into my rate of gimlet consumption rather than my friends.

The only person who looked more miserable than me was Tawny. She wore a strapless red dress, almost identical in cut to the satin sheath I still had on from the ballet. Unlike mine, hers was made of spandex—what was it with her and that fabric anyway?—and about six inches shorter. Mine also fit.

"Why so glum?" I asked, hoping the others would find someone else to obsess on.

Her lower lip trembled, either from sadness or an inability to hold its own massive collagen-filled weight. "I still haven't, you know . . ."

It was enough to allay my own distress. It also meant Niphon was still in town, as I'd suspected upon seeing her. "How? How is that possible?"

She shrugged and leaned forward wretchedly, her elbows resting on knees that were spread open guy-style. With grace like that, no wonder she couldn't get laid.

I waved my hand around us. "Well, go out there, young succubus. This place is a buffet. Grab a plate and take your pick."

"Oh, yeah, like it's that easy."

"It is that easy. You might not be up to scoring a priest or anything, but you can definitely get some sort of fix."

"Maybe you can. I don't . . . I don't really know what to say to them."

I honestly couldn't believe this conversation was happening. It was weirder than me trying to convince Dante I was a succubus. Maddie had trouble talking to guys too, but a giant, crazily proportioned blonde throwing herself at men could get someone to sleep with her. It was a basic law of the universe.

"Well . . . if you really don't know what to say, just try going up and asking them if they want to have sex. Crass, but it'll probably work for someone."

She scoffed. "Right. That's all there is to it."

"That *is* all there is to it," I said. Hugh returned from the bathroom, and I glanced over at him. "You want to go have sex?"

He didn't even blink. "Sure. Let me pay my bill."

I turned back to Tawny. "See?"

"Wait," said Hugh, one hand on his coat. "Was that a joke?"

"You were an instructive example," Peter explained.

"Fuck."

Tawny shook her head, tousled blond curls fluttering. "I can't do that."

"Oh my God." I resisted rubbing my eyes, lest I muss the makeup. "Tawny, this isn't rocket science."

"Weren't you telling us how hard it was to do your job, back when your incubus buddy was around?" asked Peter. My friend Bastien's recent visit had elicited a veritable cheerleading squad of admirers for him and what my male friends deemed "the hardest job ever."

"Shut up," I snapped. "You're ruining my mentoring."

"I don't want a bad one," Tawny said petulantly. "I want to corrupt a good one. One that'll give me lots of energy."

"Start small. Don't worry about the good ones when you probably can't even pick them out in the first place."

"How *do* you find one?"

"It's an art. One you'll learn. I'm telling you, though, just start small."

I did give her a few pointers, recalling my alleged role as mentor. We studied some of the men in the bar, spotting wedding rings and one bachelor party. A guy about to get married was a really nice hit. I also advised on demeanor, how a quiet man was often (but certainly not always) a better bet than a loud, obnoxious one—if you were going for good ones. Of course, serial killers tended to be quiet too. Really, it came down to reading people, which wasn't a skill she could learn overnight. Keeping this in mind, I tried to reiterate how she should just try easy fixes for now.

"I really like how you've got the entire male population pegged," said Peter when I'd finished lecturing. "I'm glad you don't believe in stereotyping or anything."

I shrugged. "I've been doing this for a while."

"Okay, prove it," said Hugh. He and I were at about equal levels of intoxication now. "Find three decent souls in here."

I grinned. Imps could gauge the strength and goodness of a person's soul with a glance. Accepting the challenge, I scanned for a long time. When I picked my three, he shook his head.

"You got two out of three. The two that are right are really good. The one you got wrong is pretty bad. At least you're dealing in extremes."

Tawny moaned. "You see? This is hard."

"For Christ's sake," I exclaimed, finishing another gimlet. "It's not. Not in the rookie leagues you're playing in. Look, you want a tip? Go get a job that gives you easy access."

"I am not going to go stand on a corner," she said huffily.

"Then go . . . I don't know. Go to Hugh's date auction." The imp glared at me. "Or go work at a strip club. It's about the easiest thing a succubus can do. Hang out at the bar after your number, and they'll come to you. A stripper's a hot commodity, particularly when a lot of those guys'll think you're a prostitute anyway."

"I don't know. It still sounds degrading."

"You're going to be fucking to sustain your existence for the rest of eternity! Get off your high horse. You wait much longer, and your first-one's-free energy stash will dry up. Stripping's easy. And fun. And you get to wear pretty costumes. Trust me, it's a good racket."

"I guess," she said at last. She exhaled heavily, the motion pushing her breasts out even further than usual.

"Georgina's a pro," said Hugh, reaching over to give her a comforting pat. Considering he really wasn't a warm and fuzzy kind of guy, I suspected he just wanted to brush her breasts. "Or so I hear. I guess I'll never find out." He gave me a bitter glance.

"If that's true," Tawny said, "then how come her own boyfriend blew her off?"

The guys let out a collective "ooh" and glanced eagerly between the two of us, apparently in anticipation of the catfight they'd long predicted. All of my earlier fury resurfaced, fueled now by alcohol and Tawny's incompetence.

Grabbing my glass, I strode up to the bar to get a refill in person. Hanging out with my friends was rapidly losing its charm. A newbie succubus didn't have any right to mock me about my dating difficulties, particularly when she couldn't land *one* guy. I could have landed a dozen if I'd wanted to tonight. At the same time.

And, glancing over beside me, I realized I might very well have an easy score right here.

The guy from the bookstore, the one with the fetish books, stood at the bar, talking to the bartender. He didn't appear to be with a group. Hastily, I turned away so he wouldn't recognize me. After I got my drink, I set it on my friends' table and retreated to the bathroom without another word to them. I'd had to use bathrooms as shape-shifting hideouts for years, but there was nothing to be done for it in these situations. Inside a stall, I changed into a long, graceful body with flowing gold hair—not unlike some of the ballerinas I'd seen tonight. I'd show Tawny how to do blond right.

Walking back out, I caught Cody's eye. My friends could recognize me in any shape, of course, and he gave me a puzzled look as I strode back to the bar. Standing beside the guy from the bookstore again, I ordered another drink. This time, he turned and caught sight of me. I smiled.

"That any good?" I asked, nodding to the red concoction he was drinking.

"I guess." He lifted up the glass and peered at it. "It's a pomegranate cosmo. I think. Kind of girly, honestly—no offense."

"None taken."

The bartender slid my whiskey on the rocks to me. The guy beside me laughed.

"I suddenly feel emasculated," he said.

I grinned and extended my hand, speaking the first name that came to mind. "I'm Clara."

"Jude."

"Hey, Jude."

He sighed.

"Sorry," I said. "Couldn't resist."

"You and everyone else."

"You here alone?" I asked.

He looked embarrassed and absentmindedly rubbed the empty finger his wedding ring had been on the last time I saw him. "Yeah."

"Me too."

He looked me over, attempting covertness and not doing a good job. "I find that hard to believe."

"Well . . ." I looked down at my drink, playing with its edge. "It's kind of a long story . . ."

And slowly, skillfully, I crafted a tale about how I'd come here to meet a guy and how he'd stood me up. He was supposed to go to a sex club with me, though I didn't come right out and say that immediately. That would have been too much for someone like Jude, someone who was intrigued but still nervous about the whole idea of exotic sexuality. So, I spoke vaguely at first, using innuendoes, hinting at my own interest in exhibitionism, how I just wanted to go see what a place like that was all about.

As I concluded, I used the same line he'd used in the bookstore. "I feel like such a pervert. Honestly . . . I don't know why I'm telling you this. I don't even know you. It's just . . ." I looked up at him with big blue eyes. "You're easy to talk to."

A long silence followed as Jude held my gaze. "I don't think . . . I don't think there's anything wrong with what you're saying . . . what you want . . ."

Snick! I started reeling in the line.

"Really?"

"Yeah . . . I mean, sometimes . . . I've kind of . . . you know, wanted . . ."

"Really?"

He nodded.

I allowed a five-second hesitation. "You want to go with me? Just to, you know, watch?"

After a bit of rumination, Jude agreed. Unsurprisingly, he didn't know where any sex clubs were in the city. Also unsurprisingly, I did.

I didn't even look back at my friends as Jude and I left the bar. I hadn't clocked it or anything, but I was pretty sure my solicitation had been accomplished in record time. That'd teach the gang to question my pro status.

The club we went to was one I'd visited a number of times before. I'd been to better ones in my day, but I liked this one simply because of its name: Insolence.

Establishments that catered to sex and fetishism all operated in different ways. In places where everyone expected to participate—like swingers' clubs—admission was strictly regulated. Single girls always got into places like that, and couples usually only had a few requirements. Single guys had a harder time. In a place like Insolence that was focused primarily on watching, admission was more lax. We simply had to pay our cover, and we were in. Mine was still cheaper, though.

The place was packed and had a dance club kind of feel. Techno music pulsed through the darkened room, the only illumination coming from recessed lights that shone blue and purple. Most of this light focused down on roped off areas that were reserved for those who wanted to "perform." They were like small stages that the club-goers could gather around. Some of the stages were themed—one with a doctor's office and operating table setup—while most were couches and beds. There appeared to be no system about who could use them. It was a first-come, first-served system, and since about half the platforms were empty, there didn't seem to be too much urgency. But the spectators eagerly crowded around those areas that were occupied, people craning their necks to get a better view.

"There sure are a lot of guys here," Jude told me as we pressed our way through the people.

"It's the way of the world," I told him.

"You think guys are more interested in this stuff than women?"

"To a certain extent, yeah. Guys tend to be more visual, so stuff like this is about as good as it gets. Plenty of girls are into it too—just harder to get them to come out to something like this." I promptly shut up, immediately realizing I sounded a bit too knowledgeable for a shy novice.

We finally made our way up to the edge of a roped-off area. There, we watched a man thrusting eagerly into a woman bent over an elegantly set dining room table. Jude and I studied them for a while, neither of us saying a word. We then moved on to the next couple, a man and woman going at it on an ordinary bed. She wore a shiny leather bustier and hiked-up skirt. After the third couple—pressed up against a wall—Jude finally spoke.

"These people aren't what I expected."

"How so?" I asked.

"They just look . . . ordinary."

I laughed. "Because they are. What'd you expect, porn star couples coming in off the streets?"

"Well, no." I suspected he was blushing in the darkness.

"Everyone's entitled to do what's sexy to them. And really, when you see how they're getting into it . . ." My gaze drifted to the couple going at it against the wall. Their eye contact was so powerful, so intense . . . you could totally see how much they aroused each other. I shivered. "Yeah, this is all sexy, even if it's not airbrushed. This is real. That's what gives it its edge."

He didn't answer but glanced around as though he was re-assessing it all. As he did, I studied his profile. He wasn't quite six-foot, but he had a nice upper body and neatly styled, sandy blond hair. He turned toward me, sensing my scrutiny.

"You know," I said, "if you're so concerned about raising the bar around here . . . well, *we're* pretty attractive."

He didn't get it at first. "Yeah, I suppose we—oh. *Oh.*" His brown eyes went wide.

I looked back at the wall couple. "We're already here. We could really give these people something to watch."

His eyes grew wider still, like they might pop out. "I . . . I couldn't. I mean. God. Not in front of all these people. And what if someone I know is here . . ."

"I doubt it. Besides, what are they going to do? If they tell anyone, they'd have to acknowledge that they were here too." I caught hold of his hand. "Come on, I know you're interested."

"Yeah," he admitted. "But I've never . . . I don't think I could . . ."

I tugged him toward one of the stages. "You gotta start sometime. It's easy."

Jude looked terrified but let me drag him. "You act like you've done this before. I thought it was all new."

"It is."

"You sure? Maybe you just play innocent and then seduce random men into crazy sexual acts."

I scoffed. "That's ridiculous."

We'd barely ducked under the stage's ropes when a mob suddenly swarmed around us. I doubted this had as much to do with us in particular—yet—as it did the fact that we were a new couple. Ah, variety. The spice of life.

Jude still looked terrified, but I didn't have the patience for his hesitancy anymore. The performer in me had clicked on. All those people were waiting and watching, and I had to deliver.

One of our props was a chaise lounge covered in white velvet that glowed blue under the lights. White, I decided, probably hid certain stains better than other colors.

"Come on," I said, pushing Jude toward the chaise. "Lie down."

He did, but still looked panicked. "Clara—"

"You're already here," I said sharply. "What are you going to do? You going to slink off in front of all these people? You didn't strike me as a coward when I first met you."

I'd become someone else now, someone commanding and terrifying. He shook his head.

I climbed onto the chaise with him, straddling his hips with my legs. The lack of energy within me suddenly burned and ached, and I didn't want to be gentle. Leaning down, I kissed him hard, my teeth scraping his lips as I thrust my tongue into his mouth. He let out a small sound of surprise that was lost in the kiss. Meanwhile, my hands were already frantically unfastening the buttons of his shirt. I think I ripped one of them off.

Jude lay there limply, still in shock. It didn't matter to me, though, so long as he didn't fight me. And from the feel of him underneath my hips, not *all* of him was limp.

I ran my fingers down his chest, digging my nails into the flesh there. A kindly part of me wondered how he'd explain scratch marks to his wife. The rest of me didn't care. I'd given "Clara" a black tank top and gray skirt—simple but sexy. I yanked the top off over my head, shaking my hair out afterwards like a golden veil. I contemplated taking off the black lace bra underneath but decided to leave it on.

My mouth moved down from his lips, traveling to his neck and chest, pausing to tease one of his nipples. Then I kept going, down to the edge of his khakis. While there, I undid his belt and unfastened his pants in one swift motion. I pushed them and his underwear down to his knees, just enough to give me access to the erection underneath. I took it into my mouth, letting its long shaft glide into me, almost to the back of my throat. He gasped, a noise echoed by some of the appreciative spectators.

I felt the early twinges of his life force. It twinkled like starlight, seeping into me. As it did, I got a taste of his thoughts and emotions, as well as his strength and character. When I'd gleaned enough of his energy to assess its quality, I almost laughed. This wasn't the first time he'd done anything like this with a strange woman. He'd actually done it twice before. He was still shy about it all, but some of his innocence had been faked, a lure for dominant women like me. Hugh had been right—I couldn't always gauge a soul. But, infidelity still didn't sit right with Jude, so he had enough goodness and life force to fill the void that the dream had left inside me.

My mouth moved with more urgency, sucking and teasing. He groaned as my lips slid back and forth. His back arched, and I pulled away, fearing this might end right now if I wasn't careful. Climbing off him, I stood up and pulled my skirt off, letting it fall in a crumpled pile on the floor. Jude looked at me with pleading eyes, not proactive yet, but definitely wanting more.

An ornate wooden chair stood near the chaise. I moved over to it and knelt on its cushioned seat, pressing my breasts up against its carved slats. I peered back at Jude over my shoulder.

"Showtime," I said.

I expected hesitation or reluctance, but Jude had apparently overcome his initial reticence. Good. I didn't want to feel like I was raping him or anything. He clambered off the chaise and walked over to me. I had pushed his pants to his knees earlier, and now he finished the job, kicking the khakis off. Positioning himself behind me, he ran his hands along the sides of my hips, letting his fingers slide along the edges of the black panties I still wore.

I shifted, pressing my ass up closer to him. He sighed. "You are so sexy."

"I know," I told him impatiently.

He pulled the panties down, letting them rest near my knees. I ground against him even more and felt him push into me, the penetration forceful and deep. Gripping my hips, he began moving in and out, shoving me into the chair's hard back with each thrust. I moaned loudly, but whether it was for his benefit or the crowd's, I couldn't say.

And speaking of the crowd, I was now literally in a position to look at them, at the faces and eyes all directed toward me. I'd shed most of my self-consciousness over the years, and God only knew this wasn't the first time I'd had sex in public. Sometimes, I appreciated privacy, but tonight I loved being the center of attention. Maybe it was simply my longing for more life energy. I would have taken it under any conditions right now. Whatever the cause, I found myself getting turned on by making eye contact with different guys in the audience while Jude continued pumping away at me.

As I'd noted earlier, eye contact was a powerful thing. It took you away from the realm of superficial study and moved you into something deeper and more intimate. I favored the guys watching me with a heavy, sultry look—the look of a woman being fucked within an inch of her life and who wanted nothing more than to do it with *them* next. It thrilled me to think of all the men I was arousing, of all of them aching for sex—of all of them aching for *me*.

In meeting the gazes of my admirers, I almost forgot that it was Jude who was behind me. It could be any of these men, and their expressions clearly showed that they'd be happy to trade places with him. I looked from face to face, imagining what each man would feel like, how each one would fuck differently. The thrill of it was so arousing that my wandering mind soon fantasized about having more than one at the same time. One in back, one in front . . .

One of Jude's hands gripped my hair and jerked my head back while the other hand still steadied itself on my hip. The rough maneuver pulled me out of my daydreams, but I was so turned on now that I welcomed his aggression. He thrust harder, driving me painfully into the chair, and I hoped it wouldn't fall over. The sweetness of his life energy coming into me continued building, and I felt his thoughts stream into me as well. *So good, so good, so good.*

And it *was* good. The voyeurs around us and him fucking me on my knees had aroused me to dizzying heights. The whole act was dirty and exciting and thrilling.

"So good, so good," I cried, echoing his thoughts. "Don't stop, don't stop, don't—oh."

Talk about irony.

The trick I'd used on Bryce or Bruce or whatever his name was had worked here too. Only, I hadn't actually wanted it to end this time. Maybe this was Jude's normal style—short and sweet—and not actually my doing. Regardless, it was done, and I hadn't even come. Damn it.

But I'd gotten my energy fix, a burst of life and wonder that had exploded into me with his orgasm. Ecstasy or no, he'd felt a pang of guilt at the last minute, regret over this continued desire to cheat on his wife. That guilt had been a bonus for me. Sin was subjective, and often, the magnitude

of a sin was in the eye of the beholder. I'd gotten him to sin—
which Hell always liked and gave me bonus points for—and
I'd cracked his morals, giving me more energy than I would
have stolen if he were completely corrupt. I felt that life rein-
vigorate my essence, fueling my immortality and ability to
shape-shift.

He pulled out. I stood up from the chair, catching his hand
as he started to stagger. A few people whistled and clapped.

Jude wore a look of wonder—and exhaustion. I handed
him his pants.

"Wow," he gasped. "That was . . . wow."

"Yeah," I said with a grin. "I know."

Chapter 6

I hadn't realized how late it was until I showed up at Seth's around two. He actually wasn't writing for a change, and I found him sprawled on the couch, flipping through late night television programming.

"Hey," I said, dropping my coat and purse near the door. He glanced up from the TV. Its light cast ghostly shadows on his face in the darkness. "Sorry it's so late. Something came up."

"Yeah," he said, voice still flat. "I can tell."

Immediately, I caught his meaning. It was a sign of how well he'd come to know me and recognize subtle succubus signals. I was wreathed in Jude's life energy. Immortals would actually perceive it as a literal glow. Mortals couldn't see it, but they could sense something insanely alluring and attractive about me. Usually, they just wrote it off as a sign of my beauty. Seth knew better. When he sensed it around me, he knew what I'd been doing.

I hated for him to see me like this, but it was inevitable. "Sorry. It's what I do. You know that."

"Yeah," he agreed, sounding tired—mentally tired, not physically tired. He straightened up. "But did you have to do it tonight? You trying to punish me for standing you up?"

I sat down in the armchair across from him. The energy

from Jude burned through me and made me feel alive. I didn't want a fight with Seth to ruin my good mood, particularly after I'd been so annoyed for most of the evening.

"I did it to survive. I wasn't trying to get back at you."

He sighed and stared off into a dark corner. "It's so hard sometimes."

I moved over to the couch, scooting up beside him. "I know."

He slid his arm around my shoulders and regarded me with a look both tender and exasperated. Leaning down, he brushed his lips against my neck. The small touch made my blood burn.

"God, you're beautiful. I just wish it wasn't the result of some other guy."

"Yeah," I said. "Me too."

"Sorry I blew up."

"You call that blowing up?" I asked. "That was nothing."

"And I'm sorry I stood you up. That wasn't right."

Seth had moved up my neck and now nibbled my ear. I closed my eyes and tilted my head back.

"It's okay," I assured him. "Really."

"You're awfully forgiving."

"Hey, what can I say? Christmas love and kindness, right?"

He laughed and ran his fingers through my hair. "For someone allegedly so evil, you sure are good."

"Well," I said, pressing into him. "I'm not that good. I'm thinking some very bad thoughts right now."

"Yeah. Me too. If our thoughts condemn us, I think I'm headed straight for Hell."

"No, you aren't. Hugh says your soul's like a supernova. You're going straight to the pearly gates."

Warm love and desire enfolded us, supplanting the cold tension. Yet as we curled up and chatted about light topics, I couldn't help but morosely think this was a common scene

between us. Fight. Brood. Apologize. Snuggle. In all the fan-
tasies of a stable relationship that I'd harbored over the last
millennium, this pattern had never been a part of them.

After a while, we sort of surpassed snuggling and moved
onto something of a more adult nature. At least I did. Sometimes Seth could be coaxed into sating his lust, though it always made him incredibly self-conscious. Me, I loved watching
him come. He was always so damnably blasé that seeing him
lose control in an orgasm almost did more for me than my
own climax.

He apparently had the same feelings toward me and was
content to simply watch me touch myself tonight. After not
getting off with Jude, I was more than happy to take things
into my own hands. When I finished, languid and content afterward, he lay down on the couch beside me, lacing his fingers with mine.

"I don't think I'll ever get tired of that," he sighed.

"You should finish yourself off."

"I'm okay."

"You sure?"

He smiled. "Self-control, Thetis. Self-control. Besides, I
have a good imagination. Sometimes it's enough to pretend
I'm the one doing that to you."

I shivered as an image of Seth played in my mind, his body
inside of me while I came, muscles clenching around him as I
cried out his name and dug my nails into his back.

"Jesus," I said softly, closing my eyes.

"Yeah."

We realized then that it was *really* late and started getting
ready for bed. When I emerged from the bathroom after
brushing my teeth, I found him waiting for me in the bedroom with a small box. He handed it over.

"I told you I had an early present."

I turned the package over in my hands, running my fingertips over the edges. It had been wrapped in gold paper and
had a red bow. Judging from the sloppy wrapping and mis-

aligned ribbon, I was willing to bet he'd wrapped it himself. I offered up a small grin.

"It's way too early. Presents before Christmas? That's not right. I mean, I'm not that evil."

He sat back on the bed, leaning against the headboard, looking supremely pleased with himself. "Well, I am. I guess my soul just dimmed a little. Open it."

Sitting down as well, I hesitantly tore the paper. There was no question in my mind that this was a jewelry box. The question was: What kind? Seth occasionally showed a romantic spirit, but he wasn't the type to do anything crazy like propose. At least I didn't think so.

Hoping for a tennis bracelet, I instead found a ring. But it wasn't an engagement ring, not in the current way of thinking. It was one of the modern recreations of the Byzantine rings. Only this wasn't one of the ones we'd seen at Erik's, not exactly. It was platinum for one thing, glowing soft and silvery in the dim lighting. The smooth disc on top had a dolphin engraved in it, decorated with a few tiny, embedded sapphires.

I stared at it, unsure what to say.

"Do you like it?" Seth asked, a hint of nervousness in his voice.

"I . . . yeah. Yes, I do. Very much." My words came out haltingly.

"You seemed so sad about losing the other one that I thought maybe this would be a nice substitute."

He looked so rapt and excited that I couldn't bear to tell him that not only had I *not* lost the original ring, I'd actually hidden it away in the closet so as never to see it again. This one was very different, true, but the similarities were strong enough to dredge up all the dark feelings I tried to keep buried, memories of a sunny day long ago when my husband—the husband I'd eventually betrayed—had slipped the other one onto my finger at our wedding.

"It's beautiful," I said after a long stretch of silence, needing to reassure him. It had been very kind, after all. Seth didn't know my history or the pain intertwined with it. "Why a dolphin?"

"Yeah . . . it's kind of cutesy and trendy, but . . . well, none of those Greek letters meant much to me. But I read something about dolphins being important in old religions on Cyprus, so . . ."

That brought a true smile to my face. "Yeah. They were. Messengers from the sea gods. Good fortune and all that." Something occurred to me. "We saw these at Erik's, like, a couple days ago—but not this one. How'd you get it? Did he have more in stock? Or did you go somewhere else?"

His eyes crinkled with amusement. "Hey, I'm learning your powers of persuasion. I got in contact with the artist and commissioned it."

Good lord. Seth had had a custom ring—a *platinum* custom ring—made right before Christmas. And he'd had it done in a matter of days. The cost must have been through the roof. The queasy feeling in my stomach intensified. Observing my silence, his smile faltered.

"You sure you like it?"

"Yeah, yeah . . . of course. I just . . . I'm sorry, I don't know what to say. It's great." I slipped it onto my right ring finger. It fit perfectly. Hesitantly, I met his eyes. "This is a, uh, friendship ring right?"

"Yeah, don't worry. If I propose, you'll know it. For one thing, I'll be hyperventilating." A sly smile—surprisingly sexy—turned up his lips. "And it'll be a ruby."

"Rubies? No diamonds? Too expensive for the old writer's salary, huh?"

He made a disparaging grunt at that. "No, I just think diamonds are common, that's all. If I get married, it'll be because something uncommon is occurring. Besides, you wear a lot of red, right? I know how important it is for your accessories to match."

I snorted at that and let him draw me into the bed. He fell

asleep quickly, as always, but I lay there, touching the ring. Its metal had warmed to my skin, and I could trace the dolphin and sapphires with my fingertip. The unpleasant memories the ring stirred up hadn't abated, but somehow, lying in his embrace, they seemed a little less painful.

Sleep finally came to me, and I immediately started dreaming—*the* dream.

I was back in the kitchen, surrounded by all the same vivid sights, smells, and sounds as before. My hands in the water. The scent of orange soap. "Sweet Home Alabama."

It was a repeat of what I'd seen before, my dream-self washing dishes and humming along to the music. She glanced behind her into the other room. This was where the dream had ended last time. Now it kept going.

A little girl sat in the living room, about two years old. She was on a blanket on the floor, surrounded by stuffed animals and other toys. She clutched a plush giraffe in her hands. It rattled when she shook it. As though sensing my dream-self's gaze, the little girl looked up.

She had plump cheeks that hadn't quite lost their baby fat. Wispy, light brown curls covered her head, and her hazel eyes were large and framed with dark lashes. She was adorable. Behind her on the couch, Aubrey lay curled up in a tight little ball. Another cat—covered in orange-and-brown patches— sprawled nearby. I'd never seen it before.

A delighted smile spread over the little girl's face, creating a dimple in one check. A powerful wave of love and joy spread through my dream-self, emotions that my watching self felt. I knew then—knew in a way I couldn't explain but knew with *absolute certainty*—that this girl was my daughter.

I woke up.

Just like last time, morning had arrived with almost no passage of time for me. Sunlight again poured through the windows, and beside me, Seth still slept. Also like last time, my energy was gone. I was drained.

But the ache of that missing energy was nothing compared to the ache I felt from being ripped out of the dream, of being stripped of the powerful emotions my dream-self had felt for that little girl. Her daughter. *My* daughter.

No, that was impossible, I scolded myself. Succubi could have no children. I'd left that path behind when I sold my soul.

It had felt so real, though. So intense. It was impossible for me to have a child, but in that dream, she had been mine. No doubts. Even now, I felt that maternal tug, and not having her here *right now* tore at my heart.

And again, I told myself that was stupid. Dreams weren't real. That's why they were . . . well, dreams. And I had bigger problems to deal with. Like the missing energy.

Beside me, Seth stirred and unconsciously pulled the covers around him, leaving me uncovered. I yanked them back, and he turned toward me, opening sleepy eyes.

"Hey," he said. "What gives?"

"Not you, apparently."

"Not you either, apparently."

"Hey, I'm the evil one, remember?"

We bantered a bit more and continued playing tug-of-war with the covers. I put on a smiling face so I wouldn't have to explain my problems to him. Finally, I slipped away, though part of me wished I could stay in bed for the rest of the day. Dreaming. But Seth had writing to do, and I had an afternoon shift to work.

Back home, I found Vincent up and around, making breakfast in the kitchen with Yasmine. They greeted me boisterously, giggling over some conversation that had occurred before my entrance.

"You want some eggs?" he asked me, catching a stick of butter tossed over by Yasmine. Presumably they'd gone grocery shopping since I hadn't had any butter in my kitchen before this. Or any food, really.

"No thanks," I said, settling myself on a stool. "I already ate."

"You're missing out," she said. "Vincent makes eggs that are so decadent, they're totally sending him straight to Hell."

Setting a skillet on the stove, he turned on the burner, listening to the clicking sound made while the gas took a moment to ignite. "Oh, it's the eggs that are going to do it, huh? Last time you told me it was going to be my parking."

The angel's eyes sparkled with mischief. She'd pulled her sleek black hair up into a ponytail, making her look very young. Ironic, considering her age was beyond human or succubus comprehension.

"Oh, geez. Yeah. I forgot about that. Huh. Now there's a toss-up. I'm not sure which is going to send you down below faster. Needing a stick of butter to cook two eggs or parallel parking three feet from the curb."

He jabbed her arm with a wooden spoon. "Three feet? You know, I've never even seen you *drive* a car. The only thing you drive is me—crazy."

"Oh yeah, whatever. You were crazy before I ever came along."

Glancing back and forth between them as they bickered further, I realized they'd forgotten my presence. Feeling intrusive, I discretely backed away, down the hall and to my bedroom. Closing the door, I glanced in astonishment at Aubrey. She sprawled on my bed, warmed by a patch of sunshine.

"Has that been going on all morning, Aub?"

Yawning, she blinked at me with green eyes and then curled into a perfect white ball—similar to the position I'd seen her in in the dream. She covered her face with one paw.

Um, okay. This was unexpected. I mean, was I crazy? Or had they . . . had Yasmine and Vincent been flirting? I mean, sure she was a friendly angel and everything, but that . . . yes, the more I thought about it, the more I believed they had been flirting. More than flirting. Weirder still, it hadn't been the kind of banter two people toss back and forth during the courtship phase either. It was the familiar teasing of two people who had been together for a long time, two people so utterly comfortable in each other's presence that they could almost finish each other's sentences. It was like the phenomenon Erik had described with Seth and me.

"They're in love," I told Aubrey disbelievingly. She continued to ignore me.

How did that even work? They couldn't be sleeping together. I'd learned a while back that doing that would make an angel fall, and Yasmine was still clearly on the side of truth and justice. So what did that mean? Was it okay if an angel loved a human so long as they stayed physically apart? Something inside of me didn't think so. After seeing how prudish Joel had been, I felt pretty confident even a chaste love affair wouldn't fly with him or the others. So none of them probably knew, not even Carter. And honestly, I didn't know if *I* wanted to know. I was a sucker for star-crossed lovers, but those relationships never actually ended well.

Grabbing some clothes and heading for the shower, I realized I might be witnessing a romance even more fucked up than my own. Who'd have thought that could happen? I guessed with angels, miracles really were possible.

I finished showering and drying my hair, still pondering the puzzle of this love affair. I headed back out to the living room, wondering if I'd find more flirtatious behavior. Instead, what I found was a familiar and unwelcome immortal signature. Slimy and musky.

Niphon was sitting on my couch.

Chapter 7

"Get out," I said immediately.

Yasmine and Vincent, finishing their breakfast at my table, looked up in surprise. Niphon gestured toward them.

"I was invited in. I didn't think it'd be a problem."

Angel and human looked distinctly uncomfortable, and I could guess what had happened. Niphon had turned up, and they'd let him inside, not knowing about our animosity. They'd probably figured he was a partner in evil which, in the most technical of ways, he was.

Vincent hastily stood up and took his empty plate to the sink. Yasmine followed.

"Well," said Vincent. "We should probably get going."

"Yeah," agreed Yasmine, grabbing her coat. Fools rushed in where angels feared to tread, apparently. "Great seeing you guys."

They left so fast that they might as well have teleported out.

I fixed my attention back on Niphon. "Get out," I repeated.

He leaned back against my couch, draping his arms over the back of it. "Letha, Letha—"

"And stop calling me that."

"Whatever you like. And don't worry, I'll be out of your hair soon. I just wanted to give you a Tawny update."

Oh God. Tawny. *Please, please let her have scored last night*, I silently begged. Her attitude at the bar hadn't really inspired confidence, but maybe me leaving with Jude had set a good example.

"She hasn't taken a victim yet."

Damn.

"Alright, thanks," I said, pointing at the door. "You can leave now. And next time, it's really okay if you call to give me an update. Preferably when you're in the taxi that's taking you to the airport so I don't ever have to fucking see you again."

He rose from the couch, giving me a wounded look. "Fine, fine. But there *is* one other thing I wanted to talk to you about."

"There is nothing at all I want to talk to you about." I was on the verge of growling.

"Oh, I'm not so sure about that." His hand rested on the doorknob, but he showed no intention of actually leaving. "I think you'll be very interested. It's about your love life."

"No! We are not talking about this."

"Le—Georgina, I just want to help you," he whined. "I think it's terrible that you two can't fully express your love."

"We. Are. Fine. And don't lean against the door. I don't want your hair to leave an oil stain."

Niphon straightened up and ran a solicitous hand over the back of his head. "Look, I get why you don't want to sleep with him. It's admirable. You want to protect his lifespan, not wipe him out, etc., etc. But what if that wasn't an issue? What if I made it so that you could have sex without the dire side effects?"

"Right. And you'd do that out of the kindness of your heart."

"Well . . ." He shrugged and spread his hands wide. "There's always a price."

"It's not worth it. Not worth Seth selling his soul."

"I could sweeten the deal. Give him a longer lifespan . . . longer youth . . ."

"*No*. I swear to God, if you don't leave now, I'm calling Jerome." That was a bluff, seeing as Jerome was out of town.

"Like I said, just trying to help," Niphon said.

"Yeah, like you helped me?" I asked, not bothering to hide the sarcasm.

Suddenly, the mocking, teasing look vanished. Niphon's face grew hard. Angry. Scary.

"I *did* help you, Little Letha. You were no one. No one at all. Some poor fisherman's daughter in a shit, backwoods town. Some *whore* in a shit, backwoods town. You fucked up your life, and I fixed it for you. I made you who you are. Erased your problems. Saved your husband. Gave you eternal life and beauty. If anything, you owe me."

"It wasn't worth it," I said, in a voice that matched his dark expression. "It wasn't worth it."

"Wasn't it? Would you have rather watched your husband commit suicide? Would you rather have died an outcast and disgraced?"

I didn't answer. I thought about the desperate look on my husband's face when he'd found out that I'd cheated on him. Even after all these centuries, that expression still haunted me. He'd been driven to such despair that he'd been on the verge of taking his own life. In selling my soul and becoming a succubus, I'd struck a bargain with Hell that made him and everyone else I knew forget me. My husband had lived and gone on with his life, forgetting I'd ever existed. Had it been worth it?

Observing my silence, Niphon's face turned taunting once more. He opened the door. "Good-bye, Georgina. Let me know if you change your mind."

He left, and I stared at the door for a long time before finally forcing my feet to start moving. The Seth soul-selling offer held no temptation for me whatsoever. That didn't trouble me. But his other words . . . the reminders of my past . . .

I sighed. I didn't want to deal with that, not with everything else going on in my life right now. And speaking of which ... with two hours left until work, I decided to bite the bullet and again try to get more information about my dreams. From Dante.

His store looked as bleak as the last time I'd visited, but this time, he actually had a customer. She was a young woman, college-aged maybe, with layered brown hair and a gray sweatshirt. Seeing her, I started to step back outside, but he waved me in.

"No, no, it's okay. You can wait here." Dante glanced at the girl. Both of them sat at the shabby, velvet-covered table. "You don't mind, do you?"

She barely spared me a glance. "No! No! Hurry, go on. I want to hear more about the man."

Dante produced a dazzling grin that seemed a bit fake to me but which I suspected was actually very effective on her. Taking a step closer, I realized he was reading her Tarot cards. Several already lay on the table. He flipped another over.

"Ah, the Hierophant." His voice held a mysterious, knowing note.

"What's that mean?" she squealed.

"You don't know? You don't know anything about these?"

She shook her head. "Nothing."

"Well, the Hierophant is a great love card. It represents a romantic man, someone good-looking and charming who loves giving gifts and doing small gestures. You know the kind."

"I don't, actually," she said wistfully. "All my boyfriends have been jerks."

"Well, that's going to change," he promised.

I knew quite a bit about Tarot cards, actually. The Hierophant represented tradition, wisdom, and organized religion. He wasn't exactly a romantic figure, particularly considering he was usually depicted as a priest.

"Why is he dressed so weird?" asked the girl. "He looks like he's in robes."

"It's not weird," Dante said. "It's *opulent*. Remember, the Tarot is an ancient system. A guy dressed like this represented the height of fashion back in the old days. You know, a real designer label kind of guy."

I caught Dante's gaze and rolled my eyes. He maintained his poker face and flipped the next card.

"Things are looking good," he declared. "The Tower."

The Tower was pretty much the worst card in the deck.

"This shows you guys have a promising future."

"Why is it on fire?" she asked. "And why are people falling out of the windows?"

"It's all symbolic," he said hastily. "And although things look really good for when you meet this guy, it means you have to be cautious and read the signs around you."

"Oh, wow," she said. "I hope I can."

Dante gathered up the cards and stacked them neatly. "Well, I can help if you want. I could give you a package set of readings at a discount. That way, you'll have a guide as you go along. You'll be prepared for when you meet him."

I sincerely doubted she was ever going to meet this mythical guy.

"How much?" she asked hesitantly.

"Hmm, let's see." Dante turned speculative. "Well, they're normally fifty dollars. Usually, I give a five-dollar discount for packages . . . but, hell. I really want to see this work. I'm a romantic myself, you know? It's a stretch, but I'll do a set of six for forty dollars each. You can buy them now and then come in whenever you want to claim them."

The girl deliberated, and I wanted to yell at her that it was a scam. But I needed Dante's advice and didn't want to get on his bad side. Not that I was necessarily on his good side right now.

"I don't want to pressure you," he told her gently. "So, please. Don't feel obligated. Just do whatever your heart tells you to do. I mean, if the cards have told us anything, it's that you have to protect your heart now as you enter this important stage of your life."

That sold her. "Okay. I'll do it."

I watched in disbelief as the two of them walked to his register. She handed over two-hundred-forty dollars—plus tax—and he gave her a Tarot punch card, not unlike what you'd get at a coffee or sandwich shop.

"You should be ashamed of yourself," I told him when she was gone.

"Succubus. Nice to see you too."

"That wasn't a romance reading."

"Nope," he agreed, coming over to stand beside me. "It actually suggested she'd soon be having a sex change and joining a suicide cult."

"But you told her it was about love."

"She's twenty years old. Love's all they want to hear about at that age."

"You're going to Hell."

"I could have told you that. In fact, I *did* tell you that last time, didn't I? Now. What can I do for you? You change your mind about the sex?"

"No. Of course not."

He looked offended. "Of course not? What's with the attitude? I'm not that unappealing."

"No," I agreed. He looked like he still hadn't shaved in a couple days, and there was something very sexy about that and the way his indigo T-shirt fit him. I hadn't realized before what nice ab muscles he had. Probably the lack of business around here gave him lots of time to work out. "But that's not why I'm here. And honestly, if this behavior is just the tip of the iceberg, I'm thinking your soul isn't going to be worth my time anyway."

He threw his hands in the air. "She comes and insults me, then expects help. So what is it you want? Your dishwasher finally break?"

"No, but I had the dream again. And there was more."

I recapped it, and he listened, face unreadable.

"You sure you don't want a new dishwasher?" he asked dubiously.

"No!"

"What about kids?"

"What about them?"

"You want them?"

I fell silent, and despite his lopsided smile, I could see Dante scrutinizing me. He might be a con artist, but he was smart. The best ones always are. People like him make their living reading people and exploiting little things—like that girl's longing for romance.

"It doesn't matter," I said. "You know that. I can't have them."

"I didn't ask that, succubus. I asked if you wanted them."

I averted my eyes, studying the crystal ball. With the way the sunlight hit it, I suspected it was actually plastic.

"Sure. I did even when I was mortal. If I could have kids now, I would."

He nodded, and for the first time, I got the impression he might almost be taking me seriously. Almost. "And let me guess. You woke up without energy."

"Yes, and I'd gotten a victim the night before. Just like last time."

His face turned speculative. "Interesting. It only happens when you're charged up."

"What do you think it means?"

"Dunno. Might not mean anything."

"It has to! I'm losing energy for no reason at all."

"You're stressed," he argued. "And you're, like, one of the most uptight people I've ever met—immortal or otherwise. You've spent centuries wishing you could get knocked up. You have this celibate boyfriend thing going on. And you work for that demon, right? The one who looks like Matthew Broderick?"

"John Cusack," I corrected. "He looks like John Cusack."

"Whatever. That's enough to tax anybody. Your dreams are manifestations of the woes in your life, coming out of your subconscious in vivid, energy-sucking ways."

"You are so unhelpful. Your dream expertise is a scam—like everything else."

"Nah. Not everything I do is a scam. I know dreams. I know spells. And I know what could help you."

"What?"

He pointed to the counter. "You and me. Up there. Naked. Horizontal."

I groaned. "Wow, you really weren't lying. You are a romantic."

"A pragmatist. And an opportunist."

"A sleazy guy, treating me like a cheap whore . . ."

"Fuck, I haven't been laid in months, and now this succubus shows up wanting my help. You'd try to bargain for sex too."

I eyed him warily. "Is that what this is about? I have to sleep with you to get help?"

Dante shoved his hands in his pockets. "Nope. You'd be more fun if you were willing, I think. Besides, I have no other help to give."

Disappointed, I made motions to leave. "Okay. Thanks. Sort of."

"You know what else might help?" he called after me.

"If it involves sex—"

"A vacation. At the very least, a massage. Basic stress reliever things."

Those were actually reasonable things, and I was pleasantly surprised to see his mind wasn't always in the gutter. "They can help," I told him. "But I doubt a massage will fix the problems in my life."

"Maybe. Maybe not. But if you want a free one . . . a naked free one . . ."

I left.

I'd already felt like my romance with Seth was some infinite loop tape reel. The rest of my life apparently was too. Have the same dream, go to Dante, get no help, go to work, and ruminate. Because that's exactly how my day was unfolding, just like before.

I went through the motions of paperwork and customer service at Emerald City, all the while consumed by images of the little girl in the dream and the sweet fantasy of having a daughter. My heart ached to see her again, to see that smile. Everything at my job seemed so shallow and meaningless compared with her.

When work ended, I brought Maddie back to my apartment to make good on my promise to get her a date.

"You're going to sell me?" she exclaimed when I told her the plan.

"It's an auction," I said. "For a children's charity. You don't hate kids, do you?"

"Well, no, but—"

"Then this'll be great. Here, try this on." I tossed her a BCBG shopping bag. She eyed it warily.

"Isn't that a place for teenagers?"

"It's a place for anybody with style," I assured her.

She opened the bag and pulled out the knee-length dress I'd picked up for her the other day. It was silk chiffon with a dark pink geometric print. The empire waist had a slightly gathered top, and the V-neck had a bow that tied underneath it. Fluttery cap sleeves finished it off.

"I can't wear this," she said immediately.

"Why? Because it'll look good?"

She shot me a glare. "There's hardly anything there."

"What? There's plenty." I owned lots of dresses that had "hardly anything there." This was elegant and tasteful. Amish country compared to some of my clothing. "Try it on, and we'll see."

She did, reluctantly, and I could have crowed with delight when she stepped out of my bathroom. I'd totally nailed the size. It fit perfectly.

"There isn't an extra inch here," she fretted, pulling at the fabric around the waist.

"Exactly."

"Doesn't it make me look fat?"

"It makes you look great. If it were spandex or something, there might be a problem, but this is light and drapey."

"The neckline's awfully low—"

"Oh, be quiet," I snapped. "And let's finish the rest of you."

I did her makeup and arranged her hair down for a change. It shone like black silk when brushed out, and I thought it was a shame she wore it in a haphazard ponytail so often. Besides, everyone knows that in the movies, shy girls always become beautiful by letting down their hair and taking off their glasses. Maddie already wore contacts, but the principle was still sound. I finally finished her off with half-heeled shoes I'd bought to match the dress. Higher ones would have looked better, but even I knew when not to press my luck. Satisfied with the results, we headed out to the auction.

"You're like my fairy godmother," she muttered as we walked into the hotel the event was being held at. "But I'm still a pumpkin."

I elbowed her. "How did you get so negative? You should start some angstful emo rock band to compete with Doug's."

"Oh, yeah. That'd go over—hey, is that Seth?"

We were cutting across the open room the auction would take place in, heading toward the volunteers' area. Lots of people had gathered, filling most of the round tables facing the stage. I followed her gesture to where Seth sat at one of the few tables that wasn't already full. Seeing us notice him, he held up his hand in greeting.

"He wanted to come support you," I told her. Actually, Seth had been appalled at me strong-arming Maddie into this and had attended mainly out of a perverse fascination at what he thought might end in disaster.

But Maddie, not knowing his motives, was pleasantly surprised. She smiled, and I nearly swooned.

"That," I said. "That right there is what you need to do."

The smile dropped. "That what?"

Hugh practically skipped over when he saw us. "I knew you didn't hate kids. I knew you'd cave and come help—"

"Not me," I said. "Maddie." I rested a hand on her shoulder.

Hugh's face turned perfectly blank. "Oh?"

Just then, a tall brunette in a black satin evening dress strolled over. The "fucking fox," presumably. She extended her hand. "Hello, I'm Deanna, the coordinator. You must be Hugh's friend?"

"Georgina," I said, shaking. "But Maddie here is your volunteer. She's a journalist for an important women's magazine."

Deanna's eyes lit up. "Ah! We love celebrities. Let me take down your information."

She led Maddie away. As soon as they were gone, Hugh turned on me. "What the hell? I wanted Georgina, and you give me Georgy Girl."

"You are such an asshole. That's a horrible thing to say."

He shrugged, eyes on Maddie. "I call 'em like I see 'em. She's huge."

My eyes were on Maddie too. She actually looked quite slim in the dress, but Hugh was one of those guys who liked bony types—so long as their chests were big enough.

"You're the reason women have such horrible self-esteem issues. You tear them apart. Women, I mean. Not the issues."

"Look, I'm sure she's not all bad," he said. "She probably gives good head."

I rolled my eyes. "Flatterer. Why do you say that?"

"Fat girls always do. They have to. Only way they can get men."

I punched him in the arm. Hard.

"Ow! Fuck, that hurt."

"You're a jerk," I told him. "Maddie's beautiful."

"She's okay," he said, rubbing his injured arm. "And I can't exactly have just okay tonight—not with *that* liability already on deck."

He pointed over to where some of the other volunteers waited. Immediately, I found what he referred to. It was easy because Tawny towered over the other women by about a foot.

"Holy Christ," I said. "How did that happen?"

He threw up his hands, looking miserable. "She latched on to the idea when you mentioned it at the bar."

"I didn't even think she heard me," I said apologetically.

Hugh waved me toward the crowd. "Too late now. Go have a seat, Brutus, so this disaster can get under way. You've ruined the night. I don't know why you hate kids so much."

I gave him a parting glare and went off to find Seth. The vampires had joined him since I'd come in.

"You guys here to get a date or a victim?" I asked.

"Neither," said Peter. "We're here to see the Tawny Show."

I sighed. "This is supposed to be a charity event, and people are treating it like a freak show. Hugh already accused me of ruining it by bringing Maddie."

Seth looked surprised. "Why? She looks great."

I pointed her out to Peter and Cody, who also concurred about her cuteness. "She'll be fine," said Cody. "Tawny's going to be the one to watch. I haven't really been able to see what she's wearing. I hope it's up to her usual standards."

"Maybe her Secret Santa will get her some nicer clothes," said Peter. He glanced at me. "You bought for yours yet?"

"Huh?" Right. Carter. I'd completely forgotten. Buying something for that cynical angel hadn't exactly been at the top of my priority list. "I, um, have some ideas. Still thinking about it."

"What about a Christmas tree? You got one of those?"

"Um, haven't done that either."

"I didn't know you wanted a Christmas tree," said Seth. "Do you need help picking one out?"

"Well, I don—"

The auction started, cutting me off. The auctioneer, Nick, was a young guy in his early thirties who probably had a second job doing minor modeling contracts that would never actually get him out of Seattle. He smiled non-stop and did a good job flirting with the women and making guy-jokes to the men. Bids flew fast and furious, and it was easy to get caught up in the excitement.

"Next up," said the auctioneer, reading from a card, "is Tawny Johnson."

"Johnson?" asked Cody. "Kind of boring."

"She made up both her names," I said. Succubi often did. "She probably didn't have any mental energy left after choosing the first one."

"Ouch," said Seth. "Who's being mean now?"

"You haven't met her," I warned.

Tawny pranced up, wearing seven-inch high-heeled shoes that appeared to be made out of stainless steel. They looked like medieval torture devices but matched her super-tight, silver lamé hot pants and jacket.

"She didn't disappoint," said Cody, studying the outfit.

Unsurprisingly, she stumbled the last couple of steps, and Nick reached out to steady her.

"Careful there," he said, flashing his brilliant white teeth. "Men are supposed to fall all over *you*."

It took her a moment to get the joke, and then she burst into small, high-pitched giggles. The noise grated on my nerves, but Nick seemed quite pleased to have someone appreciate his jokes.

"Why don't you tell us a little bit about yourself, Tawny," he said. "It says here you're currently unemployed. Does that mean you're out looking for something right now?"

"Well, Nick, I'm out looking for *someone* right now—if you know what I mean."

"Oh my God," I said.

"That was kind of funny," Peter noted.

"No, it wasn't."

Nick apparently agreed with Peter. He threw back his head and laughed. "Careful there, guys . . . we got a dangerous one on our hands. Tell me, Tawny, what is it you're looking for in a man?"

She pursed her red-lacquered lips in deep thought. "I'm looking for heart, Nick. Heart and soul. Those are the most important things."

There was a collective "aww" from the audience. Beside me, Peter said, "Okay, the soul thing really was funny. Only to us, of course, but still."

Tawny then winked at the crowd. "But stamina and a big checkbook can make up for that sometimes."

Nick waited for the audience's laughter to fade. "Okay, let's start the bidding at fifty—oh my God."

Tawny had taken off her jacket, revealing a zebra-print bandeau top underneath. 'Top' was a dubious term at best, though. When wrapped around her enormous bust, it looked more like a rubber band and really only served to cover her nipples.

Bids exploded from the audience, much to the astonishment of my friends and me. More surprising still was when Nick the auctioneer actually joined in.

"Folks, I know this is a bit unusual . . . but, well, I just can't help myself. Three-hundred dollars."

"Three-fifty!"

"Four-hundred!"

In the end, Nick was the one who ended up winning her, paying a startling five-fifty.

"Well, I'll be damned," said Peter.

I would have made a joke about his comment if I wasn't so shocked. When I finally found my voice, it was to say, "Well . . .

this is a good thing, right? That guy looks like he'd sleep with her right now."

"And," added Cody, "it was all for the kids."

Slowly, my astonishment faded into relief. This was an unexpected twist to the evening. The Tawny problem was fixed. Apparently, all we'd needed to do was essentially run an ad for her. She'd sleep with him, and Niphon would get off my back. One less thing for me to worry about—which was good, because I certainly had plenty of other things. Like Maddie.

It was her turn next. She walked out, face grim and set for battle. She looked both terrified and terrifying. In spite of that hard countenance, I still saw a few interested faces in the audience.

"Smile, smile," I muttered to no one in particular.

"Maddie Sato," said Nick cheerily. "You write magazine articles. Anything I'd know?"

"Probably not," she said, still wearing that grimace. "Not unless you read feminist publications."

"Feminist," he said, clearly amused. "Next you'll be telling us you hate men."

She gave him a blank look. "I only hate stupid men who don't actually understand what 'feminist' means."

He laughed. "You run into a lot of men like that?"

"All the time."

"Really?"

"Even as we speak, Nick."

"Oh no she didn't," said Peter. I groaned.

It took Nick a full ten seconds to realize he had just been insulted. Then, for the first time that night, he stopped smiling. Turning to the crowd, he said flatly, "Okay, let's start the bidding at fifty."

Silence met him. The interested faces no longer looked so interested. I swallowed a scream. No, this couldn't be happening. I'd promised her a date. This would destroy her. After what seemed like an eternity, I heard a voice in the back of the room.

"Fifty."

Relieved, I craned my head and looked. The guy who had bid was about fifty years old and looked exactly like this pedophile I'd once seen on a news special.

"Fifty," said Nick. "Do I hear seventy-five?"

Silence. I turned to Seth.

"Do something!" I hissed.

He flinched. "What?"

"Going once . . ."

I elbowed him, and his hand shot up. "Seventy-five."

There was a collective "ooh' in the room. Apparently no one, including Maddie, had expected a bidding war for the belligerent man-hater. Her eyes widened in surprise.

"One hundred," said the pedophile look-alike.

Then, either to end this quickly or because he felt sorry for Maddie, Seth said, "Three hundred."

More sounds of astonishment followed. The other bidder couldn't compete; he must have spent all his money on bail.

"Sold to the gentleman in the *Welcome Back, Kotter* T-shirt."

"Nice," said Cody, as Maddie exited the stage.

I reached out and squeezed Seth's hand. "Thank you."

He gave me his half-smile. "Anything for the kids."

Nick flipped to his next card. "And now we have . . . Georgina Kincaid."

My head shot up. Across the room, I saw Hugh's smirking face.

"Oh no he didn't," I said through gritted teeth.

Nick, puzzled, glanced toward where the other auctionees were. "Georgina Kincaid?"

"No avoiding it," Peter told me. "Might as well go up there. Otherwise people'll think you hate kids."

"That joke is getting old," I hissed.

Vowing to slap Hugh later, I reluctantly rose from my chair. Upon seeing me, Nick turned on the supernova smile. "Ah, there she is. Fashionably late."

On the subject of fashion, I wished I'd worn something as nice as Maddie's dress. I might have just gotten tricked into this thing, but now I wished I could do it right. I still looked good; my normal sense of aesthetics would allow for nothing less. I had on a black skirt and a purple cashmere sweater, my hair in a ponytail. In tiny increments—too slow and small for anyone to notice—I tightened the sweater around my figure and made the neckline bigger. I put a saunter into my hips and pulled out my ponytail tie, shaking out my hair. It had worked for Maddie and countless nerdy movie girls. It would work for me because I suddenly had a serious issue at stake here.

There was no way on God's green earth that I was going for less than Tawny.

"Georgina," said Nick, helping me onto the stage. "My notes say you prefer Georgie." Yeah, Hugh was definitely getting slapped. "And that you run a bookstore."

If I'd taken a victim recently and had succubus glamour on me, I wouldn't have to do a single thing except stand there. I wouldn't even have to smile. Now I'd have to work a little. Quickly, I assessed this crowd. The kinds of guys who came to events like this tended to be white-collar professionals with disposable income. Some would be here simply because philanthropy was trendy and good for the image, and this was a stylish way to do it. Others, while perhaps not desperate, were nonetheless intellects and introverts who found this a good opportunity to meet women. These men all wanted smart, competent women—women who were also pretty, of course. And wit . . . wit always went over well.

I gave Nick, then the audience, a heart-stopping smile. "That's right. I organize events, bring in money, make sure everything looks good, and whip people into shape."

"Sounds like a lot of work," he said.

"Or," I said, "an excellent first date."

There was no cymbal crash, but my punch line elicited the

laughs I'd hoped for. "You have some high expectations," said Nick.

"Well, I think everyone should. Why settle? If a guy meets my expectations, I'll meet his. And in the end, it's all about sense of humor and a conversation that won't put me to sleep." I realized I sounded vaguely like a Miss America contestant, but maybe there wasn't much difference. I could see from the intrigue in the audience that I'd made a good impression.

"This one's a keeper," said Nick. "Let's start at fifty for Georgie."

I got my fifty and then some. Bids flew around the room. At one point, I glanced at Seth. Our eyes met, and I could tell by his expression that he was on the verge of bidding. I shook my head. He was the only one I wanted to go out with in this room, but I didn't want to taint Maddie's win. I wanted her to feel special. Besides, I also didn't want Seth to blow that much money.

I went for seventeen-hundred dollars.

"I can't believe that," Maddie whispered to me afterward. "I think you're the highest one so far. The guy looked cute too."

He had. Late thirties. Armani suit. Harmless. Nobody I planned on establishing anything meaningful with, but he'd do for a casual date. Maybe an energy fix if I decided to use this body.

"You brought in some money yourself," I teased.

Her eyes found Seth, sitting across the room, and studied him speculatively. "Seth probably did it because he felt sorry for me."

"Of course not," I said quickly. She still looked skeptical.

"Well, it doesn't matter. I'd rather drink coffee and talk shop with him than go out with some sleazy guy. That other bidder reminded me of this sex offender I saw on TV once . . ."

When the auction wound down, I exchanged contact info with my buyer for a future date. Hugh attached himself to

Deanna and stayed as far away from me as possible. No worries. I'd have plenty of time to deal with him later. Tawny, fortunately, also stayed away from me and clung to Nick's arm. I watched them like a proud parent. Tonight was going to be a great night.

Chapter 8

"Succubus."

Dante's laconic voice was the last thing I'd expected to hear when my phone rang the next day. I'd forgotten that I'd left him my number. My surprise quickly gave way to eagerness. Maybe he'd found something for me. No energy loss had occurred after the auction, but then, I hadn't taken a victim either. It wasn't much to go on, but that small pattern Dante had pointed out was still a place to start, and I hoped he'd have more to offer now.

"Hey! What's up?" I sat down on the couch. I'd been getting ready to go out with Seth later, applying makeup the old-fashioned way in order to conserve shape-shifting energy. I'd need to cash in on my auction date sooner rather than later to get some power back.

There was a pause from the other end of the line before Dante spoke again. "I've been thinking . . . I've been thinking we're going about all of this the wrong way."

Very unexpected. "Really?"

"Yeah. I wasn't taking it seriously, so I understand why you were getting pissed off."

Hearing him admit how he'd been blowing my problems off wasn't exactly cheering, but I appreciated his honesty.

"Well . . . it's okay. I'm just glad we can maybe figure something out now. I'm getting anxious."

"Me too." More silence, then I heard him take a deep breath. "So, have you ever been to El Gaucho?"

The reference to one of Seattle's downtown steakhouses was such a non sequitur that I couldn't respond for several seconds. When I did speak, it wasn't very articulate.

"What?"

"It's a restaurant. Down on First—"

"Yeah, yeah. I know what it is. What's it have to do with the dreams?"

"Dreams? What are you talking about?"

"What are *you*—oh, Jesus Christ. Are you asking me out?"

"Of course I am. What the fuck would El Gaucho have to do with those dreams?"

I groaned. "I can't believe this. I actually thought you had something useful for me."

"I'm trying to be nice here! Look, the dreams are a lost cause, but we aren't. You were right when you said I was being sleazy and treating you like you were cheap. So give me a break! I'm trying to have sex with you the right way."

I found this even freakier than when Dante had suggested the place with the happy hour beer. "I don't want to have sex with you, okay? I want your help with my problems. And how many times do I have to tell you that I have a boyfriend?"

"As many times as you want. I just don't buy that that's a real relationship. Particularly after you sold yourself for seventeen-hundred dollars last night."

"How do you know about that?"

"It was in the paper."

"That date doesn't count."

"Can a date with me not count?"

"No! For the last time, I have a boyfriend. I'm going out with him tonight."

"To El Gaucho?"

I hung up.

I was working my hair over with a curling iron later on

when I heard knocking at my front door. Walking toward the living room, I felt immortal signatures on the other side. Fortunately, there was nothing musky or slimy here. These were familiar and welcome.

Of course, they weren't exactly welcome tonight.

"What are you guys doing here?" I asked, opening the door to admit Peter, Cody, and Hugh. My three stooges. The dwarves to my Snow White. "And why do you always show up when I'm about to go out?"

Like always, they made themselves comfortable in my living room without any further invitation. Cody handed me a slip that had been stuck to the door from my building's office manager, saying I had a package. I made a mental note to pick it up the next time the office was open.

"We're going over to that place that makes the unholy margaritas," he said. "Thought we'd stop by and see if you wanted to go."

"And here you are, ungrateful and mean," said Peter. He glanced around the living room. "I don't see a Christmas tree here."

Hugh was eyeing my red-silk robe. "You going out in that?"

"Of course not. I'm just getting ready, that's all."

The three of them exchanged looks.

"Is it business or Seth?" asked Hugh.

"Seth."

"Damn it," swore Peter. He pulled some crumpled money out of his pocket and handed it to Hugh.

"You guys bet on my love life?"

"Yeah," said Hugh. "All the time. You should see the stakes we've got riding on when you and Seth are finally going to sleep together."

"Well, keep 'em riding, cowboy. It's not going to happen." I crossed my arms and leaned against the wall near my TV. "Of course, Niphon's trying pretty hard to make it happen. Is he in on the bet?"

"Not yet. What's he doing?" asked Cody.

I told them about the offer Niphon had made for Seth's soul. To my surprise, they didn't share my shock and outrage.

"I don't know," said Hugh slowly. "I've kind of thought about that before."

I gaped. "Thought about what before? Buying Seth's soul?"

"Sure. It's what I do, and hey, if it'd help you . . ."

"Oh dear lord."

"But if you decide to do it," said Hugh warningly, "come to me first. I can beat any offer Niphon makes."

"If you broker the deal, you're disqualified for the bet," warned Peter.

"Hey!" cried Hugh. "That's not right."

"Sure it is. You'd have an unfair advantage—"

"Christ. Be quiet, all of you. I can't believe you guys are seriously talking about buying my boyfriend's—"

A new signature swept through to us. A scent liked candied apples. Warm honey on the skin.

"Tawny," we all said in unison.

I opened the door, and Tawny threw herself into my arms, bawling. I yelped and tried not to fall over.

"Oh, Georgina," she sobbed, mascara running in black rivers down her cheeks. "I'm never going to do it. Never ever ever."

I tried to pull out of her Amazonian embrace. "There, there," I said weakly. "I'm sure you will."

Sniffling, she stepped away and ran a hand over her eyes, making the mascara situation even worse. "No, I can't. I've tried and tried . . . nothing works."

I glanced over at the guys. They were all looking at me expectantly, like I should be able to explain how one succubus couldn't get laid. I doubted anyone could, though.

"Okay," I said at last. "Calm down, and we'll get to the bottom of it. But first, pull yourself together. You're a mess."

"I can't," she wailed.

"You're thinking like a human," I chastised. "You can shape-shift that makeup mess away."

"No," she said more adamantly. "You don't understand. I *can't*."

I stared at her, puzzled, then I understood. It was nearly impossible to see, but a faint shimmer was fading in and out around her body. She was having trouble holding this form. Her energy was so low that she was losing her shape-shifting power.

"Whoa," I said. I'd never seen a succubus that bad. I'd been that low once, but it had been after engaging in a major battle of shape-shifting.

Tears started welling up in her eyes again. "What's going to happen? What if I run out and—" On and on she went.

I sighed. There is a moment in every girl's life when she must choose between the lesser of evils. When you're a succubus, those moments come quite often. And right now, I had to choose. I could risk Niphon never leaving town or I could kiss Tawny.

Lesser of evils.

Standing on my tiptoes, I pressed my lips to hers and cut off her babbling. Her lips tasted like bubble gum, probably from the lip gloss. It wasn't a big kiss or anything—barely any tongue—but it was enough. A surge of power poured out of me and into her. Breaking the kiss, I stepped away and looked at her. Her form had stabilized. Meanwhile, I was now down even more in my own energy, but nowhere near the low she'd just experienced.

Her blue eyes widened to an impossible size. "How . . . what was that?"

"A kiss," I said dryly. "Something you've apparently got to learn about too." Seeing her still-stunned look, I shook my head. "We're vessels for power and life, Tawny. Usually, it passes *into* our bodies, but sometimes it can be transferred out to other creatures. Succubi and incubi can share it with each other. What I just gave you should keep you going a little longer."

"I don't know," said Cody suddenly. "I think you should give her some more, just to be safe."

Tawny touched her lips, like she could still feel my kiss. "Wow." Her form shifted, and the mascara mess vanished. Her normal, eerily perfect face reappeared.

I sat down on the arm of the couch, near Peter. "Okay. Now let's figure out how in the world this is even possible. What happened to Nick the auctioneer? You guys seemed pretty close last night."

"Well," she mumbled, staring down at her feet. "That kind of fell apart."

"How could it fall apart? He was drooling all over you!"

"Yeah, but he had to stay and close up there, so we couldn't go out last night. I left without him. Today, I called to set up a date, and he said he didn't want to. That he was cool just giving the money to charity and not to bother with anything else."

"He said that?" I asked incredulously. I eyed her suspiciously. "What did you say to him beforehand?"

"What do you mean?"

"Did you just call and ask him out right away?"

"Well, no . . . we made small talk. Not that it did much good. He seemed kind of bored by the end."

Surprise, surprise. Tawny didn't strike me as the world's greatest conversationalist. I could only imagine what she must have babbled about to scare him off.

"Okay," I said, disappointed. Nick had seemed like a sure thing. "Maybe you shouldn't, like, talk to them. What about the strip club job? Did you follow up on that?"

She jerked her head up and looked like she might cry again. "I tried! They said I wasn't qualified."

Even the guys couldn't stay out of this now.

"How can you not qualify for a job as a stripper?" asked Cody.

"Yeah, don't you just have to take off your clothes?" asked Hugh.

"They said I couldn't dance," she explained.

We all stared.

"Okay . . ." I wondered if maybe I should have read the mentor's handbook after all. "Let's see it."

"See what?"

"You. Dancing."

Tawny looked around the room in terror. "Here?" she squeaked. "In front of all of you?"

"If you can't take your clothes off in front of your friends," said Peter, "who can you take them off in front of?" I elbowed him.

"I can't," she whispered.

"Tawny," I barked. My voice held the authority of a drill sergeant. She jumped. "I am *not* making out with you until the end of time. You want to do this, then you've got to work for it. Now, *take off your clothes.*"

"Oh," said Hugh. "I've waited ten years to hear you say that to another woman."

I found my stereo remote and turned it on. "Tainted Love" started playing.

"I can't strip to the eighties!"

"Tawny!"

With a terrified look in my direction, she moved to the center of the living room. At first, she just kind of stood there, and then, slowly, she tried to step in time to the music. I say *tried* because she was so off the beat, it was astonishing. I don't think I could have been that out of sync if I'd tried. Finally, she gave up moving her feet at all and simply focused on her upper body, swaying her arms and torso slightly. It was the most awkward, uncomfortable spectacle I'd ever seen.

At last, she decided she'd "danced" enough and began removing her clothing. She apparently couldn't multitask, however, and gave up all pretenses of moving to the music. Instead, she stood still and started unbuttoning her zebra-print blouse. Her fingers fumbled on the third button down, and it took her almost thirty seconds to unfasten it.

"Stop, please stop," I said, turning off the music. "Your goal is to take years off people's lives, but not like this."

"Was I bad?" she asked.

"No," I said. "You were terrible."

She stuck her lower lip out in a pout.

"Oh, come on," said Cody, ever the kindly one in our group. "That's kind of mean."

"Hey, I'm supposed to be a teacher, not a friend."

"The School of Georgina is a harsh one," intoned Peter solemnly.

"It's not that easy," Tawny said, looking at me accusingly. "If you really are my teacher, then show me how to do it."

Four faces watched me expectantly. I started to protest, then remembered that helping Tawny meant Niphon would leave Seattle that much faster. Getting up off the couch arm, I took her place in the center of the room.

"Okay, first off, you're missing two things. One, listen to the music and move with it. There's a beat. Find it. Move your feet and your body—your whole body—to it. Become part of it." Tawny's blank look told me I was getting too esoteric for her. "Then, when it comes time to take off your clothes, remember that you're not doing it to be practical. You're doing it for someone else. Make it dramatic. Make it artful."

I turned the stereo on and clicked to the next track on my mix CD. It was "Iron Man."

"Hey!" Tawny said. "How come you get metal?"

"Not even you can strip to Ozzy," scoffed Hugh.

I gave him a sidelong glance. "I can strip to anything, baby."

I started moving. For me, there was no thought required at all. I'd been a dancer since my mortal days. I loved it. There was no music. There was no me. We were the same being.

My body flowed to its melody and rhythm, every one of my movements graceful and sensual. I didn't even pay attention to my friends. I just let myself get lost in the dance.

I didn't have much on to begin with. I had panties and a bra underneath the robe, but I intended to leave them on. I was close to my friends but not *that* close. But, I made the most out of taking off the robe, letting my hands slide over my silk-covered body. I slowly untied the sash, drawing the experience out, and finally let it slip to the floor. I took my heels off with equal deliberateness.

Literally never missing a beat, I told Tawny, "When you've got this down, we'll move onto lap dances."

I moved over to where Hugh sat on the loveseat and positioned my legs so that I straddled him while barely touching him. A stripper's art. I ran my fingers through my hair, my body still rippling like a ribbon.

"Hey, big spender," I said.

He looked appreciative but more amused than anything else. He reached into his pocket and pulled out a one dollar bill.

"Hugh," I said. "Don't insult me."

With a sigh, he produced a five and tucked it underneath my bra strap.

"Hey, Seth," Cody suddenly said.

I looked up and saw Seth standing in the doorway. When Tawny had come barreling through, I'd left the door ajar. A look of comic bemusement was on his face.

"Hey," he said, studying me. "So . . . you're paying for dinner?"

I crawled off Hugh's lap and pulled the five out of my strap. "Only if you want to go to Taco Bell."

Cody handed me a twenty. "Make it a Red Lobster."

My friends got up and moved toward the door, and I assured a distraught Tawny that I'd think of something to help her. Giving up any more attempts at manually getting ready, I shape-shifted into jeans, low boots, and another cashmere sweater. A three-quarter-length gray wool coat covered it all. I grinned at Seth, who was shaking his head ruefully. Compared to the other things he knew I did, an impromptu striptease was pretty low-key.

"And you thought I didn't earn my keep."

"No comment," he said, taking hold of my hand.

Chapter 9

"I don't understand this," said Seth good-naturedly. "I catch you stripping in front of other men, yet I'm the one who gets punished."

Clasping his hand, I led him onto the ice skating rink. Just like with dancing, I glided with practiced ease. Seth's movements were jerky and uncertain. Without my hand, I suspected he would have fallen already.

"This is good for you, Mortensen. You sit at a desk—or table or whatever—all day. This'll get your muscles working again. Get the old blood pumping."

His teasing smile turned into a grimace, his hold on my hand turning into a death grip. "There are a hundred other ways I could do that."

"But none as fun," I assured him.

Seth was brilliant and funny, but coordinated he was not. During the early days of our acquaintance, I'd tried to teach him to dance. It had been grueling. After a very long time, he'd learned the basic steps, but the process had never been easy—or, I suspected, enjoyable—for him. I'd let him off easy since then, only making him go out dancing once. He'd grown complacent now, which was why I felt this experience would be so good for him.

"Men were not meant to wear blades on their feet," he told me as we trudged further toward the rink's center. We were outdoors, at a small park, and our breathing made frosty clouds in the air.

"Women weren't meant wear to stilettos," I told him. "But you don't hear me bitching about it."

"That's different. They do great things for your legs. This? This just makes me look stupid."

"Well, then," I said. "You better learn. Time to take off the training wheels." I released his hand.

"Hey! What the—"

But I was gone, slipping away from his grasp with a laugh. He stood there frozen while I skated away, circling the rink in graceful loops and figure eights. After a few rounds, I skated back up to him, finishing with a neat pirouette. He hadn't moved from the spot where I'd left him, but he no longer appeared annoyed.

"Look at you," he said, touching my face. "Rosy cheeks. Snowflakes in your hair. You're the Snow Queen."

"God, I hope not. That's a depressing story. Hans Christian Andersen had issues."

"All writers have issues," he assured me.

I laughed and took his arm, leading him around in more awkward skating. My legs and feet protested the slow movement, but the rest of me was happy to have quality time with Seth.

"Speaking of writers with issues," I said. "How can I get in trouble for stripping in front of other men when you have a date with another woman?"

If not for the fact he would have fallen over, I suspect Seth would have elbowed me. "That's your own fault," he said. "You made me do it, so don't get all jealous now."

"I'm not jealous—but I think Maddie does have a crush on you."

"Unlikely. It's probably just author worship." He gave me a pointed look. "Like some people I know. If anything, she's got a crush on you."

"Oh, for God's sake, stop with the lesbian fantasy thing."

"Nah, nothing like that. She just idolizes you, that's all. You're chipping away at that insecure exterior of hers, and I think she's starting to really see how much she's capable of. You're sort of setting the example."

I hadn't considered that. "Really?"

"Yup. Keep training her up, and we'll have a mini-Georgina on our hands." Seth chuckled as we made a painstakingly slow turn. "Between her, that new succubus, and my nieces, you should start a Ladies Finishing School. How can you be such a good influence and have such a . . ."

"Demeaning job?" I supplied.

"Something like that. Of course, I suppose it could be worse."

I gave him a sidelong glance. "Could it?"

"Yeah, you could, like, sell Amway or be trying to get me to move large amounts of money out of Nigeria."

"Definite deal breakers in any relationship," I said solemnly.

He looked over at me, rather brave considering the intense attention he'd been giving his feet. Under the rink's soft lights, his expression was tender. His lips curled into a small, fond smile, and his eyes shone with an affection that almost made me go weak in the knees. Maybe it was a trick to get me to fumble my skating. It nearly worked.

"For you?" he said, coming to a stop. "It might be worth it."

"Worth cleaning out your bank account?"

"Yes."

"Worth being part of a pyramid scheme?"

"They say they don't do that anymore."

"What if they're lying?"

"Thetis," he said with a sigh. "I'm going to say something to you I've never said before."

"What is it?"

"Be quiet."

And then he leaned down and kissed me, bringing warmth to my cold lips. Nearby, I heard children giggle at us, but I didn't care. I felt the kiss down to my toes. It was brief, like always, but when Seth pulled away, my whole body was filled with heat. Every nerve in me tingled, alive and wonderful. I barely noticed the chilly temperature or the way our breathing formed frosty clouds in the air. He laced his fingers through mine and lifted my hand to his lips. I had gloves on, but he kissed exactly where I wore his ring.

"Why are you so sweet?" I asked, my voice small. My heart beat rapidly, and every star peeping through the clouds seemed to be shining just for me.

"I don't think I'm that sweet. I mean, I just told you to be quiet. That's one step away from asking you to wash my laundry and make me a sandwich."

"You know what I mean."

Seth pressed another kiss to my forehead. "I'm sweet because you make it easy to be sweet."

We linked arms again and continued our circuit. I had a sappy urge to rest my head against his shoulder but figured that might be asking too much of his coordination.

"What do you want for Christmas?" I asked, my thoughts spinning ahead to next week.

"I don't know. There's nothing I need."

"Oh no," I teased. "You aren't one of those, are you? One of those people who are impossible to shop—"

One of Seth's feet slipped out from under him. I managed to stay upright, but he went down, his legs crumpling underneath him.

"Oh my God," I said, kneeling down. "Are you okay?"

"I think so," he said. The tight set of his lips informed me things were a bit more painful than he was letting on. Putting my arm around his hip, I helped him up. The leg he'd fallen on started to buckle, but he managed to keep it steady in the end.

"Come on," I said, steering him toward the gate. "We should go."

"We just got here."

"Oh, suddenly you're a fan, Scott Hamilton?"

"Nope, but you are. It was just a fall."

Maybe it had been just a fall, but the thought of Seth getting hurt had made my heart seize up. "No, no. Let's go. I'm hungry."

The expression on his face informed me that he knew I wasn't *that* hungry, but he didn't fight me anymore. When we'd shed our skates for normal shoes, I was pleased to see he didn't walk with a limp or anything. That would have really been too much: him getting hurt and having it be *my fault*.

"I'm not made of glass," he told me as we drove to dinner. He was remarkably good at guessing my thoughts. "You don't have to protect me."

"It's instinct," I said, lightly. But in my mind, I recalled the grim conversation he'd had with Erik. They were mortal. They could get hurt. They could die.

It was something I'd witnessed over and over throughout the centuries. Each time I grew close to a new mortal, I'd try to pretend that it wouldn't happen to him or her. But it always did, and eventually that cold reality would hit me, no matter how hard I tried to push it aside.

In fact, that knowledge consumed me for the rest of my night with Seth. I knew it was stupid to make such a big deal out of one fall, but I'd seen too many small things lead to disaster in my life. Lying in bed beside him later on, I found myself thinking back to a series of events that had also started small and ended in tragedy.

Several centuries ago, I lived in a small town in southern England. I'd called myself Cecily then and worn a body with flaming red hair and big, man-eating eyes the color of sapphires.

Funny thing about the Middle Ages. Modern folk always harbor this image of devout, God-fearing people strictly adhering to the letter of divine law. While they were certainly devout back then, that whole adherence thing left something to be desired—even among the clergy. No, scratch that. *Espe-*

cially among the clergy. Powerful churchmen often lived very well in an age where commoners desperately tried to scratch out a living. Ironically, that desperation contributed to the Church's wealth since the population hoped their lots would improve in the next world and gave money accordingly. Wealth and power lead to corruption, however, and the bishop of the town I lived in was one of the most corrupt around.

And I was his mistress.

Ostensibly, I worked as a servant in his household, but most of my laboring occurred in bed. He fawned over me and kept me supplied with nice clothes and other trinkets, and everyone knew about our relationship. People accepted that it was technically wrong, but most just lived with it. A lot of other bishops—and popes—had mistresses too, and like I said, not everyone was as devout as modern romantics like to believe.

Simply living in sin with a crooked bishop didn't satisfy my job requirements. After all, I was a real go-getter in those days, and it hadn't taken too much to lead him astray. If I hadn't done it, someone else would have.

So, I slept around on him when I could, getting regular fixes and a great deal of entertainment along the way. One day of said entertainment came from two monks who pulled knives on each other after discovering I'd slept with both of them. I don't know what good they thought it would do. I hardly ever saw them anyway since their monastery lay so far outside of town. Besides, considering how mediocre both liaisons had been, I didn't have much interest in revisiting either one.

Nonetheless, they fought ferociously, drawing a lot of blood until a local priest managed to separate them. I watched the conflict with an innocent face, hidden among the enthusiastic crowd. No one suspected my involvement, save the intervening priest.

His name was Andrew, and I adored him. Bishops performed masses and other sacraments, but they also had administrative responsibilities. Consequently, Andrew performed a lot of day-to-day ministering. He frequently visited the house where I lived and would speak to me both as a friend and a pastor while traveling to and from his duties.

"Do you hate me?" I asked him after the fight.

We sat in the garden outside the bishop's house. A couple other servants tended the grounds nearby but were still too far away to overhear us. Andrew hadn't specifically cited my involvement in the fight, but he had mentioned the incident when he arrived, lamenting what a shame it was that two brothers had been driven to such extremes.

Closing his eyes, he tipped his head back into the sunshine. A heavy gold cross—a gift from my bishop that Andrew continually wanted to sell—rested on his chest, gleaming in the light. "No, of course not."

I studied him, admiring his young, handsome face and thinking the real shame was his celibacy. Wind ruffled his silky brown hair, and I imagined running my fingers through it.

"You sound disapproving."

"I disapprove of sin, not of you." He straightened back up and opened his eyes. "You I pray for."

I shifted uncomfortably. I didn't like being prayed for. "What do you mean?"

He smiled at me, and I nearly sighed at his beauty. I longed to have him as a conquest, but he'd proven resistant so far. Of course, that only added to his appeal. I sometimes felt that if I could ever taste it, the energy from his soul would feed me for a lifetime.

"I pray for your physical and spiritual health. I pray you will sin no more. I pray you will find some man you can marry and have children with." He hesitated. "Although, I'd prefer it more if you took vows."

I arched an eyebrow of surprise. "Why?"

"Why not? You read and write. You're more educated

than half the brothers at the monastery. You'd be a great asset to the abbey."

I tilted my head so that some of my hair spilled over my face, knowing how the light would set it ablaze. I held onto his gaze tenaciously. "Is that the only reason why? Or do you just like the idea of me never being with another man?"

Andrew looked away and took a long time answering. "I'd like you to be my sister in Christ," he said finally. "We all struggle with temptation, and I would like to see you removed from it." With that, he stood up and straightened the kinks from his body. I remained sitting. "I should leave. It's getting late."

He started to walk away, but I called after him. "What about you? Do you struggle with temptation?"

He stopped walking and glanced at me over his shoulder. A small smile, rueful and sad, played at his lips as he regarded me. "Of course. You are my great temptation, and you know it. I'd like to be free of that as well."

"Are you sure?" I asked softly. Shaking his head, still smiling, he left the garden.

That had been our last truly happy day together. . . .

Back in the present, in bed, sleepiness started to take over and interrupt my recollections. I put a bookmark in my thoughts, reluctant to leave the memory of when life with Andrew had still been sweet and good. I hadn't been able to stop *that* story's ending, but as I rolled over and studied Seth's sleeping form, I vowed history wouldn't repeat itself.

Chapter 10

When I came home from Seth's the next day, there was another note stuck to my door reminding me about the package. I plucked it off and went inside, surprised to find Vincent there again. I'd figured his angel business would be keeping him busy elsewhere.

"How's it all going?" I asked. I rummaged through my cupboards, looking for food. I'd skipped breakfast. "I mean, if you can tell me without having to kill me."

He sat at my kitchen table, leafing through newspapers. "Ah, well, still can't give you details, of course, but I can say that . . . um, well, progress isn't being made as quickly as we'd like. There's leftover lasagna in the refrigerator if you want it."

I opened the refrigerator door. Sure enough. "Wow. Did one of the angels conjure this up for you?"

"Only if you consider Yasmine's cooking a type of conjuring."

I uncovered the casserole dish. It looked great. There might be magic afoot after all. I put a piece in the microwave and set the timer.

Sitting down across from him, I peered at the spread out newspapers and remembered finding them left out the other day. "You sure like your news."

He grimaced. "Most of it's depressing."

Glancing at the headlines, I had to agree with him. Murder. Corruption. Theft.

"You hear about the cop shooting the other day?" I asked. "That one was really depressing."

Vincent turned his attention away from a story about domestic abuse. "No, what happened?"

"This cop was outside a convenience store and claims someone was inside shooting his partner. So, he ran in, gun in hand, and started shooting. He ended up killing his partner himself."

Vincent frowned. "Huh. I hadn't heard that one," he murmured. From the distracted look in his eyes, his mind had clearly latched onto something I wasn't privy to.

I gave him a sidelong glance. "That mean anything to you? Maybe to this mission from God you're on?"

His easy smile returned. "You're good but not that good. You know I can't say anything."

The microwave dinged, and I retrieved my food. As I stabbed a piece of cheesy pasta, I recalled what he'd said about Yasmine's cooking. My curiosity got the better of me. As it often did.

"Vince . . ." I began slowly, carefully keeping my eyes on my food. "I know it's none of my business . . ."

He laughed. "I always love it when people introduce topics like that—and then go ahead and dive in anyway."

Blushing, I shut my mouth.

"No, no," he said, clearly entertained. "Go ahead. What were you going to say?"

"I . . . well, nothing really. It's just, I mean, it doesn't matter to me . . . but I just sort of noticed that you and Yasmine seem, um, close."

His levity faded. I quickly looked up and met his eyes apologetically.

"I'm sorry," I blurted out. "Forget I said anything."

"No . . . it's, I don't know." He folded up the newspaper, staring at it without really seeing it. "Yeah, I guess. I've known her for a long time, and after a while, it's easy to . . . well, she's easy to like."

"Yeah, she is."

A few pregnant moments passed. When he spoke again, I heard affection in his voice. "I first met her at this fair in Akron, of all places . . . about, oh, fifteen years ago. Not sure what she was doing there—you never do with them—but I found her walking away from a concession stand. She had this giant tower of cotton candy. I swear, it was taller than she was. And, since I could tell she was an angel, it made the situation that much more absurd."

The story made me smile too. It also shed light on why he was here with the A-Team. *I could tell she was an angel.* He was another gifted human, like Erik and Dante, who could sense the immortal world. "And you went and talked to her?"

"I hadn't planned to, but then the cotton candy started to fall over, so I went to help her and ended up eating half of it myself."

"That's sweet," I said. "Er, no pun intended." It didn't matter that in the last few months, I'd fucked one guy in an office chair, used a leather whip on another, and gone down on another in the back room of a seedy club. I still loved romantic stories.

"She started asking for my help after that, off and on, once she realized what I could do. It was supposed to just be that . . . nothing more than her, you know, professional cases. But after a while, we couldn't help it. We're together all the time now."

I swallowed another piece of lasagna. It was divine. Seriously. "Do any of the other angels know?"

"Yeah, right. Joel barely tolerates me now . . ."

"But obviously, you guys aren't, um, you can't be—"

"No, but it doesn't matter. It doesn't have to be physical.

Really, it's ironic. Angels are creatures of love. They're supposed to love everyone. They're just not supposed to love one
person so much more than another."

"That's stupid," I stated adamantly.

"To you, maybe. And to me, I suppose. But to her . . . well,
she devotes her entire existence to the service of a power and
cause bigger than all of us. To be so in love with something—
or someone else—is distracting. You can't serve two masters
without eventually betraying one."

I looked down again, turning over his words. "And yet
you guys still stay together. Sort of."

He shrugged. "In as much as we can. Maybe I should
move on with my life, but, honestly, there's no one else I want
to be with. I accept what she is. It's why I love her. I'd rather
be with her in a limited capacity than none at all."

Goosebumps rose on the back of my neck. He'd just stated
a variant of what Seth used to tell me all the time, back when
I would continually urge him to leave me and find someone
else. I'd accepted his choice by now and honestly couldn't
imagine not having him in my life. But still. Sometimes I didn't
entirely get how he could be okay with everything between
us; hearing another person support such a choice was re-
freshing.

As though reading my mind, Vincent gently asked, "Am I
hitting too close to home? Carter mentioned a boyfriend . . ."

"No. Yes. I don't know. He—Seth, my boyfriend—says the
same thing as you. That if it can't be any other way . . . well,
then this is the way he wants it."

"Exactly. And thus, life goes on." Vincent started gathering up the newspapers. "I tell you though, I think your side
and hers are both so fucked up, it's not even funny. Why the
rules? Why does a succubus always have to take away someone's life when she's with them? Why can't you have the
choice? And why can't Yasmine make love? Why can't she *be*
in love?"

Good question. I don't think Vincent really expected an answer, but I had to give one anyway.

"Because that's the way it is. The way the system works. The way it's always worked."

"The system is fucked-up," he said.

I thought about it and nodded. "No arguments."

Smiling, he reached for his coat and slipped it on. "You're okay for a succubus."

Vincent left, off to do whatever it was one did with a posse of angels. I almost envied him because I had something to do that I wasn't looking forward to at all. It was another necessary evil.

I had to get Tawny a job.

After that debacle of a dance lesson, I'd told her I'd help. I might not be able to do much about my mysterious energy loss or angelic romances, but I sure as hell could do something to expedite Niphon's departure.

I drove down to Seatac, a city that owes its entire existence to the Seattle-Tacoma International Airport. It's more of a shadow, really, spreading around the airport in a blanket of long-term parking lots and cheap hotels. It also has a couple of strip clubs because really, what else are out-of-town businessmen supposed to do in their downtime?

It was late afternoon, so business was slow when I stepped inside Low Blow. A few bored-looking men sat scattered throughout the place, which was dingy and in need of some serious redecorating. Or, well, any decorating. A couple of the guys glanced up with interest as I walked through. Apparently, I held more appeal than the poor brunette trying her damnedest to fuck a pole in time to the dulcet sounds of Pink Floyd's "Young Lust."

I opened my mouth to speak to the bartender, but a voice behind me interrupted.

"Ho . . . ly . . . shit. I don't believe it. I don't fucking believe it."

I turned and looked into the long, narrow face of Simon Chesterfield, the proud proprietor of this dive. Between his face and lanky body, he always reminded me of a weasel. His black mustache never quite seemed able to grow in completely, and he dressed in brand name clothes that were always one size too small. He was chummy with the local Hellish players, and rumor had it he was in line to be an imp, eventually selling his soul for immortality and the chance to be a diabolical salesman.

"You finally come to dance for me, doll?"

"You wish."

For a sleazy guy who ran a sleazy establishment, Simon actually had a legitimate appreciation for dance. I'd once seen him trying to choreograph his strippers and had been impressed by his sense of aesthetics and rhythm. His employees hadn't really caught on. Such talents were kind of wasted here, and I used to wonder why he didn't take his business to one of the more affluent suburbs where he could get a higher caliber of dancers. The reason he stayed, I'd later learned, was that this was a better venue for all sorts of other shady business he conducted.

Still, Simon had a sharp eye and knew what a good dancer I was. He'd been on me for years to come work for him.

"We need to talk," I explained. "Business."

"It's what I do." With a sweeping gesture, he pointed to a doorway beside the bar. "Let's go to my office then."

His 'office' was barely a broom closet, but it had a stool for me to sit on. Resting my heels on a mid-level bar, I brought my knees up to my chest. It made my gray linen skirt slide up a bit. Simon watched with an interest that was more professional than personal.

"Fuck, woman. You come dance for me, and I could make a killing." He shook his head and collapsed into a rolling faux leather chair. "A succubus on my stage. Fuck."

I tilted my head to the side. "It's funny you mention that because that's kind of why I'm here."

I think my innocent tone set his alarms off. He eyed me suspiciously. "I thought you said you didn't want a job."

"Not me. We just got a new succubus, and she's looking for a gig. Didn't you hear?"

"No . . ." He frowned. "And she wants to dance? Here?"

"Yep," I said glibly. "She can't wait to take her clothes off." Wasn't that the truth.

Simon leaned back in the chair and put his feet on the desk. Casual pose or not, he was still on guard. "What's the catch?"

"Why does there have to be a catch? You should be excited about this. We're doing you a favor."

"You're offering to drop a succubus into my lap. That sounds too good to be true, so it *is* too good to be true." He paused, still thinking. "And why are you here instead of her?"

"I'm altruistic."

"Georgina," he said warningly.

"Okay," I admitted. "She's kind of . . . new."

"How new?"

"Really new. Still under warranty."

"There's still a catch here somewhere."

"Well . . . she's . . ." I spun through my mental rolodex of adjectives. "Inept."

He raised one narrow eyebrow. "Inept?"

"She's still learning how to get men." Since Simon probably wanted sexy women working for him, I figured it wasn't worth mentioning that Tawny wasn't so much learning as she was still trying to find her way to class. "And she's a, um, bad dancer."

"How bad?"

"Bad."

"Can you be a little more specific on what level of bad we're dealing with?"

"Remember *Gigli*?"

"Jesus. So, why do you think I'd want to take on a shitty dancer?"

"Simon," I exclaimed. "*All* your dancers are shitty."

"Not all of them," he said. "And it's not like I'm trying to get more. We have standards."

I gave him a pointed look.

"Alright, alright." He ran a hand through his gelled black hair. "What do I get in return?"

Now I was the indignant one. "What do you mean? You're getting a succubus dancer. What else do you need?"

"I'm getting a succubus charity case. I'm the one doing *you* a favor." His eyes were shrewd. Yeah. He'd make a good imp someday. He was this close to breaking out a contract. "I want you. Dance for me two nights this week."

"No."

"One night."

"Simon, there is nothing in this world that's going to get me to dance here, not even a succubus charity case. Pick something else."

"Okay, fine." He pondered. "You. I want you."

"Hey, I just told you—"

"No, no. Not as a dancer. As in right now. On the desk."

I sighed. That kind of want.

"Look, if I've gotta hire a bad succubus, I might as well fuck a good one."

"Interesting logic. Aren't you worried about your soul?"

He looked at me like he couldn't believe I'd had the audacity to ask such a thing. It was similar to the look I'd given him when he said Low Blow had standards.

"Noted." I stood up. "But not this body. Pick another shape."

Simon snorted. "You think I'm interested in a pinup girl crossed with an Ann Taylor model? Fuck that. I want a sixteen-year-old version of Liza Minnelli. In a school girl's uniform."

I stared. "I have no idea what that would look like."

He started undoing his pants. "You're a smart girl. Figure it out."

Sighing again, I shape-shifted, taking on a small body with a black pixie haircut. Baby smooth skin. Green plaid skirt with matching vest. Simon grunted his approval.

Turning, I rested my hands on the desk and bent over, thrusting my ass out toward him. I hoped it would be over soon. If I could just get the weasel comparison out of my head, this would probably be a lot easier.

I felt his hands slide along my legs as he pushed the skirt up. Suddenly, he froze.

"A thong? Are you insane, woman?"

"You're a sick bastard," I told him. The thong changed to white cotton panties.

"Don't I know it."

He pushed the panties down and thrust forward. Well, I guess it was a thrust. Simon wasn't that well-endowed. I was on the verge of saying something like, "Are you there yet?" Alas, the Tawny situation was too dire. I couldn't risk Simon changing his mind about her for the sake of a joke, no matter how funny.

But, whatever Simon lacked in size, he made up for in enthusiasm. He gripped my hips, nails digging into my bare flesh as he pounded away. I had to keep a fierce hold on the desk. Eventually, seeking variety, Simon flipped me over to my back. He unfastened my blouse and bra, exposing small, perky breasts that had just "blossomed into womanhood." Eyes on them and not my face, he grabbed my legs and spread them so that my ankles practically rested on his shoulders.

He returned to the task at hand, and when he finally came, I have to admit I welcomed the energy burst. It wasn't a lot—the guy practically worked for Hell already—but I needed it. Simon pulled out of me, and I sat up, mildly sated from an energy standpoint, if not a physical one. I honestly hadn't done much but lie there the whole time, but he regarded me as though we'd just gone through the entire *Kama Sutra*.

"Definitely worth putting up with an inept succubus," he said happily, pulling his pants back up.

I wanted to say that he might want to withhold judgment until he actually met Tawny, but instead, I just smiled. I knew when to keep my control switch on.

Chapter 11

Simon hadn't had a lot to give me, but just like every other time I'd gotten an energy fix recently, I had the dream.

It played out the same as always, starting with the dishes, going all the way up to when my dream-self looked into the living room to smile at the little girl. After a few more moments, my dream-self returned to her dishes. Silently, I screamed at her to look back. I couldn't get enough of the girl. I wanted to drink her in. I could have watched her forever, taking in those long-lashed eyes and wispy curls.

Then, as though she could hear me, my dream-self glanced back into the other room. The girl was gone. My dream-self jerked her hands out of the water, just in time to hear a thump and a crash. The sound of crying followed, and then I woke up.

It was late morning, and my energy was gone. That honestly didn't surprise me anymore. Coupled with that loss, however, was a new sensation. I felt cold, chilled to the bone. My skin also felt wet, like I'd been submerged in water. When I ran my fingers over my arm, it was perfectly dry. Nonetheless, I put on the heaviest sweater I could find, and eventually the chill abated.

Work was busy and not particularly eventful until the end, when Maddie casually reminded me about us hanging out afterward. I nearly walked into a display when she said that. In my haste yesterday, I'd gone ahead and made plans with both Maddie and Seth for after work. I had a tendency to do that kind of thing when I was stressed. I felt so popular. And, as I often did in this kind of situation, I solved it by combining both of my mistakes into one solution.

"Maddie wanted to hang out tonight," I told Seth. "I think she's lonely. Mind if I bring her in for the babysitting thing?"

"Sure," he said, not looking up from his laptop.

"Seth wanted help babysitting tonight," I told Maddie. "Do you mind if we sort of make that our evening activity?"

Maddie gave the proposition a bit more thought than Seth had. She didn't look upset so much as puzzled. "I haven't really been around many kids. It's not that I don't like them . . . just that it's always kind of weird."

"His nieces are great," I assured her. "You'll be a convert."

I felt a little bad about strong-arming her into the Mortensen family adventure. She stayed silent for most of the ride up, keeping her thoughts to herself. Seth's family lived up north of the city, in Lake Forest Park. Their house looked exactly like the other ones on the street, but I suspected it was a necessary sacrifice in order to accommodate two adults and five girls.

"Oh my God," said Maddie when we stepped inside the house. All five Mortensen daughters were there. They ranged in age from four to fourteen, all sharing their mother's blond hair and blue eyes. We seemed to have walked into the middle of an argument. "Maybe . . . this wasn't such a good idea . . ."

I looked around the room. Seth had gotten there earlier, and Terry and Andrea had already left to do their shopping. Fourteen-year-old Brandy tried to make her voice heard over that of Kendall, who was nine and the twins McKenna and Morgan who were six. Only four-year-old Kayla, sitting on the couch beside her uncle, listened quietly. I couldn't even tell what the others were fighting about.

"It can spin webs!" cried Kendall.

"No, it can't. That's just its name." Brandy looked weary. The others weren't paying attention to her.

"The horn would slice the webs!" cried McKenna. Morgan backed her by making a chopping motion with her hand.

"Not if the monkey trapped it first," retorted Kendall.

"The unicorn can run fast. The monkey couldn't catch it."

"Then it's a coward!" Kendall looked triumphant. "It loses automatically if it doesn't show up for the fight."

Both twins appeared stumped by this bit of logic.

"This is a stupid argument," said Brandy. "Unicorns aren't real."

The other three girls turned on her and started shouting their protests.

"HEY!" I yelled over the cacophony. Everyone fell silent and looked at me. I don't think the girls had noticed my arrival. "What's going on?"

"A debate over who would win if a unicorn got in a fight with a spider monkey," said Seth.

Beside me, Maddie made a strange noise that sounded suspiciously like a squelched laugh.

"It's been compelling and well thought out," added Seth, his voice deadpan.

Brandy groaned. "Unicorns aren't real."

"Spider monkeys aren't real!" McKenna shot back.

"Yes, they are," said Brandy. "This is all pointless."

Kendall glared at her. "It's hypocritical."

"Hypothetical," I corrected.

"Don't worry," Seth told Maddie and me. "It's downright civil compared to the mermaid-centaur debate."

"Guys," I said. "This is Maddie." I ticked off the girls' names for her, one by one.

"Hi," said Maddie nervously. She eyed each girl, then looked at Seth uncertainly. She'd been acting differently around him since the auction, and I made a mental note to harass him about their date. "This might have been a bad idea . . ."

He smiled one of those sweet smiles that could make any-one feel better. She smiled back, relaxing a little. "Nope. We need all the help we can get around here." He rose, scooping up Kayla as he rose. "What I actually need is a distraction while everyone under age nine gets put to bed." The twins cried out in dismay.

I glanced at Brandy and Kendall. "Sounds easy enough."

"Don't speak so soon," warned Brandy.

Kendall was already in motion. She tore out of the room and returned with a long cardboard box that she nearly shoved into my face. "Look what Grandma sent me." It was a Monopoly game.

"The Industrial Revolution edition?" I asked dumb-founded.

"It's about the only edition they hadn't made yet," re-marked Seth. "I think they're kind of grasping at straws."

"You got that for Christmas?" I asked. "You *wanted* it for Christmas?"

"I want to be a real estate mongrel when I grow up," she explained.

"Mogul," I corrected. "And I thought you wanted to be a pirate?"

She gave me a pitying look. "They don't have very good health insurance."

I pointed to the box. "But why the Industrial Revolution? Wouldn't you have rather had, I don't know, the Barbie edi-tion? Or the Sephora edition?" I kind of wanted that last one for myself.

"The Industrial Revolution was an important period in Western Civilization. The developments in production and manufacturing forever changed the face of our culture and socioeconomic status." She paused. "You wanna play?"

"Is one of the pieces a spinning jenny?" asked Maddie.

Seth laughed. "Actually, it is."

"I'm in," she said.

Kayla, who was in Seth's arms, appeared on the verge of

falling asleep then and there. Her cuddly form reminded me of the dream girl, and my heart lurched. Suddenly, Monopoly held little appeal. I walked over to Seth. "Tell you what. You play, and I'll take bedtime duty."

"You sure?"

"Positive."

He passed her off, and she wrapped her little arms around my neck. With the twins in tow, I left the others to set up the game. Maddie looked distinctly uncomfortable at being abandoned, but I knew she'd do fine. Sometimes being forced to socialize was the best way to learn.

The twins were surprisingly easy to put to bed, probably because they slept in the same room. Going to bed wasn't such a big deal when you had a sister to whisper to and giggle with. I supervised the brushing of teeth and putting on of pajamas, then closed them in with warnings that I'd check back.

Still balancing Kayla on one hip, I carried her to the room she shared with Kendall. Kayla almost never said anything, so I wasn't particularly surprised when she didn't protest having a pink nightgown pulled over her head and being tucked under the covers. I sat on the edge of her bed and handed her a stuffed unicorn I'd found on the floor. She wrapped it in her arms.

"I think it could take the spider monkey," I told her.

Kayla said nothing but just watched me with those huge blue eyes. They were filled with such trust and sweetness—just like my daughter in the dream. How amazing would it be to do this every night? To tuck someone in and kiss her forehead, then wake up with her each morning?

Suddenly, fearing I might cry in front of a four-year-old, I started to rise. To my complete astonishment, she held out her hand and touched my arm.

"Georgina."

Her voice was small and soprano and sweet. I sat back down. "Hmm?"

"Don't leave," she said.

"Oh, honey. I have to. You need to sleep."

"Monsters will come."

"What monsters?"

"The bad ones."

"Ah. I see. Are they under your bed?" I was pretty sure that's where most monsters lived. Aside from the ones I played poker with and bought Secret Santa presents for.

She shook her head and pointed up at the ceiling. "They live there. In space."

"Are they aliens?" As much as I hated the thought of her being afraid to go to bed, I was rather enchanted to be having a conversation with her for the first time ever. She was as articulate as all the other girls—not that I should have been surprised by that.

"No. They're monsters. They swoop in the air and go in people's dreams."

I caught on to her reluctance to sleep now. "Have you been having nightmares?"

"No. But the monsters are there. I feel them."

Something about her words and the serious set of her face sent a chill down my spine. "You want me to stay until you fall asleep? Will that keep them away?"

"Maybe," she said. She touched my arm again. "You're magic."

I wondered then if Kayla might be a psychic in the making, like Erik or Dante. The way she spoke implied more than a childhood belief in magic. There was almost an authority there. She'd be worth keeping an eye on, but I wouldn't pursue anything now. I certainly wasn't going to start quizzing her about auras.

"Okay," I said. "I'll stay."

I lay down beside her, and she studied me in silence. I began humming an old song, which made her smile and close her eyes. When I finished, she opened her eyes again.

"What are the words?"

"Eh . . ." That was hard to answer. It was a song from my mortal life, one that had been composed in an ancient Cyprian dialect no one spoke anymore. My husband used to sing it to me. Knowing I couldn't reproduce the rhymes or any sort of good translation on the spot, I simply sang it to her in the original language. The syllables, familiar yet strange, came awkwardly to my lips.

When I finished, Kayla didn't say anything or move. I waited a couple more minutes and slowly got out of the bed. She continued sleeping. Turning off the light, I left the room and returned to the Monopoly players. Seth smiled at my approach and made room for me beside him on the floor.

"Luddites burn your mill. Pay five-hundred dollars." Brandy grimaced at her Chance card. "Weak."

"That's not as much as I had to pay when the Factory Acts cut my child labor force a couple turns ago," Maddie pointed out. As I'd hoped, she seemed perfectly at ease now.

Kendall rolled the dice and moved her miniature pewter *Oliver Twist* book ahead three spaces. "I wish I had a job, so I could save capitalism for my investments."

"Capital," the rest of us said in unison.

Kendall glanced up at me. "I could work at your bookstore. Under the table."

"Like stacking books under the table?" asked Brandy.

Kendall ignored her. "Don't you need extra help?"

I ruffled her hair. "Not until you're of age, I'm afraid."

Maddie moved her pewter spinning jenny. "Yeah, haven't you learned anything from this game? You'd get us shut down. Georgina doesn't need that kind of paperwork."

"How's your manager job?" asked Brandy. "Is it harder?"

"Mostly it's . . . different."

Kendall brightened. "I could have your old job."

"Sorry. No vacancy. Maddie took my place."

Kendall sighed.

Seth landed on a silk mill no one had purchased yet and began rustling up money. "The girls go to bed okay?"

"Yeah . . . Kayla had a hard time, though. She was worried about nightmares."

He looked up in surprise. "She told you that? She, like, spoke?"

"Yeah, we had a whole discourse. Laughed, cried, shared our hopes and fears. I think she has an oratorical career ahead of her."

"What's 'oratorical' mean?" asked Kendall.

"It refers to speaking in public," Maddie explained. "Giving speeches. Talking in front of others."

"Oh. Uncle Seth doesn't have an oratorical career."

We all laughed. "No," agreed Maddie. "He doesn't. I certainly don't either."

Seth high-fived her. "Introverts unite."

Brandy picked up another Chance card and groaned. "Cholera outbreak! Not again!"

When the night finally ended and Seth's brother and sister-in-law came home, I was happy to learn that Maddie had had a really good time.

"Kids aren't so bad as long as they're brainiac Mortensen offspring. Terry and Andrea were nice too. Good genes in that group."

"Yup," I agreed. Maddie definitely needed more socialization, I decided. She was cheerful and upbeat, her eyes sparkling and excited. This had been a good night.

I dropped her off at Doug's and drove back to my apartment. The parking gods weren't with me tonight, and I ended up about five blocks away. As I walked, I passed a newspaper dispenser for the *Seattle Times*. I usually read the headlines at the store but hadn't today. I paused in front of it, one article catching my eye.

It was a weird story about a local man who'd turned delusional. He'd had a dream that if he swam across Puget Sound, it would bring wealth and security to his struggling family. Sadly, he hadn't made it very far before drowning in the freezing waters. The ironic part was that although some might consider the feat suicidal, his massive life insurance policy was going to pay out. His family would get their wealth and security after all.

Staring blankly at the paper, I thought about the poor man succumbing and disappearing under the dark waves. I suddenly flashed back to this morning, and it was like I could feel the cold, wet sensation all over again. For half a second, I couldn't breathe. It was as though my lungs were filling with water, suffocating me. I shuddered and absentmindedly ran my hands over my arms, the déjà vu nearly overpowering me. Water. Water everywhere. Cold. Black. Smothering . . .

I shivered and finally made myself start walking again, needing to find someplace warm.

Chapter 12

"I can't believe you keep coming back," Dante told me when I showed up at his shop the next day. To no one's surprise, the place was empty.

"Me either," I admitted. I never felt welcome here, yet I didn't feel I had anywhere else to go. "How do you stay in business?"

"Beats me. I don't suppose you're here to give me the best night of my life? You missed your El Gaucho chance, though."

"I'm here because I had another dream."

"You're using me, succubus." He sighed and sat down at the chintzy table. "Okay. Give it to me."

Settling down across from him, I recapped the latest dream events.

"Not really much in the way of new developments," he pointed out afterward. "You got, like, thirty more seconds of plot."

"Does it mean anything?"

"Hell if I know."

I narrowed my eyes. "You are the worst dream interpreter ever."

"Nah." He rested his chin in his hand, elbow propped on the table. His expression was typically lazy. "I'm a very good interpreter. There's nothing to interpret in your dream, though, unless it's just your subconscious lamenting your infertility. Which is likely. It also suggests you have bad taste in music. Is 'Sweet Home Alabama' really playing each time?"

Now I sighed.

"The dreams clearly aren't prophetic either since we know it's impossible for you to have a kid." He drummed his fingers on the table, face thoughtful. "You sure you might not adopt or something?"

"She was mine," I said firmly. "My own flesh and blood. I could *feel* it."

"Okay. Far be it from me to argue delusional maternal instincts. But like I said, it doesn't really matter. The content, I mean. What matters here, I guess, is the energy loss."

I could have hugged him. "Finally, someone fucking thinks that's important."

"It's a pattern now. Can't really blame it on anomaly anymore."

"So what's it mean?"

"You sure you want the opinion of the worst dream interpreter ever?"

"Good grief! Get on with it."

"If you were human, I'd say without a doubt that you were being preyed on."

I flinched. "What? What do you mean?"

He reached across the table and caught my hand, flipping it over absentmindedly while he thought. I was too caught on the word *preyed* to care about him touching me. Little Kayla's words popped into my head.

They're monsters. They swoop in the air and go in people's dreams.

"You and I both know there are plenty of supernatural beings walking the world. Some walk the dreamworld and don't really have humans' best intentions at heart. Not that you do either. And honestly, some aren't too different from you. They crave human life and energy, and they can suck it out of dreams."

"But they can't do that to me?"

"Mmm." He let go of my hand. "I don't see how. You don't make your own energy. You steal it too. But who knows?"

I shivered. The idea of some creature—some parasitic creature—latching on and sucking out my life made me ill. I was fully aware of the hypocrisy, however, seeing as I did the exact same thing all the time.

"So . . . what kind of creature might be capable of doing that?"

"Dunno. Not my specialty."

"But you're a dream expert! Shouldn't you know about dream . . . creatures?"

"Supernatural creatures are Erik's thing, not mine. You should ask him."

"You're the worst dream interpreter ever."

"So I hear." His earlier seriousness flitted away. "So . . . are we going to have sex now?"

I stood up. "No! Of course not."

Dante threw his hands up. "What more do you want? I actually gave you useful information this time. And it's not like you couldn't use the fix—small or no."

"It's more than that," I said. Suddenly, I hesitated. "I . . . I know you now."

"What's that supposed to mean?"

"If you were some anonymous guy, there might be a chance. But now you're like a . . ." *Friend* wasn't quite the word I was looking for. ". . . an acquaintance."

He appeared genuinely baffled for once. It was almost amusing. "I'm really not following this, succubus."

"I've got a boyfriend, remember? When I have anonymous, casual sex, it's not really cheating. But if I do it with someone . . ."

". . . you like?" Was it my imagination, or was there something hopeful in his eyes when he asked that?

"No, I don't think I like you. But I don't exactly dislike you either. The point is, you aren't anonymous. It would be cheating."

He stared at me for several moments, and whatever glimmer of hope I thought I'd seen was definitely gone. "No wonder succubi are so good at passing as human women. You've certainly got the head games and complete lack of rationality down."

"I've got to go."

"You *always* have to go. Where to now? Some anonymous guy?"

I rose. "No, I'm going to find Erik and see if he can actually give me useful information."

"I did give you useful information!"

"Debatable."

"Well, let me lock up, and we'll see what Lancaster has to say."

I froze. "What do you mean 'we'?"

Dante grabbed some keys from behind the counter. "You've piqued my curiosity. I want to see how this turns out. Besides, you owe me for my help, seeing as you won't put out."

" 'Help,' indeed," I muttered.

He walked to the door with me. "Did it ever occur to you that in spite of how unuseful you think I am, I'm still kind of concerned about what happens to you?"

"No," I said. "It actually hadn't."

But I let him go with me over to Arcana, Ltd. When we stepped inside, we found Erik unpacking a box of books. He smiled without looking up, having sensed me.

"Miss Kincaid, always a—" He stopped when he noticed Dante. For the first time in our friendship, I saw Erik look angry. It was disturbing. Frightening, even. "Mr. Moriarty."

Dante nodded his greeting. "Always nice to see you."

The expression on Erik's face showed the feelings weren't mutual. He straightened up from his work and walked over to the counter. Crossing his arms over his chest, he peered at both of us.

"What can I do for you?" No cordial host or tea chats

today. The air between the two men suddenly felt thick and oppressive.

I spoke uncertainly. "We . . . that is, Dante thinks he has an answer to my dream problems."

Dante laughed, wearing his trademark smirk. If he bore Erik the same animosity, he was hiding it well. "I wouldn't call it an answer, succubus. More like a theory."

"I've had the dream again," I told Erik. "More than once now. And I still keep losing my energy. Dante says it could be some kind of . . . dream creature preying on me." I stumbled over the words. The concept was still too ludicrous. "But he didn't know what kind. He said you might know."

Erik shifted his eyes from Dante to me. I could tell the old man was still unhappy about us being there together, but he cared about me too much and couldn't stop himself from helping me. I wondered at what point over the years I had earned such regard. And how. He sighed and gestured us to the table. We all sat down, but no tea was offered.

"Something like that going after a succubus is hard to imagine," Erik said at last.

"That's what I thought," said Dante.

His lighthearted mask had slipped a little. He looked much as he had in the store, thoughtful and curious. He reminded me of a mechanical engineer I'd once known. The guy couldn't help himself when it came to fixing some technical problem. Give him something in pieces, and he *had* to analyze it and figure it out. Dante might give me a hard time, but his nature, corrupt or not, couldn't stay away from this.

Erik's eyes studied me, hard and intent. I was an intriguing puzzle for him too.

"If I had to pick . . . I'd say the symptoms most match Oneroi."

I'd heard of them. They'd been in the Greek myths I'd grown up with. "Dream spirits?"

Dante considered. "More than spirits. They're the children of Nyx and Erebus."

I shuddered. I'd heard of them too. Nyx and Erebus. Night and Darkness. Primordial entities of chaos. They were powerful and dangerous. The world had been born of chaos, true, but it was also a fact—even science agreed—that the universe was always trying to move back toward chaos. Nyx and Erebus were destructive—so much so that they were now locked away, lest they tear the world apart. The possibility that their children could be sucking away my life made me feel sick again.

Dante was still turning this theory over in his head. "Yeah, that'd be the closest. But they still don't match one hundred percent."

"Nothing does," admitted Erik. "I've never heard of anything attacking a succubus."

"What do Oneroi do exactly?" I asked.

The two men exchanged glances, each waiting for the other to explain. Erik was the one who stepped up.

"They visit mortals in their dreams and feed off the emotions such dreams stir up. Victims of Oneroi wake up drained and sick." More irony. Legend said that succubi visited men in their dreams too and took their life.

"That's what's happening to me," I argued. "Why couldn't it be them?"

"It *could* be them," agreed Dante, "but like we said, the details don't fit. Oneroi can seize control and shape what you dream. But the dreams they stir up are usually nightmares. Fear and other dark emotions tend to be more intense—they offer more for the Oneroi to feed off of. Your dreams are short, and they're . . . fluffy."

"Fluffy?"

"Well, I don't know. Not nightmares. They're intriguing to you. They bring out emotions—fascinated, happy emotions. They're giving you visceral reactions, I suppose, but not the type that the Oneroi usually go after."

"And," continued Erik, "there's also the fact that you aren't an ideal choice for them. You're inefficient. You're a conduit, a link to the mortal world and their energy. If Oneroi are stealing from you, they have to wait for you to get your power from someone else first. Far simpler for them to take directly from a human."

I suddenly realized I'd forgotten something. "One other weird thing happened . . . more than the energy loss . . ." I explained about waking up feeling cold and wet.

"I guess that's kind of weird," said Dante, "but I don't know that it's really related to this."

"Well, except later that day, I read this article about a guy who went crazy and tried to swim across the Sound. He thought it would help his family—and it did because he drowned and they got his insurance money. When I read the article, the wet and cold feeling came back. It was like . . . for a second, I was him. I felt exactly what he'd felt. Like I was drowning too."

"Empathy," said Dante. "You read it and imagined what it must be like."

"No." I frowned, trying to bring the feeling back. "I . . . I *felt* him. I knew it was him I was feeling. That guy. The same way I knew the girl was my daughter. It was in my gut."

Dante looked annoyed. "Would have been helpful to know this earlier."

"I forgot. I didn't really see it as relevant until now."

"Have you ever had anything like this happen before? Knowledge of something you didn't experience?"

"I don't think so."

Erik glanced at Dante. "Clairvoyance?"

"I don't know. Unlikely. Too many variables. None of them mesh." Dante turned his gaze back on me. "Have you talked to your own people about this?"

I shook my head. "Jerome's been gone. I mentioned the first dream before he left, but he didn't seem very concerned."

"Well, I don't know what to make of it," Dante said.

"Nor I," said Erik kindly, "But I will look into this for you."

"Thanks," I told him. "I really appreciate it."

We stood up, and like that, the momentary truce between Erik and Dante vanished. Erik looked stormy once more. Dante appeared smug and condescending.

"Miss Kincaid," Erik began stiffly. "You know I have nothing but the highest regard for you, and I am more than happy to assist you in any way you need. I also recognize that Mr. Moriarty can also offer you help. But I would prefer it if . . ."

". . . if you don't bring me around anymore," finished Dante. He saluted. "Noted, old man. Meet you at the car, succubus." He turned and walked out of the shop.

Erik's mood didn't vanish with Dante's departure. I could still sense the fury radiating from him. Erik had said Dante was corrupt, but really, so was I. Erik didn't have this kind of reaction around me. There was something I was missing here.

"I'm sorry," I told Erik. "I didn't know it would bother you so much."

"You couldn't have known," he replied wearily. "And after all, I was the one who directed you to him."

"I'll keep him away," I promised.

I thanked him again and went out to meet Dante. He leaned against my car, his thoughts obscured by a lazy smile.

"Why does Erik hate you so much?" I asked.

Dante glanced down at me. "Because I'm a bad man who does bad things."

"There's more to it than that," I said. "And you don't seem *that* bad. The worst things you've done are trick customers and offer useless information. Although . . . well, you actually were pretty helpful just now. But like I said, I don't think you're as bad as your reputation implies."

"How would you know?"

I shrugged. "Instinct."

In one swift motion, Dante snaked his hand behind my neck and pulled me to him. I put a hand on his chest and started to push him away and then stopped. There was a warmth in his body, the eagerness of a man who'd been deprived of something for a very long time. To my surprise, I felt arousal burning in me—a yearning of my own to touch someone who wasn't all business. I experienced that feeling a lot, and it usually got me into trouble. My succubus nature woke up, wondering if energy might be on its way.

And despite my lofty talk earlier about not sleeping with people I was acquainted with, I suddenly wanted him to kiss me. I wanted his energy—just a taste.

His mouth moved toward mine. I started to close my eyes and part my lips—then, abruptly, he stiffened. Releasing me, he stepped back. I opened my eyes, staring in astonishment.

"What the hell?" I asked. "You backed off. And after all the grief you've given me about sleeping with you."

"You're drained and hungry, succubus," he said. "It'd be like taking advantage of a drunk girl."

"Right. And you've never done anything like that."

"Yeah, well, I'm not eighteen anymore." He opened the car door. "Are we going or not?"

I studied him a bit longer, thinking again I saw that hope and compassion from earlier. I was starting to wonder if a lot of his cattiness was just bravado, hiding the same insecurities everyone in the world had. I kept my psychoanalysis to myself, however, and joined him in the car. We drove back to his shop, our usual flippant banter obscuring anything serious that might have happened.

Chapter 13

"**I**'m really not a serial killer. It just seemed like too good a chance to pass up."

"Man," I said. "If I had a dime for every time I heard that . . ."

Liam, the guy who'd bought me at the auction, laughed and opened the car door for me. He drove a shiny black Lotus Elise that he'd had imported from the UK. I found that impressive. It appeared to have just been freshly washed. I found that impressive too—and a little sad since it looked like it was going to rain at any moment.

"It's supposed to be really good, though," he added, starting up the engine. "So, I hope you'll like it and not think it's too demented for the holidays."

I hadn't been keen on following up with my charity date, but I'd known it would have to happen sooner or later. When Liam had called earlier to say he'd gotten tickets to a dramatic production of three Edgar Allan Poe stories tonight, I figured it was as good a time as any to get it over with. Besides, I liked Poe. It was kind of a creepy date to have around the happiest time of the year, true, but that would be the theater's fault, not Liam's.

It was an early show, so we planned to attend first and catch dinner later. On the drive there, he turned out to be a lot like I'd expected. Intelligent. Nice. Moderately funny. He worked for an investment company downtown and had enough sense not to bore me with the details. We traded light banter, sharing anecdotes and experiences. I still would have rather been with Seth, but Liam was a fine guy for one night, and I figured he should have a fun time after donating so much money.

The play was about as twisted as I'd hoped. They started with "The Masque of the Red Death," followed by "The Cask of Amontillado." "The Tell-Tale Heart" closed the night off because honestly, what sort of Poe festivities would be complete without that crowd pleaser?

"I've never heard of 'The Masque of the Red Death,' " Liam said afterwards. We'd decided to leave the car and walk the six blocks to the restaurant he had reservations at. "I read the others in high school. I guess it's some kind of allegory about how you can't escape death, huh? You can lock yourself away, but it doesn't work."

"More than an allegory, actually," I mused. "Historically, that wasn't an uncommon way for people to deal with plague and disease. Lock themselves up. Or else leave town and run away. Sometimes they'd throw the sick people out of town and lock the doors, so to speak."

"That's horrible," said Liam. We stepped inside the restaurant, a small Italian one that was almost always booked. I had to admit, he was doing a good job with this date thing.

"People didn't know any better," I said. "They didn't know what caused diseases, and aside from good hygiene and luck, there were few treatments for ancient and medieval epidemics."

"That auctioneer didn't say anything about you being a history buff," he teased.

"Yeah? Would you not have bid?"

"Are you kidding? A beautiful woman who uses the words 'ancient and medieval epidemics' on the first date? I would have bid more."

I grinned and let the maitre d' lead us to our table. I was glad Liam appreciated my historical knowledge, but I'd have to be careful not to get too nerdy. I knew more than the average girl should and could get into levels of detail that modern people had no way of knowing about. I shifted to something else.

"Well, I think the auctioneer was kind of distracted by the other contestants."

"Oh, you mean the feminazi who went before you?"

I frowned. "No, I mean the giant blonde in silver that he bid on."

"Oh, yeah," Liam agreed. "She was crazy. Attractive, but crazy."

"You actually thought she was pretty?"

"Sure. Not as pretty as you, of course," he hastily added, mistaking my meaning. "But the auctioneer apparently thought otherwise. He couldn't keep his hands off of her."

"Oh, come on. He barely touched her."

"Well, not during the auction, of course. I mean afterward."

"What?"

I was interrupted when the waiter came by. I had to wait for Liam to order wine before he could finish the story.

"After the auction. I was there helping wrap things up. Deanna's a friend of my ex-wife's. When we all finished, Nick and that blonde were all over each other and left together."

"That . . . that isn't possible."

Tawny had said they'd left separately. There was no way she and Nick could have been hot and heavy the night of the auction. The following night had been when she showed up for the dance lesson. Even if she was lying about things falling apart with Nick—and really, why would she?—she'd obviously had no recent energy fix. Massive shape-shifting, on the scale of nonhuman shapes, could burn through energy that quickly, but a new succubus wouldn't have that skill yet. None of this made sense. Liam, obviously, didn't catch my confusion.

"Why's it so hard to believe?" he asked.

I shook my head. "It's . . . never mind. I hope they had a great time. Now . . . what kind of wine did you order? I missed it."

Not wanting to ruin dinner, I put the Tawny conundrum into a holding bin in my mind and did my best to give Liam his seventeen-hundred-dollars worth. When dinner ended, we walked back toward his car, enjoying a leisurely pace. The weather, though damp, had warmed to about fifty. Seattle's fickle winters did that sometimes, only to freeze up a day or so later. When Liam slipped his hand into mine, I let him, but it presented me with a dilemma.

He was no one I really planned on seeing again. As a courtesy to Seth and an attempt at a normal life, I avoided casual affairs in this body. All of those reasons meant I shouldn't let the night escalate into anything more than a friendly handshake good-bye. But suddenly, I was feeling the loss of my energy. It had felt so good to have Simon's—yet it had been stripped from me before I could even do anything with it. It'd be so nice to have that feeling back, to go home with Liam and get what I needed.

When we reached his car, he kept holding my hand and turned me so that I faced him. "What now?" he asked.

"I don't know." I was still torn on what to do. "I'm open to suggestion."

Liam smiled, a cute smile that showed in his blue eyes too. "Well, how about this?" He leaned down and kissed me, much as Dante had nearly done.

Oh, Liam. Liam was a good man. A good, good man. Seth caliber. The moment our lips touched, I felt the sweetness of his life energy trickling into me. My desire woke up, and I pressed myself to him. I might not like to use this body, but these were unusual circumstances. I made my decision. I'd sleep with him and part ways. He was a nice guy, not a psycho stalker. He might be disappointed, but he wouldn't give me grief for wanting to be friends in the morning.

He kissed me harder, pushing me against the side of the

car. All that energy from just one kiss. The sex was going to be great.

Yes, yes. More. Get more. Feed me.

I jerked away from Liam.

He looked down at me, legitimately concerned. "What's the matter?"

It had been a whisper in my head. Faint but real. It had been paired with a longing, a deep longing for Liam's energy that rivaled my own need—but it hadn't been mine. It had belonged to someone—or something—else. Suddenly, it all came back to me. The conversations with Dante and Erik. Some creature preying on me and stealing my energy. True, it was what I did to men . . . but, well, I couldn't help how I felt. And just then, I felt nauseous at the thought of some parasitic creature coming to me tonight because I was full of energy. It made my skin crawl. Bad enough this thing was using me. It was also using me to use Liam.

I looked back at him; he was so cute and so nice. I shook my head. I couldn't do this. I needed the energy, but I was going to put if off as long as possible. I wouldn't give this thing what it wanted.

"Liam . . ." I said slowly. "I should tell you something. I, um, just recently got out of a long relationship, and I went to the auction because I thought I could, you know . . ."

He sighed, not appearing angry so much as regretful. "You aren't ready."

I shook my head. "I'm really sorry. I wanted to help at the auction, and I thought I could move on."

He squeezed the hand he was still holding and released it. "Well . . . I'm sad, but I understand. And I like you . . . if we went out, I'd like to work on something serious. That can't happen until you're ready, and I'd never want to force you."

Oh, God. Nice, nice guy.

"I'm so, so sorry," I said. I meant it. I so wanted his energy.

"Nothing to be sorry about," he told me, smiling. "Come on, I'll take you home."

He returned me to Queen Anne, and I kissed him on the cheek before leaving the car. He told me to call him when I was ready to date again, and I told him I would.

Once he was gone, I didn't go inside. Instead, I called Dante.

"It's your favorite succubus," I said when he answered.

I heard him yawn. "Debatable. What do you want? It's late."

"I need to talk to you. Something weird happened."

"I'm in bed, succubus. Unless you plan on joining me, I'd rather not receive visitors right now."

"*Please*, Dante. It's important."

He sighed. "Fine, come on over."

"I don't know where you live."

"Of course you do. You've been here a gazillion times."

"You live in your store?"

"Why would I want to pay rent for two different places?"

I drove down to the shop. The sign read CLOSED, but there was a faint light inside. Dante opened the door when I knocked. He wore jeans and a plain T-shirt, nothing unusual, but the disheveled hair suggested he had indeed been in bed.

"Sorry," I told him. "Maybe I should have waited."

"Too late for regrets. Come on in."

He led me through the storefront, back to the small door I usually saw closed. On the other side was a large room that appeared to be a combination living space, office, supply closet, and . . . workshop.

"Erik was right," I said, walking over to a high set of shelves. They were filled with jars and bottles of herbs and unidentifiable liquids. "You are a magician." I considered. "Or at least you're pretending to be."

"No faith in me. Probably smart." He pointed to a bean bag chair and a plaid ottoman. "Take your pick if you don't want the bed."

I chose the ottoman. "Well, it's not that I don't trust you . . . but everything else you do is a scam. Of course, Erik has to hate you for something legitimate, and he wouldn't have sent me to you in the first place if you didn't have some kind of skill."

"Interesting logic. Maybe he hates me for my charming personality." He rubbed his eyes and yawned again. With the motion of his arm, I noticed faint punctures in the middle of his arm that I'd never seen with long sleeves.

"Maybe he hates you for your vices."

Dante looked at where I was staring. He shrugged, unconcerned. "Nah, Lancaster has better things to worry about than a casual hit now and then."

"From my experience, there's no such thing as a casual hit."

"What, are you here to do an intervention now, succubus?"

"No," I admitted. I had neither time nor interest to reform Dante. "But I heard a voice tonight."

"I heard a voice too. It called and woke me up."

"Dante!"

Angrily, I explained the situation. A hint of his sarcastic smile remained, but otherwise, he actually seemed concerned.

"Huh. Interesting. It actually raised its ugly head."

"What do you think that means?"

"Not a clue until we know what it is. The only thing I can guess is that it was desperate for some reason. Until now, it's done a pretty good job at hiding itself—aside from your energy loss, obviously." He brightened a little. "I don't suppose it's here now, urging you to jump me?"

"Sorry."

"Ah, well. I'm probably not as good a catch as Seventeen-hundred-dollar Man. Your predator has standards."

I shuddered, hating the idea that I actually had a predator. I looked up at Dante and must have looked truly pathetic because a startled look crossed his features.

"Dante, you have to help me. I know we don't have the answers yet . . . but, well, I'm scared of this thing. I can't bring myself to take a victim because I'm afraid of this monster coming back. I don't even want to go to sleep."

His gray eyes assessed me, and to my astonishment, he almost looked gentle. It completely transformed him. "Ah, succubus. You can sleep tonight. No energy, no visit. I doubt the kiss was enough of a lure."

"But eventually . . . eventually I'll have to get another fix . . . and until I'm able to talk to Jerome about all this . . ."

"Well, I could maybe make you a charm or something. Protection to ward this thing away."

"You can do that?" I tried to keep the skepticism out of my voice but failed. His face turned wry once more.

"If you don't want the help . . ."

"No! I do. I'm sorry. That was wrong of me. I asked for your help, then backed off."

"Well, as you said, I haven't inspired much faith in you."

"I'll take whatever help I can get," I said honestly.

He stood up and stretched, then walked over to his shelves, studying their contents. "You sure about that? You might not like what I have to do to make this. How badly do you want it?"

I thought about that voice, that creature's need inside my head. "Pretty badly. Provided you don't, like, give me a necklace made out of goat entrails, I think we're good."

His eyes were still on his shelves and jars. Several moments passed while he considered. "I'm going to need some time on this, I'm afraid. It'd be a lot easier if I knew what it was we're dealing with. Without that, I've got to try to make some sort of catch-all charm that may or may not work. The broad spectrum ones are always hard, too."

"So nothing tonight."

He strolled back over to me. "You're fine tonight, remember? Of course, you're welcome to stay here, and I'll stay awake and make sure nothing happens to you."

I couldn't help a smile. "Just like Kayla."

"Who?"

"My boyfriend's niece . . ." I'd nearly forgotten about our weird conversation. "She said some funny things. But I don't know if it was just kid imaginings or if she maybe has some kind of psychic ability."

"Fine line with kids," he said. "If she has any powers, I'm sure science and discipline will work them out of her. What'd she say?"

"She said that I was 'magic.' And that there were monsters in the air who got into people's dreams." When he didn't respond, I exclaimed, "Do you think she could help with this?"

He shook his head. "No. If she is psychic or gifted or whatever, she's too young and inexperienced to know what she's perceiving to be of any real use."

"But she could be sensing what's following me."

"Sure. If she's a really astute psychic, she'd be sensitive to anomalies in the magical and spiritual worlds."

Interesting. Tiny little Kayla, possibly with the potential for great spiritual powers some day. "What's your advice?"

"Huh?" he asked.

"For someone like her. To develop her abilities and make sure science and discipline don't beat it out of her."

"My advice?" He gave a harsh laugh. "Let them beat it out of her. You'll be doing her a favor."

I sat quietly for a long time, studying my feet. When I finally looked back up at him, I asked, "Why are you so unhappy?"

"Who says I'm unhappy? I make money by doing nothing."

I gestured around. "Everything says you're unhappy. Your attitude. Your arm. The pile of beer bottles over there. The fact that even though you claim I annoy you, you keep helping me and always seem glad to have me around."

"Misery loves company. You aren't exactly all that chipper yourself."

"I'm very happy with my life," I argued.

"Well, then, go back to it, and let me sleep." In a not too subtle signal, he walked over to the door and opened it. "I'll work on your charm and get back to you."

I started to snap back at the abrupt dismissal, but he looked so weary, I couldn't bring myself to do it. Besides, I knew I'd been right. Dante Moriarty was a very unhappy man who used sarcasm and substances to hide it. I wondered what it was that plagued him so much—what it was that had darkened his soul.

"Are you ever going to tell me why Erik hates you so much?" I asked quietly.

Dante pointed at the door. "Good night, succubus. Sweet dreams."

Chapter 14

I worked an evening shift that day and had made plans to have lunch with Maddie. She and I had worked several shifts together in the last week or so, but things were getting so crazy at the store that we hardly had a chance to talk anymore.

"Well, aren't we the rebels?" she said when the waiter set two margaritas on the table. We were at the "unholy" place Peter, Cody, and Hugh had tried to lure me out to a few nights ago.

"Nah," I said, licking the edge of my glass. Salt and lime juice were proof of God's existence. And tequila was proof of Satan's. "We don't work for three more hours. We'll be sober by then. Besides, I'm your superior, and I say it's okay." We clinked glasses and drank up.

"I feel like I'm boring," she told me halfway through our meal.

"Not true."

"It is. I don't do anything with my life." She held the glass by its stem, swirling the contents around and around. "Doug goes out every night, either to practice or party or whatever. Me? If I'm not at work, I'm home writing articles or watching reality TV."

"What do you wish you were doing instead?"

"I don't know. There are lots of things I've thought about. Skydiving. Travel. Always kind of wanted to go to South America. But it's hard, you know? Those kinds of things force you to break out of your comfort zone."

"There's no reason you can't do those things. You're smart and capable, and I think you're braver than you give yourself credit for."

She smiled. "Why are you such a cheerleader for me?"

"Because you're awesome." The truth was, I was starting to realize, Maddie reminded me of myself when I'd been mortal. Not entirely comfortable with my body (I'd been insanely tall). Not always so adept socially (my sharp attitude had gotten me in trouble a lot). That version of me was centuries gone, but a kernel of it would always be within me. I gestured the waiter over and shook my glass at him. "Hey, Josh. Can you hook me up?"

Josh the waiter, who looked too young to drink, took the glass with a grin. "You bet. Same thing?"

"Yep. Although . . . I hate to tell you this, but it was kind of weak."

Josh adopted an offended air. "Was it? I'll yell at the bartender immediately. Maybe I'll make him come over and apologize on bended knee."

"No need," I said magnanimously. "Just have him add an extra shot this time."

He gave a gallant bow and winked. "As you command."

Maddie groaned when he was gone. "See? I could never flirt that way. Certainly not with jailbait like him."

"Sure you can."

She shook her head. "No. I have the worst luck with men."

"How is that possible? You're always saying funny things to me."

"You're not a man. And I'm not afraid of you," she explained.

"You're afraid of Josh the waiter?"

"Well . . . no, not exactly. But I just get so self-conscious. All flustered and stuff."

I leaned forward and spoke in a conspiratorial tone. "Trade secret. Everyone's self-conscious. Act like you aren't, and you'll be a superstar."

Josh brought me my margarita. I thanked him with more flirting while Maddie looked thoughtful.

When he went to check on another table, she sighed. "Did you know that I've only ever slept with two guys?"

"So?"

"So, I'm twenty-nine! Isn't that sad?"

I thought about my track record. No point even trying to count. "Just means you have standards."

She grimaced. "You haven't met the guys."

"So find a good one. Plenty of them out there." I had a weird flash of déjà vu to past conversations with Tawny.

"Not that I've seen. Well, except maybe Seth. He's one of the good ones." She sighed. "He still hasn't mentioned our date."

"Hasn't he?" I'd have to get on him about that.

"Yeah. Unless babysitting his nieces counts." She shrugged. "It's okay. Like I said, I know he just did it because he felt bad. I appreciate the gesture. Oh hey, I overheard Seth saying something to Doug about how you wanted a Christmas tree. Are you having trouble finding one or something?"

I groaned. "Not that again."

"So . . . you don't want one? Or do you? You seem like the kind of person who would."

"Honestly? I'm indifferent." I shook my head. "It's something my friend Peter started, then he told Seth."

She cut me a suspicious look. "You know, you sure seem to hang out with Seth a lot."

"Hey, you can be friends with nice guys too." I had no idea why I still felt the need to keep my relationship with Seth a secret. Some instinct told me it was the right thing to do.

"Too bad," said Maddie, finishing her own margarita. "I bet he'd treat his girlfriend like a princess."

"Yeah," I agreed wryly. "So long as that princess doesn't mind a mistress. Sometimes I think his writing will always be his first love."

To my surprise, Maddie didn't laugh or look outraged. "Well, I think that's the price you've gotta pay if you want to be with a man like that. It might be worth it."

Now I became pensive, wondering if this was true. Was I too hard on Seth and his distractibility? When lunch wrapped up, we walked back—not *too* tipsy—to the bookstore. I nudged Maddie as we stepped inside.

"Okay, here's the deal. In the next week, I want you to do three adventurous things."

She looked startled. "What kind of adventurous things?"

"I don't know." I pondered, thinking I might be drunker than I'd suspected. "The adventurous kind. Go out clubbing. Wear red lipstick. Doesn't matter. All I know is that there's going to be a pop quiz later, okay?"

"That's ridiculous. It's not that easy," she said with a scowl, turning away. "You can't just make something like that happen."

"Did I just hear you tell Maddie to go clubbing?" Seth's voice asked a moment later. She was already halfway across the store, and I doubted she'd take me up on my challenge. Too bad. I turned around to face him.

"I'm helping her live life."

"By drinking in the middle of the day?" he teased.

I pointed upstairs. "Don't you have a book to finish? I'll talk to you later. I have important things to do."

I felt only a little bad about dismissing him, seeing as we had dinner plans and would see each other later. He wandered off to write, and I threw myself into my work. Someone was home sick, so I got to be out amid the holiday shopping frenzy. Maddie worked a register beside me, and I was pleased to see how cheery and charismatic she was with customers.

When closing time came, I stopped in front of the newspapers, looking for . . . well, I didn't know what. But I hadn't forgotten about that poor drowning victim. I wondered if there might be more about him—or more about anything that might help me figure out what was happening to me in my sleep. Sadly, the headlines offered no insight today.

Seth and I drove to Pioneer Square for our late dinner and unsurprisingly couldn't find parking. We ended up several blocks away and were freezing by the time we entered the restaurant. The trek was worth it, though. This place was one of my favorites, serving up Cajun food spicy enough to chase away the winter chill. With gumbo and étouffée, it was hard to brood for too long.

We'd almost finished dessert when my cell phone rang. I didn't recognize the number.

"Hello?"

"Hey, Georgina. This is Vincent."

"Hey," I said, surprised to be hearing from him.

"Look, I really need to talk to you in person. Is there any way I can see you?"

"Right now?"

"Yeah . . . it's kind of important."

I glanced over at Seth, who was finishing the last of his bread pudding. He was so easygoing, I doubted he'd mind if Vincent stopped by.

"I'm out with Seth . . ."

"It'll just take a few minutes," Vincent promised.

"Okay." I told him where we were, and he told me he'd be there shortly.

He wasn't kidding. I'd barely explained the situation to Seth when Vincent walked into the restaurant.

"What'd you do, fly over here?" I asked as he slid into a chair beside us.

"Nah, I was just close." He gestured to the remnants of our desserts. "Looks good."

"It was great," I said. "Now, what's up?"

He hesitated and glanced in Seth's direction.

"It's fine. Seth knows everything," I assured him. The waitress came by and dropped off our receipt and change.

Vincent studied Seth a moment more, then turned back to me. "Okay. I just have a quick question for you. We can talk about it on our way out."

The three of us set out into the cold again, heading toward Seth's car.

"So," Vincent began. "Remember that story you told me a little while ago? About the cop shooting his partner?"

"Yup."

"Where'd you hear it?"

We walked in silence for a few moments as I tried to remember. "I don't know. Probably on TV. Maybe I saw the headline at the store. Can't recall."

"Are you sure?"

I frowned. "Positive."

Vincent sighed. "Well, here's the thing. I looked into that story and had a hard time finding out anything. It was never made public. I actually had to go investigate with some police sources."

"It had to have been made public. How else would I have known?"

"That's what I'm trying to figure out."

I racked my brain. Where *had* I heard it? No clue. I'd just known it when I talked to Vincent that day. But, obviously, it hadn't sprung up in my head out of the blue.

"Do you know anybody in the police department?" he suggested.

"No one I would have talked to. Maybe I overheard someone. Seriously, I just . . . I just can't remember."

"What's the story?" Seth asked me.

Puzzle pieces suddenly fell together. The cop was just like the guy who'd swam Puget Sound. Both had had a vision of something that wasn't true, but their subsequent actions had brought it about. And I had known about both stories before I should have.

"Georgina?" asked Seth.

"This cop went crazy in a store and started—"

"Okay, just stop. *Just fucking stop.*"

The three of us jerked to a halt as the voice came out of the darkness. In heading toward our remote parking spot, we'd strayed quite a ways away from the hustle and bustle of Pioneer Square. And from around a corner, a man in need of a shave and clean clothes had emerged. He made Carter look genteel. Muggings were rare in Seattle, but statistics meant little when actually being mugged. The man had a gun aimed at us.

"Give me everything you've got," he growled. He had kind of a wide-eyed, paranoid look, and I wondered if he was on something. Again, it meant little. He had a gun. We didn't. "Every fucking thing. Wallet. Jewelry. Whatever. I'll shoot. I swear to God, I will."

I took a step in front of Seth and Vincent, small enough not to raise the guy's alarms but enough to put me in the line of fire. I'd been shot before. It hurt, but it couldn't kill me. My humans were the ones in danger.

"Sure," I said, reaching into my purse. I kept my voice low and soothing. "Whatever you want."

"Hurry up," he snapped. His gun was aimed squarely at me now, which was fine.

Behind me, I heard Seth and Vincent rustling around for their wallets as well. With a pang, I realized I'd have to give up Seth's ring, which I'd worn on a chain around my neck tonight, but that was a small price to pay if we all walked away from this unscathed.

Suddenly, I saw movement in my peripheral vision. Before

I could stop him, Seth lunged forward toward the man and slammed him into the side of the brick building near us. I had never taken Seth for the fighting type, but it was actually pretty impressive. Unfortunately, it was *not* needed at the moment.

Vincent and I sprang into the fray, moving at exactly the same time. The guy had been forced to lower his gun while Seth pinned him against the wall, but the attacker was struggling with the ferocity of a bear. Vincent and I tried to add our own strength, mainly hoping to wrest the gun away. It was one of those moments in time that seemed both really long and really short.

Then, the gun went off.

My two companions and I stopped moving. The guy used the brief lull to wiggle away from us and ran off into the night. I exhaled a breath of relief, grateful it was all over.

"Georgina—" said Vincent.

Seth sank to his knees, and that's when I saw the blood. It was all over his left thigh, dark and slick in the watery light of a flickering streetlight. His face was pale and wide-eyed with shock.

"Oh, God." I fell down beside him, trying to get a look at the leg. "Call 911!" I screamed at Vincent. Having anticipated me, he already had his cell out.

Some part of my brain listened to him speaking frantically into the phone, but the rest of my attention was on Seth.

"Oh God, oh God," I said, ripping off my coat. Blood was pouring steadily out of the wound. I pressed my coat into it, trying to slow the bleeding. "Hang with me. Oh, please, please, hang with me."

Seth's eyes looked at me with both tenderness and pain. His lips parted slightly, but no words came out. I lifted the coat and looked at the wound. Vincent knelt beside me.

"It won't stop, it won't stop," I moaned.

Vincent peered over my shoulder. "Femoral artery."

After over a millennium, I knew the human body and what could kill it. I would have realized what kind of a shot this was if I hadn't been so hysterical.

"It'll drain him," I whispered, pressing the coat into his leg again. I had seen it happen before, watched people bleed to death right in front of me. "It'll kill him before they get here. That bullet hit perfectly."

Beside me, I heard Vincent take a deep, shaking breath. Then, his hands covered mine. "Take it away," he said softly.

"I have to slow the bleeding."

But he gently lifted my hands away, taking the coat up as well. There was blood everywhere. I imagined I could see it steaming in the cold air.

Vincent rested his hands on Seth's thigh, oblivious to the mess. Words formed on the tip of my tongue but never came out. The air around us began burning, and a prickling feeling raced across my skin. For a moment, Seth seemed to be bathed in white light. From Vincent, I suddenly had the sensation of dried lavender and humidity. It was tinged in something else . . . something I'd never hoped to sense again.

Then, it all faded away. Vincent removed his hands, and when I looked down, blood no longer oozed from Seth's thigh.

"I'm sorry," gasped Vincent. "I'm not so good at healing, and if I do any more, the others will sense me. This will keep him alive until the ambulance gets here."

In the distance, I heard the faint sounds of sirens. In my chest, my heart thudded. The world slowed its pace. How long had Vincent said he'd known Yasmine? Fifteen years. Too, too long. He didn't look any older than thirty. They hadn't met when he was a teen. The timing didn't make sense. Neither did the fact that he had just healed a major injury.

But none of that was as telling as what else I'd already discovered. For just a moment, he'd let his defenses slip, and I'd felt—an immortal signature. And while immortals have unique features of their own, all *types* of immortals have certain attributes that identify them by creature as well. Succubi. Vampires. Angels. Demons. Vincent's signature had given him away.

The others will sense me.

I stared at Vincent as red flashing lights rounded the corner. My eyes were as wide as Seth's had been.

"You're a nephilim," I breathed.

Chapter 15

The doctors at the hospital said Seth's survival was a miracle. Which, of course, it was.

The police officers who talked to all of us believed Seth's actions had been rash—but also admirable. Defending a fair maiden tends to elicit that reaction, and since Seth hadn't been killed, no one else viewed his gallant defense quite the same as I did. Because honestly?

I thought it was stupid.

I thought it was *so* stupid, and I was furious. Beyond furious. I'd surpassed it and moved into an uncharted area of enragement.

What had he been thinking?

"I wasn't thinking," he told me in a low voice, when I questioned him in the ER. The others had stepped out for a moment, busy with other things, and it was just the two of us. Seth lay on the bed, face still pale, but otherwise alive and well. "That guy had a gun. You were in his line of fire."

I opened my mouth to argue the poor logic there, but one of the doctors stepped back inside. She needed to check Seth, and I backed out of the room before I said something I'd regret. Seth might have acted like an idiot, but he was in the hospital with a major injury. Blowing up right now probably wasn't the most appropriate course of action for the healing process.

Instead, I sought out Vincent. After his interview with the police, he'd stationed himself down the hall, back against the wall and hands stuffed into his pockets. He tilted his head back, face staring miserably up at the ceiling.

"Hey," I said, careful to keep a safe space between us.

He glanced down at me. "Hey. How is he?"

"Fine—considering everything. The doctors are amazed the bullet 'missed.'"

Vincent turned away and gazed blankly down the hall. He stayed silent.

I didn't know what to say. *So . . . you're a nephilim. How's that working out?*

Frankly, I could guess how that was working out. Horribly. Nephilim were the offspring of angels and humans. Those angels were now demons, of course. You couldn't sleep around with hot humans and still play for heaven's team—as I'd noted with Yasmine. It was why Jerome had fallen. In what had to be the most unfair deal in the world, many nephilim had been hunted and killed by angels and demons—even their own parents. Heaven and Hell viewed nephilim as dangerous abominations. The fact that nephilim tended to have unruly natures and poor impulse control didn't really help their reputation.

As a result of their persecution, nephilim usually walked the earth disguised, hiding the full brunt of their power—which rivaled their parents'—as well as the immortal signatures that could give them away. And while I felt bad for them, they nonetheless scared the hell out of me. Many of them held grudges against angels, demons, and anyone else immortal. Jerome's son Roman was like that. He had come to Seattle a few months ago and embarked on a revenge killing spree. Looking at Vincent now, I wondered if I was dealing with the same sort of thing.

"Does . . . Yasmine know?" I asked after several more awkward moments.

His eyes flicked back to me. "Of course." He said it with the same matter-of-fact tone he'd used when we'd talked about their relationship. It was a tone that implied how could she *not* know? Like it was absurd that he would keep anything from the woman he loved.

"It kills her," he said with a sigh. "It's eating her up inside."

"Because . . . of . . . what you are . . . ?"

"No." His eyes were so sad that I almost forgot he came from a race of uber-powerful psychopaths. "She doesn't care about that part. What she can't stand is that it's a secret. That she has to hide everything. You know they can't lie . . . but she's not exactly telling the truth either. It's deceitful, and she hates that. And *I* hate that she hates it. I've tried to end our . . . thing a couple of times, but she won't do it because . . ."

"Because she loves you," I finished.

Vincent shrugged and looked away from me again.

"I'm sorry," I told him at last. And I was. How horrible. Yasmine loving anyone was dangerous enough, but for her to love one of the most despised creatures in our world . . . well, yeah. That took it to an entirely different level. An angel should have been reporting Vincent's existence, not hiding it.

Vincent turned his attention back to me. "Who will you tell? Carter? Jerome?"

I stared into those dark, dark eyes, those eyes filled with so much sorrow and so much love. I stopped being afraid of him. He wasn't Roman.

"No one," I said quietly. "I'm not going to tell anyone."

He turned incredulous. "Why? You know what I am. You know you could get in trouble for hiding me. Why wouldn't you tell?"

I thought about it. "Because the system is fucked up."

I went back to Seth's room after that, and when I stepped out into the hall later, Vincent was gone. He wasn't at my apartment when I returned home that night.

Seth was released the following morning, and I stayed home from work with him.

"I don't need to be coddled, Thetis," he told me gently—though I could swear there was the *tiniest* hint of annoyance in his voice. "I'm fine. I won't break."

We were sitting in his living room, side by side on the couch. He had his laptop, and I had a novel. I folded a corner of the page I was on and shut the book.

I wanted to tell Seth that he would break, that that's what it meant to be mortal. I wanted to tell him a thousand things, just like I'd wanted to in the hospital, but once more I swallowed my feelings.

"You just need to take it easy," I said. "And I want to make sure you don't do anything too crazy."

"Right. Because my usual lifestyle is so physically vigorous."

He had a point. Most of his days were spent sitting and writing. He wasn't too likely to burst another artery that way.

"I just want you to be careful," I said obstinately. "You were shot last night, remember? That's not the same as falling on the ice."

"You overreacted to that too."

"Is it so wrong to care about you?"

He sighed and returned to his work. I had a feeling I wasn't the only one biting back angry words. We spent most of the day like that, talking little. Whenever he expressed any interest in something—food, drink, etc.—I was quick to jump up and get it for him. I was the perfect nurse/servant. Finally, around dinnertime, he looked like he was nearing a breaking point.

"Arent your friends doing something tonight?" he asked stiffly.

"Are you trying to get rid of me?"

"Just asking."

"They're having a card game."

"You aren't going?"

"No, I'll stay here with you."

"You should go."

"I don't want to leave you. In case you need something."

"Then take me with you."

"What?" I exclaimed. "But you need to—"

"—take it easy, rest, not strain myself. I know, I know. But look, I'm kind of getting cabin fever here, and honestly, I think you'd benefit from a little distraction."

"Seth—"

"Georgina," he interrupted. "It won't be much different than this. More sitting around, except with—"

"Better company?"

"That's not what I mean," he said.

We went back and forth, and as we did, I wondered when we'd reached this point in our relationship. Hitherto everything had been giddy and sentimental with us. How had we crossed the line into nagging? When had we started getting on each other's nerves? In movies, life-threatening experiences are supposed to bring people together.

I finally relented, and we went over to Peter and Cody's place. The gang—consisting of Hugh, Peter, Cody, and Carter tonight—was surprised to see us since Seth often avoided immortal social events. But socially inept or no, Seth liked playing cards. It was the kind of analytical activity he enjoyed, and he could often get by without talking very much.

Just before the game started, Niphon showed up. He and I exchanged brief glares and then proceeded to ignore each other.

Inevitably, Seth getting shot came up in conversation.

"You threw yourself in front of a gun for her?" asked Peter, clearly impressed.

"Well," said Seth, a little uncomfortable at all those eyes on him. "Mostly I tried to jostle it away."

"You mean, disarm him?"

"Well . . . no. More like . . . jostle. I don't really know how to 'disarm' anyone."

"I figured maybe you took combat classes in order to write those fight scenes in your books," explained Peter.

Seth shook his head. "Never been in a fight in my life. Until last night."

"That's awesome," said Cody. "Risking your life in the name of love."

I stared at the vampires disbelievingly while they babbled on about how amazing Seth's feat had been. They peppered him with more questions about the attack, and the anger I'd been trying to squelch since last night kept building and building. Across the table, Niphon listened with a smirk. Carter, in his usual way, concealed his feelings. I wanted to know why he wasn't out with the other angels, but the Seth thing was taking precedence over my curiosity.

One thing struck me as odd. Hugh, listening quietly, seemed as angry as I did. I would have expected him to jump right in with the vampires, blithely pestering Seth for action-packed details and waxing on about how cool Seth's heroics had been. But the imp's face looked dark and stony, his eyes fixed pointedly on his cards.

"The guy was probably high," remarked Peter. "Never know what that might bring out. You jumping in like that was pretty ballsy when you think about it."

I couldn't take it anymore.

"It was stupid!" I cried. Everyone's heads jerked in my direction. I ignored them, my eyes on Seth. "It was foolish and idiotic and, and—" I couldn't think of any more synonyms, so I let it go. "You shouldn't have done it. He couldn't have hurt me. He couldn't have killed me. You should have let me handle it!"

I knew that Seth despised being the center of a commotion

like this, but he returned my gaze with a surprisingly fierce one.

"Georgina, there was a man with a gun in a dark alley. You were in front of him. Do you really think I was running through all sorts of logical scenarios at the time? 'Oh, let's see. She's immortal, so even if she gets shot, there's nothing to worry about.'"

"Yes," I growled. "That *is* what you should have been thinking."

"What I was thinking was 'The woman I love is in danger, and I would rather die myself than see anything happen to her.'"

"But *nothing would have happened to me*!"

"It's a basic human instinct to protect the ones you love. Even if they're immortal."

"That doesn't make any sense."

"That's because it's been too long since you were human," he snapped.

It was like being hit. I shot up from my chair and stalked off to the bathroom. Angry tears were welling up in my eyes, and I refused to let them show in front of my friends. Leaning my forehead against the mirror, I tried to do all the standard tricks for calming down. Deep breathing. Counting to ten. None of it worked.

I didn't get it. I just didn't get it. And apparently, Seth didn't either. Why couldn't he understand? Getting shot—in my head, in my heart, whatever—would fucking hurt. The pain would be excruciating. But in a day or so, I'd recover. I'd go on.

But Seth wouldn't. Why did he not see how serious this was? Death was forever. Squeezing my eyes shut, I tried to block out the image of Seth dead. Cold. Still. No more spark in those brown eyes. No more warm hand to hold mine. A sob built up in me, and I forced it away.

After more deep breathing, I finally felt like I could return to the others. But as I stepped out of the bathroom and started to round the corner back to the kitchen, I heard more shouting. Hugh.

"It was brave, okay? Noble. Gallant. Worthy of a gold star. But she's right. It was stupid. It was so fucking stupid, and you're even more fucking stupid for not realizing it."

"I get it," said Seth. I could hear the weariness and exasperation in his voice. "I could have died. I know, okay? But I wasn't thinking about the larger workings of the universe. I was thinking about *her*."

"No," said Hugh. "You weren't. I am so goddamned tired of hearing everyone talk about how hard it is to be you. They all go on and on about how amazing it is that you can handle this relationship with her. But, Christ. Really, what's hard about it? You have this beautiful, brilliant girlfriend who doesn't fucking age. She loves you. I know you can't have sex, and everyone acts like that's the end of the world, but come on. She's given you the green light to go get it somewhere else. I don't really see you suffering that much."

"What's your point?" asked Seth.

"My point is that *she's* the one who suffers. She knows your life is a ticking time bomb. What have you got, another fifty years maybe? And that's if disease or an accident doesn't take you first. Fifty years, and you're gone. She has to live with that every day, knowing that in one breath, your life could be snuffed out like that." I heard Hugh's fingers snap. "Not hurt. Not injured. *Gone*. She is going to watch you age, watch you gray and wither away, and when you do finally die, it's going to destroy her."

There was a moment's silence, then I heard Seth say uncertainly, "Fifty years isn't anything compared to the scope of her life. She'll get over me. As everyone keeps reminding me, she's immortal."

"All that means is that she has more time to mourn. If you had any fucking regard for her, you would have ended this

stupid romance a long time ago. You would have never gotten involved. She was uncertain at first, but now she's in. She
isn't going to give you up. You could turn into the world's
biggest asshole, and she still wouldn't do it—not with all
these romantic ideals she has now. She loves too easily—and
gets hurt too easily."

I finally forced myself to move in the ensuing silence.
Everyone looked away from me, except Niphon. He was obviously enjoying all of this. I sat back down, and the card
game commenced. None of us were really into it, though.
The atmosphere was stiff, the conversation forced and halt-
ing. It was the proverbial elephant in the room situation.
When Peter awkwardly said he was getting tired, the rest of
us practically flew out of our seats to leave.

As I was putting on my coat, Carter strolled over to me.

"Seth makes his own choices, as is his right," Carter said
softly. The angel was regarding me in that way that always
sent chills down my spine. Someone wearing such an ugly
baseball cap really shouldn't have that kind of ability. Honestly, how did his hats always get so dirty? "You can rage all
you want, but in the end, mortals live their lives the way they
decide to. It's not our place to interfere with that."

"Of course it is," I said. "It's what you guys do. It's what
we all do. That's the whole point of the Heaven and Hell battle—we purposely interfere with people's lives."

"Yes, but this is different."

"No, it's not." Beyond him, I saw Niphon saying something to Seth. Great. The imp was probably trying to buy his
soul. That was so not what I needed right now. I turned back
to Carter. "Look, I've got to go. Say hi to the Get Along
Gang when you see them."

I dragged Seth away from Niphon, and we headed home. I
hadn't thought things between us could be any more uncomfortable than they had been at Peter's, but the car ride proved
me wrong. Earlier, Seth and I had discussed him staying over
at my place, but as I merged onto I-5, he asked, "I'd kind of

like to get some more work done. Do you mind if I just go home?"

The elephant had apparently joined us in the car now. I smiled tightly and kept my eyes on the road. "Sure. No problem."

Chapter 16

As I walked into my building after dropping Seth off, I was surprised to see the guy who staffed the front desk still working. He usually went home at dinnertime. A sheaf of papers in his hands indicated some sort of mandatory overtime. He brightened when he saw me.

"Miss Kincaid! I have something for you."

I blanked for a moment, then remembered the daily Post-it reminders on my door. There'd been a total of three now. "Oh, yeah," I said. "Sorry I haven't had a chance to pick it up yet. I keep forgetting."

He was already rustling around for something behind him on the other side of the window. I strolled over, just as he heaved a huge box up onto the counter. The printing on the side was upside down, but I could still make it out: *Christmas Tree—Austrian Fir*.

"Oh, man," I grumbled. "This is somebody's idea of a—"

But the guy was busy hauling *another* box up to the counter, a smaller one with pictures on the side depicting the 'pre-decorated fiber optic tree' inside. It was followed by another box, a bit smaller than the Austrian Fir, and a smaller one still that was about two-by-two feet. These last two boxes were wrapped in glittery green paper, with a wrapping job so perfect that only one being on earth could have managed it: Peter.

The desk guy surveyed the boxes. "You must really like Christmas."

"I thought each of those notes was a reminder for the same package."

"Nope. New one each day. Want some help?"

We hauled the trees up to my apartment and deposited them on the living room floor. I thanked him, and as soon as he left, Aubrey emerged and began stalking the boxes.

"That's a lot of tannenbaum," a voice behind me suddenly said.

I jumped and turned around. Yasmine. "Don't do that. Carter does exactly the same thing."

"Sorry," she said, looking sheepish. "Wasn't intentional. I just got here." She walked over to the boxes, tilting her head to read them. She wore jeans and an LSU sweatshirt, her black hair pulled into the trademark ponytail that made her look seventeen. "What's up with all these?"

I took off my coat and flounced onto the couch with a sigh. "My friend Peter started this whole buzz that I needed a Christmas tree after Carter burned mine down. So I guess everyone made good on it."

"Wait," she said. "Did you say Carter burned down your Christmas tree?"

"Yeah, it's a long story."

"He must feel bad."

She pointed to the little fiber optic tree, the one that was already decorated. Words were scrawled on the side of the box in spidery, nearly illegible writing:

G—
Figured you could handle this one. Ready and decorated!

—C

P.S.—And flame retardant.

"Hmm," I mused. " 'C' could be Cody too."

"Nah. I recognize the poor attempt at penmanship. It's Carter."

"Okay, so the angel repents. But who are the rest from?"

We soon found out. The wrapping job on the two matching boxes had already given Peter away. The larger box contained a very beautiful, very expensive tree with 'winter moss green' needles that were lightly dusted with silver glitter. The smaller box contained a matched set of lights and ornaments all done in purple and fuchsia. Peter apparently hadn't trusted me to decorate his gift myself.

The Austrian Fir turned out to be from the bookstore staff. A card from Maddie read: *Surprise! We all pitched in for it. Now you can't be a Scrooge.* It was signed by other store workers, as well as Seth.

I looked back and forth between the boxes. "It's a Christmas miracle. I had no tree. Now I have a forest."

"C'mon," said Yasmine. "I'll help you set them up."

I looked at her in surprise. "Aren't you here to meet up with Vince or something?"

She shook her head. "I'm here to talk to you."

Uh-oh.

I didn't really want to set up the Christmas trees, but a being vastly more powerful than me did, so I set to it. Carter's tree was the easiest since all I had to do was plug it in. I placed it in a window sill, one with an outlet right underneath. The tree's fiber optic needles lit up to pale pink, then purple, then teal, then white.

"Good God," I said. "It's the Christmas tree equivalent of a lava lamp."

"I like it," declared Yasmine. "It's got moxie." She looked really excited. She could have been a kid on Christmas morning. You'd think after seeing so many Christmases (and trees) in her existence, they'd get kind of old. She pointed at Peter's tree. "Let's do the prissy one now."

We were stringing purple lights on the 'winter moss green' tree when she finally started The Talk.

"So. Vincent told me what happened." She paused as she looped the lights over a branch. "I'm glad your guy is okay."

"Me too. He was lucky . . . if Vincent hadn't been there . . ."

More silence. I didn't entirely know where Yasmine was going with this. My guess was that she was concerned I'd tell someone about Vincent. I felt absolutely certain, however, that she wasn't going to threaten to break my kneecaps or anything to keep me silent. In fact, I realized then that what she wanted was reassurance. It was a crazy and startling idea. She was an angel, after all. A being of hope and peace, a being that *others* prayed to for comfort. Yet, here she was, seeking it from me—a creature of Hell.

"I meant it," I told her. "What I said to him. I'm not going to tell anyone."

"I believe you," she said, confusion all over her face. Angels knew when others were telling the truth. "But I don't understand it. Why? Why wouldn't you? You could get into big trouble if your superiors—if Jerome—found out you knew and weren't telling." Vincent had said the same thing. It was true. "Your people tend to get pissed off over stuff like that."

"What, and yours don't? Would they be forgiving if they found out?"

She looked away from me, diverting her attention to hanging a pink glass dove.

"Look," I said. "I work for Hell, but I don't, like, delight in others' suffering. Especially since I like both of you. I don't want to see you get into trouble. I don't even think what you're doing is wrong. Dangerous, maybe, but not wrong."

"Which part? The loving part or the nephilim part?"

I shrugged. "It's all risky."

She smiled at me. "You talk about nephilim pretty calmly. Most people—in our circles—go running for the hills."

"I met one once. Dated him." I hung a bejeweled purple

orb on the tree. "He was scary as hell, yeah. Had this whole homicidal revenge thing going on, which kind of negated his sexiness a little. But at the end of the day . . . I don't know. He wasn't much of a monster. He couldn't help being born what he was."

I was glad to be free of Roman, glad he was somewhere far away from me. He'd posed too much of a threat to both me and those I loved. Still, there had been something in him I found appealing. It was why we'd connected before things literally blew up. I understood his weariness with the games Heaven and Hell played. He'd offered to take me away and free me from it all, and there were days I would still wake up and long for that.

"No," Yasmine agreed. "They can't help what they are. And it's not their fault. But their existence is a reminder of *our* faults . . . of our weaknesses." She held her hands open in front of her, studying them as though they held answers. "None of us higher immortals want to be shown that we're weak. That's our hubris, I guess. Especially the angels. No one's perfect, but we like to play that we are." She sighed and let her hands drop. "I should walk away from this. I should have a long time ago."

I jerked my head up. "But you love him."

"Sometimes loving someone means you have to do what's ultimately good. What you need instead of what you want."

"I suppose. But ending it seems so extreme. There must be a way to . . . I don't know, have it all."

The door opened, and Vincent walked in. He didn't look surprised to see either of us, but then, he would have sensed our auras. His eyes met Yasmine's, and it was like lightning crackling through the room. Both of them lit up, shining in a way that I doubted my succubus glamour could even begin to compete with.

He expressed surprise over my Yuletide Forest but jumped in to help us, appearing just as excited as Yasmine over the activity. The two of them never touched, but I noticed the same thing that I had at breakfast: an intimacy in the way they interacted with each other. They didn't need to touch. Their relationship was obvious, and I wondered how it was possible none of the other angels had ever noticed this. Maybe it was like what Yasmine had mentioned about angels and hubris. Maybe angels always assumed they were perfect and were too blind to see flaws in each other, whereas someone like me—who exploited weakness—knew what to look for.

We finished Peter's tree, and then I found my ornaments from last year—the ones that hadn't been destroyed in the fire—and used them on the bookstore's tree. When my woodland paradise was finally complete, Yasmine and Vincent made their farewells and left. I still had no idea what their divine mission in Seattle was, but I assumed it had universal consequences. I felt a little weird that it had been put on hold to decorate my home.

As I cleaned up the boxes, I kept thinking about what Yasmine had said about needing versus wanting. In some ways, that was what Seth and I did. We wanted to have sex. We needed to avoid it.

I also found myself recalling Andrew again, that annoyingly good priest who'd caused me so many headaches. I hadn't thought much about his story since last week, but as my body mindlessly completed chores, the images began replaying in my mind.

Despite my best efforts, he'd remained a bastion of purity and willpower. While frustrating, it nonetheless continued to make the game fun. And although I didn't appreciate it as much back then as I did now, I sort of took pleasure in just hanging around him. He was good company, and he came to mean more to me than just a sexual conquest. It was obvious he cared about me too.

It would figure that things went bad between us on a beautiful, sunny day. I remembered it distinctly. I had wandered over to the church he ministered out of and sat with him in the vegetable garden. I stayed clear of the dirt, conscious of the yellow silk dress my bishop had just had made for me. Andrew, less concerned, worked on his knees, unhesitatingly digging in—literally—and cultivating the church's small crop.

"Don't you have other people who could do this for you?"

Squinting up at me in the bright light, he smiled. "Nothing compares to the satisfaction of doing something yourself."

"If you say so."

He returned to his work, and I continued to sit quietly, watching him and the lazy vista of that golden afternoon. Not far away, the sounds of daily hustle and bustle carried over. I liked this town—it was a nice break from the large, busy cities I'd spent most of my succubus time in. Eventually, though, I knew I'd grow restless and move onto some place with a little more excitement.

I turned back to Andrew. "Thomas Brewer just got back from Cadwell. He says they're all getting sick there."

Andrew nodded. "People are getting sick everywhere. There have been outbreaks in a lot of the western towns."

"Are you worried?"

He shrugged. "What comes will come. None of us can change God's will."

I grimaced. I'd heard about this illness, what later generations would call the Black Death. The rapid onset. The blackened skin. The swollen lumps. Even if it couldn't technically hurt me, I didn't want to see it spread here.

"I don't think God can be as merciful as you say in mass if He's inflicting something like that on his people."

"It's a test, Cecily. God is always testing us. It makes us stronger."

"Or dead."

He didn't respond.

"What will you do if it comes?" I pushed. "Geoffrey says he'll leave. Will you go with him?"

His dark eyebrows rose in surprise, like I'd asked if the sun would take tomorrow off. "Of course not. I mean, as bishop, I'm sure Geoffrey must . . . do what is necessary to continue fulfilling his duties, but me? I serve the people. I will continue to serve the people. If they're sick, I'll tend them."

My sarcasm gave way to shock, and I leapt to my feet, striding toward him. "You can't do that! Haven't you heard about this? People don't come back from it. The only thing to do is get out and let it run its course."

It was true. Call it cruel, but as I'd told Liam on our post-auction date, that was the way the world had dealt with epidemics for a lot of human history. Certainly, some people cared and ministered unto others, but when disease grew really terrible, with no clear answer in sight, ignorance and fear reigned supreme. Most people of that era saw the simplest solution as putting as much distance as possible between them and the illness.

Andrew stood up as well, wearing an expression so annoyingly wise and serene as he faced me. "If that's what you must do, then you must do it. My place is here."

I didn't even have seduction on my mind when I reached out and grabbed his hands. He flinched with surprise but didn't let go.

"It's stupid," I told him earnestly. "You can't stop it. You'll die, and I—I can't watch that."

"Then go. Go with Geoffrey. Or go . . . out to the convent. It's isolated. You'd be safe there."

I scowled. "Not that again."

"I just want what's best for you, that's all." One of his hands reached up and cupped my chin. "I don't want to see you suffer either."

It occurred to me then how close we stood. The heat building between our bodies rivaled that of the sunshine pounding down on us from above. Andrew, realizing this too, started and tried to pull away. I held on to his hand, anger flaring up in my chest.

"So that's how you'll let it end then? You spend your whole life living in poverty and chastity, only to die in a pile of stinking corpses with oozing sores and rotting skin?"

"If that's what God—"

"Stop it," I said, leaning forward. "Just stop it. Don't you get it? God doesn't care. He's not even paying attention."

"Cecily—"

I didn't let him finish. Instead, I pressed my mouth against his mouth, molding my body to his. I don't know if he'd ever kissed anyone else before, but if not, he was a quick study. He didn't break from me. In fact I would have sworn there was an eagerness to his lips as they explored mine, willingly letting my tongue stroke and dance with his.

And oh, God help me, he was so very good and noble that I tasted a sunburst of energy just from that kiss alone. It poured into me like honey, glorious and sweet.

And surprisingly, it was me who finally broke the kiss, though I still stayed pressed against his body, my arms encircling him.

"Don't you see how stupid it is?" I whispered, our lips so close we shared each other's breath. "Are you going to die without having lived? Without having tasted everything that's out there? Are you really just going to rush into death like that?"

His eyes weighed me, his own hands resting on my waist. "I don't need fleshly pleasures to complete my life."

"You're lying," I told him. "You want to."

"Wanting and needing are two different things." He stepped away from me, and I suddenly felt incomplete without his body against mine. I had a fleeting flash of some connection bigger than both of us, and then it was gone. "A long life means nothing if it's empty and has no purpose. Better to live a short one filled with the things that are important to you."

"You're a fool," I snapped. "I'm not going to stay and watch you die."

"Then go."

And I did.

Chapter 17

The next day was only a partial shift at work for me, but when I saw how busy things were, I suspected I'd have a hard time dragging myself away. Seth wasn't working in the café, but I found a note on my desk. He'd apparently already been there earlier.

> *Thetis—*
> *Have some errands to run, but I'd like to see you later. I miss you and don't like how we left things. Come on over later when you get the chance. I'll be home all night.*
>
> > *Love,*
> > *Seth*

I had some things of my own to take care of, and after reading his note, I suddenly wanted them done as soon as possible so that I could go see him. As I was about to leave, Maddie caught a hold of me and covertly led me into the history books. To my astonishment, she pushed down her shirt collar, baring her shoulder.

"Whoa," I joked. "Don't you think things are moving kind of fast?"

"Look," she whispered, pointing at the lacy bra strap that had been revealed. "It's *red*."

"That it is," I agreed, still a little puzzled.

"It's number one."

"What?"

"My three adventurous things. I bought a red bra."

I stared in astonishment. "I thought . . . I thought you said my idea was ridiculous?"

She averted her eyes. "I thought it was . . . but then, well . . . I heard about Seth. What happened to him. You were there, right?"

My favorite topic. "Yeah, I was there."

"Didn't it freak you out? I mean . . . right there in front of you: life and death."

"Yeah. Kind of."

Shaking her head, she looked back up at me. "Hearing what happened to him just kind of shook me up. I told you it wasn't that easy to be adventurous, but suddenly I decided that maybe it was. I just had to take control."

I smiled. "With a red bra."

She flushed. "Hey! All your lingerie may be red and edible, but this is the first bra I've ever bought that isn't white or black."

I reined in my humor and gave her a genuinely pleased smile. "I'm proud of you, Maddie. I really am."

"Don't patronize me," she warned.

"I'm not. It looks great. You get matching underwear?"

Now she really looked embarrassed. "A thong."

I repressed the urge to whistle. "Nice work, soldier."

She wandered off, back to the registers. Moments later, I felt an immortal signature and a touch on my shoulder. Spinning around, I found Tawny's enormous chest practically shoved into my face. I'd heard little from the succubus since I'd called to tell her she had a job at Simon's. Niphon's presence at the poker game had been the only indication that she still hadn't bagged a guy.

"Georgina—" she wailed, lower lip trembling.

"No, no," I interrupted. I grabbed her arm and dragged her toward my office. "Not here."

I managed to close the door just before she burst into tears. I groaned.

"Now what's happened?"

"I met a guy last night." She flounced into my chair, and it was a wonder her breasts didn't hit her in the face.

I leaned against the wall, crossing my arms over my own chest in a sort of protective gesture. "Okay . . . that's not a bad thing."

She swallowed a sob, and it was all I could do not to clean up the mascara smudges on her face. Honestly, how much did that woman wear? "We had a great time . . . had drinks and talked and all that."

"That's not a bad thing either."

She shook her head. "But at the end of the night, he told me he just wanted to be friends."

"He—wait. You got the friends line from someone you just met?"

Tawny nodded.

"What did you say to him? Like . . . did you proposition him?"

"Yeah . . . I asked him if he wanted to meet me in the bath-room and try out this edible mint chocolate warming gel I have."

"You—what?"

Tawny reached into her purse and started to pull out a tube of something. I waved her off.

"No, no. I don't need to see it."

"What went wrong?" she cried.

"Well . . ." I wasn't sure if I should laugh or weep. Tawny was never going to pull this off. Never. "You might have come on too strong. And honestly . . . that gel thing? That's just weird."

"I thought guys were into that kind of thing."

"Some are . . . but, I don't know. What kind of guy is he? What's he do for a living?"

"He's a cashier."

"Hmm. Okay. That's not too bad."

"Over at Blessed Images."

"Over at—you propositioned a guy who works at a religious supply store?" I exclaimed.

"I wanted a good one," she told me. "There's no better place."

"Oh my God. Tawny . . ." I didn't even know where to start. There were so many nuances to seduction, so many tactics and strategies. She didn't know any of them, and seriously, I didn't even know if she could learn. "I got you the strip club job . . . why are you trolling religious supply stores? Guys should just be coming up to you after your sets." Something troubling occurred to me. "You do still have the job, don't you?" I believed Simon would stick to his word, but one never knew for sure with his type.

"Yeah . . ." she mumbled. "But those guys aren't—"

"For the last time! Forget the good ones. You can't afford to be choosy." I studied her. She was clearly low on energy again. Frowning, I recalled my date with Liam. "So . . . Tawny . . . things really didn't work out with Nick the auctioneer?"

She took a tissue from the box on my desk and blew her nose loudly. "Nope. I told you. I called, and he said he wasn't interested."

I was good at reading people, very good. It was, well, what made me a star succubus. And looking into those teary blue eyes, I searched for some sign of deceit. Any sign. I found nothing. So who was lying? Tawny or Liam? And why would either one of them lie? Liam had no reason to—not about Tawny. Tawny, I supposed, could be in league with Niphon. Maybe he wanted to prolong things simply to annoy me. That was a dangerous game for both of them. His animosity couldn't be strong enough to risk pissing off Jerome. And I knew Jerome *would* be pissed off if he found out Tawny's orientation was being used for ulterior motives.

There was also the fact that Tawny's energy had shown no

post-sex glamour the day after Liam saw her and Nick together. She hadn't gotten any. That was my only hard evidence in all of this.

All of these thoughts flitted through my mind in a heartbeat. If Tawny really was pulling a poker face on me, she'd
soon learn that she wasn't the only one who could do it.
Keeping my expression exasperated and unsuspecting, I said,
"Tawny . . . I . . . I just don't get this. Any of this."

"That's it?" she asked. "You're my mentor, and that's all
you've got for me?"

"I got you the job! I don't know what else to do. Maybe
we can go out together and . . . God help me . . . do a three-
some or something." I could imagine few things more horrible than that, but these were desperate times. The expression
on Tawny's face showed similar sentiments.

"I don't know about that," she said. "I don't think I really
do that."

I rolled my eyes. "In another century or so, you'll find you
do *everything*."

She blew her nose again. "Well . . . I want to keep trying
on my own before anything like that. Until then . . . do you
think . . . do you think you could . . ."

"Could what?"

"You know."

"No, I really don't." From her, a request could be anything.

Tawny gulped. "The kissing thing again."

"No! I told you that was a one-time deal."

"But . . . but . . . I'm so low . . ."

She burst into tears again. And yeah, she was low on energy. Really low. By tomorrow morning, she could be in danger of losing her shape again. Fuck. This wasn't possible. I
had to be getting played here, but why and how? Was all this
hassle worth it to Niphon, just to keep irritating me? Fuck.

"This is the last time," I growled.

She stopped mid-sob. "Really?"

I sighed. "Come here."

With a sense of dread, I kissed her again. My discomfort had less to do with the act of kissing her than it did with me realizing I'd just pushed myself into dangerous energy limits. I was the one who'd need a fix before morning now. And if I got an energy fix, it was likely my dream stalker would return. . . .

With the influx of life, Tawny was able to shape-shift away her disheveled appearance. "Thanks, Georgina! You're the best!" She started to hug me, and I jerked away.

"Just go out and get laid, okay?"

Doug stuck his head in just then, asking for my help. He didn't seem to have heard my charge to battle, thankfully. His eyes widened when he saw Tawny. I shooed her out, warning her not to forget what we'd talked about.

"Is she single?" he asked, watching her walk away. Her pleather pants were riding up.

"Yeah," I said. "Very. But she's high maintenance."

After I finished my survey of the bookstore, I went off to take care of assorted errands. When I finally made it to Seth's place, I found him lying lengthwise on his couch, laptop open as usual. He sat up and closed it when I stepped inside.

"Hey, Thetis," he said.

"Hey," I said.

I sat down beside him, and silence fell as we regarded each other. The air between us wasn't angry, but it wasn't bursting with love either. It was speculative. We were sizing each other up. He reached into the V-neck collar of my sweater, and I flinched. Then, I felt his fingers brush by the chain I'd been wearing his ring on. He pulled the ring out and ran his fingertips over the dolphin.

"Around your neck, huh? What is this, high school?"

"Might as well be," I said, "seeing as how we haven't even made it to second base yet."

He smiled and released the ring, moving his fingers up to my cheek. "Yes, we have." He sighed. "We sure do seem to be fighting a lot lately, huh?"

"Yeah." I settled back into the couch's softness. "It's not even about sex anymore."

"I noticed that. It's boring stuff, actually."

"Boring?"

He shrugged. "You know. Typical relationship stuff. Spending time with each other. Trust. Communication. Love isn't always about grand forces of the universe keeping us apart."

Unless, I thought, you considered the difference in length between a mortal life and an immortal one. I didn't know why Seth's lifespan was bothering me lately. I'd understood the complications on an intellectual level when we'd first started dating, but I hadn't really had such visceral reactions until recently. Him getting shot hadn't helped, I supposed. And speaking of which . . .

"I never thanked you," I told him.

"For what?"

"For risking your life for mine."

"But you can't di—"

"Yeah, yeah. We've already established that, like, a hundred times. And the wisdom—or lack thereof—of your actions aside, it was sweet and brave and . . . and, well, thank you."

Seth moved his hand over mine and squeezed it. "There's nothing to thank me for."

I stood up. "Well, now that we've got the sentimental stuff out of the way, let's get down to business. Take off your clothes."

Seth started. "Wai—what?"

"Well," I amended, "except for your boxers."

"Are we going to second base after all?"

"Just do it."

While he stripped, I gathered some things from his kitchen, as well as from a tote bag I'd brought. When I returned to the

living room, he was sitting in the center of the couch in boxers only. They were soft gray flannel. Adorable.

I sat down on the floor in front of him, moving a bowl of
warm water beside me. After dipping a washcloth into the
water, I slowly began rubbing it over his feet.

Seth was quiet for several moments. Then: "You getting
Biblical on me? Didn't somebody wash Jesus' feet?"

I rewet the cloth and began moving up one of his legs. "Don't
worry," I told him. "I don't expect you to turn this water into
wine. At least not until I'm done." I moved the washcloth over
Seth's calf. It was leanly muscled, covered in tawny brown
hair. "The foot washing tradition is bigger than the Bible.
You find it everywhere, long before New Testament times, in
lots of other cultures. Kings. Generals. They all got this treat-
ment."

"You wash a lot of kings' and generals' feet?" he teased.

"Yeah, actually."

"Oh. Well. I don't think I'm really in that league."

I smiled and moved on to the other calf. "Not true. Poets
and bards used to have as much prestige as kings. Lots of
them got this too."

"I miss the good old days. Now we're lucky if we get
paid."

I washed his thigh, careful to avoid the bandaged wound.
"Yeah, true. But people also don't threaten to behead you if
they don't like what you wrote."

"You obviously haven't read some of my reviews."

"I only read the good ones."

I finished both legs and dropped the washcloth into the
water. I scooted the bowl away. Seth started to get up, but I
shooed him back down.

"Nope. Not finished." I reached for a bottle of massage oil
I'd brought and poured some on my hands. It smelled like al-
monds. "That was just to get you clean."

With as much deliberation as I'd performed the washing, I
massaged the oil into his skin, starting with his feet once

again. Washing can be sensual, but rubbing someone with oil is doubly so. Triple, even. The light banter faded between us. Seth simply watched, wonder and arousal on his face as I worked my way up. And as I met his gaze, I saw more than just those feelings. The love in his eyes was so powerful, I needed to look away. Seth had an amazing grasp of the English language, but there were days when that skill was nothing compared to what he told me in his looks.

When I finished his legs, I climbed up behind him on the couch and worked on his back and chest too. I'd been giving massages almost as long as I'd been dancing. I knew exactly what to do, knew where all the muscle groups were and how to unkink them. Seth had a lot of stiffness and knots in his back, either from bad laptop posture or stress. Maybe both.

At last, the job was complete. Heedless of oil on me or the couch, he leaned back and pulled me to his chest. My cheek rested on his smooth, slick skin, and the scent of almond and Seth enveloped me.

"Ah, Georgina," he sighed. "I wish I could return that."

"I'll just pretend you did."

He sighed again. "I hate the pretending."

"Yeah."

"I mean it. *Really* hate it."

The vehemence in his voice startled me. I lifted my head up. "You okay?"

"Yeah . . . I'm just . . . I don't know." He shook his head. "Frustrated, I guess."

"Sexually frustrated?"

"Sure . . . but it's more than that. Do you ever think about us . . . just, you know, doing it maybe once?"

"No," I said immediately. "Absolutely not."

"I'd take the risk."

"The shooting addled your brain. You've always been the strong one, remember?"

"The shooting's made me think about what life means, that's all." He sounded just like Maddie. How could such a foolish gesture on his part be inspiring so many people? Was I too jaded? Could I no longer relate to humans? "And I mean, I can't even reciprocate a simple massage. You perform all the time for me . . . but what do you get? You must be the one who's sexually frustrated. The stuff you do on the side . . . well, that doesn't matter. Sometimes I think Hugh was right. You do suffer more than me."

"No, I don't. The sex stuff bugs me, but I can handle it."

"I hope I can," said Seth. "When I was in the hospital, I had this weird moment where I started thinking about how I write about all these action-packed things but don't live any of it. O'Neill has dozens of great romances, but me? I can't even have one."

"It sucks," I agreed. "But with the risks . . . well. We know this is how it has to be."

"What about the rest?"

"Hmm?"

Seth shifted slightly so that he could look into my face. "Do you really think about me dying? Do you worry about me?"

"Sometimes."

"Am I going to cause you pain in the end?"

"No," I said breezily. "Of course not."

He pulled me back to his chest. "I love you, Georgina. You give me more joy than I ever expected to find in this life. I want to be with you . . ." He ran a hand through my hair, tangling it in his fingers. "But not if it's going to do more harm than good. I don't want you to hurt. I don't want you to spend the rest of my life worrying about my body and my soul. I don't want you to cry when I'm gone."

A lump formed in my throat, and I thought I might actually start crying then and there. There was something in his voice, a strange and ominous note that scared me for reasons I couldn't entirely explain. I dug my fingers into his skin and pressed myself closer to him.

"No more," I whispered. "I don't want to talk about this anymore. It isn't relevant."

Seth tightened his grip on me and didn't respond. We went to bed after that, speaking little. He snuggled against me, resting his head on my chest. I ran my fingers through his hair, taking in his scent and his feel. As he slipped into sleep, I thought about what he'd said about what puts meaning into life. I thought about wanting and needing.

And what I needed right then was energy. Tawny'd wiped me out, and there was no way I was going to start shifting back to the body I'd been born with. Still touching Seth's hair, I thought how easy it would be to just lean down and kiss him. *Really* kiss him. And kiss him and kiss him . . .

Wanting and needing.

Regretfully, I slipped out of bed. Seth was a heavy sleeper and simply rolled to his side, never coming close to waking. With a wistful look, I left the condo and used my last bit of energy to put on a different shape. Finding a victim wasn't hard—further reinforcing how absurd the whole Tawny thing was—and in less than two hours, I was back in bed with Seth and recharged. That creepy voice didn't speak to me, for which I was grateful. Sad but sated, I fell asleep.

And I dreamed.

Chapter 18

My dream-self sprinted out of the kitchen and toward the sound of the crying. Aubrey and the mystery cat jerked their heads up, surprised at my sudden movement. On the other side of the living room, the little girl sat on the floor beside an end table with sharp corners, a small hand pressed to her forehead. Tears streamed down her checks as she wailed.

In a flash, my dream-self was on her knees and had wrapped the little girl up in a tight embrace. I could feel what the other Georgina felt, and I nearly wept as well over the feel of that soft, warm body in my arms. My dream-self rocked the girl, murmuring soothing, nonsensical words as she brushed her lips against the silken hair. Eventually, the girl's sobs stopped, and she rested her head against my dream-self's chest, content to simply be loved and rocked.

I opened my eyes and stared at Seth's plain white ceiling. He lay beside me, curled up near my body and still smelling like the massage oil. Even awake, the dream's images were still strong and so real. I knew *exactly* how my daughter's hair had felt, the way she smelled, the rhythm of her heart. My own heart pined so much for her that I could almost ignore the fact that last night's energy was now gone.

This was turning into a real problem.

I sat up, gently pushing Seth off of me. But as I tried to figure out what to do about this latest dream, a strange thought kept pressing into the back of my head.

Erik. I couldn't stop thinking about Erik. It was nothing in particular, either. No specific problem. But, whenever I tried to think about something else—my job, the energy loss, Seth—it was Erik's face that appeared in my head. I didn't understand it, but it worried me.

Seth's arms reached for me as I slipped out of bed, but I skillfully avoided them. Grabbing my cell phone out of my purse, I headed off toward the living room. No one answered when I dialed Arcana, Ltd. It was almost ten . . . usually he was open by then. I called information in search of Erik's home number, but it appeared to be unlisted.

A sense of dread was building in me. Desperate, I dialed Dante's store.

"Dante, I think something's happened to Erik, but I don't have his home number and—"

"Whoa, whoa, succubus. Slow down. Start from the beginning."

Backing up, I explained how I'd dreamed again and woken up obsessed with Erik.

"Maybe it's nothing, but after the drowning thing . . . I don't know. Do you have his home number?"

"Yeah," Dante said after several moments. "I do. I'll . . . I'll check on him for you and give you a call back."

"Thanks, Dante. I mean it."

I disconnected as a sleepy Seth stepped out of the bedroom. "Who's Dante? Was that a collect call to the Inferno?"

"They won't accept the charges," I murmured, still troubled. Seth's face turned serious.

"What's wrong?"

I hesitated, not because I was afraid to tell him about Dante but because I didn't know if I wanted him caught up in all of this.

"It involves immortal intrigue," I warned. "And the higher workings of the universe."

"I live for those things," he said wryly, settling into an armchair. "Tell me."

So, I did. He knew about my first energy loss but not the rest. I didn't tell him about the content of the dreams, merely that they drained me of energy. I also explained about the self-fulfilling prophecies and how I'd woken up damp one morning and thinking about Erik today. When I finished, I stared at the cell phone accusingly.

"Damn it. Why isn't he calling?"

"Why do you always tell me this at the last minute?" asked Seth. "It's been giving you trouble for a while. I thought it had been a one-time thing."

"I didn't want to bother you. And I know how funny you are about immortal stuff."

"Things that affect you—that may be harming you—don't bother me. I mean, well, they do, but that's not the point. This all goes back to commun—"

The phone rang.

"Dante?" I asked eagerly. I hadn't even bothered to check the number.

But it was him. His voice sounded grim.

"You need to come over here. To Erik's."

"The store?"

"No, his house. It's close to my place here."

"What's going on?"

"Just come over."

Dante rattled off an address and directions. With quick shape-shifting, I was dressed and ready to bolt out the door in an instant. Seth told me to wait, and in less than a minute—not as good as me, though still good—he was ready too.

I'd never thought much about Erik having a home of his own. To me, he just always sort of existed in his store. The address was about a mile from Dante's, in an old, yet well-maintained neighborhood. Erik's house was one of the small bungalow types so common in Seattle neighborhoods, and the front yard was filled with roses gone dormant for the winter. As we walked up the steps, I entertained a brief vision of Erik out there tending the flowers in the summer.

Dante opened the door before I could knock. I wondered if he'd sensed me or had simply seen us through the window. He displayed no particular reaction to Seth's presence and ushered us in toward the house's one bedroom.

The house's interior looked like it hadn't been updated in a while. In fact, a lot of the furniture reminded me of mid-twentieth-century styles. A plaid sofa with rough fabric. A worn velvet armchair in seventies gold. A TV that dubiously looked capable of color.

None of that triggered any sort of reaction in me, though. What startled me was one framed picture sitting on a bookshelf. It showed a much younger Erik—maybe in his forties—with fewer wrinkles in his dark skin and no gray in his black hair. He had his arm around a thirty-something brunette with big gray eyes and a smile as large as his. Dante nudged me when I stopped, an odd look on his face.

"Come on."

Erik lay in bed. To my relief, he was alive. I didn't realize until that moment just how worried I'd been. My subconscious had feared the worst, even though I'd refused to let it surface.

But alive or not, he really didn't look so great. He was sweating and shaking, eyes wide and face pallid. His breathing was shallow. When he saw me, he flinched, and for half a second, I saw terror in his eyes. Then, the fear faded, and he attempted a weak smile.

"Miss Kincaid. Forgive me for not being able to receive you properly."

"Jesus," I gasped, sitting on the bed's edge. "What happened? Are you okay?"

"I will be."

I studied him, trying to piece together what had taken place. "Were you attacked?"

His gaze flicked over to Dante. Dante shrugged.

"In a manner of speaking," Erik said at last. "But not in the way you're thinking."

Dante leaned against the wall, appearing a little less grave than he had earlier. "Don't waste her time with riddles, old man. Spill it."

Erik's eyes narrowed, a bit of fire flaring in their depths. Then, he turned back to me. "I was attacked . . . mentally, not physically. A woman came to me tonight . . . wraithlike, inhuman . . . wreathed in energy. The kind of beauteous, enthralling energy I see you glow with sometimes." It was a sweet way to describe my post-sex glamour.

"Was she bat-winged and flame-eyed?" I asked, recalling Dante's long-ago joke about the mythological description of succubi.

"Not a succubus, I'm afraid. That might be easier. No, this . . . I believe . . . was Nyx."

"Did . . . did you say Nyx?" Of course that was what he'd said, but I'd been waiting for him to launch into a discussion of Oneroi, not their mother. Nyx made no sense. It was one thing for dream spirits to appear in your bedroom and in your dreams. It was an entirely different matter for a monstrous primordial entity of chaos who had been instrumental in creating the world as we know it to appear in your bedroom. It was like saying God had stopped by for waffles on the way to work. Maybe Erik was still delirious.

"Nyx," he confirmed, no doubt guessing my thoughts. "Chaos herself. Or, more accurately, Night herself."

From the corner, Dante laughed softly. "We're all fucked now."

"She's the mother of the Oneroi," Erik reminded me. "And, although dreams aren't her sole domain, she too is connected to them."

"Then . . ." I tried to grasp the implications. "Are you saying she's been responsible for what's been happening to me?"

"It almost makes sense," said Dante.

Erik apparently agreed. "She's linked to time and all the myriad potential fates that exist for the universe. Fate and time are forever moving closer to chaos—to entropy—and that's what she feeds off of. She's trying to create more of it in the world, to bring us that much nearer to ultimate disintegration. But she's a long way from bringing anything like that about, so she settles for small acts of chaos."

I wasn't following. "My dreams and energy loss are acts of chaos?"

"No." Erik glanced at Dante again. "We believe you're her instrument. Since she's connected to time as well as space, she has the ability to see pieces of the future. And there is no greater way to cause chaos in this world than by revealing the future to mortals. Such visions prove consuming, and if crafted in a certain way, they can drive a person to madness. That person will obsess on it, struggling to either stop it or bring it about in a way it's not actually meant to unfold. Both acts are futile. The future plays out as it is meant to. In trying to alter it, we only make it happen that much more quickly."

"Like the Oedipus story," noted Seth. "His father's attempts to change the prophecy's outcome are what actually made it happen."

Erik nodded. "Exactly."

I understood now too. "Just like the cop who saw his partner getting shot. And the man who saw his family benefiting by him swimming the Sound."

"It's how Nyx operates. Everything she shows them is true . . . just not true in the way they expect. The ensuing madness and destruction brought about by showing mortals their futures—futures that *they* end up bringing about—feeds her."

"But where do I fit in?" I demanded. "She isn't showing me my future or making me do crazy things."

"That's where the theory ends, succubus," Dante said. "You're part of it, absolutely. And she needs you to do all this . . . but we don't know the mechanics of it."

"This is insane," I said blankly. "I'm the instrument of an all-powerful primordial deity's wave of chaos and destruction."

"That's kind of extreme," said Dante jovially. "It's not like you work for Google or anything."

Seth gently touched my shoulder. "Can I ask a question here? I'm confused by . . . like, how is it possible that you're just now realizing that this . . . Nyx . . . is out there? I mean, if she's as powerful as you claim . . . I don't know. Why didn't you think of her right away? Why hasn't this happened before?"

"Because she's locked up," I said. "Or well, she's supposed to be. Heaven and Hell have their own agendas for the world; they don't want her running loose and messing it all up. If this is her, I have no idea how she got loose. She's supposed to be guarded by angels, and if there was ever a group that could—" I let out a gasp that turned into a groan.

The others stared at me. "What's wrong?" asked Seth.

"That's why they're here," I said. "I'm such an idiot. There's a monstrous regiment of angels in town. I knew they were looking for something, but I didn't know what." That would also explain Vincent's interest in local news—he was looking for Nyx-patterns that would provide them with a trail. He'd even started to pursue my knowledge of the cop story, but Seth's shooting and his outing as a nephilim had distracted us all.

"Yeah, well, they're doing a bang-up job," said Dante.

I rose from Erik's bedside. "I have to tell them what we know. Maybe they'll understand what she's doing to me."

"Be careful," Erik warned. "She's suspicious now . . . I think that's why she came after me. I was looking into this, and she didn't want me to succeed."

Something else suddenly occurred to me. "Erik . . . did she show you a vision?"

He nodded.

"What was it?" It must have been horrible, whatever it was. He'd clearly been in shock when Dante had found him.

Erik looked at me, and for an instant, I saw a flash of the terror he'd shown when I first walked into the room. Then, it was gone.

"It doesn't matter, Miss Kincaid. She wanted to scare me, to stop me from helping you . . . but it didn't work. The future will unfold as it's meant to." Seeing my doubtful look, he smiled again and pointed toward the door. "Stop worrying about me. I will be fine. Go find your angel friends before anything worse happens."

I gave him a quick hug before stepping into the other room with Seth and Dante. Once again, I paused to study the picture of Erik and the woman. Just as I'd always imagined Erik living in his store, I'd also never pictured him having any sort of personal life. Obviously, that was a foolish thought on my part. Who was this woman? Wife? Lover? Just a friend?

Beside me, Dante held out his hand to Seth and introduced himself. The two men sized each other up.

"I've heard so much about you," said Dante cheerfully.

"I never heard of you until this morning," remarked Seth.

My eyes were still on the picture. Near the edge of the frame, I noticed a crease in the photograph. I don't know what made me do it, but I picked the frame up and pulled the picture out. The right-hand third of the photo had been folded, obscuring another person who had been with Erik and the woman. Dante.

I looked up in surprise. Dante took the picture and frame from me and reassembled them. "There's no time for this, succubus."

"But—"

"We have more important things to deal with than your own curiosity right now."

I cast an uneasy look at Erik's closed bedroom door. Dante was right. "Do you think you could maybe . . ."

Dante sighed, anticipating my question. "Yes, succubus. I'll check in on him today."

For a moment, I thought I saw something in his face . . . something that wasn't just him grudgingly humoring me. Like that maybe—*maybe*—he cared about Erik too. It was weird, but then, they'd all looked pretty happy in the photograph. The worst enemies were often those who had been friends. This Erik-Dante puzzle just got weirder and weirder.

I started to turn away, then Dante called, "Oh, hey. I can probably make your charm, now that we know what this is."

Hope surged up in me at the thought of finally having safe dreams again. "Really?"

"If you still want me to," he added warily.

I presumed he was subtly referencing my skepticism—which hadn't entirely abated. Still, now that I had a name for my predator, I was more anxious than ever to take whatever protection I could get. "Definitely. If you think it'll work."

"In theory, at least. Nyx isn't exactly a run-of-the-mill spirit. I'll see what I can do."

I drove Seth back to his condo, anxious to let him off, so I could do some searching. "I have to go find the angels," I told him. "I'll catch up to you later."

"So . . . no movie tonight?"

"I—what? Oh, damn it." I'd forgotten about the plans we'd made. He'd gotten tickets for an indie movie that was showing one night only here. "I'm sorry . . . I really am . . ."

"Well," said Seth wryly, "considering life and death are literally on the line, I think I can forgive it this time."

"You know what you should do? You should take Maddie. You still owe her a date."

He smiled. "I have the best girlfriend in the world, always trying to push me into the arms of another woman."

"I'm serious! She's feeling unwanted. She thinks you don't like her."

"I like her a lot. The whole thing is just weird, that's all. I think I'm going to see if Terry can go to the movie. Don't give me that look," he warned. "I'll still take her somewhere. Just not to this."

We kissed good-bye, and Seth promised to check on me later. Once he was gone, I set out to find my guardian angels.

Chapter 19

Finding them wasn't so easy. No one was at my apartment, and Vincent didn't answer his phone. I drove down to the Cellar, hoping maybe they'd all decided to start drinking mid-day. Nope. The pub was barren, with only a couple bored patrons sitting at the bar.

Frustrated, I called Hugh, deciding it was time to get help from my own resources.

"Is Jerome back yet?"

"No," the imp said. "Do you need him?"

"Kind of."

"Kind of?"

"It's a long story."

"I'm in the city for a meeting. You want to have lunch and explain? I'm practically down the street from your place. I'll meet you there, and we'll go eat."

It was the first time I'd talked to Hugh since the blowup at Peter's over Seth and me. I was still reeling from all that, but I did kind of want to get feedback from another immortal source. Besides, I was rapidly running out of options.

It only took ten minutes for him to show up, but it felt like an hour.

"Holy shit," said Hugh, spotting the Christmas trees when he walked in. "Your apartment's a national park."

"Be quiet."

"I'm serious. You need a ranger working in here."

"Come on. Let's go."

We walked to a deli down the street. Once we were seated with our food, I began explaining to him why I needed Jerome. By the time I finished the Nyx story, Hugh's mirth had faded.

"Fuck," he said, biting into an enormous Reuben. "That might be worth bugging Jerome after all."

"Where is he?" I asked. "Another training?"

Hugh shrugged. "Not entirely sure. He was vague about it. Grace and Hiroko insinuated he's having 'a personality conflict' with another demon and went to settle it."

"Oh, God," I said. "Not a duel?"

"I don't know. I hope not. Those crazy bitches seemed pretty smug, so they're probably hoping for some opportunity to pull a power play out of all this. You know how they are. Still . . . you could probably go to them for help with all this."

I could . . . but if Jerome had something weird going on, I didn't want to get enmeshed with his lieutenants and possibly be used in some way. The two demonesses worked for him but would seize any chance for promotion, and when political tremors shook our world, everyone was quick to exploit everyone else.

"I'll hold out for the angels," I said. "As long as I can space out my energy fixes, there shouldn't be a problem. If I can't find Carter and friends in another day or so, I'll think about talking to Grace and Hiroko."

"I *can* get a hold of him if you really need it," said Hugh.

I smiled at the uneasy tone in his voice. "Yeah, but your instructions were to avoid bothering him at all costs, right?"

The imp nodded.

"It's okay. I'll wait on the angels. If I have to go to Grace and Hiroko, they can be the ones to decide if it's worth interrupting Jerome for. I mean, the evidence is pretty solid . . . but, well, if we're wrong, and it turns out to be nothing . . .

Jerome's going to be pissed that I bothered him based on the word of two humans."

"Pissed at all of us."

"Yeah." I idly picked holes in my sandwich with the toothpick that held it together.

"Are you scared?" asked Hugh. "Of Nyx?"

"Yeah. I am. I don't like the idea of anything invading my sleep. Certainly not something that powerful. That guy I mentioned—Dante—is going to try to make me a charm or something to ward her away."

Hugh snorted. "No human can make a charm like that."

"He's a magician. He said he could."

"Sweetie. Nyx is a fucking deity—no, more than that. An uber-deity. A force of the universe that was instrumental in creation. She's been weakened over time, yeah, but some strung-out, psychic sham can't make a charm powerful enough to scare her off. There are probably only a handful of humans in the world who could, and to get that kind of power . . ." Hugh shook his head. "I don't know. Based on what you've told me, I'm just not seeing it."

I'd had my own doubts about Dante, but I'd thus far managed to push them aside and keep hoping for the best. Hearing Hugh, I felt all of my misgivings return.

"Fuck," I said.

Silence fell as we munched on our sandwiches a bit. Rain fell outside, and hungry customers ducked in to avoid it. Hugh watched a cute brunette order at the counter, then he turned his attention back to me.

"Any idea when Niphon's leaving?"

I frowned. "Whenever Tawny gets a victim."

Now Hugh frowned. "But she did, didn't she?"

"Did she?"

"I don't know. That's what Simon said. Or at least, he thought she did. He said she was up there dancing with a glow a couple nights ago. Made up for the shitty job she was doing."

A couple nights ago . . .

"No . . . that's impossible. I saw her right around then, and she still hadn't taken anybody. She was so low, I had to kiss her again. He's wrong."

"Maybe she got a glow from the kiss." Hugh sounded kind of hopeful. "You use a lot of tongue?"

"It wasn't that big of a kiss. No glow. Just enough to get by."

"Huh." He swirled the ice around in his Diet Coke. "I guess Simon was wrong. Figured he'd be good at spotting that stuff."

I would have thought so too. "Hugh . . . this is going to sound weird, but I think Tawny may be faking how inept she is."

He looked rightfully startled. "Why the fuck would she do that?"

"I don't know. I think it's to help Niphon. But none of this makes sense. This is the second time I've heard of her possibly getting a fix, but then I've seen her shortly thereafter, and she was *way* too low to have burned through so much so quickly."

"Maybe she's got your problem."

"I have a lot of problems."

"Your Nyx problem. Maybe Tawny's losing her energy too."

Whoa. Interesting idea. And why not? If Nyx was preying on one succubus, why not two? And it would explain how Tawny was losing energy so quickly. Except . . .

"If Nyx is taking her energy, that means she's actually *getting* it to begin with. But Tawny keeps telling me she isn't having sex."

"Huh. A servant of Hell lying. Go figure."

"Yeah, but why? Niphon's risking getting both of them in a shitload of trouble if Jerome or anyone else finds out. He's gambling a lot just to stick around and annoy me. And if Hell thinks Tawny isn't doing her job, they'll recall her."

Hugh gave me a funny look.

"What?" I asked. "What's that for?"

"You didn't read the book, did you?"

"What book?"

"The succubus manual."

"You know I didn't."

"And I even got you the abridged one," he said, sounding wounded.

"Hugh," I growled. "What's your point?"

"The point is that as her mentor, you're accountable for her actions. If she can't bag a victim, you're the one they'll call in."

"*What*? That's ridiculous."

"Those are the rules now."

"So, what, I get slapped on the wrist for her screwing up?"

"Slap on the wrist? For being a succubus who can't teach another one to have sex? It's so ludicrous, it's probably never happened before. I don't know what they'd do. Censure you at the very least. Transfer you to work under a senior succubus."

"I *am* a senior succubus."

He shrugged.

"But if she's lying . . ."

"Then prove it."

I rubbed my eyes. "This is utterly insane. Why does Niphon hate me so much? He already bought my soul, for God's sake. What more is there?"

I expected some smartass remark. Instead, I received silence. I looked at Hugh. "What? What is it now?" He pointedly glanced away. "Hugh!"

"I don't know, Georgina." Hugh rarely called me by my first name. I was usually *honey* or *sweetie*. "Sometimes we make deals, and they seem airtight, but something goes wrong."

"What do you mean?"

"I worked with another imp when I lived in Dallas. Raquel. She brokered this one deal with a guy who was pissed off when his wife left him because he found out he was sterile. Couldn't have kids." Hugh helpfully illustrated the meaning by pointing down toward his lower torso.

"I know what sterile means, Mr. Wizard. Get on with it."

"So, he sold his soul under the conditions that his ex-wife couldn't have kids either. He was bitter and into the poetic justice thing, apparently. Wanted to punish her with what she'd punished him over. So, he gave up his soul, and our side gave her some kind of inflammation thing that totally destroyed her fallopian tubes and scarred up her uterus. I don't know. Girl stuff." I had to hold back an eye roll. Hugh might feign ignorance about 'girl stuff,' but he'd found time in his years of corruption to go to medical school. He knew more about this than I did.

"Harsh," I said. "But fitting from the guy's point of view, I guess."

"Yeah. Should have been a done deal, but something went wrong. Or, well, right. Her ovaries still worked—she was making eggs, even if she couldn't carry a baby. She and her new husband found a surrogate mother. The wife donated eggs, they mixed up a Petri dish cocktail, and the surrogate carried the baby. Bam!"

"The wife had a child after all," I mused. "Wow. Hell gets defeated by science. All those philosophers from the Enlightenment were right."

Hugh scoffed at my joke. "It was stupid. Someone—by which I mean, Raquel—should have thought of that when they picked the infection as a way to make that lady infertile. Raquel fucked up. The guy was able to take his case back to Hell and won his soul back for breach of contract."

"Oh, wow," I said. "I bet that went over well. What's Raquel doing nowadays?"

He grimaced. "I think we're all happier not knowing."

I agreed. "But what's this have to do with me? That's kind of a rare case."

"Eh, it happens more than you'd think. Most of the time,

the seller doesn't even notice something got messed up. But if the imp or someone else in authority catches it, I've seen them move Heaven and Earth—no pun intended—to fix it."

"So, you're implying that Niphon's here, finagling all this stuff with Tawny, because he did something wrong in my purchase?"

Hugh spread his hands out. "I don't know. All I know is that when an imp shows up and is going to this much trouble over something, the evidence suggests it's big. Maybe not a situation like Raquel's, maybe not a breach of contract, but something."

"My contract's long since done," I murmured. "Everyone it involved is dead now. If there was a problem, I would have had to bring it up back then."

"Like I said, I don't know. Maybe I'm jumping to conclusions."

"Could you look? Could you get a hold of the contract?"

"No." Hugh's answer came almost before I finished speaking. "Absolutely not."

"But if there's some wording I didn't know about—"

"You think I can just go walk into Hell's records and pull a contract I'm not involved with?" he exclaimed. "Fuck. If I got caught, it'd make what happened to Raquel look like a promotion."

"But—"

"No," he said again, voice like stone. "No debate. I love you, sweetie. You know I do. You're like my sister, and I'd do almost anything for you, but not this. I'm sorry." I glared. He glared back. "Look, you want my advice? Get rid of Niphon. And Tawny, if you can. Expose them if they really are pulling something here, and Jerome will take it from there."

"Jerome's not even around! Damn it. Why can't you help me with this? You were so quick to help with my love life when you were talking to Seth the other night."

Hugh narrowed his eyes. "It was probably the best thing I've ever done for you."

"Are you insane? He's walking around talking about that now—all worried about how he's going to hurt me and make me miserable!"

"Good," snapped Hugh. "He should be."

I shoved my trash onto my tray and stood up. "See you later. Thanks for . . . well, nothing."

Hugh followed me over to the garbage bins. "You're behaving irrationally. On all of this."

"I'd never treat you the way you're treating me," I said, dumping my tray. "I'm your friend."

"Friendship has nothing to do with this."

"It has everything to do with this!"

He stacked his tray on the others and looked at his watch. "Look, I have to go. I'm sorry I can't give you the answers you want. Am I going to see you at Peter's?" Peter, unable to pass up party-giving opportunities, was hosting a Christmas dinner, weird as that seemed.

"No. I'm going to be with Seth. Unless he breaks up with me because of your great advice."

Hugh bit his lip on some remark that probably would have been uncomplimentary. Shaking his head, he turned around and left.

Chapter 20

I didn't expect to hear from Dante so quickly. Based on what he'd said about the difficulty of the Nyx-charm, I'd figured it would be a while—if at all. Hugh's observations on the matter had only reinforced my growing skepticism about Dante's abilities.

"I've got your protection," Dante told me on the phone. "Or at least as close as I can get. You want it, come pick it up." He disconnected.

I drove to Rainier Valley, finding Dante's shop empty as usual. "Guess you don't see a lot of business so close to Christmas, huh?"

"Actually," he told me, emerging from the back room, "you'd be surprised at the kind of desperation the holidays can bring out in people. Here, catch."

He tossed me something baseball-sized. I caught it, feeling a little disappointed when I studied it closer. It looked like a wicker ball, made of very thin, dark branches. Through the gaps, I could make out a few things inside. One looked like a rock. Another looked like a feather. The whole thing rattled when I shook it.

"This is it?" I asked. "This is going to keep away an uber-powerful dream entity? It looks like a prop from *The Blair Witch Project*."

"It can't force her away," he said. "Nothing can. But it might make her think twice. It's more of . . . a repellent."

"Like citronella?"

He rolled his eyes. "Yes, like citronella. Depending on her energy charge, she might blow past it. If she's weak enough . . . well, it might hold her back."

I examined the ball again. It still didn't look like much to me. I sensed no power or magic off of it, but not all objects had an aura I could sense. For reading inanimate items, a psychic mortal tended to be more adept than a lesser immortal. My silence appeared to further annoy Dante.

"Look," he snapped. "You don't have to use it, but it took a fuckload of power for me to craft it, okay? It'd be nice if you could maybe withhold your customary sarcasm for a whole five minutes to thank me."

"*My* customary sarc—"

I stopped the burst of temper starting to flare in me. Dante ranked near the top of my list of cynical acquaintances, but I wasn't exactly Pollyanna myself. I'd given him nothing but a hard time since I first came to him for help. And now, studying him, I noticed he was pale and tired-looking. His eyes were bloodshot. The ball might be worthless, but he'd clearly exerted some sort of effort in making it.

"You're right," I said. "I'm sorry. Thank you. Thank you for this."

His eyebrows rose, and I could actually see the self-control it took for him not to mock my sincerity. He nodded. "You're welcome." We each waited for the other to speak. I don't think we knew what to do without the sarcasm. "So . . . did you find your angel friends?"

"No. I apparently need a fucking Bat Signal or something. Jerome's gone too. Hugh—this imp friend of mine—could get a hold of him, but it'd probably piss Jerome off if we were wrong about all this." I scowled, recalling the conversation in the deli. "Anyway, Hugh's pissing *me* off right now, so I don't even know if I want his help."

Dante smiled. "I thought succubi were supposed to make friends everywhere they went. Or is that a myth like the bat wings and flame eyes?"

"He's just being an asshole about Seth."

Dante looked at me expectantly. I sighed.

"He thinks us dating is a waste of time. And *not* because of the sex thing. He thinks I'm going to get hurt."

"Terribly altruistic of an imp. But then, considering your quasi-morals, I'm starting to think it's a bad idea to assume anything about you guys." He took a few steps toward me and playfully tapped my nose. "And what about you? Do you think you're going to get hurt?"

"No. And if I do, that's for me to deal with. Hugh shouldn't be worrying about it. And he shouldn't make Seth worry about it either!"

"Don't get so upset about people worrying about you. It means they care. If enough of us were like that, there'd be a lot less pain in the world."

That was an unexpected observation from Dante. "Maybe. But there'd also be a lot less unnecessary stress."

He chuckled and caught hold of my hand. Flipping it over, he looked at the palm. "A random assortment of lines for this body?" he asked.

I nodded.

"Can you change it to your original?"

"What, so you can read it? I thought this was a bunch of bullshit."

"Sometimes."

I waited for more, but it didn't come. His gray eyes were serious and thoughtful as they met mine. Something in them compelled me, and with great reluctance, I shape-shifted my hands back to the ones I'd been born with. I hadn't worn my original body since the day I'd become a succubus, and this small change felt unnatural. I hated this form. While my original hands weren't gargantuan, they were larger than was proportional to this petite frame I carried and appeared weird and mismatched.

Dante held my hands in his and glanced back and forth between the palms. After just a few seconds, he snorted and dropped them both. "Surprise, surprise."

I shape-shifted them back to the way they had been. "What?" I asked.

"Right-handed?"

"Yeah."

He pointed to the left hand. "Those lines represent what you're born with—your inherent traits. The right hand is the hand that shows how you grow and change and adapt to what you're born with. Nature and nurture."

"So?"

"Yours are identical on both hands. Your heart line is high on the palm—which means you have an intense, passionate nature. No surprise there. But it's broken into a million pieces. Sliced and diced." He tapped my left hand. "You were destined for heartache." He tapped my right hand. "And you are going to repeat that pattern forever. You aren't learning. You aren't changing."

"If I'm *destined* for it, then what does learning or changing have to do with anything? Isn't it a done deal?" I didn't like the censuring tone in his voice, like I'd done something wrong by having these palms.

"Don't start," he said. "I'm not a philosopher and don't want to get into any pre-destination or free-will debates. Besides, palm reading is a bunch of bullshit."

"Yeah," I said dryly. "So I hear."

To my surprise, Dante put his arm around me and drew me close in a sort of half-hug. "Be careful, succubus. You've got a mess o' dangerous things in your life right now. On all fronts. I don't want to see you get hurt either."

I stayed in the embrace and rested my head on his chest. "When did you get so nice? Are you still trying to get me into bed?"

"I'm always trying to get you into bed." He pressed a kiss to my forehead, to my nose, and then to my lips. "But I kind of like you too. Just watch out."

I drove home after that, a bit confused over Dante's surprising behavior. Thinking about him, I soon arrived in Queen Anne before I knew it. I found neither Vincent nor the angels in my apartment and decided to go to the bookstore. I had today off too, but I knew they were busy and could use the extra help. I needed the distraction.

Just before closing, Seth called my cell and asked if I could pick him up at his brother's. He and Terry had indeed gone to see the movie, but Seth's car was actually here in Queen Anne and he needed a ride now since Terry had originally picked him up. I finished what I was working on in my office and headed out.

Terry and Andrea greeted me warmly when I showed up, reminding me to come to Christmas dinner—even though I'd long since told them I'd be there. They always regarded my relationship with Seth as a tenuous, fragile thing (which it was) and felt compelled to do all they could to protect it. The girls were as thrilled as always to see me, and they assaulted me with questions and chatter.

All except Kayla. She'd apparently gotten to stay up late tonight. In some ways, her silence wasn't surprising. Aside from the startling conversation the other night, she almost never spoke anyway. But usually, she'd come forward with the other girls to see me. Tonight, she simply stayed on the couch, watching me solemnly. When Seth made motions to leave, I broke from the girls and went over to Kayla.

"Hey, you," I said, sitting down beside her. "How's it—"

I hadn't touched her, but Kayla suddenly jerked away from me as though she'd been burned. Backing up, she scrambled off the couch and tore out of the room. We heard her small footsteps on the stairs as she ran to her room.

Startled, I looked at the others. "What did I do?"

"No idea," said Andrea, puzzled. "She's been fine all night."

"Something must have gotten into her," said Terry. "No telling with kids. *Especially* with girls." He mussed Kendall's hair, and she yelped.

Everyone promptly forgot about Kayla and continued to make farewells to Seth and me. I spoke to them half-heartedly, though. Kayla was always happy to see me, and last time, she'd demonstrated a special trust and belief in me. Tonight, she had looked at me with abject terror. Why? Was it a little girl mood? Or was there something hanging on me from another plane that I couldn't see?

Just before we left, I asked if I could go say good-bye to Kayla and give talking to her another shot. Upstairs, I found her curled into a corner of her bed, clutching the unicorn. Her eyes widened in terror when she saw me, and I stopped in the bedroom door.

"Hey," I said. "You okay?"

No answer, just wider eyes.

"I won't come any closer," I said. "Promise. But, please . . . just tell me. What do you see? Why are you afraid of me?"

For a moment, I didn't think she'd answer. Then, finally, she spoke in a voice I could barely hear.

"You're bad," she whispered. "Why are you so bad?"

That wasn't what I'd been expecting. I'd thought maybe she'd tell me there was a ghostly hag hovering above my head. Something in Kayla's words made my stomach sink. I knew I was evil—it was kind of the definition of a Hellish servant. I lived day to day with my eternal task, seducing and corrupting men. But somehow, a little girl telling me I was "bad" hit me harder than the cruelest, most profane accusation could. Without another word to her, I headed back downstairs.

As I drove Seth back to my place, I gave him the scoop on the angels and my subsequent lack of progress.

"You've got some creature stalking you, and you decided to go into work?" He sounded both amused and exasperated. "You might as well have gone to the movie with me."

"Oh." I felt kind of stupid. "I didn't want to interrupt any brotherly bonding."

"And," he added, "you forgot."

"I never forget about you," I said stoutly. "But I was kind of distracted."

"Funny how that's never a good excuse when the roles are reversed . . ."

My apartment was still empty when we got there. I left my coat and Dante's charm in my bedroom and then went to sit on the couch with Seth. "I hate waiting," I told him. "Why does this always happen? Some big, supernatural crisis pops up in my life, and I always end up sitting around and feeling useless. I'm always dependent on others."

"No, you aren't," he said, lacing his fingers through mine. "You're wonderful and capable. But you can't do everything."

"I just wish I could do something else besides shape-shift and look good. I wish I could, I don't know, shoot laser beams out of my fingers or something."

"You think that'd stop Nyx?"

"No. But it'd be cool."

"Me, I always wanted frost power."

"Frost power?"

"Yeah." Seth gestured dramatically toward my coffee table. "If we're talking superhero abilities. If I had frost power, I could wave my hand, and suddenly that whole thing would be covered in ice."

"Not frost?"

"Same difference."

"How would frost and/or ice power help you fight crime?"

"Well, I don't know that it would. But it'd be cool."

I laughed and snuggled into Seth, feeling better. I could wait this out.

"Are you hungry?" I asked him. "Yasmine and Vincent have been waging their own version of *Top Chef* around here."

We went to the kitchen and found it stocked with more food than it had ever had since I moved in. I unwrapped a plate of what appeared to be slices of freshly baked short-cake. Seth pointed to the refrigerator.

"If there are strawberries in there, it's proof of God's existence."

I opened the door and peered around. "Get ready for a religious experience," I told him, pulling out a bowl of chopped-and-sugared strawberries. With the other hand, I pulled out a larger bowl covered in plastic wrap. "And homemade whipped cream."

"Hallelujah," he said.

We piled plates high with shortcake and strawberries, and suddenly, dream entities seemed downright comical. I unwrapped the whipped cream, and Seth promptly dabbed a finger in it.

"Savage," I scolded.

"Heavenly," he countered, licking off the cream.

He stuck another finger into the bowl and held it out to me. I leaned forward and ran my tongue over the tip. Rich sweetness flooded my mouth.

"Mmm," I said, closing my eyes.

"Mmm," said Seth.

I opened my eyes. "Are you talking about the whipped cream?"

"Not exactly."

"You talking about this?"

There was still whipped cream on his finger. I took it into my mouth and sucked gently on it, cleaning up the last of the cream and stroking Seth's skin with my tongue. When I finished, he exhaled a held breath.

"Thanks for the cleanup."

"Cleanliness is next to godliness, I hear."

"I think I have more on me, though," he said.

"Really?" I asked. "Where?"

He swiped his finger through more whipped cream. "Right here."

I licked that off too, sucking and kissing all of the fingers on his hand—not just the guilty one. Finished, I flipped the hand over and kissed the top of it.

"There. Sparkling clean."

Seth shook his head. "Oh no."

"What?"

"You've got some on you too."

"Do I? Where?"

He dipped into more whipped cream and dabbed it on my lips, my chin, and the side of my throat.

"Everywhere," he said.

Before I could formulate a response, his mouth was on my neck, licking and kissing with as much sensuality as I had just used on his fingers. The eroticism of it astounded me—and I was hardly one to be caught by surprise with such things. I instinctually moved my body toward his, arching my neck back as his lips continued moving up. I felt his tongue, warm and amazingly skilled, clean up every drop of the whipped cream on my throat before sliding to my chin and finally to my mouth.

We kissed harder, dessert (of the food nature) now forgotten. I felt his lips fit perfectly with my own. My back was against the counter, and Seth pressed his body against mine, trapping me. When I finally pulled back from the kiss, I could scarcely breathe.

"Wow," I said, eyes wide. "This is why I don't cook. It only leads to trouble."

Seth, still right against me, glanced left and then right. There was a heated, feral look in his eyes that made me shiver. "I don't see anything too bad happening."

"Not yet," I admitted. "But you know the drill."

He shrugged. "Yeah. But nothing bad is happening *now*."

"It will if we—mmphf!"

Seth was kissing me again, and this time his arms went around my waist, pulling us closer still. I wrapped my own arms around his neck, tilting my face upward to get more of the kiss. It was hot and dangerous and amazing, and I couldn't get enough. I knew, though, that I'd *have* to get enough of it pretty quickly here and was contemplating how to stop it when Seth broke away first.

"Ah," I teased. "You've come to your senses."

Seth smiled at me, and my heart raced at the juxtaposition of the animal desire and trademark laidback look on his face. "Nope," he said. "Let's see how far we can go."

"You already know," I said. "We've timed this before."

That was a bit of an exaggeration. We'd never had a stopwatch or anything, but we'd gained a good sense of how long and how deep a kiss could go before it was time to part.

He shook his head. "Not kissing. This."

I wore a black tank top with a red cardigan over it. Seth reached out and unfastened the sweater's three large buttons and pulled it off of me. Letting it drop to the floor, he then rested his hands on my arms, fingers warm against my bare skin. He looked at me expectantly.

"We're timing how quickly you can take off my sweater?" I asked.

"Wrong answer. It's not always about you."

Removing his hands, he caught the bottom edge of his Cap'n Crunch T-shirt and pulled it over his head. He'd pulled me to his chest before it even hit the floor, and suddenly, I was face to face with golden, delicious-smelling Seth skin. Lots of it. Resisting the urge to start kissing his chest then and there, I looked up into his face and attempted levity.

"Is this like strip poker? Except . . . without the poker part?"

"This, Thetis," he said, grabbing the edge of my tank top, "is a test. A test to see how far we can go on all dimensions. *Not* just kissing."

I should have stopped him, but the feel of his hands sliding up my torso was too intoxicating. The tank top went over my head and joined the other clothing on my kitchen floor.

I laughed. "So . . . we know how much kissing we can do. Now you're trying to see how much naked we can do?"

"Yes," he said. He was attempting a dignified air. "It's a scientific experiment."

"Mostly it seems like you pulling off my clothes."

"That's part of it. We know how much we can kiss. But can we kiss naked? How long can we kiss naked? Is it the same?"

"I don—"

Again, he cut me off with a kiss, and my whole body tingled as my breasts pressed up against his chest. There was nothing between us, just skin on skin, and it was incredible. Between that and the kiss, I felt dizzy.

And so, Seth's experiment progressed. He removed articles of our clothing one at a time, then would kiss me, pause, and examine the results. When we were both completely naked, he stepped back and admired my body, his face gleeful and smug.

"I don't think the succubus thing is working," he said.

"Oh, it works, believe me," I said, suddenly nervous. Every inch of me wanted to be touched and caressed and ravaged. My skin burned. And the hunger within me—the instinct that urged me to feed off human energy—was raging, realizing just how close it was to dinnertime. This had started out as an amusing game, but it now occurred to me how dangerous this had become. "It's less about naked and more about us not kissing so much. Remember that time we started making out in bed? I got some of your energy then, and we were dressed. Push this enough—or start doing things with other parts of our bodies—and it'll be game over." I stepped back and reached for my shirt. "But you made good scientific progress tonight, I'll give you that."

Seth caught my wrist before I could get the shirt. He pulled me back to him. "Just a little bit more. Just to see." He still had the same intensity and arousal all over him. I'd seen it in him before but never like this.

"What more is there?" I asked.

"Just one more kiss," he said, feigning innocence. "A . . . parting kiss."

"Oh good grief."

"One kiss, Thetis. That's it."

I hesitated, then nodded. "Okay. Fine. But I'm onto you, so don't think you can get away with anything here."

"Noted."

At least that's what I think he said because it came out kind of muffled with his mouth crushing mine. I was pressed back against the counter again, and his hand was moving down my ass, down the back of my thigh. We were so close. So, so close. We'd never been this close, this naked, before. We'd certainly never been this naked and kissing before. I felt alive and on fire, craving him both as a succubus and a woman in love. The floodgates burst, and all the passion we kept restrained flowed forth. I could feel him, how hard he was and how much he wanted me. My own body responded in kind, pushing closer and grinding against him. His hand on the back of my thigh tensed and then pulled my leg up. It was barely around his hip when I felt . . . it.

It.

Seth's life. Sweeter than kissing, sweeter than whipped cream. It came into me pure and bright, unlike anything else I'd ever tasted—well, other than the *last* time I'd stolen some from him. I would have moaned if my mouth wasn't preoccupied.

Reason seized me, and I did my best to squirm free. My best wasn't good enough, and all I could do was slide my mouth away from his. He simply moved down, kissing my neck. The energy didn't stop.

"Seth. *Seth*. We made the point. We saw how far we can go."

His eyes, full of so much longing and passion, held mine. "Please, Georgina . . . we're so close . . . just this once . . ."

We were so close. Too close.

"No." I pressed my palms to his chest. "Seth! Stop." I shoved hard. "*Stop*!" I broke free all at once and staggered a few feet back, my hand catching the counter for support. The energy transfer cut off abruptly.

He reached out a hand to help steady me, but I stayed out of reach. "Are . . . are you okay?" he asked.

"I'm fine," I said, breath heavy. "But you aren't. I got a little—a little of your energy."

"A little is nothing."

"Not to me," I said, still keeping my distance.

"It's not *your* energy," he said. His eyes were still heated and hungry. "It's mine. And I think it was worth it." He took a step forward. "And I'd think it was worth it, even if I lost more."

I held out my hand, palm-first. "Stop. Don't come closer. I don't trust you."

His expression became less aroused and more dumbfounded. "You . . . don't trust me? I never thought I'd hear you say that."

"That's not what I meant. Exactly. I mean, I don't know. I don't think you're going to rape me or anything, but you're . . . uh, persuasive. And you haven't been yourself lately. Ever since you got shot. You've been . . . I don't know. Risky. Like you're having a mid-life crisis."

"I'm having a life crisis, Thetis. I don't want to be one of those people who discovers on my death bed that I didn't do anything. Why can't you understand this? You're so quick to encourage Maddie to do exciting things, but you're still trying to protect me."

"It . . . it's different."

"How?" he asked. "Why is it okay for her to take risks but not me?"

"Because there's a big difference between going rock climbing and sleeping with someone who's going to take years off your life. How long is this phase going to last? You always said it wasn't about sex between us."

"It's not," he said stoutly. "Not at all. I love you for . . . so many reasons. More than I can even begin to describe. But I don't want to die never having touched you. Really touched you."

I stared. He was serious. How could he say he didn't want to die without touching me when touching me would only lead him closer to death?

"You're only saying this because you haven't had sex in so long," I accused. "You got all turned on and now you're not thinking straight."

"I am turned on," he agreed. "By you. The woman I love." He took another step toward me but still stayed far enough away so we didn't touch. "I want you, Georgina. So badly it kills me. I know you want me too. How can we go on being afraid of something we never tried? I'll take a hit for it, yeah, but if we go on for years . . . without ever knowing . . ." He shook his head and sighed. "Please, Georgina. Just this once. Let us be together—*really* together."

I swallowed. He was so earnest. So sweet. So sexy. And so help me, he sounded reasonable. The calm way he spoke almost made me believe it didn't matter, that if I gave in and let our bodies come together, the loss would be small and inconsequential. I looked into his eyes and tried to convince myself of his rationalization, bringing up what Carter and others had said. That it was Seth's choice to make, nothing for me to worry about.

But, of course, it was.

"No," I said. "I can't. Please, Seth. Don't do this. Don't look at me like that. I love you too—so, so much. But we can't do this. I'm telling you, you just need to have sex. Go out and find someone—anyone. It doesn't matter. I don't care. It'll fix all this and make it easier for us to go on."

"You would care," he said, voice deadly calm. "You say you wouldn't, but you would."

"Not if it protects you."

"Protecting me doesn't matter."

"Damn it, it does!" I yelled, lunging forward. I drove my fists—lightly—into his chest, and all the emotion that had been building up throughout this argument suddenly burst out. "Don't you get it? I have to protect you! If anything happens to you—if I'm responsible for anything happening to you—it will kill me. *It. Will. Kill. Me.* I can't handle that. I can't handle anything happening to you. It will kill me!"

I stopped my yelling and met Seth's eyes. Neither of us said anything. And as he stared down at me, I knew what he was thinking. Because I was thinking exactly the same thing. I had just given voice to what Hugh had said, what Seth had been worried about. In my outburst, I'd changed the balance of risk. It wasn't about Seth hurting. It was about me hurting.

Gently, he reached out and caught my wrists. He removed them from his chest and let go. Backing up, still not speaking, he picked up his clothes and began dressing. I stayed where I was, naked and frozen.

"Seth . . ." I said slowly. "I didn't mean it."

"It's okay, Thetis," he said, fastening his pants and not meeting my eyes. "I understand. I'm sorry. I'm sorry I pushed you."

"No, no . . . it's not . . ."

"It's okay," he repeated. His voice was so, so neutral. So, so steady. It wasn't natural. "Really. But I think I need to go. I think it's better for both of us, and God only knows you have enough going on without me to worry about."

I felt tears starting to fill my eyes. "I didn't mean . . ."

"I know what you meant," he said. He straightened his shirt and finally looked at me. "But seriously . . . I should leave. We'll talk . . . I don't know. We'll talk later." He held out his hand, like he might touch my cheek, and then let it drop. With another sigh, he said good-bye and left.

I stood exactly where I was, still not moving. My heart felt like it had just had acid thrown on it. It was burning and raw. Finally, finally, it all caught up with me. My knees gave out, and I sank to the floor. It was cold and hard against my bare skin. I drew my knees up to me and buried my face in them, wondering what I had done. Part of me screamed to go follow him, to beg him to come back, to tell him we could make love and have everything we had ever wanted. Another part, half-reason and half-pride, held me back.

It was that same part that had stopped me from going after Andrew that day back in the garden after we'd fought about the Black Death. I'd let him go and gone out of my way to avoid him after that. When the plague finally came to our town, my bishop was one of the first to leave. I went with him and the rest of our household. Just like in *The Masque of the Red Death*, there was no true place to hide from sickness. Still, some places were better than others, and my bishop took care to keep to the better places. He survived.

Months went by, and stories and rumors trickled in about the town we'd lived in. By that point, I'd grown weary of Geoffrey and decided it was time for me to move on. I got permission from my archdemon for a transfer to Florence and sneaked out of Geoffrey's house one night to make the long journey. Our old town was along the way, and a week later, I passed through it.

A plague town wasn't quite like what modern people might imagine. It wasn't as though there were piles of bodies lying in the streets or anything. Not always. After all, Europe had survived the Black Death in the end, and civilization had still functioned through the worst of it. Crops were still grown, houses still built, babies still born.

But the town seemed quieter and more melancholy than when I'd lived there. Andrew wasn't at the church when I stopped by, and an old man tending the grounds told me that Andrew was off helping some of his parishioners in one of the poorer districts.

I found him there, inside the home of a brewer. The brewer had a large family—eight children—as well as a couple of brothers living with him. The house was small and cramped and filthy. Everyone in it was sick except for the brewer's wife who wearily tried to help Andrew take care of her family.

"Cecily?" he asked in astonishment when he saw me. He was kneeling by a teenage boy. Something inside my chest blossomed with both joy and relief. Andrew was alive. He'd stayed, fought disease, and won.

I strode forward and knelt beside him. The wife, giving water to a small girl, watched me uneasily. I wasn't in silk or anything, but I was clearly from a different class than theirs, and she didn't entirely know how to treat me.

"You're alive," I breathed. "I've been so worried. So worried I'd never see you again."

He smiled that gentle smile of his, and I saw more lines around his eyes than I'd seen before. "God didn't want to separate us quite yet," he said.

I looked down at the boy. I'd figured Andrew was feeding him or something, but I realized then that the priest was actually giving him last rites. The boy wore no shirt, and I could see on his neck and in his armpits the tell-tale dark pustules that had given the plague its name. The plague usually did what it was going to do in about a week, but from his emaciated look, you would have thought he'd been dying for years. His eyes were fever-bright, and I didn't know if he even knew we were there.

Bile rose in my throat, and I averted my eyes. Standing up, I told Andrew, "I'll let . . . I'll let you finish this and wait outside." I left the house, going out to where it was warm and things weren't dying.

A while later, Andrew found me. I didn't ask if the boy was

still alive. Instead, I said, "How many of them live? Out of all the ones you stay and risk your life for, how many of them actually survive?"

He shrugged. "Three-quarters. Sometimes half, if they're very young or very old."

"Half," I repeated flatly. "That's not very good."

"If one more person lives because of me, then that's very good."

I looked at that confident, serene face and sighed. "You're so damned frustrating."

He smiled. I sighed again.

"What can I do to help?"

The smile disappeared. "Don't make light of this, Cecily."

"I'm not. Tell me what to do."

And that was how I found myself playing nurse in a small town in backwoods England. Honestly, there wasn't anything glamorous one could do to fight the plague. It was all about basics, keeping the people clean and supplied with as much food and water as they could take in. The rest was in the hands of their immune system and—if you believed Andrew—God. When my patients began declining past the point of no return, I usually stopped helping. I couldn't stand to watch and left them to Andrew and his prayers.

But sometimes I'd see people come back around, people whom I'd given up on, and then I could almost believe there was a higher power at work. At least, I believed that until Andrew got sick.

It started slowly at first, a fever and aches, but we both knew what that meant. He ignored it and kept working until the symptoms began compounding. Finally, he couldn't fight it. Neglecting my other patients, I devoted myself fully to him.

"You should help others," he told me one day. His skin was pink and blotchy, and he was starting to get the dark spots around his lymph glands. Through all the sickness and fatigue, he was still beautiful to me. "Don't worry about me."

"I have to worry about you. No one else is." It was true. Andrew had helped so many, but no one had come to his side, despite the fact that plague survivors tended not to catch it again.

"It doesn't matter," Andrew told me, voice frail. "I'm glad they've survived."

"You will too," I said obstinately, even though the signs were starting to suggest otherwise. "You have to go on so you can keep doing your annoying good works."

He managed a smile. "I hope so, but I think my time in this world may be drawing to a close. You, though . . ." He looked at me—truly looked at me—and I was astonished at the love I saw there. I knew he'd been attracted to me, but I'd never expected this. "You, Cecily . . . you won't get sick. You will go on, strong and healthy and beautiful. I can feel it. God loves you."

"No," I said sadly. "God hates me. That's why he lets me keep living."

"God only gives us tasks he knows we can handle. Here, take this." He touched the gold cross around his neck, but he was too weak to take it off. "Take it when I'm gone."

"No, Andrew, you won't—"

"Take it," he repeated in as firm a voice as he could manage. "Take it, and whenever you see it, remember that God loves you and knows that no tragedy you face is ever too much for you to bear. You are strong. You will endure."

Hot tears spilled down my cheeks. "You shouldn't have done this," I told him. "You shouldn't have helped them. You would've lived if you hadn't."

He shook his head. "Yes, but then I wouldn't have been able to live with myself."

Andrew lingered a few more days after that. I stayed with him, but every moment of it was agony. I hated watching what happened to him and was more convinced than ever that there really was no benevolent power looking after humans.

He died peacefully and quietly, much as he'd lived. Another priest came to administer last rites when it happened, and Andrew's final conscious moments reflected hope and absolute faith in what would come next. I stayed to make sure the funeral arrangements were taken care of, not that there was much fanfare or anything. There were no viewings or fancy funeral halls in those days—at least not for men like him.

I soon left England for the continent, and after a while, the pain of his death began to take on a new form. Oh, I still missed him—still burned and ached and felt like part of me had been ripped away. But added to that, guilt was starting to create a pain of its own. I felt like I should have taken better care of him. I should have insisted on him leaving with me when the plague came. Or maybe I should have gotten my hands dirtier while helping him tend the sick; it might have kept him away from whomever had infected him.

Florence was a beautiful city, on the verge of the Renaissance when I got there. Yet even while living amongst all that splendor and art, Andrew's death tormented me for many years, the pain of guilt and missing him digging into my heart. It never entirely went away, but it did lessen—it just took a really, really long time. As Hugh had said, a long life simply means having more time to mourn.

Chapter 21

Five minutes after Seth left, I realized I'd made a mistake. Not about refusing him—that was the right thing to do. But I shouldn't have let him walk out like that. It was no way to end a fight.

I was still angry after all these years that Andrew had died helping those people. I was still pained by his loss. To this day, I believed my stand in the garden had been correct, but nonetheless, I'd always regretted the separation that followed. Anger and pride had come between us, keeping us apart until it was almost too late. Even disagreeing with each other, we shouldn't have stayed away. We should have talked and tried to find some compromise.

I refused to let this fight foster more bad communication and confusion between Seth and me. I wouldn't let it take away from the time we could have together. I had to fix things. Resolved, I grabbed my coat and purse and headed out the door after him.

I half-walked, half-jogged down to the bookstore, where he'd left his car, but it was gone. I'd missed him. I stared at the empty parking lot for a few moments and then went inside. I'd finally bought Carter's stupid Secret Santa present and had left it in my office earlier. But when I went back inside and stuffed the gift in my purse, I found I didn't have the will to head back out. Instead, I sank into my chair and

buried my face in my hands. How had things gotten so mud-
dled with Seth and me? Had the shooting really given him
such a new perspective on life? Would this have happened
anyway?

Yasmine's signature suddenly filled the room, and I looked
up just in time to see her and Vincent materialize in front of
me. Immediately, Seth left my mind.

"Hey, Georgina," Vincent said. "I got your mess—"

"I know about Nyx," I blurted out.

Astonished silence hung in the air. I couldn't say for sure
with nephilim, but I knew angels were rarely caught by surprise. Yasmine clearly had been.

And, being an angel, she didn't try to deny anything about
Nyx. She simply asked, "How?"

"Because she's using me to do her dirty work." Their looks
of amazement grew. "Only . . . I'm not exactly sure how she's
doing it."

The two of them glanced at each other, then back at me.
"Start from the beginning," said Yasmine. "That's usually
the way to go."

And I did, first telling them about the dreams and the energy loss. After that, it was on to my weird knowledge of
tragic events and the residual feelings of Nyx's activities. Finally, I explained how Erik and Dante had pieced it all together, linking what was happening to me with all of those
unfortunate news stories.

Yasmine sat down in a folding chair, tipping her head back
as she thought. It was kind of like what Vincent had done in
the hospital while ruminating. I wondered if it was one of
those unconscious gestures couples sometimes picked up
from each other. "Hmm . . . brilliant. That's how she's doing
it without us finding her."

"I never would have even thought of that," agreed Vincent, pacing. "Which, of course, is the point."

"You know what she's doing to me, then?" I asked eagerly.
The not-knowing was killing me.

"Yep," said Yasmine. "But let's get the others first."

"The other—"

The question faded from my lips as three figures materialized in the room: Carter, Joel, and Whitney. Angelic auras crackled around me. I couldn't help a little envy. It might take me days to hunt down higher immortals, but Yasmine could do it with a thought.

Carter smiled when he saw me. Joel looked outraged. Whitney looked confused.

"What's going on?" Joel demanded. He seemed as angry as the last time I'd seen him. It was a good thing he was immortal, or he probably would have died from high blood pressure ages ago. "Why have you brought us to this . . . this . . . *place.*" You would have thought he stood in an opium brothel, as opposed to a tiny office with badly painted walls.

Yasmine leaned forward in the chair, hands clasped under her chin and elbows on her knees. Her dark eyes sparkled with excitement. "We've got her. We found her—or rather, Georgina found her."

Joel and Whitney appeared flabbergasted. Carter didn't. From the look on his face, I felt like he'd been expecting it.

"I can't believe it took you this long to figure it out," he joked.

Whitney was not amused. "Explain this."

Yasmine did, and when she was finished, the others were as impressed as she and Vincent had been earlier. Even Joel looked a little less pissed off.

"Ingenuous," he murmured. "Every time she escapes, she always thinks up a new way to elude us."

I looked from face to face. My emotions were raw after the blowout with Seth, and I was really low on patience at the moment. "Will someone finally tell me how I fit into this?"

Carter walked over to me. He wore a beat-up blue flannel shirt and a Mariners baseball cap that looked like it had been put through a wood chipper. He was still smiling.

"You must know by now that Vincent's a psychic. He's attuned to our world and in some ways has a higher sensitivity to supernatural activity than some of us do. It happens with humans sometimes." It was true. Angels weren't omnipotent and didn't possess all gifts. I nodded along, not letting on that I knew Vincent was actually a psychic nephilim. "Normally, he'd be able to find her trail pretty quickly. When she runs amuck feeding off mortal chaos, there's a kind of, I don't know . . . magical residue left where she's been. The energy she steals only sustains her; it isn't actually enough to obscure her. Someone like Vincent can . . ."

Vincent helped him out. ". . . sniff her out. I'm a paranormal hound." Yasmine snickered.

"He hasn't sensed anything so far," Carter continued, "which is why we were having to do more mundane searches, like looking for telltale patterns in the news."

"So . . . she was hiding her trail." I shrugged. "How do I fit in?"

"She was using you to hide it. In a couple different ways. Kind of a fail-safe, really. In taking energy from you and human victims, she was able to double her stash. It made it easier to hide from us. When her power dipped, I think she was actually . . . hiding *in* you."

"Ew." I suddenly felt violated. "How is that possible? Is she . . . is she there now?" I glanced down at my lower body, as though I might actually see something.

He peered at me. "No, I don't think so. She's probably got enough energy to run loose for a while. As for how she does it . . . well, life and energy move in and out of you, and at some level, she's both of those things. You're a conduit for those forces."

"I wish people would stop calling me that. It makes me feel like a machine."

"Hardly. The merging she does with you is how you occasionally get a sense for what she's been doing. Some of the details of her mischief leak into you, though she goes to great pains to hide it—and herself."

"How?"

"The dreams," said Vincent. "She's distracting you with them. Happy, consuming dreams that you're starting to obsess on. Your subconscious is so enmeshed in them at night that you don't notice her leaching the energy while you sleep."

I leaned back in my chair, dumbfounded. I'd dealt with a lot of weird shit in my life—an exceptional amount of it occurring in the last few months, actually—but this was shooting to the top of the list. My skin crawled, and I had the surreal sense that my body was no longer my own.

I was also kind of bothered by the fact that my dreams had been red herrings, meant to throw me off the path of what was going on. They were so sweet . . . so powerful. I treasured them, yet it seemed they were nothing but lies. Illusions created by a monster to hide her parasitic control of me. That knowledge cheapened the beauty of what I'd seen. I loved the little girl. I wanted to believe in her. I wanted her to be real.

"Well," said Joel brusquely, narrowed eyes fixed on me. "We've got to use the succubus to lure Nyx out." He gestured to me. "Go. Go out and seduce some poor soul, so Nyx'll come back."

I flinched. Yasmine glared at him. "Can't you see she's upset? Show some compassion."

"Denizens of evil deserve none," he muttered.

Across the room, Whitney stood by the door. She'd spoken little, so her voice startled me. "All creatures deserve compassion." I looked up and met her eyes. They were dark and bottomless, filled with power and emotion. I had the sensation of falling into that blackness, much like I experienced with Carter sometimes. I decided I didn't like hanging out with angels. They did a lot of soul searching—and usually it involved mine.

More awkward silence fell. "Okay, okay," I said. "We don't all have to spill our feelings and hold hands here. Tell me what you need me to do."

"You're going to be bait, Georgina," said Carter.

"I'm *always* bait," I grumbled. "Why is that? Why do these things keep happening to me?" Not too long ago, I'd had to play bait for a date-raping demigod. I hadn't been any happier then than I was now.

I expected a joke, but Carter's response was serious. "Because you're one of those unique individuals whom powers in the universe tend to gather around."

That was worse than being a conduit. I didn't want any of those things. I didn't want to be a target. I wanted my quiet life back where I worked in a bookstore and had a blissful, perfect relationship with my boyfriend. Okay, I'd never had such a relationship yet, but a girl can dream.

Dream.

Bad choice of words.

"Unfortunately," said Yasmine delicately, "Joel is right to a certain extent. We do need you to, um, replenish your energy in order to lure Nyx out." Joel grimaced.

I sighed. "I know this is important . . . I don't want her to hurt anyone else, but well, does it have to be tonight? Can we do it tomorrow? I just . . . I just don't feel up to it." Not after Seth. Not after any of this. I was so, so mentally exhausted. Sex sounded nauseating, energy or no.

Joel clenched his fists. "Don't feel up to it? This is no time for whims! Lives are at stake—"

"Joel," said Carter. It was one word, but it was hard and powerful. I'd never heard lax, sarcastic Carter speak in that sort of tone. He and Joel locked gazes. I couldn't assess higher immortals' power, but I knew Carter was pretty damned strong. Stronger than Jerome, even. "Leave her alone. Nyx only attacks when she steals more energy anyway. We should be okay for one night."

If I didn't know better, I'd say Joel was afraid of Carter. Joel looked very much like he wanted to say a lot more, but he backed down.

"Fine," he said through gritted teeth.

I shot Carter a relieved glance. With the way I felt tonight,

I probably would have had about as much luck trying to seduce someone as Tawny. Thinking of the other succubus, I wondered if I should mention my suspicions about Tawny being drained by Nyx too. In the end, I decided against it. That whole situation was still circumstantial. I let it go.

Yasmine stood up and laid a hand on my shoulder. "Rest up. You look terrible. You need to be ready for tomorrow."

"Yikes. I can look like anything I want. When someone tells me I look terrible, it's pretty serious."

She smiled. "It's more than physical."

She vanished. Whitney and Joel did the same a few moments later. Only Carter remained with Vincent and me.

"It's going to be okay," Carter told me.

"I don't know. There's a crazy chaos-eating monster flitting in and out of me," I said. "You're going to try to frisk her out. Seems like there's a high likelihood things might end up pretty not okay."

"Ye of little faith." He too disappeared.

Vincent and I stood there for several moments. Finally, I sighed once more.

"Fucking angels."

He touched my shoulder. "Let's go back home."

We ventured back into the cold and walked to my apartment, saying little. Vincent look tired and thoughtful, no doubt from all the Nyx stuff. As we approached my apartment, however, his expression began to change. At first, he simply looked puzzled. Then he grew surprised, then startled, then horrified, and finally, disgusted. We stopped on the building's steps.

"What's wrong?" I asked.

He pointed upward. "There's something . . . evil in there."

"Like . . . my apartment? Because, you know, I'm technically evil . . ."

Vincent shook his head. "No, no. It's a different kind of evil. You're evil by nature—no offense. This is something different. A created evil. It's black and wrong. Unnatural. You know of anyone else who lives in the building that plays for your side?"

"No. Just me."

He grimaced. "Well, let's go in then and see where it's coming from. Ugh. To my senses, it's like . . . rotting garbage."

We went inside, and it didn't take him long to figure out where this different evil was coming from. My own apartment.

"Told you I was the only evil thing in here," I joked. But I was a little uneasy at his reaction.

Vincent didn't respond and simply pushed past me, searching in a way that brought the earlier hound reference to mind. He disappeared into my bedroom and reemerged with Dante's arts and crafts project.

"This," declared Vincent, holding it at arm's length.

"That?" I asked, astonished. "That's . . . nothing."

"Where did you get it?"

"This guy I know made it. The one who was helping me. He's, I don't know . . . a pseudo psychic. Maybe a real psychic. Interprets dreams and claims to be a magician." I stared at the wicker ball. "Are you saying he really is a magician?"

"Oh, he's something all right. This thing is so filthy, I can't believe you can't feel it. Well, I can believe it . . . I mean, it's a different sort of magic than you're attuned to, but Jesus. It makes me feel like I just . . . I don't know, went swimming in a sewer."

"Well . . . I know he's supposed to be, like, bad . . . he and another friend have said as much. But . . . I don't know. I thought it was just hype."

"There's bad and there's bad," Vincent said. "And this is *bad*. This thing's a repellent, right? Did he give it to you to keep Nyx away?"

"Yeah . . . but he wasn't sure if it'd work . . ."

"Oh, it'd work. It'd keep about anything away. To make something like this . . . man, Georgina. It's incredible—the kind of power required. Very few humans are born with this kind of power. He certainly wasn't. This is stolen power."

"Everyone steals power," I noted dryly. "Me, Nyx . . ."

Vincent's eyes were hard. "You and she suck it from people. This was *ripped* out of someone. The way you'd rip someone's heart out of their chest."

"So, what . . ." I stared. "Are you saying Dante killed someone to make this?"

"To make this specifically? Perhaps. But someone would need to already possess great power—independent of what he might put in this—to even attempt making it. And to be someone with that kind of power in the first place, he had to have done something, at some point in his life, that was bad."

"Like . . . killing someone."

"More than that. A special killing—something sacrificial. You know the kind of power those can yield."

I did. I didn't have a choice in the succubus soul-stealing thing, but I tried to keep my hands clean of other atrocities. Still, you couldn't work for Hell and not know about the full range of evils out there and how to achieve them.

"And," continued Vincent, "you know that the greater the impact—the greater the meaning—of a sacrificial killing . . ."

"Right. The greater the power." Goosebumps rose on my neck as I started to see where Vincent was going with all this.

"Whatever he did to get this kind of power wasn't just some random, clean killing. It had meaning for him. And it was horrible. He would have had to turn on himself—give up part of his humanity—to get this kind of power."

I stared at the wicker ball. I couldn't sense what Vincent could, but now I too was feeling disgusted and uneasy by its presence. And suddenly, Kayla's repulsion suddenly didn't seem so strange after all. I'd had the charm in my purse when I saw her. She'd said I was 'bad' because I was probably covered in the charm's power. What had Dante done? What act could sarcastic, laconic Dante have done to achieve the kind of power both Vincent and Hugh had said would be needed to make this kind of charm? Whatever it was, it was the reason Erik hated him.

I shivered. "Can you destroy it?"

Vincent nodded. "You want me to?"

A tiny part of me remembered that it had the ability to repel Nyx. But it wouldn't make her disappear, and we needed her to come back if we were going to stop her for good. Swallowing, I nodded. "Yeah, go ahead."

It took only a few seconds. Green light encased the wicker sphere, then Vincent's hand was empty. I'd felt no change in power or anything, but the nephilim looked relieved.

I exhaled. "Well. There's nothing to stop her now, huh?"

"Nope," he said, rubbing his hands together. "Get ready."

Chapter 22

Seth wasn't at the bookstore the next day, which I took as a bad sign. It was usually his passive-aggressive reaction to whenever we had a fight.

I thought about him a lot while I worked, thinking of that awful blowout. We'd had a lot of uncomfortable talks in our time together, but we'd never had anything like that. I couldn't put my finger on exactly what about it bothered me—aside from the obvious—but I kept feeling like it was a pivotal moment, something that was going to have long-reaching effects. It scared me, and I wanted to fix things.

And, of course, there was Nyx to worry about. I was going to find a victim after work, and then Vincent said the angels would come while I was asleep—when Nyx made her move.

"You okay?"

I looked up from the stack of checks I was signing in my office. Maddie stood there in a black pencil skirt and fitted white blouse that made her look super amazing. She'd worn her hair down too.

"Wow," I said. "What's the occasion?"

"Nothing," she said, with a shrug. "Wardrobe overhaul." She lifted one foot, revealing three-inch black heels.

"Holy shit," I said. "You don't do anything in halves."

She beamed, and I noticed something about her that had nothing to do with the new clothes. There was joy in her eyes—a happiness that made her confident and even more radiant. She was a far cry from the bitter woman who'd shown up at the auction.

"What's going on?" I asked, not fixating on myself for the first time today.

Her grin widened, revealing her phantom dimple. A moment later, she turned more serious. "I'll tell you later. My news is good. But you . . . what's the matter? You look awful."

Yasmine had said the same thing last night. It really was a sad day when a succubus couldn't stay on top of her game. I shook my head.

"It's . . . complicated." I offered a weak smile. "I'll deal with it, don't worry. Now, come on. I'd rather hear something cheerful. Tell me what's going on."

"Can't. They need me out there. I just came to drop these off." She set a stack of papers on my desk. They practically melted into the other stacks I already had. My office was so chaotic, it could have been a lair for Nyx in and of itself.

"Come on, the suspense is going to drive me crazy," I teased.

"Well . . . you think you can give me a lift to the airport tomorrow? I'm going home for Christmas."

"You taking Doug with you?"

"Nope. He's your holiday gift. But I'll give you the scoop then if you can give me a ride. I'd probably need to leave around five."

"Five o'clock traffic on the Friday before Christmas. We're going to have a lot of time to talk."

A bit of her normal nervousness reappeared. "If it's a problem . . ."

"Nope. We're closing early anyway. We'll go then."

Maddie left, and I found myself momentarily distracted by whatever her news could be. Whatever it was, it was a good thing. I liked the change it had brought about. That sort of happiness and confidence suited her.

My thoughts were interrupted by the phone ringing. I answered and found Seth on the other end.

"Hey," I said, hoping I sounded cool and confident and not desperate and relieved.

"Hey." A long pause followed. "I . . . just . . . wanted to make sure we were on for Christmas."

My heart sank. No: "I've missed you." No: "I'm sorry."

"Sure. Wouldn't miss it."

Thinking about Christmas. I experienced a weird sense of déjà vu. We'd also been with his brother on Thanksgiving. And like now, we'd also been fighting. There it was again: my life, the endless loop. *You aren't learning. You aren't changing.*

Of course, Seth and I had patched up the other fight. Maybe that kind of resolution would repeat itself too. After all, holidays were supposed to be magic, right?

"Okay," he told me. "I'll pick you up."

"Okay."

Another long pause. "I'd come by today, but . . . well. The book . . ."

The book. Always the book. Then again, I was busy with chaos deities today. "Yeah, I know. It's fine."

"We'll talk on Christmas."

"Okay."

We hung up. A chill ran through me. There it was again. I had no gift for premonition, but an inner instinct—one that had nothing to do with Nyx's visions of the future—told me there was something big coming.

After work, I drove over to Bellevue, Seattle's richest and most pretentious suburb. A city in its own right, Bellevue was pretty much the polar opposite of SeaTac. Hotels, restaurants, and shopping were continually being added to its downtown strip, and the influx of money from Boeing and Microsoft was steadily replacing older, plain buildings with sleeker and more stylish architecture.

Bellevue was also home to a guy I knew named Kevin. I'd met him years ago in a bar. There was nothing overly extraordinary about Kevin. He was neither a sinner nor a saint, instead occupying some happy ground in the middle that yielded a decent amount of energy whenever I slept with him. His most notable trait was that he was perpetually available. He worked at home—some Web business, I believed—and never seemed to go out, despite being good-looking and sociable. I didn't question that too much, though, because it suited my purposes whenever I needed quick and easy sex with someone I didn't completely loathe.

"Sandra," he said happily, opening the door of his condo for me. He had dark brown hair and a closely trimmed, very new beard that I approved of. Dark brown eyes regarded me with amusement. "Been a while."

My "Sandra" form had a petite build similar to the one I usually wore. After that, the resemblance ended. My hair was now curly and black, my eyes a blue that looked violet sometimes. Underneath my long black coat, I wore a sleeveless navy blue dress that fit snugly and was far too skimpy for this kind of weather.

"It has been," I agreed. "Does that mean you aren't going to let me in?"

He smiled and stepped back, grandly waving me inside. "What, do you think I'm crazy or something? Only an idiot would turn you away."

I followed Kevin down the hall and into his living room. He'd redecorated since the last time I was here, and the change was nice. The furniture and décor were now all done in shades of a grayish blue that reminded me of winter twilights. A fireplace crackled on one side of the room, and a large bay window looked out to another set of condos. I draped my coat over a chair and smoothed miniscule wrinkles out of the dress.

"You want something to drink?" he asked, hands in his pockets.

I shook my head. "I don't have much time."

He gave me a rueful smile. "You never do. You know, sometimes I feel used."

"Is that a problem?"

"Problem?" he asked with a snort. "A beautiful woman who wants to have sex with me and no commitments? Hardly a problem." He took a few steps toward me. "Use me all you want."

He came closer still, and we met in a kiss. No delay, no preamble. I wrapped my arms around his neck and parted my lips, eager to feel him and taste him. His hands rested on my hips for a moment, then slid upward. He caught my dress's straps and pulled them down, baring my breasts and still kissing me the whole time. Pushing forward, he pressed me against the wall, near the fireplace. I felt its heat against the bare skin of my legs. His hands cupped my breasts, thumbs sliding to my nipples and squeezing them. He varied the intensity, sometimes hard and sometimes gentle.

I broke the kiss long enough to incline my head toward the uncovered window behind him. "The window—"

He crushed his mouth back against mine. Our tongues danced together briefly, and then he pulled back just long enough to say, "I know." The tone of his voice told me that he not only knew—he also wanted it that way. I didn't question it. This apparently was the season for exhibitionism.

Eventually, he moved his mouth away from mine and trailed kisses down my neck. I tilted my head back and arched the rest of my body toward his. One of his hands continued cupping a breast as he nibbled on its nipple, teeth and tongue stirring it to arousal. His other hand pushed up my skirt, eagerly seeking my panties and what lay within.

The ache for his energy and his touch coursed through me. I moaned softly as he moved his lips down my body. Shifting to the floor, he settled on his knees while still keeping me standing against the wall. He pulled the panties down all the way, so they hung around my ankles. Sliding his hands between my thighs, he pulled them apart slightly and then buried his face between them, his stubble tickling me. I was burning and wet, more so than I'd realized, and when his tongue touched my aching clit, I moaned more loudly and felt my knees tremble slightly.

I started to tell him that he didn't need to do this, that it was okay if he just wanted to get straight to the main event. But as his tongue gently moved back and forth, building the heat and ecstasy within me, I swallowed my words. The last three guys I'd slept with hadn't made me come, and although this visit was strictly utilitarian and part of the Nyx plan, I suddenly and selfishly wanted to get more than his life energy out of it.

Back and forth his tongue moved, speed and intensity continually shifting. As his thoughts began to trickle into me, I could tell that he liked doing that not simply for the sake of novelty, but also because he liked seeing the way I reacted to each slight change. He was one of those men who truly enjoyed making a woman happy. The burning spot he'd brought to life between my legs grew and grew, expanding beyond where his tongue touched, beyond my thighs. Steadily, it spread into my whole body, all the way to my fingertips. I felt like fire in human—or rather, succubus—form and writhed against the wall, against him. My knees buckled as the searing pleasure reached a critical point inside me, and his hands moved down to steady my legs and keep me upright.

At last the core within me exploded, the fire turning to pure light, pure bliss. I cried out at the way the orgasm consumed me, at the way his tongue still kept teasing me even in the throes of my climax. Finally, even he couldn't keep me upright. My legs had turned to jelly, and I sank to the floor in front of him. He smiled, genuinely pleased, and leaned forward to kiss me. I could taste me on his lips.

"Come on," he said, taking my hands and helping me up. He led me over to the window and peeled off the rest of my dress. He eased me onto a high window seat. Removing his own clothes, he murmured, "I should go find a condom."

My breathing was rapid, my heart pounding away. "No, I want to feel you—just you." I took his hand and brought it between my legs, guiding his fingers into me. "I want you to feel me."

I'd been wet before starting all this and was now doubly so after what he'd just done. His fingers glided easily inside of me, and his eyes widened at what he felt. Indecision played on his face, and then he nodded. If counseling any of my human friends, I would certainly advocate safe sex. It didn't matter for me personally, however, since I couldn't catch anything or get pregnant. Often with victims, I'd talk them out of any sort of protection in order to increase their guilt. With Kevin tonight, I didn't want to bother with condoms simply because I didn't want to waste the time. My urgency and desire were too strong. I wanted him *now*.

I slid my hands down his stomach and felt how hard he was. He wanted me too. I wrapped my fingers around him, stroking and massaging and loving the way he swelled within my hand. Pressing my back against the cold glass, I drew my knees up to me and then spread them wide, feeling rather like a butterfly. The window seat was exactly the perfect height, putting us hip to hip as I led him inside of me.

We both gasped at the contact. He pushed in as far as possible, our hips pressed skin to skin. The way he filled me up was exquisite. Shape-shifting meant I could make myself as tight as possible, and I loved how he tested the limits of it. He paused a moment, simply savoring the way our bodies felt together, and then slowly began moving in and out of me, rocking me against the window with each thrust.

And with that, his life began pouring into me in earnest. I nearly exhaled with relief. The sensation of that energy filling me up rivaled the feel of his body inside me. I had missed it so much, missed the wonder and joy of that pure, indescribable energy generated by the human soul. Nyx had been stealing a part of me, and I was glad to have it back, if only for this moment. The thoughts coming through with his energy were happy and content ones as he reveled in the pleasure of being with me. A secret, kinky part of him was turned on by hoping that his neighbors across the way might be watching. He hoped they were. He hoped they were jealous.

His thrusts grew harder and harder, and he murmured over and over how wonderful I was, how beautiful. Still sensitive from him going down on me, I came twice more, my body melting as the orgasms' spasms shook me. At last, I felt his body tense and saw his expression signal he was about to lose control. I dug my nails into his arms and begged him to come in me. He did, shoving me so hard against the window that I hoped the glass would hold. The peak of his energy hit me with his climax, and as it faded, we both sighed happily.

I didn't abandon him quite as quickly as I had Bryce, but I didn't spend time lounging in the afterglow either. I helped him get dressed and made sure he was situated comfortably on the couch before I left. I liked him, after all, and hoped I'd see him again in some other casual situation. His face was languid and content as we made our good-byes.

"You are the most exhausting woman I've ever been with," he told me, eyelids flickering with fatigue.

I couldn't help a smile. Of course I was. Other lovers didn't steal his soul—at least not literally.

"Does that mean you want me to stay away longer next time?"

He smiled and yawned. "No. Absolutely not."

Still smiling, I left and headed back to the city. But as I drove closer to downtown, brimming with energy, my happy feelings faded. I remembered why I'd had to go see him in the first place and what would happen tonight. My body, so achingly hot an hour ago, grew cold.

When I arrived back at my apartment, Vincent, Carter,

and Yasmine were already waiting for me. None of them commented on my glow. Instead, they launched right into the plan.

"Nyx will probably come trolling around tonight," Carter explained. "And when she sees you've got energy again, she'll do her thing."

Yasmine nodded along. "We can't be here when it happens. Vincent will be around, out in the living room. She won't suspect him of anything; she'll figure he's an ordinary human. But when he senses her feeding off of you, he'll let us know. Then, we'll show up and bind her."

I didn't like the sound of any of that—neither the feeding nor the binding. "What's that mean?"

"We'll pull her out and trap her," said Carter. Presumably "out" meant out of *me*. Yikes.

"Then we'll take her away, back to her prison," added Yasmine.

Their confidence inspired confidence in me, and I suspected I was being influenced by angelic charisma. But there was no way out of this, not if I wanted to shake my nighttime visitor.

"All right," I said. "Let's do this."

The angels left. It was still early evening, so I hung out with Vincent. We played a couple games of cards and watched bad movies. Hanging out with him in such a casual way made it easy to forget he was a nephilim. When midnight loomed, I stood up and stretched.

"I don't think I can sleep," I remarked. "It's like trying to go to bed on Christmas Eve. Too jittery to settle down. Except . . . it's not Santa I'm waiting for."

He smiled. "Well, try. If we need to, we can probably give you a sedative or something, but this whole thing will be more efficient without."

It took a long time—lying in bed for almost two hours—before I fell asleep. It wasn't easy to relax when you were inviting a creature of chaos to come feed off of you. And yet, as I drifted off, I couldn't help a small flicker of eagerness. I'd be dreaming the dream again.

And I did.

It started from the beginning, like always, running all the way to the part where the little girl fell and my dream-self comforted her. The girl's tears were drying when we both heard the faint sound of a car door closing. My dream-self straightened up. A smile blossomed on her face as she regarded her—my—daughter with the kind of over-exaggerated excitement adults often use with children.

"You hear that?" my dream-self asked. "Daddy's home."

Mirrored excitement showed on the girl's face as my dream-self stood up, still holding the girl and balancing her on one hip. It was an act of some coordination, considering how small my dream-self was.

They walked to the front door and stepped outside onto a porch. It was nighttime, all quiet darkness, save for a small light hanging on the porch. It shone onto a long stretch of unbroken white snow on the lawn and the driveway. All around, more snow fell in a steady stream. I didn't recognize the place, but it certainly wasn't Seattle. That much snow would have sent the city into a panic, putting everyone on Armageddon alert. My dream-self was perfectly at ease, barely noticing the snow. Wherever she was, it was a common occurrence.

In the driveway, a car had just pulled up. I felt my dream-self's heart swell with happiness. A man stood behind it, a non-descript dark figure in the faint lighting. He took out a rolling suitcase and slammed the trunk shut. The little girl clasped her hands in excitement, and my dream-self waved a hand in greeting. The man returned the wave as he walked toward the house, and my waking self tried desperately to see his face. It was too dark. I needed him to get closer, just a little closer—

I couldn't get any closer because just then, I felt my soul get ripped out of me.

I sat up in bed, nearly screaming in agony at the pain coursing through me. All four angels, plus Vincent, ringed the room. The power pulsing around us felt like smoke. I could barely breathe.

And there, beside my bed, was Nyx.

She looked a lot like Erik's description: an old, emaciated woman. Her skin and hair were white, her dark eyes sunken and inhuman. A tattered, gossamer dress wrapped around her body. She had an almost translucent look, like she wasn't entirely solid, and a sparkling aura shone around her.

I couldn't see the forces being wielded, but I felt them distinctly. The angels temporarily had her enclosed in walls of power, but she wasn't bound, not yet. She pushed back against their restraints with considerable power of her own, and I gaped. Any one of those angels dwarfed my own power—yet, their combined force was still an even match for hers. It was a staggering thought, and I couldn't understand why she'd need my energy since she had so much of her own. And actually, she did have some of mine. She'd taken about half before they'd pulled her out of me.

Nyx shrieked in rage, still pushing back on them. Then, bit by bit, I could see the balance shift. Her power was fading the more she used it. The angels' was steady. They were weakening her. She realized this and panic showed on her face. Casting frantic eyes over all the angels, she finally rested her gaze on Yasmine. There was still enough of a faint connection between us that I realized what Nyx was going to do. She'd sought out the least powerful of the foursome. Mustering the last of her power, she blasted it toward Yasmine, hoping both to smash the angels' united front and hurt Yasmine enough to cause a distraction.

A heartbeat before Nyx unleashed her attack, I saw Vincent's face. He too realized what she was going to do. He moved forward, and I felt his mask drop. The telltale nephilim signature washed over me, and his power filled the room as well. There was a lot of it. He'd held back in the alley.

Invisible energy rushed from Nyx toward Yasmine, trying to destroy the angel. But Vincent was there, blocking the attack. It rebounded back on Nyx. She screamed again, her defenses shattering. The other angels seized the opportunity, and bands of light snapped into place around her. A moment later, the light faded, but the restraints were there, even if I could no longer see them. She clawed around her, like a twisted version of a mime in a box, but she was trapped. She couldn't get through the walls they'd locked her in.

They'd done it. They'd recaptured Nyx. But none of the angels were paying attention to her.

They were all looking at Vincent.

"You," gasped Joel.

He didn't hesitate. He strode toward the nephilim, and I saw Joel's body start to shimmer with light. He was about to transform into his true form, a form of terrible beauty and power.

But Yasmine was faster.

The slim, dark-haired woman became pure light. She was all the colors of the rainbow and none of them. A sword of flame appeared in her hands. She stepped in front of Vincent—who was screaming at her to stop—and swung toward Joel. The blade hit him, and he screamed.

An awful, burning sensation was starting to flood me. Hastily, I shielded my eyes and looked away, realizing what I'd almost done. An angel's true form was an indescribable thing, requiring senses a human—or a human-turned-succubus—didn't possess. Staring at her could cause me major damage. Even being in the same room with her hurt.

But I'd seen what I'd needed to before looking away. I'd seen the sword fall. Yasmine had attacked Joel. Nyx had pegged her as the weakest of the four, but Yasmine and Joel must have been incredibly close in power. Catching him by surprise like that tipped the scales.

The air in the room swirled, reaching hurricane levels. Power exploded around me, like a sun going supernova. Everything was fire and wind. And screaming. Twin screams: Yasmine's and Joel's. I wrapped my arms around me, burying my face, certain I was going to die. The energy exploding toward me reached a point in which it would surely blow up the building, blow up the world. Stronger and stronger it grew.

Suddenly, it all reversed. Power rushed away from my side of the room, back toward the angels. It was like a black hole had formed, sucking everything toward it. Of course, it was only pulling energy, not physical objects, but I nonetheless felt like it was dragging me in too. I clutched the bed's comforter, using it like an anchor to hold me down. Time ceased to have meaning. Ten seconds or ten hours could have passed for all I knew.

Finally, the rushing stopped, and everything went still. The atmosphere returned to normal. No more insane power levels. There was only what you would normally expect in a room with three angels, a nephilim, a succubus, and a primordial entity of chaos. The latter had suddenly moved to the backburner of everyone's attention.

Yasmine had returned to her "human" form. It was safe for me. I looked up, expecting Carter and Whitney to swoop in and attack her. But they stood frozen. No trace of Joel remained. He was gone, destroyed. The typhoon of power had marked his death.

Yasmine was on her knees, fingers digging into the sides of her face. She sobbed, murmuring words that sounded like frantic prayers. Vincent, like the angels, kept his distance from her. She had just killed Joel. I didn't understand why no one was acting. Why were they just standing there? Everyone seemed to be waiting for something.

Suddenly, a voice hissed beside me, more in my mind than spoken aloud.

"Succubus."

I looked into Nyx's cavernous eyes. Like Vincent and the angels, I'd forgotten about her. She extended her hand toward me, and I cringed. Fortunately, the invisible binds kept her from getting any closer.

"Succubus," she repeated. "Touch the walls. Use the last of your power to set me free."

"What? No!" I was dividing my attention between her and the others. The angelic group still stood motionless.

"Free me, and I'll help you exact your revenge."

"Revenge? Who are you talking about?"

"The one who sent me to you when I escaped," she rasped. "The one who promised you to me."

I had no clue what she meant.

"Like . . . who freed you?"

She cast an uneasy look behind her. Time was ticking down on her distraction.

"No, you were promised to me! But I can help you. Help you punish—"

"No," I said. She was too dangerous. Whatever insane revenge she was talking about wasn't worth what she could do to mortals if she was freed.

Her desperation grew. The angels were eventually going to remember her, and we both knew it.

"I will show you the end of the dream!" she cried. "I'll show you the man. The man in the dream."

My heart stopped.

"He isn't real," I whispered. "It was all a lie. You used it to trick me."

"No! Everything I show is true. Always true."

"It can't be . . . it's impossible." I swallowed and felt tears starting to fill my eyes. I wanted it to be true. More than anything. "That can't ever happen to me."

Nyx beat her hands on her unseen prison walls. "It's real! It's the future! I've seen it. Touch the walls, and I will show you. *I will show you the man in the dream!*"

I wanted to. I wanted to see him. I needed to see him. The man in the dream. The man who could maybe truly make this future happen. . . .

My hand moved forward, like it was being controlled by an outside force. Nyx's eyes widened, eager and hungry.

All of a sudden, a scream split the air.

No, it was more than a scream. When Yasmine had destroyed Joel, *that* had involved screaming. This was more than that. It was the most horrible noise in the universe, a phenomenon that went beyond mere sound. Much as my eyes couldn't exactly perceive an angel's appearance, my ears couldn't fully comprehend this.

My hand dropped from Nyx, and I jerked my gaze to the angels. Yasmine was still on her knees, and flames were starting to consume her. It was no ordinary fire, though. It reminded me of the light of her true form: all colors and none. Carter and Whitney watched, faces unreadable.

Vincent also watched. He'd taken a few steps toward me, backing away from the fire. The look on his face was filled with a jumble of emotions, none of them good. I didn't understand what was happening to Yasmine yet, but I knew what would happen to him.

"Get out," I told him in a low voice.

His face was pale, as pale as Nyx's. He looked like he'd aged a hundred years. "I can't . . . I can't leave her . . ."

"You have to. They'll destroy you. Or if they don't, someone else will. Someone else in the city will have noticed this. You know I'm right."

His eyes were still on Yasmine. I could no longer see her, though. She was all flame—flame that had turned black.

"Go!" I exclaimed. "It's what she'd want. She did this for you!"

Vincent flinched at those words and finally looked at me. The full force of his grief made the held-back tears spill down my cheeks.

"Go. Please," I begged. Joel had been destroyed. Yasmine looked like she was about to be. I couldn't stand anymore death.

He said nothing, but after several seconds, he turned invisible. I felt his aura go.

Across the room, the flames were starting to fade. Yasmine was slowly reappearing, completely unscathed. She looked no different, but something about her signature had changed. I felt the same golden light, the impression of saffron and frankincense. But it was edged in something else. It no longer had the sharp, crystalline quality of angelic auras. That was gone, replaced by a dark and smoky feel—a smokiness that had nothing to do with the fire.

The flames finally disappeared altogether, and Yasmine still knelt on the floor. Seconds later, another signature joined us, one I knew well. Jerome stood in the room, apparently back from whatever clandestine matters he'd needed to oversee.

He looked from face to face, finally focusing on mine. "Jesus Christ. What have you done now?"

I ignored him, unable to tear my gaze from Yasmine. She looked the same, exactly the same. And yet, she wasn't . . .

She'd noticed the change too. She held her arms out in front of her, studying them as though she'd never seen herself before. Horror flooded her features.

"No," she moaned. "No . . ." She began sobbing again.

Carter finally looked away from her and met Jerome's eyes. "This is yours now, Charon."

Jerome nodded and stepped toward Yasmine. "Time to go."

She looked up at him, face glistening with tears. She said nothing, but she didn't need to. Her expression said everything. It was a plea, a plea that none of this was real, that maybe—just maybe—Jerome could make it all go away. He shook his head and touched her shoulder. They vanished.

The room was quiet, an unnatural quiet that felt almost oppressive. My voice seemed strange and out of place.

"Wh-what happened?" I asked Carter. I noticed now that Whitney was crying.

"Yasmine has fallen," he said softly. "She's a demon now."

Chapter 23

I couldn't stay in my bedroom after that, not after seeing two angels die—one physically and one spiritually. I had to get out of there, out of the apartment. None of the others seemed to notice or care that I fled. With Nyx captured, there were bigger things to worry about in the universe than one distraught succubus.

I'd been driving in the car for about ten minutes before I realized where I was going. Dante's. Vincent's talk about the evil charm suddenly seemed unimportant. What I needed right now was to talk to someone about what I'd seen. Seth wouldn't entirely understand, and besides, matters still weren't fixed between us. Discussing serious things with the vampires was hard for me sometimes. I was still mad at Hugh. I wouldn't bother Erik since he was still recovering. Dante was all I had left.

He opened the door to his store after I banged on it for about five minutes. The messy hair and wrinkled clothing showed me that I'd woken him again. He looked annoyed, as usual, when I walked inside.

"Didn't it work? I told you—" He took a closer look at me. "What happened?"

I staggered to one of the chairs and collapsed into it, hands resting on the side of my forehead. I could have been a mirror of Yasmine. I opened my mouth to speak, to explain what had happened . . . but no words came out. He knelt beside me.

"Succubus. You're freaking me out here. What happened?"

I stared blankly at him for several seconds before finally focusing on his concerned face. "She fell."

"Huh? Nyx?"

"No . . . Yasmine."

"Who?"

My eyes went unfocused again as I remembered that black flame. The horrible sound. Blinking, I tried to shake it off and turn my attention to Dante. "She's an angel. Was an angel. Maybe she still is. I don't know. Fuck, I don't know. I don't know what she is."

He reached out and gripped my arms, shaking me slightly to get my attention again. "Look, you're losing me. I don't know how an angel falling ties into Nyx. *If* it ties into Nyx. You've gotta calm down and start from the beginning. Take a deep breath." I did. "Now another." I did. "Now talk."

I did.

It was hard at first, and I had a few false starts. Finally, however, I was able to back up and explain the cast of angels to Dante. The story slowly spilled from my lips, and I told him all about what had happened: Nyx's capture, Joel's death, and Yasmine's fall.

He kept his hands on my arms when I finished, and I later realized it was to steady me. I was shaking. Several quiet minutes passed as we sat there. He exhaled at last and shook his head.

"Fuck, succubus. That's a lot for one night. Even for you." He touched my chin with his hand and tilted my face up. "But you know angels fall. You know they *still* fall. All the time."

"But I've never seen it," I whispered. "In all this time . . .

I've never known anyone who was an angel and then became a demon. All the demons I know . . . well, they've *always* been demons. I never saw them when they were angels."

"First time for everything."

I met his eyes. "But I *liked* her."

I expected some comment like, "Bad things happen to good people." Instead, he just shook his head. "I'm sorry."

I swallowed back tears—I'd already cried enough tonight— and leaned forward, resting my head against his chest, just as I had the other night. He ran a hand down my hair and rocked me.

"What hope is there?" I asked. "If even angels fall, what hope is there for the rest of us?"

"There isn't," he said. "We're on our own. And we have to make the choices we think are best for our own survival. If your angel friend had been thinking like that, she wouldn't have fallen."

"But that's the thing . . . angels don't think about themselves, right? They're selfless."

"Maybe," he said doubtfully. "She let things get that far with the nephilim . . . that wasn't really selfless. Now they're both fucked, and we've got another member in the club."

"What club?"

"*The* club. Our club. The one for people who make one mistake and are punished forever because of it." He paused. "It's a pretty big club."

I gently pulled out of the embrace. "What did you do?"

"Hmm?"

"Your one mistake. Vincent found the charm . . . he said it was horrible. Black magic. He said you had to have done something really bad to make it."

Dante's eyes were sad as he regarded me. "You really want to know?"

I nodded.

"No. You don't. Right now, for the first time, you're talking to me like maybe I'm not the biggest asshole on earth. I tell you the truth . . . and you'll lose all respect for me."

"I won't. I'll respect you more."

He rolled his eyes. "People always say noble things in hypothetical situations. 'I'd never cheat on my spouse.' 'I'd return the million dollars that I found on the street.' It's bullshit."

"It's not," I argued. "I respect the truth."

"But you won't like it. Why do you think I didn't kiss you that day outside Erik's? I joke about wanting to sleep with you—hell, I do want to sleep with you—but if we'd done it, you'd have felt how little energy I really have."

"I buy the low energy thing, but I still want to know the story behind it."

His eyes narrowed in frustration. "Look, succubus. I don't even think I could tell the story if I wanted to. It's too hard."

His comment about kissing suddenly inspired me. "Can you show me?"

"What?"

I moved toward him. "Kiss me. I can hardly get any energy from you, but if you open yourself to the memory, I should be able to feel pieces of it."

I hoped that was true, at least. While my lovers' thoughts and feelings came through to me during sex, it wasn't exactly a system we could control. I couldn't summon up specific things. Usually what I felt was whatever the guy was thinking about just then. More often than not, it was amazement or perhaps a guilty conscience over the lover he was cheating on.

But maybe . . . maybe if Dante was specifically thinking of whatever he had done, it would come through. It was worth a shot. I leaned closer to him. He didn't move, so I went in all the way and kissed him.

Initially, it was just a kiss—all physical. Gradually, I started to get a bit of his life force—but it was just like he'd said. His soul was too dark. The life energy that flowed into me was barely a trickle. It was only a few drops, like a leaking faucet. Then . . . once I'd assessed the energy, I felt something else. I felt his soul—felt why it was so black, so devoid of the shining life most humans had. That blackness began pouring into me, that sickening and oozing evil . . . and there, behind it, was despair and anger and hopelessness and frustration. It was nauseating. Blackness and blood. I wanted to pull away, but I had to see what he was hiding.

The memory came through to me in disjointed images, but I was able to piece them together and form a narrative. I saw a sister. Older than him by ten years. She'd taken care of him throughout his childhood—both in a motherly way and as an instructor. She was a psychic too. She'd taught him how to harness his power, to tap the magic of the world that was unseen to most humans. She had been powerful, but he was even stronger. It hadn't been enough, though. He'd wanted more than to simply control his power—he'd wanted to enhance it. But as Hugh and Vincent had told me, few humans were born with the magnitude of power that he'd craved.

So, he'd taken it. Ripped it out.

From her.

I saw his face when he killed her, felt his pain as the dagger touched her throat. She was half-mother and half-sister to him, but he stole her life anyway. And with that act, his power had grown by magnitudes—both because he'd gained hers and because of the spell involved. The blood of the innocent always brings power, and the black magic intertwined in this death brought it in spades. It had left him feeling like a god.

And wishing he were dead.

He'd damned himself. He still loved the power, still loved wielding it . . . but after killing his sister, he'd hated himself. He'd withdrawn from the world, trying to bury his memories in drugs and alcohol, only occasionally using his powers for small, nickel-and-dime con jobs.

I broke the kiss, not wanting to see or feel anymore. If we went further, I'd probably see what he had to do to make the charm. It wouldn't be as bad as what he'd done to his sister, but I was through with all this. Wide-eyed, I scooted away from him on the floor.

"She was Erik's lover," I said softly. I'd had a brief glimpse of Tanya—that was her name—and Erik together. "She was the woman in the picture. That's why he hates you."

Dante nodded. "The three of us . . . we were going to do great things. We were all so fucking talented, you know?" He rested a hand on his head, eyes full of grief. "Unsurprisingly, Erik chose to end our friendship after this. He wanted to kill me . . . he should have. He really should have. But, well. He's not that kind of guy."

"No," I agreed, voice cold. "He's not." I stood up and backed away from Dante, who was still sitting on the floor.

He looked up and realized what I was doing. The miserable face turned angry. "Leaving so soon?"

"Yes."

"Well. Thanks for stopping by. And thanks for proving me right."

"About . . . ?"

He threw his hands in the air. "This. I told you you'd hate me."

"I don't—" I stopped. I did hate him. I couldn't help it, not after seeing how much he and his sister had loved each other. Not after realizing how much this must have hurt Erik. "Dante . . . what you did . . ."

"Was a mistake. One I would take back if I could. One mistake to damn me forever. Just like your angel friend. Just like you."

"No," I said. "It's not the same. Yasmine fell because of love."

"She fell because of selfishness," he argued. "But I won't challenge that point. Tell me about you. Did you fall because of love?"

I didn't say anything. I'd fallen because of lust. I'd cheated on my husband because I was hurt and lonely and bored and . . . well, because I could.

Dante regarded me sharply. "You see? I get it. You fucked up too. I understand you—you're not going to find too many people who do. I bet your boyfriend doesn't."

"He accepts me."

"But does he understand? Have you ever told him in painstaking detail what you did?"

"No, but it doesn't matter."

Dante stood up and approached me. "It does matter! Being with him is a joke. It can't work. I'm not saying you have some great romantic future with me either, but at the very least, you should stick with people who know where you've come from."

"Right. Hanging out with you means I'd just drink and hate life."

"Your point?"

"Seth makes me hope for better things. Makes me want to be better."

"But there's no point!" exclaimed Dante. "Why don't you get that? Things can't change for you. Even your own fucking palms say so."

"No . . . Nyx said . . . Nyx said the dream could come true. The man in the dream—"

"—was her scamming you. You would have fallen for it, too, if your angel hadn't fallen first."

I clenched my teeth. "Her dreams are true. Seth and I—"

"—are going to get married? Run off into the sunset? Have babies? Succubus! Wake up!" Dante was shouting, his face inches from mine. "It can't happen. Not for you. Maybe it can for him—but not *with* you. Every day you spend with him just ensures his life is going to be as empty and meaningless as yours."

"That's not true!" I screamed. "We're happy. We're going to be happy together, and I don't care if you don't believe me.

I'm never going to see or speak to you again. I know why Erik hates you, and I hate you too." I kicked the door open. "You deserve to burn in Hell."

I left him, but I still couldn't make myself go home. With nothing else to do, I simply found a twenty-four-hour diner and drank coffee, pointedly ignoring anyone who talked to me. I watched the sun come up over the Olympic Mountains and finally went to work when the bookstore opened. I helped out with the last-minute Christmas rush, doing mindless and mechanical tasks. We were closing early that day, and everyone was finishing up their shopping. It was hectic and crazy, but it gave my zombie-like body something to do.

When we closed, it was nearly time for me to take Maddie to the airport. She needed a few more Christmas purchases herself and asked if I'd swing downtown with her. After witnessing the death of an angel, shopping seemed like the most trivial thing in the world. Still . . . I had nothing else to do, so I agreed. I probably would have agreed to anything.

Downtown Seattle was decked out in its Christmas finery, with lights and wreaths strung along the shopping nexus that centered around Fourth Avenue. At four in the afternoon, it was already dark outside. Rain pounded down on the pavement, the kind of torrential downpour most people believed we had year-round. Really, it only rained in the winter, and that was usually a drizzly type. This heavy stuff was a rare event, as though perhaps the heavens mourned Joel's passing.

Through a window, I watched the rain and pedestrians fighting with umbrellas while Maddie searched in Banana Republic for something for her sister. I'd half-heartedly looked for a present for Seth, but my motivation eventually faded, and anyway, there was no way to compete with the ring. I still wore it around my neck. It felt heavy today.

Along with my grief over what had happened to Yasmine, I still kept thinking about Nyx. In particular, I kept thinking about what she'd said to me. *The man in the dream.* Who was the man in the dream? The question consumed me, as futile as it was. I kept repeating Dante's words, trying to tell myself it didn't matter—that the whole thing had been a hoax. But that dark silhouette still haunted my mind's eye, and some part of me believed that if I knew his identity, then maybe it could all be real.

"Georgina?"

I turned from the rainy street and saw Vincent standing in front of me. Beyond him, a preoccupied Maddie flipped through a rack of cardigans. I'd thought he looked grief-stricken in my apartment, but that was nothing compared to what I saw now. His face was pinched and pale. His eyes were glassy and red, but whether from crying or lack of sleep, I couldn't say. Probably both.

He handed me my apartment key. "Just wanted to give this back."

I took it. "You didn't need to find me for that. You could have left it."

"Yeah." He stuffed his hands in his pockets and looked at the ground. "I guess I just . . . wanted to talk to someone."

"Have you, um, seen Yasmine?"

He shook his head. "Nope. I don't know what happened to her. I mean, I *know* . . . she's off somewhere in Hell. Maybe they have orientation or something. I don't know. Whatever it is, it must be awful. And it's my fault."

"It's not," I said automatically. "It was her choice."

"She did it for me, though."

"It doesn't matter why. The point is that she did it willingly. It isn't your place to question the decisions she makes."

As the words left my mouth, I had a total *holy shit* moment. I was saying exactly what everyone had been telling me about Seth. I was saying exactly what Seth himself had been telling me for so long.

"I guess. I don't know." He sighed. "It's so fucking stupid too. All these years, we've been so cautious to stay at arm's length, so she wouldn't fall. We were so good—holding back from what we wanted. And then, we get the same results from a stupid moment of confusion and passion. It just happened so fast, you know? I acted to protect her, she acted to protect me . . ." He trailed off and looked as though he might weep. I kind of felt like that myself. *It's a pretty big club*, Dante had said.

"But . . . if she's already fallen . . . well. Maybe you guys can be together now."

Vincent shook his head and gave me a small smile that made him look sadder than when he hadn't been smiling. "I don't know. I don't even know if she'll meet with me now. Something tells me she won't want me to see her like that."

"And how do you feel?"

"I love her unconditionally . . . or, well, at least . . . I loved Yasmine the angel unconditionally. She's not that woman anymore. I mean, she may hate what's happened . . . she may be miserable. But eventually, she'll settle in. They always do. And then she'll be one of them. She won't be the same Yasmine, and I don't know if I can love her or if she can love me. Part of what made her such a great person was that she resisted that temptation . . . and I think she felt the same about me."

I forgot Vincent for a moment as my attention turned inward, toward my own situation. Again, it was like Seth and me, I realized. The continual tension in our arrangement was a pain, yet the morals it was based on were part of what attracted us. He might have said he was okay with us not having sex, but I think some part of him loved me because of my continual refusal to give in to that. Likewise, I loved his steadfastness—not only in abstaining from me but from other lovers as well. It was part of what had made the fight so shocking. I didn't expect him to be weak.

And yet . . . even if we admired each other for our principles, was it worth it? And had that really been weakness on his part? Vincent and Yasmine had been together much longer than Seth and I had, torturing themselves in the same way. In the end, it had done them no good. Things had unfolded as they had.

"Star-crossed love isn't as glamorous as it seems," Vincent said, perhaps guessing my thoughts.

"I never believed it was."

"Sometimes I think . . . well, maybe it would have been better if she and I had never been together at all. These years have been wonderful . . . but well, she'd still be the woman I loved if I'd never gotten involved."

I didn't know about that. Surely, brief moments of joy were worth the pain that might follow? Wasn't that why I was with Seth, despite knowing he'd eventually die? Maybe Seth had been right about taking chances. Life was short. Maybe you needed to seize what good you could. It was all so confusing, and all of a sudden, I wanted to talk to Seth about all of this—about living life and taking risks, about what made us love one another, and about what made our relationship worth fighting for. I didn't want to make the mistakes Yasmine and Vincent had. Seth and I needed to sit down with open minds and make this thing with us work.

"What are you going to do now?" I asked Vincent. I didn't think now was the best time to argue relationship philosophy with him.

He gestured vaguely behind him. "Leave town. Even being masked, I know they're looking for me. I need to hide out somewhere."

I nodded. I was sad to see him go, but I knew what the other angels and demons would do if they found him. So, I wished him well and shared a brief hug before he departed. As I watched him leave, I again pondered the cautionary tale he represented. Growing anxious, I hoped this airport trip would go quickly so that I could call Seth.

Wandering to the other side of the store, I found Maddie paying for her purchases.

"Who was that guy?" she asked me, handing over her credit card. "He was cute. Bedraggled . . . but cute."

"He's had a long day," I told her. And a long eternity to go. "He's just a friend."

"Is he single?"

I thought about it. "Yeah, I guess he is."

While I waited for her, I looked over at a nearby mirror. Maddie was still going strong with her new cute and stylish self. She'd gotten a haircut too, the layering of which made her face appear delicate and lovely. The slacks and sweater, though simple, looked sleek and elegant on her.

By contrast, I looked kind of like the ugly stepsister. Oh, I still had the nice figure and pretty face born of shape-shifting, but I'd thrown on jeans and an old coat, not really concerned with high fashion today. I also hadn't bothered to shape-shift my hair. I'd simply brushed it into a high ponytail. Most telling of all was my face. I wore as much grief as Vincent. There was a hollowness to my eyes that startled me. It counteracted all the other beauty of my features. Glancing back at Maddie, I realized she was the hot one today.

When we finally hit the road to the airport, traffic was as horrible as I'd expected. I-5 was at a standstill, and with my luck lately, there was probably an accident up ahead to compound the rush hour and holiday mess. Sighing, I settled back into my seat.

"Okay," I told Maddie, desperately needing distraction. "What's the report? What adventurous things have you done? I'm pretty sure you've more than met your quota."

"Well," she began. "There's the new clothes, of course. You've seen a lot of them, and I own more lingerie than I ever have in my life. I was always kind of afraid of it, but there's so much cute stuff out there, you know?"

"Yup. I sure do."

"I got a bunch of high heels too. I'm still kind of learning to walk in them, but I'm doing okay, I think." She groaned and looked like the snarky feminist writer she was. "I feel like . . . well, like a *girl*."

I smiled and looked at the cars ahead of me. All the variables were in place for an accident, so I had to be careful. In this kind of stop and go, people tended to cease paying attention and fall into a lull. That was how cars got rear-ended. It was also an oddity that Seattle drivers had trouble driving in the rain.

"You seemed fine in the heels to me. What else have you done? Other than shopping?"

"I signed up for a judo class."

"You did not."

"I so did," she said, laughing. "It was the craziest class I could think of. Besides, I can finally get back at Doug after all those years he used to pull my hair."

"Well-deserved," I said. I moved over to the farthest lane, with the futile hope that it might move a fraction faster. "Anything else?"

"Mmm . . . well. I started looking for my own place."

"That's a good idea."

"And checking out flights to some places I've always wanted to see."

"Another good idea."

"And I slept with Seth."

I nearly drove into the median.

"What?" I said, jerking the wheel back to my own lane. Maddie had her hands stretched out protectively. "Did you say Seth?"

"Yeah . . ."

"Seth *Mortensen*?"

She sounded incredulous. "Of course. Who else?"

It was one of those things that was so ludicrous, I couldn't even fully react. It was like saying, "Hey, did you notice the earth just exploded?" It wasn't real because all the rest of the data in your known world said it was impossible. My brain wasn't going to bother processing it yet. Wasted cells.

"How . . . I mean, what . . ." I shook my head. "Explain."

I could see by her face that she was dying to. This was what had been bursting in her in my office yesterday.

"Well, two nights ago, I ran back to the bookstore after closing because I'd left something. I saw Seth out in the parking lot. He'd been out somewhere and was coming back to get his car."

"Somewhere" was my apartment. That had been the night of the fight.

"Anyway," she continued. "He looked kind of down, and I remembered what you'd said about taking risks. Plus, he still owed me the date, right? So, I asked him out for a drink, and he said sure."

I tried not to drive into the median again. "He didn't *drink*, did he?"

"No, not alcohol. But we stayed out really late, and we had a great time. You can't even imagine how great he is to talk to. He comes across as shy, but once you get to know him . . ." She sighed happily. "He thinks like I do too . . . wants to do all sorts of things, go places . . . Anyway, the place finally closed, and he asked if I wanted to go hang out at his place for a while."

I couldn't even look at her now. "Seth . . . asked you back to his place?"

"Well, if we went back to mine, we'd have to hang out with Doug, and we just wanted to talk more. And we did . . . except, well, after a while . . . we stopped talking. And one thing kind of led to another." She exhaled, like she still couldn't believe it herself. "I never do things like that. Not so soon. But, well, he's a nice guy, you know? And I wanted to do something adventurous . . ."

No, no, no. This really wasn't happening. This was a dream. This was Nyx getting back at me for not helping her. She was sending me a nightmare, one I hoped I'd wake up from soon.

I didn't realize how long I'd been quiet until Maddie hesitantly asked, "Georgina? You still with me? You don't think . . . you don't think I was too easy, do you?" There was fear in her voice, fear of my disappointment and disapproval.

"Huh? No . . . no . . . of course not." I took a deep breath. "So, um, it was good?"

"Oh, yeah!" She gave a nervous giggle. "I can't believe I'm even talking about this. But, yeah, Seth's a great lover. He's really attentive."

"Yeah, I imagine he would be."

"God, I can't believe this happened."

That made two of us. "What's going to happen now? Was it . . . a fling?" After all, what else could it be? Seth was with me, right? I had no reason to be upset. I'd given him the go-ahead to get sex elsewhere. In fact . . . I had *told* him to that night. If he wanted to sleep with her, that was fine. But obviously, it meant nothing. It *had* to be a fling, right?

Right?

"I don't know," she admitted. "I hope not. I really like him . . . and it was so great. I feel like we really connected . . . like the auction hadn't just been because he felt sorry for me. He said he would call and we'd go out again sometime." Once more, she turned timid and unsure. "You don't think . . . you don't think he's the kind of guy who'd just say something like that and not mean it, do you?" She was the Maddie I'd known before, the one who looked up to me and wanted my guidance. The one who didn't trust men.

I stared ahead and decided maybe the heavens were weeping for me now. After several moments, I finally said, "No, Maddie. If he says he wants to go out, he means it. That's the kind of guy he is."

Chapter 24

Iknew I was going to live forever, but sometimes I had a hard time really understanding how long *forever* was. During that ride to the airport, however, I got a taste of what eternity might feel like.

Maddie spent almost the entire time talking about Seth. In fact, I'm pretty sure the only time she didn't was when she stopped to check her watch and ponder whether we would make it on time. I knew we would make it on time because I would stop the car and carry her on my back before I'd risk her missing her flight and needing to ride back with me to the city. Once she'd decided we were still okay with time, it was back to Seth. Seth, Seth, Seth.

I'm pretty sure there were only about three people in the world I wouldn't have suspected of fucking with me if they'd come telling a story like this. Unfortunately, Maddie was one of them. She was telling the truth. It was written all over her, and something in me—maybe the part that really understood how serious the fight between Seth and me had been—could feel it.

After a while, my mind sort of went numb, and I stopped thinking about it all. I finally dropped her off at the airport and went home, barely aware of the traffic I once again had to fight my way through. When I got back to my apartment, I ate dinner and watched *A Christmas Carol*. A long, hot bath followed, and five shots of vodka finally put me down for the night. I slept on the couch because I couldn't bear to go in the room where an angel had fallen. Some Christmas Eve.

Seth came over the next morning to take me to dinner at Terry and Andrea's. Uneasiness radiated around him, but he still smiled when he saw me.

"You look great."

"Thanks."

I knew I did. I'd spent two hours getting ready, the last thirty minutes of which had been me simply standing in front of the mirror. I'd stood there, taking in every detail of my appearance. The clinging red dress. The curve of my neck under the glittering black choker. The way my golden-brown hair, worn sleek and smooth today, hung down my back. Gold eye shadow and black liner framed my eyes. My lips glowed under pale peach lip gloss. Even at five-four, my legs looked long and supple. My face, carved with high cheekbones and flawless skin, was beautiful.

I was beautiful.

Call it vanity or egotism, but it was true. I was so, so beautiful. More beautiful than Maddie. More beautiful than any mortal woman. Staring at that gorgeous reflection, I begged it to tell me that Seth would want me. He had to want me. How could he not?

But I knew all the beauty in the world couldn't mask the pain in me. And after a couple more moments, Seth noticed too. His smile vanished.

"How did you find out?" he asked.

I dropped the coat I'd been holding. "How do you think? She told me. She couldn't wait to tell me."

He sighed and sat on the arm of my couch and stared into space.

"That's it? You have nothing else to say?" I asked.

"I'm sorry. God, I'm really sorry. I didn't mean for you to find out like this."

"Were you ever going to tell me?"

"Yeah . . . of course."

His voice was so sweet and so gentle that it momentarily defused the anger that wanted to explode out of me. I stared at him, looking hard into those amber brown eyes. "She said . . . she said you didn't drink, but you did, right? That's what happened?" I sounded like I was Kendall's age and suspected I wore the pleading expression Yasmine had given Jerome.

Seth's face stayed expressionless. "No, Thetis. I wasn't drunk. I didn't drink at all."

I sank down into the armchair opposite him. "Then . . . then . . . what happened?"

It took a while for him to get the story out. I could see the two warring halves within him: the one that wanted to be open and the one that hated to tell me things I wouldn't like.

"I was so upset after what happened with us. I was actually on the verge of calling that guy . . . what's his name? Niphon. I couldn't stand it—I wanted to fix things between us. But just before I did, I ran into Maddie. I was so . . . I don't know. Just confused. Distraught. She asked me to get food, and before I knew it, I'd accepted." He raked a hand through his hair, neutral expression turning confused and frustrated. "And being with her . . . she was just so nice. Sweet. Easy to talk to. And after leaving things off physically with you, I'd been kind of . . . um . . ."

"Aroused? Horny? Lust-filled?"

He grimaced. "Something like that. But, I don't know. There was more to it than just that."

The tape in my mind rewound. "Did you say you were going to call Niphon?"

"Yeah. We'd talked at poker . . . and then he called me once. Said if I ever wanted . . . he could make me a deal. I thought it was crazy at the time, but after I left you that night . . . I don't know. It just made me wonder if maybe it was worth it to live the life I wanted *and* make it so you wouldn't have to worry so much."

"Maddie coming along was a blessing then," I muttered. Christ. Seth had seriously considered selling his soul. I really needed to deal with Niphon. He hadn't listened to me when I'd told him to leave Seth alone. I wanted to rip the imp's throat out, but my revenge would have to wait. I took a deep breath.

"Well," I told Seth. "That's that. I can't say I like it . . . but, well . . . it's over."

He tilted his head curiously. "What do you mean?"

"This. This Maddie thing. You finally had a fling. We've always agreed you could, right? I mean, it's not fair for me to be the only one who gets some. Now we can move on."

A long silence fell. Aubrey jumped up beside me and rubbed her head against my arm. I ran a hand over her soft fur while I waited for Seth's response.

"Georgina," he said at last. "You know . . . I've told you . . . well. I don't really have flings."

My hand froze on Aubrey's back. "What are you saying?"

"I . . . don't have flings."

"Are you saying you want to start something with her?"

He looked miserable. "I don't know."

No. This wasn't happening.

"What's this mean for us?" I asked.

"I don't know."

The anger returned, and I leapt up, much to Aubrey's annoyance. "What *do* you know?" I demanded. "Do you even know why you did this?"

"There were a lot of things going on . . ." he said. "A lot of factors. It just happened . . ."

I put my hands on my hips and stalked toward him. "Did it? Did it really? Because I'm not so sure."

His distraught expression turned wary. "What's that mean?"

"I think you were getting back at me for not giving in that night. I made you mad. I hurt you. So, you're trying to hurt me. Teach me a lesson."

"I—what? Are you insane? You think I'd do something

like this to teach you a lesson? You think I would *want* to hurt you? Just because you refused sex?"

"Why not?" I asked. "Guys always want sex from me. Why are you any different?"

"Georgina," he said incredulously. "You can't believe that. It's always been about more than sex. You have to know that. I've told you that over and over. I would never purposely hurt you. And yet . . ."

"And yet what?"

He looked away from me and focused on the carpet. "I don't know that we can keep going on *without* me hurting you."

"Well, if you don't sleep with my friends—"

"It doesn't even have to be that. There are so many things it could be. I could get hit by a car tomorrow or catch some disease. If you ever do crack some day and sleep with me, you'll hate yourself forever. And if *I* crack and sell my soul, that's going to upset you too. One way or another, you will get hurt. It's just a matter of when. I saw it that night in the kitchen—I saw your face when you were yelling at me. That's when I knew it was all true."

"I . . . I was upset," I told him. "And, I mean . . . we knew this relationship wouldn't be easy. You were okay with all this in the beginning . . . the sex and everything else. . . ."

"Things change," he said bluntly. He met my eyes, and I again saw warring sides within him. "And back then, I thought *I* was the one who would get hurt, not you. I can handle it."

"Are you saying I can't?"

"I'm saying I don't want to find out. And honestly, it's not even about sex either. We've got communication problems, time problems . . . I don't know. Hell, we have death problems. I don't really know if we should keep doing this."

It felt like Joel's death again, like all the energy was being sucked away from me.

"How," I demanded, "can you always lecture me about

open communication and then dump this on me *now*? If you were feeling all this . . . you should have brought it up before-hand, not in some bluff break-up at the zero hour."

"I'm not entirely sure what that last part meant, but I'm not bluffing. And I've tried to talk to you about this. I tried the night you massaged me—you didn't want to hear it." Seth took a deep breath. "Georgina . . . I really mean it. I don't think we should be together anymore."

I gaped. No, this wasn't right. This wasn't right at all. I'd expected a big fight, one we'd eventually get over, like al-ways. I'd expected him to ask for forgiveness. I'd expected to set new boundaries in the relationship. I'd expected *me* to be the one to have the high ground and decide if we were going to continue this.

I hadn't expected to be pleading.

"No. *No*. Seth . . . we've just got to make it work. Look, I'll get over Maddie, okay? And if you want to sleep with other women . . . I mean, it is okay. I always said you could. It's just this first time . . . well, it's a shock, that's all." He just continued to watch me quietly, and I found myself babbling on more and more. "But we can make it work. We always do. We'll find a way. You can't just go ahead and decide something like this on your own. There are two of us in this, you know."

"Yeah," he said. "I do know. And I'm one of the two. And I want to split up."

"No," I said frantically. "You don't *want* to. This is just some weird . . . I don't know. You don't mean it."

Seth's silence was more infuriating than if he'd shouted back at me. He just kept watching me, letting me talk. His expression had so much regret—but so much determination too.

"You were the one who told me we could overcome any-thing," I cried. "Why not this?"

"Because it's too late."

"It can't be. If you do this . . . it's all for nothing . . . you'll have ended up hurting me. Me and Maddie both."

"It's a small hurt compared to what could really happen," he said. "And as for Maddie . . . I don't plan on hurting her. I . . . I like her."

"But you *love* me."

"Yeah, I do. I probably always will. But maybe that's not enough. I have to move on. We can't do this. I think maybe . . . I don't know. I think something good could happen with me and Maddie. In some ways, she's like you, only—"

Seth had started to slip into the rambling he sometimes did when nervous enough. He bit his lip now, as though he might summon the words back, and looked away.

"Only what?" I asked. I could barely hear my own voice.

He turned his gaze back to me, firm and unflinching. "Only . . . more human."

And that was it. All the anger and sorrow vanished. There was nothing in me. Nothing at all. I was empty.

"Get out," I said.

He paled. Something in my voice and expression must have been truly terrifying. Tentatively, he extended a hand.

"I never meant to hurt you. Thetis, I'm sorr—"

"Don't *ever* call me that again," I told him, stepping away. I didn't know how any of these words were coming out of my mouth. It was like someone else was controlling me. "Leave. Now."

He opened his mouth, and I thought all that resolve he'd just shown might crumble. In the end, it didn't.

He left.

Chapter 25

I'd sworn I'd never go back into my bedroom, but just then, I needed my bed. I spent the rest of the day in it, curled up in the proverbial fetal position. Much like when I'd made Seth leave, I didn't feel anything. I was dead inside. There was nothing left, nothing in my life, nothing to keep me going. Some wise part of my brain said I should cry. I knew there was grief inside of me, grief that would eventually explode. But I was blocking it for now, afraid to acknowledge that all of this was real or face the consequences. This, I realized, was why Yasmine had screamed. It was a terrible thing to be cut off from something you loved so much. To be cut off from the thing that gave your existence meaning.

Hours passed, and light and shadows moved across my bedroom as the sun began its descent. My room grew dark, but I didn't bother flipping on the lights. I didn't have the energy or motivation.

I don't know how much time passed before I heard the knock. At first, I wasn't even sure that's what it was. Then, it sounded again—definitely someone knocking on my front door. I stayed in bed, not wanting to see or talk to anyone. *What if it's Seth?* Some small part of me clung to that hope, that maybe he'd changed his mind. The rest of me didn't believe it. I'd seen the look in his eyes. The resolve. He wasn't coming back. And if he wasn't coming back, then there was no point in being social.

My visitor knocked a third time, louder still. Beside me, Aubrey turned her head toward the living room, then toward me, no doubt wondering why I wouldn't put a stop to the noise. With a sigh, I crawled out of bed and stalked toward the front of the apartment. Half-way there, I stopped. It wasn't Seth.

"Georgina!" wailed a twangy soprano voice. "I know you're in there. I can sense you." I'd sensed Tawny too, of course, which is why I'd stopped walking. I sighed again, wondering if it would be possible to ignore her. Probably not. Even if I didn't answer, she'd probably stand out there all day, now that she knew I was here.

I opened the door, expecting to be barreled into with tears and fanfare. Instead, I found Tawny standing calmly outside my door, hesitant to enter. Her eyes were wet after all, but she seemed to be trying very hard to rein herself in. The trembling of her lip suggested that wasn't going to be easy.

And she had a glow.

"C-can I come in?" she asked.

I stepped to the side and waved her in. "You want me to take you out for a drink to celebrate your conquest?"

That was it. She lost it. Sobbing into her hands, she sank down on to my loveseat. Still numbed from the Seth fallout, I had no mental energy to deal with this. Not enough energy to hate her, not enough energy to pity her. I was living apathy.

"Tawny, I—"

"I'm sorry!" she interrupted. "I'm so, so sorry. I didn't want to. I didn't want to do it. But he told me if I did that it'd pay off for both of us, that he'd pull strings to get me faster advancement and that I'd—"

"Whoa, hang on," I said. "Who's 'he'? Niphon?"

She nodded and produced a pack of tissues from her purse. At least she traveled prepared now. She blew her nose loudly before going on. "He told me to fake it—fake being bad. I mean . . . well, actually, I am kind of bad. Okay, a lot bad. I can't flirt like you. And I really can't dance." She paused a moment, as though this caused her particular pain. "But you were right in saying it was impossible for me to not get sex from *someone*. I did. I just lied and said I couldn't."

It was just as I'd suspected for a while now, but hearing her confirm it didn't really cheer me up. It was yet another reminder of all the miserable things in my life these last couple of weeks. Staring at her, I still couldn't bring myself to feel angry at her. Partially because I was still drained of feeling and partially because it just wasn't worth it. Niphon had used her to play me, but he'd played her too.

"You're a good liar," I told her finally. "I could never be sure if you were telling the truth or not—but you seemed to be. I'm usually good at reading people."

Tawny smiled, just a little, with something almost like pride. "I hustled people a lot when I was mortal. Worked some con jobs." The smile disappeared. "Until that asshole dumped me for a cheap blond whore. She had no idea what she was doing, but did he care? No. Dick. He's sorry now. They both are."

I blinked. I hadn't expected to hear that. I wasn't sure I wanted to hear that. Suddenly, Tawny's initial desire to make men everywhere suffer made a lot more sense—as did the reason she might have sold her soul in the first place. I hoped her current appearance wasn't some weird bastardization of the cheap blond whore. Because that would just be kind of creepy.

"Well, um, I'm . . . sure they are. And you know, the skills you need to hustle and con aren't that different from seduction." Maybe it was the moving and talking, but as I sat there, my sluggish brain began to stir to life and analyze the situation. "Tawny, why are you telling me this? If you're working for Niphon, he's probably not going to appreciate you blowing his cover."

"You're right. He doesn't know I'm here. But . . . but I was afraid. I know it'll all come out if you tell, and I don't want to go down with him! I thought if I came and talked to you and told you what happened that maybe . . . maybe you could forgive me. I'm starting to like it here. I don't want to leave. And if they punish him, they'll punish me too and—"

"Wait, wait. Stop again. Punish him for what? For getting you to lie?" I frowned. "And what is it I'm going to tell?"

Tawny was so surprised that she forgot to sniffle. "About her."

"Her?"

"That—that hag. The one who came into my dreams . . ."

"Nyx? Oh. That really is how you hid your glow. Hugh was right."

"I hated it," said Tawny vehemently. "Every time he made me go to her so she could suck me out. And then I'd have such weird dreams."

Think, Georgina, think! It was all coming together here if I could just put my own romantic disaster off to the side of my mind for a moment.

"You . . . went to Nyx willingly? To have your energy sucked out so I wouldn't find out that you were lying?" Tawny nodded. My brain hurt. "And he—Niphon—made you, and—" I stopped. "Niphon knew about Nyx. You both did. And how to find her."

"He's the one who got her to come here when she escaped. Promised her two succubi," sniffed Tawny. She gave me a puzzled look. "I thought . . . I thought you knew all that? I heard you were there when they captured her . . ."

Tawny looked a little nervous, like she was wondering if maybe she'd done the wrong thing in betraying Niphon. As for me, I was suddenly reliving the battle back in my bedroom and Nyx's offer to help me get revenge on the one who'd sent her after me. . . .

Niphon.

"Niphon?" I exclaimed. "Niphon sent a crazy chaos goddess after me? Why? Why does he hate me that much?"

Tawny's eyes went wide, no doubt surprised at my sudden outburst. "I . . . I don't know. He just said that he wanted to make things difficult for you. Screw up your life. Maybe get you sent away."

Hugh's words came back to me. *All I know is that when an imp shows up and is going to this much trouble over something, the evidence suggests it's big.*

My heart raced, and I grabbed hold of her hand. "Tawny. Did he ever say anything about my contract? Any contract at all?"

She shook her head frantically, tousling her blond curls even more than they already were. "No, not while I was around."

"Are you sure? Think! Think of anything, anything at all he might have said to explain why he did what he did."

"No, nothing!" She broke her hand away. "I'm telling you the truth this time. He just made it sound as though . . . well, like he didn't like you. He wanted you to be unhappy. Suffer. I don't know."

Niphon. So many things could be laid at his feet.

According to Tawny, he'd used her to make me look like a bad mentor (which I was, kind of) and possibly get sent away. The imp had also talked to Seth about selling his soul—despite my warnings. Seth's decision to leave me had been his own, true. But, I realized, Niphon had played a role in getting Seth to think about such things. The distraction Nyx had caused—which apparently Niphon had brought about too—had cut me off from spending time with Seth. Realizing how close he'd been to selling his soul had driven Seth away. The fear of how that would affect him and me both had been too strong—strong enough that he chose to walk away from me.

"Georgina?"

I made a decision then. It wasn't going to change what had happened with Seth and me, but it was going to make me feel better.

"Georgina?" repeated Tawny, peering at me. "Are you okay? You aren't going to get me sent away, are you? Georgina?"

I rose from my chair, surprised at how my muscles had become kinked. No longer wanting to be dressed up, I shape-shifted out of the dress and into jeans and an empire cut sweater. Black. Like my mood. I glanced over at Tawny.

"You want to go to a party with me?"

I drove us over to Peter and Cody's, where the "evil" holiday party was taking place. I barely noticed that it was raining again. I walked up the building's stairs like one going to her own funeral, grim and purposeful—and with enough speed that Tawny had to scurry to keep up in her stilettos. When I felt the immortal signatures within the apartment, smug relief flooded me upon discovering Niphon was still there.

Peter opened the door before I finished knocking. He wore a red sweater with an appliqué Santa on it. It matched his tree, of course.

"Look at this," he said sarcastically. "She deigns to show up and join us lowly—"

I strode past him without a word. He gaped. Moving through the room, I was vaguely aware of the others there. Jerome. Cody. Hugh. But I didn't want any of them.

Niphon, standing with a glass of wine, regarded me with curious amusement as I headed straight for him. Considering I usually avoided him if it all possible, my approach undoubtedly astonished him.

But not as much as when I punched him.

I didn't even need to shape-shift much bulk into my fist. I'd caught him by surprise. The wineglass fell out of his hand, hitting the carpet and spilling its contents like blood. The imp flew backward, hitting Peter's china cabinet with a crash. Niphon slumped to the floor, eyes wide with shock. I kept coming. Kneeling, I grabbed his designer shirt and jerked him toward me.

"Stay the fuck out of my life, or I will destroy you," I hissed.

Terror filled his features. "Are you out of your fucking mind? What do you—" Suddenly, the fear disappeared. He started laughing. "He did it, didn't he? He broke up with you. I didn't know if he could do it, even after giving him the spiel about how it'd be better for both of you. Oh my. This is lovely. All your so-called charms weren't enough to—ahh!"

I'd pulled him closer to me, digging my nails into him, and finally, I felt an emotion. Fury. Niphon's role had been greater than I believed. My face was mere inches from his.

"Remember when you said I was nothing but a back-woods girl from some gritty fishing village? You were right. And I had to survive in gritty circumstances—in situations you'd never be able to handle. And you know what else? I spent most of my childhood gutting fish and other animals." I ran a finger down his neck. "I can do it for you too. I could slit you from throat to stomach. I could rip you open, and you'd scream for death. You'd wish you weren't immortal. And I could do it over and over again."

That wiped the smirk off Niphon's face. Behind me, the rest of the room had come to life.

"For fuck's sake," yelled Jerome. "Get her off him."

Strong hands pulled me back, Cody and Hugh each grabbing one of my arms. I fought against them, struggling to get back to a cringing Niphon. My friends were too strong. I couldn't break free and didn't have the life left to shape-shift added bulk.

"Get rid of him, Jerome!" I yelled. "Get rid of him, or I swear to God, I really will rip him apart. He set me up to fail with Tawny. He brought Nyx here, for fuck's sake! *Get rid of him*!"

I saw my boss's face. He didn't like being yelled at or or-dered around—particularly in front of others. His face was hard and angry. I could tell he was about to tell me to shut up, and then something in his expression shifted. He turned his attention back to Niphon.

"Get out," the demon said.

Niphon stared open-mouthed. Very fishlike, actually.

"Jerome! You can't just—"

"Get out. I know what you were trying to do, but you shouldn't have done it behind my back. Go back to your hotel, and be out of town by tomorrow."

Niphon still wanted to protest. But then, he looked at Jerome, looked at me, and then looked at Jerome again. Swallowing, the imp scrambled to his feet and grabbed a briefcase sitting on the couch. With one more glance back at me, he ran out the door.

Jerome's gaze fell on Tawny, who was pressing herself against the wall in a futile effort to disappear.

"It's not her fault," I said quickly. "Don't punish her."

Jerome studied her a few more moments before sighing impatiently. "Later. I'll deal with you later." I wasn't sure if that was a good thing or not, but the fact that he hadn't smote her on the spot was a positive sign. Judging from the grateful look on her face, she agreed.

Cody and Hugh still had a death grip on me, but after several moments, they released me. I sagged with exhaustion, surprised to see I was breathing heavily.

Tension filled the room. Finally, Cody said, "Where did you learn to throw a right hook?"

"You don't live through the Dark Ages without learning stuff like that," mused Peter. He glanced at the spilled wine and sighed. "Club soda's not going to get that out."

"Georgie," said Jerome in a rumbling voice. "Do not *ever* speak to me like that."

I steadied my breathing and swallowed back the bloodlust coursing through me. I met Jerome's dark eyes defiantly.

"Noted," I said. Then, unable to handle my friends' looks of both astonishment and concern, I ran out of the apartment. I made it down one flight of stairs before collapsing and sitting on the landing. I buried my face in my hands and started sobbing. The grief had finally won.

A few minutes later, I heard footsteps on the stairs. Hugh

sat down beside me and put his arms around me. I pressed my face to his chest and kept crying.

"You'll get over this," he said quietly.

"No. I will never get over this. I'm alone. I wish I was dead."

"No, you don't. You're too wonderful and have too many people who love you."

I lifted my head and looked at him. I'd never seen his face so compassionate, so serious—except when he'd yelled at Seth during poker. I sniffed and ran a hand over my wet eyes.

"We broke up. This is what you wanted. You didn't want me and Seth to be together."

Hugh shook his head. "I like Seth. I want you to be happy. If you could be together without all the heartache, I'd send you on with my blessing. But I don't think that's possible. I think this is best."

"You told him the only way I'd let him go is if he hurt me, if he was an asshole. Do you think that's why he did it? Slept with Maddie? Because only something drastic would drive me away?"

Hugh looked surprised at the reference to Maddie. "I don't know, sweetie. I don't know what he was thinking."

Sighing, I leaned back into him. "I will never get over this."

"You will."

"It's going to take a lot of time."

"Well, you have a lot of time."

Chapter 26

New Year's Eve.

Warren, Emerald City's owner, had thrown a swank party at his house and invited the whole staff, along with about fifty others. His house was enormous, and he'd spared no expense. Waiters worked the crowd. A bartender made drinks with great flourish. A DJ spun music in the corner. It was probably the most elaborate party I'd been to all year. Everyone was having a great time.

Well, except me, naturally.

Maddie and Seth were there. Together. It was strange to see them out as a couple so openly, after all the time he and I had spent hiding our relationship. But when she'd arrived back in Seattle a few days ago, she'd made no attempts at secrecy. Everyone at the store had known within twenty-four hours, and it was still a source of much buzzing and speculation. The general consensus was that they were cute.

And, watching them, I supposed that if I weren't so intimately involved, I'd think they were cute too. Mostly they made me want to go throw up the caviar I'd just eaten. They stood together with a few other staff across the room, holding hands. Maddie glowed like a succubus, talking animatedly to Beth about something. Seth, dressed up for a change and looking gorgeous, listened with a small smile—though there was something solemn in his eyes. He looked uncomfortable, and I strongly suspected he'd been brought here at Maddie's urging. I didn't think he was the type who'd come and rub their relationship in my face, but then, I'd never thought he'd break up with me either.

Just then, he glanced up to scan the room and met my gaze. By accident or on purpose, I couldn't say. We held each other's eyes for a moment. His expression grew troubled, wistful. I don't know what mine looked like. A moment later, he turned his attention back to the others. But the small smile was gone.

"Makes you want to brush your teeth, doesn't it?"

Doug approached me, holding what I believed to be his fifth rum and coke. I pointed to it.

"What, all that sugar you're drinking?"

He grinned. "I mean my sister and Mortensen, as well you know."

I gave them one more glance, then turned back to him. "Everyone thinks they're cute."

"I guess. I can't decide how to feel." He knocked back his drink. "I mean, he's sleeping with my sister, right? I'm supposed to be, like, outraged and want to defend her honor. Or something. But part of me's thinking maybe they'll hit it off so well that she'll move in with him. And that kind of makes me . . . happy."

Ugh. Bad enough they were dating at all. Moving in together? I couldn't even think that far ahead. They'd only been an item for a week. I silently counted to five and tried not to say something I'd regret.

"Who can say?" I murmured vaguely.

Doug tilted his head as he regarded me. "Always figured you'd be the one going after him, what with your hero worship and his erotic stories about you." He was referring to a short story of Seth's that had appeared in a magazine not too long ago. The kinky heroine bore an uncanny—and completely coincidental—resemblance to me.

I could tell by his voice and face that Doug was joking. He'd never believed there had been anything between Seth and me. Little did he know how close to home his joke hit.

"Well," I told him. "Looks like your sister's going to be the one in the erotic stories now."

Doug paled. "Oh my God. I never thought of that." He glanced at his empty glass. "I gotta get another one."

I watched him go and felt a smile tug at my lips, despite my resolution to be miserable.

And I was definitely doing a good job at the miserable part. I didn't approach anyone at the party and only spoke a few words to those who tried to engage me in conversation. I'd already turned down several men who'd tried to fetch me a drink or get me to dance. I just wanted to be alone. Really, I shouldn't have come.

"Never thought I'd see you alone at an event like this."

I'd felt his presence behind me before I heard him. "Carter, you party crasher. I know you didn't get an invitation."

"Hey, I heard this was the place to be."

"Isn't crashing one of the seven deadly—holy shit."

The angel had stepped in front of me. His chin-length blond hair was washed and brushed, and he wore khakis and a blue polo shirt. The ensemble was utterly casual and also the nicest thing I'd ever seen him in.

He laughed, knowing what had surprised me. "I couldn't show up like I usually do. I'm still underdressed compared to you." I had on a form-fitting satin dress with a collar that went all the way up to my neck. Black. Like my mood.

"Yeah," I said, "but if we're measuring comparison to our normal ware, you're the best-dressed person in here."

"This is a great party," he said, eyeing the room. He had a drink in his hand that I swore he hadn't had a moment ago. "You don't look like you're having a very good time."

I wasn't ready to talk about that yet, not to him. Averting my eyes, I stared absentmindedly to where Doug was hitting on some woman about twenty years older than he was. The DJ's current song ended, and the guitar notes of a new one kicked up. "Sweet Home Alabama."

"Oh, fuck," I said.

"What?" asked Carter.

"I hate this song."

"Really? I've always liked it."

I sighed. "What happened to Yasmine?"

His mocking humor faded. "You know what happened to her. She belongs to Hell now. I'm sure they'll make good use of her."

"But will she do it?" I asked. "Will she really turn her back on Heaven and fight?"

"They always do." It was exactly what Vincent had said. "Once she's spent enough time shunned by other angels and denied the face of the divine . . . well, she'll want to fight against Heaven."

"That's stupid. It's like she's . . . I don't know. Like she's being forced to go bad."

"She made the decision to fall."

"She did it out of love! You're always telling me that love is the most wonderful thing in the universe."

"It is. But an angel's love must be given to the power above first, then to humanity *as a whole* second. It can't be bestowed on just one person—human or nephilim."

"That's stupid. I think the nephilim have it right thinking all of us are messed up." I handed my glass to a passing waitress. It had been empty for a while. Hesitantly, I brought up something that was still troubling me, something this song wouldn't let me forget. "Carter . . . about Nyx. Her visions . . . are they always true?"

"As far as I know. They don't always play out like people think, though. Why do you ask?"

"No reason. Well, I mean, just curious about what she showed me."

"Ah. Yeah, that's tricky." He frowned. "Since she was actually manipulating you, it's hard to say . . . I don't know everything about her. What'd she show you?"

"It's not impor—"

The music abruptly stopped, and from across the room, I heard someone shouting numbers. "Ten . . . nine . . ."

I looked at a nearby clock. Nearly midnight.

"Eight . . . seven . . ."

People were getting out noise makers and drinks. Couples were getting close.

"Six . . . five . . ."

Maddie drew close to Seth. He leaned down toward her, looking nervous.

"Four . . . three . . ."

I clutched Carter's arm. I couldn't watch this. I couldn't watch Seth and Maddie kiss. "Get me out of here," I gasped, suddenly having trouble breathing.

"Two . . ."

"Carter! Get me—"

The world exploded in color around me. Cold night air blasted my face. Disoriented, I staggered and felt Carter catch my arm to steady me. We stood on top of a roof, directly facing the Space Needle. Fireworks burst around it in showers of rainbow sparks. The accompanying noise startled me, and I gasped. Farther away, other fireworks sparkled on the horizon.

"Best view in the city," joked Carter.

I stared around, still confused, until I was finally able to triangulate our position. "We're on top of the bookstore."

He released my arm, and we stood there watching the fireworks for several minutes. We were so close to the Space Needle that I could soon smell the smoke as the wind blew over us. I started to rub my arms, then remembered to shapeshift on a coat.

"A new year has all sorts of possibilities, Georgina," Carter finally said, eyes still on the show.

"Not for me. I've lost all mine. I've lost Seth. I screwed up."

"It's not all your fault. Relationships are symbiotic. Takes two to make them work, two to make them fall apart. Seth's got plenty of blame in this."

I shook my head. "No . . . the things he did. It was my fault."

"You're missing the big picture, Daughter of Lilith. You're forgetting Niphon's role. What was he trying to do?"

"Ruin my life," I said bitterly. "He had a part, yeah, but he complicated what I'd already messed up."

"Why? Why'd he do it?"

"Because he hates me."

Carter sighed. "You're not getting it."

I turned toward him. "What do you mean? What more is there to get?"

"Only so much I can tell you. Only so much I can interfere." He fell silent as a particularly showy burst of silver sparkles lit the night sky.

The deli conversation with Hugh came back to me. "Did . . . did he really mess something up with my contract? Is it flawed?"

"That's your side's business. I can't tell you anything about that." He sighed once more. "I can tell you that eternity is an awfully long time to keep accruing and carrying around guilt."

"Why do you care so much?" I demanded. "Why do you care so much about what happens to me and Seth?"

He looked back down at me. "I like happy endings. I like helping make them happen."

"Yeah, well. You kind of fucked this one up."

His old, cynical smile returned. "You want to go home?"

I turned toward the Space Needle. "I want to finish the show."

"Okay."

"Oh, hey. Wait." I reached into my purse and pulled out a cashmere knit hat. I handed it to him. "Merry Christmas. Sorry I didn't wrap it."

Carter examined his Secret Santa present, then put it on. "Neat."

When he did finally take me home, he used the same angelic teleportation that always made me slightly nauseous. Aubrey greeted my entrance, rubbing against my legs as I fumbled for the lights. Beneath the floor, it sounded like my neighbors were having a party.

I kicked my heels off in the middle of the living room floor and walked toward my bedroom, unbuttoning my dress as I went. I let it fall to the floor, happy to be free of the tight fabric. Opening my closet door, I knelt down and began rummaging through it until I unearthed the old shoe box again.

Reaching up to the spot just above my breastbone, I found Seth's ring on its chain. I unfastened it and held the ring in one hand for a long time, staring at its smooth, shining surface and winking sapphires. I took out the old worn ring from the box and held it in my other hand. For a while, I just sat there, looking back and forth between the two. They were different . . . and yet so alike. *You were destined for heartache. And are going to repeat that forever. You aren't learning. You aren't changing.*

With a sigh, I placed both rings into the box, next to a heavy gold cross. I closed the lid and shoved it all back into the closet.

It was over. It was all over.

Still half-naked, I walked back to where I'd dropped my purse and found my cell phone. I dialed a number and waited.

"Hello?"

"Dante? This is Georgina."

"Who?"

With a start, I realized I'd never actually told him my name. "The succubus."

"Oh." I had a feeling he'd already recognized my voice. "Happy New Year."

I took a deep breath.

"Are you free tonight?"

There was a long, pregnant pause.

"What about the man in the dream?" he finally asked.

"There is no man in the dream."

Please turn the page for an exciting sneak peek of
Richelle Mead's next Georgina Kincaid novel,
SUCCUBUS HEAT,
coming in June 2009!

Chapter 1

Sleeping with my therapist was a bad idea.

I knew it too, but I couldn't really help it. There were only so many times I could hear "Why don't you explain that" and "Tell me how you feel." So, I finally snapped and decided to *show* the guy how I felt. I've gotta say, for someone so moral who had never cheated on his wife, he wasn't that hard to take advantage of. And by "not hard," I mean "ridiculously easy." His pseudo morals gave me a strong succubus energy fix, and when you consider that what we did was probably the most productive thing that ever took place on his couch, it was almost like I did a good deed.

Still, I knew my boss was going to be pissed, seeing as he was the one who'd ordered me to seek counseling in the first place.

"Do *not* tell Jerome," I warned my friends, tapping my cigarette against the ashtray. "I don't want to deal with that kind of fallout."

My friends and I were sitting at a booth in Cold July, an industrial club down in Seattle's Belltown district. Because it was a private club, they didn't have to adhere to the city's public smoking ban, which was a perk for me. In the last few months, I'd found nicotine was one of the essential things helping me cope. Other things on the essential list: vodka,

Nine Inch Nails, a steady supply of moral men, and an all-purpose bitchy attitude.

"Look, Georgina," said my friend Hugh. He was an imp, a type of hellish legal assistant who bought souls for our masters and did assorted middle management tasks. "I'm no expert in mental health, but I'm going to go out on a limb here and say that probably wasn't a helpful step on the road to healing."

I shrugged and let my eyes scan the crowded room for potential victims. There were some pretty good pickings here. "Well, he wasn't that good. At therapy, I mean. Besides, I don't think I need it anymore."

Silence met me, in as much as silence could meet me in a place so noisy. I turned back to my friends. Hugh was making no pretense of hiding his *you're fucking crazy* look. Our vampire friends, Peter and Cody, at least had the decency to avert their eyes. I narrowed mine and put out the cigarette.

"I don't suppose," said Peter at last, "that this is anybody you'd maybe, uh, like to date long term?"

"Yeah," agreed Cody. "I bet a therapist would be a great listener. And you wouldn't even have to pay for it."

"My insurance pays for it," I snapped. "And I don't really appreciate your passive aggressive attitude about my boyfriend."

"You could do better, sweetie," said Hugh.

"The guy's corrupt and going to Hell. How is this a problem for you? And you didn't like my last boyfriend either. Maybe you should stop worrying about my love life and go back to figuring out how to get your latest secretary into bed."

In what had to be a weird twist of the universe, none of my friends liked my current boyfriend, a black magician named Dante. Dante's morals were pretty non-existent, and he owned stock in bitterness and cynicism. That would make you think he'd fit in perfectly with this group of damned souls, but for whatever reason, it didn't.

"You aren't meant to be with someone bad," said Cody. Cody was young compared to the rest of us immortals. Hugh claimed almost a century. Peter and I had millennia. As such, there was almost a naivety about Cody, a charming idealism that rivaled the kind I used to have.

It had been shattered when my previous boyfriend, a human named Seth, had left me for a friend of mine. Seth was a good soul, quiet and infinitely kind. He'd made me believe in better things, like that maybe there was hope for a succubus like me. I'd thought I was in love—no, I had been in love. Even I could admit that. But being a succubus, I brought a dangerous element to any relationship. When I had sex with a guy (or a girl—it worked either way), I stole their life energy, which was the power that fueled every human soul. It kept me alive and sustained my immortal existence. The purer the guy, the more energy I took. The more energy I took, the more I shortened his life. With Dante, I had almost no effect. He had little energy to give, so our sex life was relatively "safe," and I therefore sought my fixes from meaningless guys on the side.

With Seth . . . well, that had been a different story. Sleeping with him would have had detrimental effects—and I'd refused to do it. For a while, we'd lived on love alone, our relationship being about a lot more than a physical act. Over time, however, that had taken its toll, as had a number of simple relationship complications. Things had finally blown up when Seth had slept with my friend Maddie. I think he'd done it to encourage me to break up, hoping to spare me future pain. Whatever the initial intent, he and Maddie had actually gone on to establish a fairly serious relationship in the following months.

I hadn't taken that very well.

"There's no pleasing you guys," I growled, beckoning the waiter for another drink. He ignored me, darkening my mood. "You don't like good ones. You don't like bad ones. What the fuck does it take?"

A new voice suddenly cut into our circle. "Please tell me we're discussing your romantic hijinks, Georgie. There's nothing I enjoy more."

There he was, standing beside our table: my boss Jerome, archdemon of Seattle and its greater metropolitan area. I glared. I didn't appreciate the mocking tone—or him calling me Georgie. He sat down beside Hugh, and the waiter I'd been trying to summon dashed over immediately. We ordered new drinks.

Jerome was clearly in a good mood today, which always made our lives easier. He had on a black designer suit, like always, and his hair was styled exactly the same as John Cusack's had been in a recent TV interview I watched. That probably bears mentioning: Jerome's human body of choice was a clone of John Cusack. Succubi can change shape because that's part of what helps us with seduction. Demons can change shape simply because they're insanely powerful. Because of a weird fan obsession that he adamantly denied, Jerome chose to interact in the mortal world looking like the actor. The strange thing is that when we were out like this, humans never seemed to notice.

"You haven't been out with us in a while," I pointed out, hoping to change the subject. "I thought you've been busy with demon stuff." Rumor had it that Jerome was sparring with another demon, though none of us knew the details.

He took one of my cigarettes out of the pack without asking. A moment later, the end of the cigarette lit on its own. Showoff.

"Things have actually taken a pleasant turn," he said. He inhaled deeply and then let the smoke swirl around him. "One less thing to deal with. I'd hoped the incessant babbling about your romantic woes was also going away, but I suppose that's too much to hope for. Are you still with that charlatan?"

I threw up my hands. "Why does everyone hate Dante? You guys should be embracing him as a brother."

Jerome considered, dark eyes thoughtful. "He annoys me. You can do better."

"Jesus Christ," I said.

"Maybe she'd see that if she'd stop doing stupid shit like sleeping with her therapist," noted Hugh, in what was apparently supposed to be a helpful tone.

I turned on him, eyes wide. "Did you listen to anything I just said?"

"Plenty," he said dryly.

Meanwhile, Jerome's lazy, pleased expression disappeared. He fixed his gaze on me, eyes like flame yet inexplicably making me feel cold all over. He smashed the cigarette out and shot up from his seat. Grabbing my arm, he jerked me up from own spot and started dragging me from the table.

"Come with me," he hissed.

I stumbled with him out to the hall that led to the restrooms. Once out of the sight of others, he pushed me against a wall and leaned toward me, face filled with fury. It was a sign of his agitation that he was behaving like a human. He could have simply transported both of us to some isolated place.

"You fucked your therapist?" he exclaimed.

I gulped. "I wasn't making much progress."

"Georgie!"

"Why is this a problem? He was a good soul. I thought that was what you wanted me to do!"

"I wanted you to get this fucking chip off your shoulder that you've had ever since that boring mortal dumped you."

I flinched. It was kind of a weird thing. I'd been so depressed after the Seth breakup that Jerome had finally flipped out and told me to go seek help because he was tired of listening to me "bitch and moan." The weirdness of a demon encouraging counseling for one of his employees wasn't lost on me. But honestly, how could he understand? How could he understand what it was like to have your heart smashed? To be ripped from the person you loved most in the world?

My whole existence had lost meaning, and eternity had seemed impossible to bear. For weeks, I wouldn't go out or talk much to anybody. I'd isolated myself, lost in my own grief. That was when Jerome had thrown up his hands and demanded I snap out of it.

And I had, kind of. I'd swung the other way. I'd suddenly become angry—so, so angry at the way life had treated me. Some of my misfortunes were my own fault. But Seth? I didn't know. I didn't know what happened there, and I felt wronged by the world. So, I'd started getting back at it. I'd stopped caring. I'd thrown myself into full succubus mode: seeking out the most moral men I could, stealing their life, and breaking their hearts. It helped with the pain. A little.

"I'm doing what I'm supposed to!" I yelled. "I'm scoring soul after soul. You have nothing to complain about."

"You have a bitchy attitude and keep picking fights with everyone—and you aren't getting better. I'm tired of it. And I'm tired of you."

I froze, my antagonism turning to pure fear. When a demon said he was tired of you, it often resulted in being re-called to Hell. Or being smote.

"Jerome . . ." I tried to assess my best strategy here. Charm? Contrition?

He stepped away and took a deep, calming breath. It didn't help much. His anger came through loud and clear.

"I'm sending you away. I'm going to outsource you to someone."

"*What*?" My anger returned, pushing my fear away momentarily. Outsourcing was a huge insult to a succubus. "You can't do that."

"I can do whatever I fucking want. You answer to me." A lanky guy turned down the hall, heading toward the restroom. Jerome fixed him with a piercing, terrifying look. The guy yelped and hastily headed back the other way. "There's an archdemon in Vancouver who wants someone to keep an eye on a cult he has an interest in up there."

"Up there . . ." My mouth dropped open. "You mean Vancouver, BC? You're sending me to *Canada*?" Fuck. I really had gone too far. There was also a Vancouver in Washington. That wouldn't have been so bad.

"He'd wanted a succubus since he only has one and couldn't spare her. They've got their work cut out for them up there, you know. I was going to send him Grace." He made a face at the mention of his antisocial lieutenant demoness. "She's not optimal, but I didn't have any other choice since Tawny's in Bellingham and out of my control. I hadn't wanted to give up you . . . but, well, I think it'll be worth missing my succubus for a while to get you out of my hair, so I can get some peace."

"Look, Jerome," I pleaded. "I'll go find another therapist, okay? A woman. An ugly one. And I'll try to lay off the attitude and—"

"That's my decision, Georgie. You need something to occupy you, and this'll make Cedric happy. He figures a succubus is the best choice to infiltrate his little devil worshipping cult."

I stared. "Canadian Satanists? You're sending me to a group of Canadian Satanists?"

His only answer was a shrug.

"If this were happening to anyone else, it would be hilarious," I said. "But why *are* you doing it? Since when do you help anyone—let alone another demon?" Demons tended to be insanely competitive with each other.

Again, Jerome didn't answer. He took out a cigarette—honestly, if he had his own, why'd he steal mine earlier?—and did the lighting trick again.

"Something else is going on," I said warily. "You're using me to use him. What's this really about?"

"Altruism," he said, rolling his eyes.

"Jerome . . ."

"Georgina," he returned, eyes hard. "You have no right to question this, not as much as you've pissed me off lately. Now go pack your things and brush up on the metric system."